the Crossroads

Also by Niccolò Ammaniti

I'm Not Scared
Steal You Away

The Crossroads

NICCOLÒ AMMANITI

Translated from the Italian by Jonathan Hunt

CANONGATE

Edinburgh · London · New York · Melbourne

First published in Great Britain in 2009 by
Canongate Books Ltd, 14 High Street,
Edinburgh EH1 1TE

3

Copyright © Niccolò Ammaniti, 2006
English translation copyright © Jonathan Hunt, 2009

First published in Italy as *Come dio comanda*
by Mondadori Editore s.p.a.

The moral rights of the author and translator have been asserted

 The publishers gratefully acknowledge subsidy
from the Scottish Arts Council towards the
publication of this volume

 This English translation was supported by
the Italian Cultural Institute, Edinburgh

British Library Cataloguing-in-Publication Data
A catalogue record for this book is available on
request from the British Library

ISBN 978 1 84767 037 3

Typeset in Sabon by Palimpsest Book Production Ltd,
Grangemouth, Stirlingshire

Printed and bound in the UK by
CPI Mackays, Chatham ME5 8TD
www.meetatthegate.com

CONTENTS

PROLOGUE

I

'Wake up! Wake up, for fuck's sake!'

Cristiano Zena gasped, and clutched at the mattress as if the ground had opened up under his feet.

A hand clamped round his throat. 'Wake up! You know you should always sleep lightly. It's when you're asleep that the buggers will get you!'

'It's not my fault. The alarm clock didn't . . . ' the boy murmured. He twisted free of that vice-like grip and lifted his head off the pillow.

But it's still night time, he thought.

Outside the window everything was pitch-black, except where the streetlamp shed a yellow cone of light, into which snowflakes as big as balls of cotton wool were falling.

'It's snowing' he said to his father, who was standing in the middle of the room.

A shaft of light crept in from the hall, picking out Rino Zena's shaven head, his beaky nose, his moustache and goatee beard, his neck and one muscular shoulder. Instead of eyes he had two black holes. His chest was bare. Below, his army trousers and paint-splashed boots.

How can he stand this cold? thought Cristiano, stretching out his fingers towards the bedside lamp.

'Don't turn it on,' said Rino. 'My eyes are sore.'

Cristiano curled up under the warm tangle of blankets and sheets. His heart was still pounding. 'Why did you wake me?'

Then he noticed that his father was holding the pistol. When he was drunk he often got it out and wandered round the house pointing it at the television, the furniture, the lights.

'How can you sleep?' Rino turned towards his son.

His voice was hoarse and dry, as if he had swallowed a handful of chalk.

Cristiano shrugged. 'I just do . . . '

'You're lucky.' His father took a beer can out of his trouser pocket, opened it, drained it in one draught and wiped his beard with his arm, then crushed it and threw it on the floor. 'Can't you hear him, the fucker?'

There wasn't a sound. Not even the cars which flashed past the house day and night so close that if you closed your eyes they seemed to be going right through the room.

It's the snow. Snow deadens noise.

His father went over to the window and rested his head against the pane, which was wet with condensation. Now the light from the hall caught his deltoids and the cobra tattoo on his shoulder. 'You sleep too deeply. In wartime you'd be the first to get it.'

Cristiano concentrated and heard in the distance the hoarse bark of Castardin's dog.

It was a sound so familiar his ears no longer registered it. Like the buzz of the neon light in the hall and the broken flush in the toilet.

'The dog?'

'At last . . . I was beginning to get worried.' His father turned back towards him. 'He hasn't stopped barking all night. Not even in the snow.'

Cristiano remembered what he had been dreaming about when his father had woken him up.

Downstairs in the sitting room, next to the television, there was a large phosphorescent fish tank containing a squishy green jellyfish which spoke a strange language, all Cs, Zs and Rs. And the amazing thing was that he could understand every word.

What time is it? he wondered, with a yawn.

The luminous dial of the radio alarm on the floor showed three twenty-three.

His father lit a cigarette and snorted: 'I'm pissed off with it.'

'It's punch drunk, that dog,' said Christiano. 'With all the beatings it's taken . . . '

Now that his heart had stopped pounding, Cristiano felt sleep pressing down on his eyelids. His mouth was dry and full of the taste of garlic from the takeaway chicken. A drink of water might have washed that foul taste away, but it was too cold to go down to the kitchen.

He felt like resuming the dream about the jellyfish from where he had left off. He rubbed his eyes.

Why don't you go to bed? The question was on the tip of his tongue, but he checked it. From the way his father was pacing around the room there wasn't much chance of him calming down.

Three stars.

Cristiano ranked his father's rages on a five-star scale.

No, three to four. Already in the 'approach with caution' area, where the only strategy was to agree with everything he said and keep out of his way as much as possible.

His father turned round and kicked a white plastic chair, which hurtled across the room and fetched up against the pile of boxes where Cristiano kept his clothes. No, he had been wrong. This was five stars. Red alert. Here the only thing to do was to keep shtum and blend in with your surroundings.

His father had been in a filthy mood for the past week. A few days earlier he had lost his temper with the bathroom door because it wouldn't open. The lock was broken. For a couple of minutes he had fiddled with a screwdriver. He had knelt there, swearing and heaping curses on Fratini, the ironmonger who had sold it to him, the Chinese manufacturers who had made it out of tin, and the politicians who allowed such crap to be imported, as if they all were standing there in front of him. But it was no good, the door just wouldn't budge.

One punch. Another one, harder. Another. The door had leaped on its hinges, but hadn't come open. Rino had gone to his bedroom, got the gun and fired at the lock. But it still hadn't yielded. The only result had been a deafening bang which had left Cristiano dazed for half an hour.

There had been one good thing about this: it had taught Cristiano that, contrary to what the movies would have us believe, you can't open a door by shooting at its lock.

In the end his father had started kicking the door. He had smashed it in, shouting and tearing out strips of wood with his bare hands. When he had got inside the bathroom he had punched the mirror, and shards of glass had gone everywhere and he had cut his hand

and had sat for a long time dripping with blood on the edge of the bath, smoking a cigarette.

'What the fuck do I care if it's punch drunk?' replied Rino, after thinking it over for a while. 'I'm pissed off with it. I've got to go to work tomorrow.'

He came towards his son and sat down on the edge of his bed. 'Do you know something that really gets up my nose? Stepping out of the shower in the morning, soaking wet, and putting my feet on the freezing cold tiles, and at the risk of breaking my neck.' He smirked, loaded the pistol and held it out to him by the barrel: 'I was thinking that what we need is a nice new dogskin mat.'

2

At three thirty-five in the morning Cristiano Zena left the house wearing green rubber boots, his checked pyjama trousers and his father's windproof jacket. In one hand he held the pistol, in the other a torch.

Cristiano was a slim boy, tall for his thirteen years, with slender wrists and ankles, long, bony hands and a size forty-four foot. On his head grew a towelled mop of fair hair which couldn't conceal his protruding ears, and which continued down onto his cheeks in the form of two bushy sideburns. He had two big blue eyes separated by a small snub nose, and a mouth too wide for his thin face.

The snow was falling more thickly. The air was still. And the temperature several degrees below zero.

Cristiano crammed a black woolly hat on his head, puffed out a cloud of vapour and shone the torch round the yard.

A layer of snow covered the gravel, the rusty old rocking chair, the rubbish bins, a pile of bricks and the van. The highway, which ran right past the front of the house, was a long, immaculate strip of white. The dog continued to bark in the distance.

He shut the front door and tucked his pyjamas more tightly into his rubber boots.

"Go on. It's a piece of cake. All you have to do is shoot him in the head – make sure you hit the head, or he'll start whining and

you'll have to shoot him again – then come home. You'll be back in bed in ten minutes. Go, soldier." The little speech his father had delivered as he turfed him out of bed still echoed in his brain.

He looked up. The dark shape of his father stood behind the window, waving at him to get a move on. He stuck the pistol into his underpants. The cold steel shrivelled his scrotum.

He waved to his father and stumbled unsteadily round to the back of the house, as his heart began to beat faster.

3

Rino Zena watched from the window as his son went out into the snow.

He had finished all the beer and grappa. And that's bad enough in itself, but if, on top of that, you have a piercing whistle boring into your eardrums, it becomes a real problem.

The whistle had begun when Rino had fired at the bathroom door, and although a week had passed since then, it wasn't decreasing.

Maybe I've burst an eardrum. I should see a doctor, he said to himself, as he lit a cigarette.

But Rino Zena had sworn that the only way he would ever enter an ambulance was feet first.

He wasn't going to get caught in the trap.

The bastards start by telling you you need some tests done, that way you enter the tunnel and you're a goner. If the illness doesn't do for you, the medical bills will.

Rino Zena had spent the evening slumped on a folding chair in front of the television, pissed out of his mind. With two slits instead of eyes, his jaw sagging and a beer can in his hand, he had tried to follow some crappy show which kept blurring over in front of him.

As far as he could make out it was about two husbands who had agreed to swap wives for a week, God only knew why . . .

They had no respect for anything these days on the fucking TV. Just to be original they had chosen a piss-poor family from Cosenza and a filthy rich one from Rome.

The poor husband was a panel-beater. The rich one, who anyone could see was a complete tosser, worked in advertising. And of course the panel-beater's wife was as ugly as sin and the other woman was a curvy blonde with long shapely legs who taught people how to breathe in a gym.

In the end, however, the story had caught Rino's attention and he had finished a whole bottle of grappa watching it.

At the advertising agent's home the hag from Cosenza made herself unpopular by going around with a can of Windolene, and you couldn't sit down without her scolding you for spoiling the cushions. But before the first day was out they were ordering her about like a chambermaid and she was as happy as a sandboy.

Rino was more interested in the situation in Cosenza. The repair man treated the sex-bomb as if she was Lady Diana. Rino had been hoping that, in a surge of lust, he would grab the blonde – who for all her airs and graces was clearly gagging for it – and fuck her.

'Come round here, you slag! I'll show you the way we do it in the Zena household!' he had bellowed, hurling a beer can at the TV.

He knew it was all a sham, that those shows were about as genuine as the African handbags the niggers sold outside the shopping malls.

Then he had dozed off. He had woken up again some time later feeling as if he had a dead toad in his mouth and with a vice crushing his temples.

He had wandered round the house searching for something alcoholic to alleviate the pain.

Eventually, at the back of one of the kitchen units, he had found a dust-covered bottle of Poire William. God knows how long it had been there. The grappa was finished, but the pear still seemed pretty well steeped in alcohol. He had smashed the bottle on the sink and, bending over the table, sucked the pear. It had been then that he had noticed the dog. It went on and on barking. After a while he had figured out that it was the mongrel in Castardin's furniture factory. It would lie in its kennel all day as quiet as a mouse, then when night fell it would start barking and never let up till dawn.

Old Castardin probably didn't even know about it. At closing time he would come out, drive to the club in his great hearse of a BMW and fritter his money away on poker. In the village he was known as a great gambler, one of the old-fashioned kind who showed dignity in defeat.

In other words he gritted his teeth and kept his mouth shut.

So he showed all his great dignity in losing the money he stole with his trashy furniture, and his bloody dog barked all night.

And if anyone had pointed this out to him, he would have replied, with his old-fashioned dignity, that there was nothing but factories in the area. Who could possibly object to a dog that was only doing its duty? Rino was sure it had never crossed that old-fashioned man's mind that only half a kilometre away there was a house in which a young boy slept.

A boy who had to go to school.

Okay then, Rino Zena had said to himself, taking the pistol out of the drawer, *tomorrow you'll have a chance to show the world just how dignified you can be, when you find your dog stone-dead.*

4

Cristiano decided to approach the furniture factory via the fields. Even though the highway was covered with snow, there was still a chance that someone would come along it.

The light from the lamp-post didn't reach the back yard, and the darkness was total. He shone his torch on the twisted bonnet of a Renault 5, a cement mixer, the tattered remains of an inflatable swimming pool, a plastic chair, the skeleton of a dead apple tree and a two-metre-high fence.

Cristiano had left the house in a hurry, without having a pee. He considered doing it there, but decided not to, it was too cold and he wanted to get this thing over with.

He put the chair against the wire netting of the fence, stood on the chair, put the torch between his teeth, gripped the mesh with his fingers and pulled himself up. He swung one leg over to the other side, but the seat of his trousers got caught on a piece of wire. He tried to break free, but couldn't, and in the end he threw the torch down on the ground and jumped. He heard a ripping sound and felt a pain in his leg.

He found himself lying on his back among the wet weeds, with snow melting on his face. He got to his feet and slipped his hand through the tear that ran halfway down his pyjamas. A long scratch, not deep enough to bleed, scored the inside of his thigh. The pistol was still in his underpants.

He picked up the torch and began to work his way round the fences of the factories, the mud sucking down his feet and brambles blocking his path.

He was on the edge of a ploughed field which in the daytime stretched as far as the horizon. In the distance, if there was no fog – but there always was fog in winter – you could see the grey foliage of the woods that lined the banks of the river.

If it hadn't been for the barking of the dog and his own heavy breathing the silence would have been complete.

Far away, across the river, he could see the lights of the factories hanging in the air and the yellowish glow of the power station.

His fingers, squeezed in the vice of cold, were beginning to feel numb, and the chill was rising up through his feet and biting his calves.

What a fool.

In his haste to go out, furious with his father, he hadn't put on his socks. The snowflakes were falling on his neck and his jacket was beginning to get wet along the shoulders.

The black silhouettes of the industrial buildings followed one after the other. He passed a bathroom furniture outlet. Toilets. Tiles. Basins. Neatly stacked all around the building. Then a salesroom that sold tractors and farming machinery and the rear end of a discotheque which had had to shut down because it had gone bankrupt.

It's no good, I'm going to wet my pants.

He switched off the torch, put the pistol in his jacket pocket, lowered his trousers and pulled out his pecker.

Fear and the cold had shrunk it. It looked like a little salami. The spurt of urine melted the snow and a cloud of acrid steam rose from the ground.

As he was shaking it, he noticed that the dog's bark was louder.

The next building was Castardin's furniture factory.

It seemed as if the brute ran on batteries: it didn't even pause for breath. Every now and then, though, it stopped barking and howled like a fucking coyote.

He switched on the torch and started walking again, more quickly. He was taking too long. Old baldy would already be fuming. He could just see him pacing around the house like a lion.

5

Cristiano Zena was wrong. At that moment his father was in the bathroom. Standing in front of the toilet, one hand against the wall, he was looking at his reflection in the black water at the bottom of the bowl.

His face was swelling up. Where had his cheekbones gone? His gaunt jaw? He looked like a Chinaman. He was thirty-seven years old and he looked fifty. He had put on several kilos in the last few months. He hadn't dared to get on the scales, but he knew it. His stomach had swollen up too. He kept lifting weights and doing press-ups and struggling with sit-ups on the bench, but that bulge below his pectorals just wouldn't go down.

He couldn't decide whether to piss or to throw up.

His stomach contained a dozen beers, half a litre of grappa and a Poire William.

He hated being sick. But if he got it all out of his system he would certainly feel better.

Meanwhile the dog went on barking.

What the fuck is Cristiano doing? What if he doesn't shoot it?

One part of his brain was telling him yes, the boy did have the balls to shoot a dog. But another part wasn't so sure: Cristiano was too childish, he only did things out of fear of his father. And if your only motivation is fear, not anger, you'll never be able to pull a trigger.

A sour yellow stream gushed out of his mouth without warning. Rino only partly managed to get it into the toilet; the rest spattered over the tiles.

He sat down on the bidet, exhausted, with the reek of vomit around him.

As he sat there with the toilet spinning round and round like the drum of a washing machine, he remembered how in his childhood Castardin's furniture factory and all the other buildings hadn't been there. Back then the highway had been a rough, narrow road with poplars and weeds along the sides, not much wider than a country track. All around, there had been nothing but cultivated fields.

Not far from where their house now stood had been the Trattoria Arcobaleno, a little restaurant which specialised in polenta, kid and freshwater fish.

And on the site now occupied by Castardin's furniture factory there had been an old farmhouse, one of those square, barrack-like buildings, with a tiled roof, a large shed and a farmyard full of geese and chickens. It had been the home of Roberto Colombo and his family.

On a large tree by the roadside Roberto had put up a notice:

MOTOR WORKSHOP
LORRIES, TRACTORS AND CARS REPAIRED
ITALIAN AND FOREIGN MAKES

And from a branch of the same tree there had hung a swing on which Rino used to go and play with Colombo's daughter.

From his parents' house, down by the river, it took half an hour to get there on foot. But half an hour's walk was nothing in those days.

What was her name? Alberta? Antonia?

Someone had told him she had got married and now lived in Milan.

One day, while she was sailing back and forth on the swing and he was trying to catch a glimpse of her knickers, her father had arrived.

Sitting on the bidet, Rino couldn't help smiling.

He had never once seen Roberto Colombo dressed in anything but blue overalls, a red bandanna and a ridiculous pair of moccasins made of interwoven leather threads. He was short and stocky and wore glasses so thick his eyes looked like two pinpoints.

'How old are you, son?'

'Eleven.'

'Eleven years old and you're still playing games like a snotty-nosed kid? Your father's dead and all you can do is peek at my daughter's knickers?'

Half-blind as he was, it was a mystery how he had managed to see that.

Colombo had looked Rino over as you might appraise a horse at a fair. 'You're as skinny as a stray dog, but you're sturdy. A bit of hard work might help develop your muscles.'

So he had taken him on at his workshop. The job was simple: he had to make the cars shine as bright as the day they had left the factory. Outside and inside.

'It won't make you rich, but you'll earn enough to buy yourself a pair of decent shoes and to help your mother, who finds it a struggle to make ends meet.'

So Rino had started going to the workshop every day after school, and, armed with pump and sponge, had earned the first money of his life.

At five o'clock the girl would bring him a sandwich and a meatball with raisins.

Rino tried to get to his feet, but failed. He wanted to open the window to let in some fresh air.

A swirl of images wrapped around him like a warm blanket. Him and the girl together. Marriage. Children. The workshop. Working there with Cristiano.

What wonderful times those had been! Everything was so simple. It was easy to find a job. There weren't all these bloody laws about working practices and no trade unions to fuck you about. If you had the skill and the will you worked, if you didn't you were out on your ear. End of alternatives.

Respect for those who deserved it.

Then one day Rino had arrived to find Colombo shutting up shop. A certain Castardin had appeared out of nowhere and bought up the farmhouse and all the land around it. Even the Trattoria Arcobaleno.

'They've opened some new workshops in Varrano. They're as big as factories. Nobody comes this way any more . . . It's a good offer.'

End of story.

'Good offer my foot,' muttered Rino, getting to his feet. 'The poor gullible prick.'

6

The furniture factory was twenty metres away. Bathed in the glow of halogen lights, it stood out in the night like a lunar base. The fence was high and there were coils of barbed wire along the top.

'Shit. The barbed wire.'

They had put it up some time ago, after thieves had broken in one night.

A mechanical noise mingled with the barks. A truck.

Cristiano switched off the torch, squatted down and waited for it to pass. It had yellow headlights and was clearing the snow.

Maybe school will be cancelled tomorrow. Great!

When the truck had moved far enough away, Cristiano walked the last few metres and stopped behind the factory.

The dog was barking even louder now, if that was possible. But he couldn't see it from there.

Cristiano couldn't remember whether they let him off his chain at night, though he had been past the factory very late sometimes.

He jumped up and down to get the feeling back into his feet, which were like blocks of wood. 'I hate you! Why do you do this to me?' He bit his hand to stop himself screaming with rage. He felt a lump in his throat and it hurt as if he'd swallowed a shard of glass.

I've had enough. It's fucking cold . . . I'm going home. He took three steps, kicking at the snow, but then stopped.

Going home was not an option.

He walked round the perimeter of the fence, looking for the best place to climb up.

All the while the dog kept barking in the same monotonous way.

Near one of the posts that supported the wire netting the loops of barbed wire weren't so big.

He grabbed hold of the post, put the toes of his boots into the mesh and reached the top without difficulty. Now he had to avoid getting stuck on the barbed wire. Calmly he put over first one leg and then the other, and, holding his breath, jumped down. He landed in the carpentry area.

He took out the pistol, released the safety catch and primed the gun.

He knew very well how to use it.

His father had taught him how to shoot in a scrapyard. At first he hadn't been able to hold his aim; his arm had shaken as if he was suffering from Parkinson's disease. But constant shooting at car windows, rear-view mirrors, rats and seagulls had taught him that it was all a matter of posture and breathing.

'It's like squatting over a hole-in-the-ground toilet,' Rino had told him.

Legs apart, backside slightly protruding, arms outstretched but not too stiff. Gun in line with your eyes. And the way you breathed was crucial. You had to put the tip of your tongue against your bottom teeth, breathe out through your nose and, as your stomach deflated, count up to four and then shoot.

He looked around. No one in sight. The mongrel was barking away on the other side of the building.

If he approached slowly he would have a good chance of getting close enough to take aim at him. The snow would muffle his footsteps and the stupid mutt was so busy barking he wouldn't notice he was about to be dispatched to doggy paradise.

If it did go for him he would have to be cool enough to stop, crouch and take aim as it ran towards him.

He moved forward in a squatting position, quelling his desire to run, till he came to a pile of planks. They formed a long block more than four metres high which stretched out to the end of the yard, a few metres short of the highway. Cristiano climbed up, putting his feet between the planks and gripping their ice-cold edges with his hands. When he was on top he realised that there was a gap of about a metre between one pile and the next. Like between the carriages of a train.

From where he stood he could see a segment of the deserted car park, and the children's playground, with the roundabout and its dwarves, the swings glowing white in the lamplight, and the lampposts themselves with their glass globes emanating milky spheres.

No sign of the dog.

Crawling along the wet planks on his hands and knees, he reached the end of the first pile. He steeled himself and jumped; the planks rose and fell with a tremendous clatter. From where he landed he could see the other side of the car park, and three vans emblazoned with the words:

CASTARDIN & CO. FURNITURE LTD.
HIGH QUALITY, LOW COST

He couldn't see the dog, though. And yet he must be very near. Or was all that barking just a recording?

Then he saw, about thirty metres away, a dark shape on the ground. Near the long entrance gate. Half-covered in snow . . . From that distance it looked like an overcoat.

Cristiano moved closer, crawling over the planks.

The thing on the ground was moving. Only slightly. But it was moving.

And he understood.

The stupid beast had got himself tangled up in the long chain that was supposed to enable him to move around the perimeter of the building. Now and then he raised his head.

That's why he's barking so much.

The stupid great mutt.

Shooting him from there would be child's play. Even if he didn't kill him first shot, the dog wouldn't be able to move, and he would certainly send him to his maker with the second.

He's barking because he can't move. I could set him free, then he would stop barking.

No, he must kill him, because the truth was that his father didn't give a damn whether the dog barked or not. He hated Castardin, so the dog had to die.

Period.

7

That was precisely how things were.

Rino Zena hated old Castardin with the same devout intensity with which a Cistercian monk loves his Lord.

'It's in my character. If you cross me just once, you've finished with me for good and I'll always be out to get you. Okay, I may have a shitty character, but it's the one I was born with. It's easy to get on with me: just don't fuck me around and everything will be fine.' Such was the reply that Rino would give to anyone who gently tried to suggest to him that he might be a trifle touchy.

A few years before this story, Rino Zena had been taken on at the factory as a transporter of furniture.

He was paid in cash and earned more from tips than from the pittance he got from Castardin.

Things had gone reasonably well, with Rino grumbling to anyone who cared to listen that he was treated like dirt, until the day old Castardin in person had phoned to ask him to take the furniture for a children's bedroom to the home of Councillor Arosio.

'Please, Zena, be on your best behaviour. There's no one else I can send; they're all out doing deliveries. Arosio is an important customer. Cover up those tattoos or you'll frighten the children. And speak as little as possible.'

Rino had glared at him and loaded the furniture onto the van.

Councillor Arosio was another guy Rino couldn't stand. He was the shithead who had closed Varrano's main street to traffic. So even if you had to deliver the space shuttle the traffic police wouldn't let you through.

When he had reached the house he had learned that the councillor's flat was on the third floor and that the porter wouldn't let the lift be used for carrying heavy loads: 'I *would* let you, but if *you* used it I'd have to let everyone else use it too and the lift would get worn out.'

Fuming, Rino had hoisted the furniture onto his back. At the door of the flat he had found Mrs Arosio waiting for him in a violet satin nightdress.

She was a really attractive woman, about forty years old, with a tawny perm, two enormous tits only partly hidden by her night-dress, a slim waist and a bum as big as an aircraft carrier. She had a round face, a small nose too perfect to be the one her mother had given her, eyes tinged with light-blue shadow, and swollen, shiny lips parted to reveal some slightly gappy incisors.

Rino had seen her walking along the high street in summer and winter with plunging necklines over those huge UVA-tanned breasts, but he hadn't known that she was Arosio's wife.

While he got to work with the nuts and bolts, she had sat down in such a way that her ample frontage was prominently displayed and had remarked that muscles formed at work were much more attractive than ones that were pumped up in a gym. And what were all those tattoos? What did they mean? She wanted one too, a squirrel . . .

By now Rino had a hard-on and was finding it difficult to follow the instructions under that hungry gaze.

After the little writing-desk, the mini-blackboard and the wardrobe, he had assembled the bunk bed.

'Have you screwed it together tightly enough? I wouldn't want it to come apart . . . My son Aldo is a bit on the heavy side. Would you mind getting up onto it yourself? To try it out?'

Rino had climbed onto the top bunk and bounced up and down. 'Seems all right to me.'

She had shaken her head. 'You're too light. I think I'd better come up too. Just to make quite sure.'

Half an hour later the bed had suddenly given way. Mrs Arosio had broken her wrist in falling out and had sued the furniture factory.

Rino had sworn to Castardin that he hadn't had sex with her.

And technically speaking that was correct. Penetration had not yet taken place when the bed had collapsed. She was on all fours, with her face buried in the pillow and her petticoat pulled up, and Rino was holding her by the hair like a red Indian gripping his horse's mane, stamping her buttocks with large red slap-marks like the patches on an Apache steed.

Then the bed had given way.

Rino Zena had lost his job.

And he had sworn to get even with old Castardin.

8

Cristiano Zena lay down and aimed at the head. He took a deep breath and fired. The animal flinched, gave a little whine and lay still.

He raised his fist. 'First shot!'

He jumped down from the pile of planks and, after checking that no cars were passing by, approached slowly, keeping the gun trained on the animal.

The mouth open. The froth. The tongue hanging to one side like a bluish slug. The eyes rolled back and on the neck a red hole among the black hairs and the snow swirling lazily in the air, burying the corpse.

One fucking mongrel less in the world.

9

Cristiano returned home and ran to his father to tell him how he had killed it first shot, but Rino was stretched out on his bed fast asleep.

BEFORE

You are too just, Lord,
for me to dispute with you,
but I would like to talk with you about justice.
Why do the ways of the wicked prosper?
Why do all the treacherous live at ease?
You have planted them and they have taken root;
they grow and bring forth fruit.
You are near to their mouths
but far from their hearts.

Jeremiah 12, 1–2

Friday

10

An open cluster is a group of stars held together by gravitational forces. The number of stars can be in the thousands. Their low attraction favours a chaotic arrangement around the centre of the system.

This untidy formation resembled that of the thousands of little towns, villages and hamlets which dotted the vast plain where Cristiano Zena and his father lived.

The snow that had fallen all night on the plain had whitened the fields, the houses and the factories. The only things it had not covered were the thick, incandescent cables of the power stations, the lamps on the billboards, and the Forgese, the big winding river which linked the mountains up in the north with the sea down to the south.

But at the first light of dawn the snow changed to a thin, persistent drizzle which in less than an hour melted the white mantle that had momentarily made the plain as beautiful as a cool albino model wrapped in an Arctic fox fur. Varrano, San Rocco, Rocca Seconda, Murelle, Giardino Fiorito, Marzio, Bogognano, Semerese and all the other towns and villages re-emerged with their dingy colours, with their small or large areas of urban sprawl, with their modern two-storey houses surrounded by frost-browned lawns, with their prefabricated industrial buildings, their credit institutions, their flyovers, their motor showrooms and forecourts, and with their vast expanses of mud.

11

At a quarter past six in the morning Corrado Rumitz, commonly known as Quattro Formaggi because of his consuming passion for the pizza of that name, his staple diet for the best part of his thirty-eight years, was sitting on a shabby, flower-patterned sofa having his breakfast.

He was wearing his home clothes: dirty underpants, an ankle-length tartan dressing-gown and a pair of battered Camperos boots, a relic of the old millennium.

With his gaze fixed on the little area in front of the kitchen, he took a biscuit out of a packet, dunked it in a bowl of milk and shoved it whole into his mouth. He repeated the action with metronomic regularity.

When he had woken up he had seen from the window of his room, in the pale light of dawn, an expanse of gentle hills and white valleys, as if he was enjoying the view from a mountain lodge. If he avoided looking at the walls of the building opposite he might even have imagined he was in Alaska.

He had sat in bed, huddled up under the blankets, watching the snowflakes fall as light as feathers.

It hadn't snowed like this for ages.

Almost every winter, sooner or later, there was a sprinkling, but before Quattro Formaggi had time to go out for a walk in the countryside it had always melted.

But that night at least twenty centimetres must have fallen.

When Quattro Formaggi had been small and lived in the orphanage run by the nuns it had snowed every winter. Cars would stop, some people would even put on cross-country skis and the children would make snowmen with branches for arms, and would slide down the garage ramps on old car tyres. What incredible snowball fights they'd had with Sister Anna and Sister Margherita. And there had been sleds drawn by horses with jingling bells . . .

At least, he thought there had.

Lately he had noticed that he often remembered things that had never happened. Or he got things he had seen on TV jumbled up with his own memories.

Certainly something in the world must have changed if it no longer snowed as it used to.

On TV they had explained that the world was warming up like a meatball inside the oven and that it was all the fault of man and his gases.

Quattro Formaggi, lying in bed, had told himself that if he hurried up he could go round to Rino and Cristiano's and when Cristiano came out to go to school he could pelt him with snowballs.

But as if the weather had been listening and decided to put a spanner in the works, the snowflakes had become increasingly heavier and more liquid till they had turned to rain, and the hills had first become pockmarked and then shrunk to patches of icy mush, revealing the mass of old junk heaped up in the little yard. Beds, furniture, tyres, rusty rubbish bins, the skeleton of an orange Ape 125 pickup, and the carcase of a sofa.

Quattro Formaggi gulped down his cup of milk, his pointed Adam's apple rising and falling. He yawned, and stood up to his full height of one metre eighty-seven centimetres.

He was so tall and thin he looked like a basketball player who had been put on starvation rations. Gangly arms and legs, enormous hands and feet. There was a callused weal on the palm of his right hand and a hard brown scar on his right calf. His bony neck supported a head as small and round as that of a silvery gibbon. A greyish beard stained his sunken cheeks and his chin. His hair, unlike his beard, was black and shiny and hung in a fringe over his low forehead, in the style of an Amazonian Indian.

He put the cup in the sink, quivering with tremors and spasms as if he had hundreds of electrodes clamped to his body.

He continued to stare at the yard, cocking his head on one side and twisting his mouth, then he thumped himself twice on the thigh and slapped his forehead.

The children in the park, when they saw him go by, would stare at him in amazement and then run to their nannies and tug at their clothes, asking: 'Why does that man walk in that funny way?'

And usually they would get the reply (if the nanny was a polite person) that it was rude to point and that the poor fellow was an unfortunate who suffered from some mental illness.

But then the same children, talking to the older ones at school, would learn that that strange man, who was always in the public gardens and who would steal your toys if you didn't watch out, was called Electric Man, like some enemy of Spiderman or Superman.

That would indeed have been a more appropriate nickname for Quattro Formaggi. At the age of thirty Corrado Rumitz had had a nasty experience which had nearly cost him his life.

It had all begun with an air rifle which he had exchanged for a long fishing rod. It was a good bargain: the air rifle's gaskets were worn out and it made a farting noise when you fired it. It barely even tickled the coypu in the river. The rod, by contrast, was practically new and extremely long, so if you cast it properly you could reach the middle of the river.

Feeling very pleased with himself, Quattro Formaggi had set off, rod in one hand and bucket in the other, to fish in the river. He had been told that there was one special point, just below the lock, where the fish gathered, carried down on the current.

After having a look around, Quattro Formaggi had climbed over the fence and stationed himself just above the lock, which that day was closed.

He had never been the brightest of people. When he was in the orphanage he had caught a particularly acute form of meningitis and consequently he 'thought slowly', as he put it.

That day he may have thought slowly but he had thought well. He had made a few casts and could feel that the fish were touching the bait. There must be hundreds of them, massed by the lock gates. But they were very crafty. They would eat the worm and leave him with nothing but a hook that needed re-baiting.

Maybe he should try further out.

He had made a long, vigorous cast, describing a perfect curve through the air. The hook had cleared the foliage of the trees but not the electric cables that ran right over his head.

If the rod had been made of plastic he wouldn't have come to any harm, but unfortunately for him it was made of carbon, which on a scale of electrical conductivity is second only to silver.

The current had entered his hand and gone right through his body, leaving via his left leg.

The lock-keepers had found him lying on the ground, burnt almost to a frazzle.

For several years he hadn't been able to speak and had moved jerkily, like a green lizard. Then gradually he had recovered, but he still had spasms in his neck and mouth and a crazy leg which he sometimes had to thump awake.

Quattro Formaggi took some minced meat out of the fridge and gave it to Uno and Due, the turtles who lived in five centimetres of water in a big washing-bowl on the table by the window.

Someone had thrown them into the fountain in Piazza Bologna and he had brought them home. When he had found them they had been the size of two-euro pieces; now, five years later, they were nearly as big as cottage loaves.

He looked at the clock shaped like a violin that hung on the wall. He couldn't remember exactly at what time, but he was supposed to be meeting Danilo at the Bar Boomerang, after which they had arranged to go round together to wake Rino up.

There was just time to reposition the little wooden church by the lake.

He went through into the sitting room.

A room about twenty square metres in area, completely cover-ed with mountains of coloured papier-mâché, with rivers of tin foil, with lakes made out of plates and bowls, with woods made of moss, with towns dotted with cardboard houses, deserts of sand and roads of cloth.

And the surface was populated by soldiers, plastic animals, dinosaurs, shepherds, little cars, tanks, robots and dolls.

His nativity scene. He had been working on it for years.

Thousands of toys retrieved from rubbish bins, found on the dump or left by children in the public gardens.

On the highest mountain of all stood a stable with Baby Jesus, Mary, Joseph and the ox and the ass. They had been a gift from Sister Margherita when he was ten. Quattro Formaggi, moving with surprising agility, crossed the scene without knocking anything over and repositioned the bridge across which a troop of smurfs was walking, with a Pokémon at their head.

When he had finished the job he knelt down and prayed for the soul of Sister Margherita. Then he went into the tiny toilet, had a cursory wash and put on his winter gear: some long johns, a pair of cotton trousers, a flannel shirt with a blue-and-white checked pattern, a brown sweatshirt, an old quilted jacket, a Juventus scarf, a yellow cape, woollen gloves, a peaked cap and some heavy working shoes.

Ready.

12

The alarm clock went off at a quarter to seven and jolted Cristiano Zena out of a dreamless sleep.

It was a good ten minutes before an arm emerged like a hermit crab's pincer from under the bedclothes and silenced the ringing.

He felt as if he had only just closed his eyes. But the most terrible thing was leaving the warm bed.

As every morning, he considered the idea of not going to school. Today it was particularly tempting, because his father had told him he was going to work. That didn't happen often these days.

But it wasn't possible. There was the history essay. And if he skipped it again . . .

Come on, up you get.

One corner of the room was beginning to brighten with the dull light emitted by the overcast, grey sky.

Cristiano stretched, and checked the scratch on his thigh. It was red, but it was already forming a scab.

He picked up his trousers, fleece and socks off the floor and pulled them under the bedclothes. Yawning, he sat up, slipped on his trainers and shuffled, zombie-like, towards the door.

Cristiano's room was large, with still unplastered walls. In one corner two trestles supported a wooden plank on which exercise books and textbooks were piled. Above the bed, a poster of Valentino Rossi advertising beer. Sticking out from the wall by the door were the truncated copper pipes from a radiator that had never been fitted.

With another yawn, he crossed the hall floored with grey linoleum, passed the tatters of the bathroom door that still hung from its hinges and entered the room.

The bathroom was a little cubbyhole measuring about one metre by two, with blue, flowery tiles encircling the floor of the shower. Over the basin hung a long shard of the mirror. A bare light bulb dangled from the ceiling.

He stepped over the remains of his father's vomit and looked out of the little window.

It was raining and the rain had eaten away all the snow. All that was left were a few useless white patches, melting on the gravel in front of the house.

School will be on.

The toilet had no seat and he rested his buttocks on the cold porcelain, gritting his teeth. A shiver ran up his spine. And in a state of semi-consciousness he crapped.

Then he cleaned his teeth. Cristiano didn't have good teeth. The dentist wanted to give him a brace, but luckily they had no money and his father had said his teeth were fine the way they were.

He didn't take a shower, but sprayed himself with deodorant. He dug his fingers into the gel and ran them through his hair to make it even more towelled, if that was possible, but taking care not to let his ears stick out.

He returned to his room, put his books in his rucksack and was about to go downstairs when he saw a dim glow under the door of his father's bedroom.

He pushed down the handle.

His father was huddled up in a camouflage sleeping bag on a double mattress on the floor.

Cristiano drew nearer.

Only the oval of his shaven head protruded from the sleeping bag. The floor was strewn with empty beer cans, socks and his boots. On the bedside table, more cans and the pistol. There was a stench of rancid sweat and dirty clothes which mingled with the smell of an old, threadbare blue carpet. A lamp swathed in a red cloth threw a scarlet glow on the enormous flag with a black swastika in the middle that hung on the plasterless wall. The shutters were down, the curtains, patterned with brown-and-white lozenges, were held together with pegs.

His father only came here to sleep. Usually he collapsed on the sofa in front of the television, and only the cold, and in the summer the mosquitoes, gave him the strength to drag himself up to his bedroom.

If Cristiano ever saw him open the windows and make an attempt at tidying up the room he knew old baldy had arranged to fuck some woman and didn't want to suffocate her with rotting socks and cigarette stubs.

Cristiano kicked the mattress. 'Papa! Papa, wake up! It's late.'

No reaction.

He raised his voice. 'Papa, you've got to go to work!'

He must have drunk a barrelful of beer.

Ah to hell with it! he said to himself and was about to leave when he heard a groan which might as easily have come from beyond the grave as out of that bundle. 'No, today . . . today . . . I'm going . . . I have to . . . Danilo . . . Quattro . . . '

'OK. See you later. I must be going or I'll miss the bus.' Cristiano moved towards the door.

'Wait a minute . . . '

'It's late, pa . . . ' Cristiano bristled.

'Give me my cigarettes.'

The boy snorted and searched round the room for the packet.

'They're in my trousers.' His father's face emerged from the sleeping bag, yawning. The mark of the zip on his cheek. 'My God, that chicken we had last night was shit . . . I'll cook something this evening . . . I'll do some lasagne, what do you say to that?'

Cristiano threw the packet to his father, who caught it deftly. 'Look, I'm in a hurry . . . I'll miss the bus, I told you.'

'Hold on a minute! What's got into you today?' Rino lit himself a cigarette. For an instant his face was enveloped in a white cloud. 'Last night I dreamed we were eating lasagne. I can't remember where, but it was delicious. You know what I'm going to do? I'm going to make some myself today.'

Why does he always talk such bullshit? Cristiano asked himself. It was as much as he could do to cook a couple of fried eggs, and he couldn't even do that without breaking the yolk.

'I'll make it with loads of béchamel. And sausages. If you do the shopping, I'll make you some lasagne so delicious you'll be forced to bow down and admit that I'm your God.'

'Yeah, like last time, when you made pasta with a sauce of clams and sand.'

'There's nothing wrong with a bit of sand in clams.'

Cristiano, as usual, fell into a reverie as he looked at him.

He thought that if his father had been born in America he would definitely have been an actor. Not a pansy actor like the guy who played James Bond. No, a hard man like Bruce Willis or Mel Gibson. Someone who went to Vietnam.

He had the face of a tough guy.

Cristiano liked the shape of his skull and his ears, which were small and round, not like his own. The square jaw and the little black dots of his beard, the small nose, the cold stare of his eyes and the little creases that appeared around them when he laughed.

And he liked the fact that he was not too tall, but well proportioned, like a boxer. With a lot of bulging muscles. And he liked the barbed-wire tattoo around his biceps. He wasn't so keen on his beer-belly and that lion's head on his shoulder which looked more like a monkey. But even the Celtic cross on his right pectoral wasn't bad.

Why can't I be like him?

They didn't even look like father and son, except for the colour of their eyes.

'Hey! Are you listening to me?'

Cristiano looked at his watch. It was very late. The first bus had already passed. 'Look, I've got to go!'

'Okay, but first you've got to give a kiss to the only man you've ever loved.'

Cristiano laughed and shook his head. 'No! You're disgusting, you stink to high heaven.'

'Hark who's talking! The last time you took a shower you were in primary school.' Rino shoved the cigarette into an empty beer can, grinning. 'Come over here at once and kiss your God. Remember that without me you wouldn't have existed, and if I hadn't been around your mother would have had an abortion, so kiss this Latin male.'

Cristiano puffed out his cheeks, muttered 'Jesus Christ' and brushed his father's rough cheek with his lips. He was about to move away when Rino grabbed him by the wrist, used his free hand to wipe his cheek and gave a grimace of disgust. 'Ugh! I've got a pansy son!'

'Fuck off!' Cristiano started laughing and hitting him with his rucksack.

'Ooh yes . . . Again . . . Again . . . I like it . . .' Rino sighed idiotically.

'You bastard . . .' And the blows rained down on his shaven pate. Rino rubbed the back of his head and then suddenly turned menacing: 'What the hell do you think you're doing? Not on the head! You little fool! You hurt me! You know I've got a headache!'

Cristiano was taken aback, and stammered, 'I'm sorry . . . I didn't mean to . . . '

With a sudden movement Rino grabbed the gun from the bedside table, yanked Cristiano towards him, bringing him crashing down on the bed, and put the barrel to his forehead.

'Fooled you again! Always keep your guard up. You'd be dead by now,' he whispered in his ear conspiratorially.

Cristiano tried to get up, but his father held him down with his arm. 'Let me go! Let me go! You bastard . . . ' he protested.

'Only if you give me a kiss,' said Rino, proffering his cheek.

Reluctantly Cristiano kissed him again, and Rino yelled out in disgust: 'It's true! I do have a pansy son!' and he started tickling him.

Cristiano giggled and tried to break free, gasping: 'Please . . . Please . . . Please . . . Stop it . . . '

At last he managed to escape. He retreated from the bed, tucking his T-shirt into his trousers, and picked up his rucksack. As he went downstairs Rino shouted after him: 'Hey, that was a good job you did last night.'

13

Forty-five-year-old Danilo Aprea was sitting at a table in the Bar Boomerang finishing his third grappa of the morning.

He too was tall, but unlike Quattro Formaggi he was large and had a stomach as swollen as that of a drowned cow. Not that he was exactly fat; his muscles were firm and his skin as white as marble. Every part of him was square: his fingers, his ankles, his feet, his neck. He had a cubic skull, a wall-like forehead and two deep-set hazel eyes on either side of a broad nose. A thin strip of beard framed his perfectly shaven cheeks. He wore gold-rimmed Ray-Ban glasses and his crew-cut hair was dyed mahogany red.

He too, like Quattro Formaggi, had a winter outfit, but unlike his friend's, his was always immaculately washed and ironed. A checked flannel shirt. A hunter's waistcoat with lots of pockets. Jeans with a pleated front. Trainers. And, attached to his belt, a pouch for a Swiss Army knife and his mobile phone.

He economised on everything else, but not on his appearance. He had his beard trimmed and his hair dyed once a fortnight by the barber.

He was waiting for Quattro Formaggi, who, just for a change, was late. Not that Danilo was particularly bothered. In the bar it was nice and warm and he was in a strategic position. The table, by the front window, overlooked the street. Danilo held the *Gazzetta dello Sport* up in front of him and now and then took a glance outside.

Directly opposite was the Credito Italiano dell'Agricoltura. He saw people going in and out through the metal detectors and the private guard outside the entrance talking into his mobile.

That guard really pissed him off. With his bullet-proof jacket, his emblazoned beret, his gleaming pistol, his sunglasses, his square jaw and his chewing-gum, who the fuck did he think he was? Tom Cruise?

But the thing that really interested Danilo Aprea was not the guard, but what was behind him: the ATM.

That was his objective. It was the most frequently used cashpoint in the village, as this bank had more customers than any other in Varrano, so it must be crammed with money.

There were two CCTV cameras positioned above the machine. One to the right and one to the left, so as to cover the whole surrounding area. And no doubt they were connected to a set of videorecorders inside the bank. But that wasn't a problem.

In actual fact there wasn't the slightest need for Danilo to sit there watching the movement in front of the bank. He had already worked out the plan down to the smallest detail. But watching that cash machine made him feel better.

The plan for the raid on the Credito dell'Agricoltura had been hatched six months before.

Danilo had been at the barber's, and leafing through the crime pages of the newspaper he had read that in a village near Cagliari a gang of crooks driving a four-by-four had smashed through the wall of a bank and carried off its cash machine.

32

While his hair was being dyed the story kept buzzing around in his head; this could be the turning point in his life.

The plan was quite simple.

'Simplicity is the basis of every well-done thing,' his father used to tell him.

And it was easy to put into practice. The night in Varrano was so quiet that if you acted fast, who would see you? And who would ever suspect that such a respectable citizen as Danilo Aprea could have robbed a bank?

With the loot he would make Teresa's dream come true. The dream of opening a lingerie boutique. Danilo was sure that if he gave her a shop his wife would come back to him, and then he would find the strength to go to Alcoholics Anonymous and dry out.

14

After Cristiano's departure Rino Zena had gone back to sleep, and when he had woken up again the whistling in his ears, as if by magic, had vanished, along with the band of pain round his head. It had been replaced by a ravenous hunger.

He lay in bed and imagined a dish of chargrilled sausages accompanied by plenty of bread.

His cock was hard and his balls were as full as hard-boiled eggs.

How long is it since I last had a fuck?

It had been at least two weeks. But when he had a headache screwing was the last thing on his mind.

This evening I'll go out on the town, he said to himself, struggling to get up from the mattress and going into the bathroom naked, with his pecker sticking out in front of him like the bowsprit of a schooner.

In the course of his life Rino had encountered difficulties of many kinds, but these did not include finding a woman to fuck or someone to pick a fight with.

And recently he had found a couple of bars where skinheads, punks and all the local freaks hung out. A bunch of rich kids who showed off riding round on Harley-Davidsons worth thirty thousand euros. Rino despised them, but their womenfolk swarmed over him like flies on a dog turd.

All the girls followed the same career pattern: most started out as shaven-headed anorexics who tattooed swastikas and Celtic crosses on their bums and for a while played at being bad girls and slept around. They would fuck up their brains with cut shit, then get sent off to some American clinic to detox, have their tattoos lasered off, marry a rich businessman and end up driving around in a Mercedes wearing a miniskirt and a bouclé jacket.

But Rino took advantage of the transitional phase and of their undiscriminating desire for sex and intense experience. He would put his mark on them, then kick them out next morning with their pussies on fire and a few bruises. And most of the slags came back for more.

Stupid cows!

He plunged into the ice-cold shower, shaved his skull and then put on a tiny vest, his trousers and his boots.

He went down the stairs into the lounge, a room of about thirty square metres. On one side of it was the front door, on the other side a hall leading to the kitchen, a toilet and a broom cupboard.

The floor was covered with reddish linoleum which rode up against the red-brick and concrete walls. On one side of the room was a table draped with a green-and-white checked plastic tablecloth, and two benches. On the other the television area. Two blue plastic crates with an old Saba colour TV on top. To change channels without getting up the Zenas used a broomstick, ramming it against the big channel buttons. Opposite the TV were a sofa bed with a filthy cover and three white folding chairs with plastic threads. There was also an orange-coloured iron bench with a barbell loaded with weights. Lastly, in one corner, next to a big box full of newspapers and a pile of firewood, there stood a cast-iron stove. A ventilator fan on a stick served in winter to spread the warmth of the stove and in summer to stir the sultry air.

Danilo and Quattro Formaggi would soon be arriving.

I can do some work on my biceps, Rino said to himself. But he abandoned the idea. His tummy was rumbling and his cock was still erect.

He turned on the TV and started wanking as he watched a blonde bitch with a pendant as big as the medallion of a turkey round her neck helping a fat man prepare some fillets of wild mullet in a sauce of raspberry, chestnut and sage.

With his pecker in his hand, Rino gave a gesture of disgust. That pansy crap they were cooking had made him lose his hard-on.

15

Danilo Aprea looked at the old Casio digital watch on his wrist.

A quarter past eight and there was still no sign of Quattro Formaggi.

He took out the purse in which he kept his coins. He had three euros and . . . He brought the small coins closer to his eyes. Twenty . . . Forty cents.

Four years had passed since they had changed the currency and he still found it confusing. What had been wrong with the lira?

He got up and ordered another grappa.

This'll be the last one, though . . .

At that moment a mother entered the bar with a little girl bundled up in a white parka holding her hand.

"How old is she?" he restrained himself from asking the woman.

"Three," she would have answered. He was sure she was three, or four at most.

Like . . .

(Stop it) Teresa's voice reproved him.

Wouldn't it be wonderful if Teresa came round this afternoon?

Teresa Carucci, a woman as insipid as a bowl of celery soup (as Rino had put it to him once) and whom Danilo had asked to be his bride one evening in 1996, had left him four years ago to set up home with a tyre dealer who she had been working for as a secretary.

Yet Teresa continued to see Danilo. Unknown to the tyre dealer she brought him trays of lasagne, spezzatino and rabbit cacciatore to put in the freezer. She would always arrive out of breath, sweep the flat and iron his shirts and he would start begging her to stay and give it another try. She would retort that it was impossible to live with an alcoholic. And, in the early days, sometimes she had felt sorry for him, and had lifted up her skirt and let him screw her.

Danilo watched the little girl happily eating a huge croissant. Her mouth all smeared with icing sugar.

He took the glass off the counter and went back to his table.

He knocked back the grappa. The alcohol warmed his oesophagus and his head became lighter.

That's better. Much better.

Until five years before the most Danilo Aprea had been able to drink was a finger of moscato. 'Alcohol and I don't get on,' he would say to anyone who offered him a drink.

This remained the case until 9th July 2001, when alcohol and Danilo Aprea decided that the time had come to bury their differences and become friends.

Until 9th July 2001 Danilo Aprea had been a different person with a different life. He had worked as a night-watchman for a freight firm, had had a wife whom he loved and Laura, a three-year-old daughter.

On 9th July 2001 Laura Aprea had choked to death, with the cap from a bottle of shampoo stuck in her windpipe.

A year later Teresa had left him.

16

Cristiano arrived at the bus stop, but the bus had just gone. And with it his chances of making the first lesson.

If only he had been a year older . . . If he'd had a motorbike he could have got to school in ten minutes. And he would have had the fun of riding across the fields and rough tracks. As soon as he finished school next year he was going to get a job – he should be able to earn enough to buy one in six months.

The next bus wasn't due for half an hour.

What do I do now? he asked himself, kicking at a little mound of snow that was melting away on the pavement.

If he could find someone to give him a lift maybe he could slip into class without being noticed.

But who's going to stop here?

Along that stretch of the highway everyone drove flat out.

He set off, with his woolly hat pulled down over his head, his headphones in his ears and his hands in the pockets of his jacket. The air was saturated with water; the drops were so small you could hardly tell it was raining.

With Metallica shrieking in his eardrums he looked around and lit a cigarette.

He wasn't really all that keen on smoking, though he enjoyed the sensation when his head started spinning. But if his father caught him with a cigarette in his mouth he'd kill him.

'One of us committing suicide by nicotine is quite enough,' he always said.

In front of him was a strip of asphalt which ran as straight as a ruler and faded into a leaden haze. To the right lay the fields of sodden earth, to the left the row of industrial buildings. When he came to the Castardin furniture factory with its red banners proclaiming special discounts he stopped. The gate was closed and the dog lay there on the ground, tangled up in his chain. Head framed by a dark pool. Jaws open. Eyes rolled back. Gums flecked with foam. Stiff as a piece of frozen cod. One paw sticking out, as straight and stiff as a walking stick.

Cristiano inhaled a mouthful of smoke as he looked at the corpse.

He didn't feel sorry for him.

He had died like a fool. And for what? To defend some arseholes who kept him chained up day and night and beat him with sticks to make him even more ferocious than he was by nature.

He threw the stub on the ground and walked on, as cars and lorries drove past him, churning up a spray of filthy water.

He remembered Peppina, a little mongrel with a long body and legs as short as jam jars.

His mother had got her from the dogs' home in the days before she left home. How often Cristiano had said to himself that a woman could ditch her son and husband if she liked, but not her dog. You had to be a real cow to do a thing like that.

Rino didn't want Peppina in the house because he said she was a stupid little beast and if he was in a particularly bad mood he would threaten to kill her. The real reason he didn't want her around, in Cristiano's opinion, was that she reminded him of mama, but when it came to it he never gave her away.

Cristiano was different, he liked Peppina. She always made a fuss of you, and if you picked her up she would nibble your earlobes. She lived for tennis balls. She woke up thinking of them and went to bed thinking of them.

You would throw a ball for her and she would keep going to fetch it and when you got fed up she would sit down beside you with the ball between her little paws and keep nudging at you with her nose till you threw it for her again.

One day – it must have been in the summer because it was very warm – Cristiano had arrived home from school, and the school bus (which brought primary school children right to their doors) had left him opposite the house, on the other side of the highway.

He had a treat in store for Peppina: he had gone all the way to the sports club and behind the fences of the tennis courts, in a drainage ditch choked with weeds and nettles, he had collected a lot of balls. He was on the point of crossing the road when Peppina emerged from behind the house, going like the clappers. She looked funny when she ran, like a furry train. How on earth had she heard him arrive? The wooden gate was usually closed, but that day it had only been pushed to.

Cristiano realised that the silly little mutt intended to cross the road to join him.

He looked right and left and saw a constant stream of lorries. In a split second he realised that if he shouted to her to stay where she was she would think he was urging her on and dash across the road.

He didn't know what to do. He wanted to cross the road and stop her, but there was too much traffic.

Peppina had pushed her nose between the gate and the gatepost and was trying to open it.

He had to stop her. But how?

Of course, he must throw her a ball. A long throw. Towards the back of the house. But not too high, or she wouldn't see the ball and it would all be in vain.

He took a tennis ball out of his trouser pocket, held it up so that she could see it, took aim and threw it, but even as it left his hand he realised he had misjudged it. For a moment he clutched at the air as if trying to pull the ball back, but it flew straight and fast and too low and hit the front of an approaching articulated lorry. The yellow sphere shot up into the air and fell back into the middle of the road, where it started bouncing wildly up and down. Peppina, who had managed to wriggle her way out, saw the ball in front of her and ran to get it. By some miracle she avoided the first lorry, but not the second; it ran over her, first with its front wheels, then with those of the trailer.

It was all over in a few seconds and Peppina was nothing but a heap of flesh and fur squashed on the asphalt.

Cristiano, rooted to the spot on the other side of the road, wanted to do something, wanted to pick her up off the ground, but there was a river of metal flowing in front of him.

For the rest of the day he stood at the window crying and watching Peppina's corpse being turned into a little mat. He and his father had to wait till evening, when the traffic had slowed down, to remove her remains from the road. There was hardly anything left of her – just a furry brown scarf, which his father had chucked in the rubbish bin, telling Cristiano to stop blubbing, because a dog that only lived for a ball didn't deserve to live.

So, Cristiano said to himself, Castardin's beast was the second dog he had killed in his life.

17

After turning the key in each of the three locks that sealed the door of his flat, Quattro Formaggi went up the steps that led to Corso Vittorio. It was cold, and his breath condensed in the air into white vapour. A solid grey blanket of clouds covered the sky, and it was drizzling.

Quattro Formaggi waved to Franco, a shop assistant in the Mondadori Mediastore, which occupied all the upper floors of the house.

The building stood in a central position, among the clothes shops and shoe shops, close to Piazza Bologna and the church of San Biagio.

The previous owner, the old notary Bocchiola, had died leaving the whole building to his children, except for a flat in the basement behind the lifts, which he had bequeathed to Corrado Rumitz, aka Quattro Formaggi, his trusted caretaker and factotum for over ten years.

His heirs, furious at his decision, had done everything they could to get rid of the tramp, offering him money and alternative accommodation and mobilising lawyers and psychiatrists, but to no avail. Quattro Formaggi wouldn't budge.

In the end they had managed to sell the rest of the building at a knock-down price to Mondadori, who had divided the three floors into the holy trinity: music, books and videos. The owners of the firm had, in their turn, made several attempts to buy the basement, wanting to turn it into a storehouse. But they had no luck either.

Quattro Formaggi put on his pea-green full-face crash helmet, unlocked the chain that tied up his old green Boxer and with one kick at the pedal started it first time.

The engine fired and the exhaust pipe belched out a cloud of white smoke, which snaked its way down the street and gathered under the red-and-black-striped awning of the Café Rouge et Noir.

Giuliana Citran and Colonel Ettore Manzini, who were sitting at one of its tables, started coughing, choked by the fetid smoke of the three-per-cent mixture. The old lady spat out a piece of croissant filled with white chocolate, which was instantly hoovered up by Ottavio, the colonel's wire-haired dachshund.

'Don't breathe in, whatever you do, Giuliana, don't breathe in! You've only just recovered from pneumonia!' said the colonel, pressing his napkin over his mouth.

'Oh my goodness, it's all gone down my throat! Help!' croaked Giuliana, sticking out her tongue.

It took them a few minutes to recover their composure, and by the time they had Quattro Formaggi had ridden off on his scooter, despite the fact that the centre of the village was strictly out of bounds, day and night, to any form of transport equipped with wheels, skates, air cushions or caterpillar tracks.

For a while the old lady and the colonel sat in silence, too indignant for words.

Finally, after taking a sip from her cappuccino, Giuliana managed to say: 'It's scandalous. Did you see what he did?'

The colonel shook his head. 'Quite disgraceful, Giuliana. I've heard the wretched man takes rubbish into his house.'

'Really, Ettore, do you mind? I'm eating . . . '

Manzini sank his teeth into a doughnut and said: 'I'm sorry, my dear, but these things make my blood boil. So much for all the fine talk about cleaning up the centre of Varrano. People like that need to be helped, locked away in some institution . . . '

Giuliana wiped the crumbs away from her mouth and asked: 'So you know who he is, do you?'

The colonel nodded: 'I most certainly do.'

It was rumoured in the village that Corrado Rumitz was Bocchiola's illegitimate son – that the late lamented notary had dumped him in an orphanage when he was a baby, but then, twenty years later, had been overcome with remorse and had given him a job and left him that flat which was worth a fortune.

18

As Cristiano Zena walked along the highway, resigned to going on foot, he heard the high-pitched drone of a scooter's exhaust pipe growing louder and louder behind him.

Cristiano looked round and his heart missed a beat.

A beige Scarabeo 50 with a big yellow smiley on the front was coming towards him.

It was Fabiana Ponticelli's scooter.

What am I going to do?

He looked around in a panic for some place to hide. But where? There was no cover anywhere.

He hated the idea of Fabiana Ponticelli seeing him walking along the side of the highway like a complete twat, three kilometres away from school.

So, on an impulse, he turned away towards the fields, hoping he wouldn't be recognised. Out of the corner of his eye he saw the scooter flash past. On the back seat behind Fabiana Ponticelli was Esmeralda Guerra. Both in phosphorescent windproof jackets. One pink, the other pistachio. Both in miniskirts. Both in black tights with embroidered seams, and Texan boots. Both wearing a helmet with a fluffy tail hanging down behind.

They were the same age as Cristiano (well, actually Fabiana was a year older – she'd been kept down for failing her exams – which is why she could ride a scooter). They all went to the same school, but were in different sections. The girls in H, he in B.

Cristiano didn't know them well.

They didn't recognise me.

He was wrong. After travelling another fifty metres the scooter slowed down and pulled over to the side of the road.

Don't worry; they've probably stopped because one of their mobiles was ringing.

The girls' long legs stuck out on each side of the scooter like the black legs of a tarantula. The exhaust pipe belched out white smoke.

He walked on, ignoring them and holding his breath, but finally, when he had almost passed them, he couldn't help turning to look at them.

Fabiana raised the visor of her helmet. 'Hey, you! Stop! Where are you going in this rain?'

Cristiano struggled to find enough air in his lungs to give a reply. 'To school . . . '

On the rare occasions when he talked to the two of them, something happened which always left him unhappy and frustrated.

He would become so shy that he couldn't string two words together, his body temperature would soar and his ears would burn.

If only he had been a little less awkward perhaps he could have made them laugh, become their friend, got them to like him. But this was impossible because there was a problem.

They were too beautiful.

They paralysed him. When he met those two his brain would seize up. He would become a complete moron, only able to stutter, nod and shake his head.

They had a way of behaving that made you feel like a worm.

They knew the whole school fancied them and they delighted in driving you crazy. They would start toying with you and then when they tired of it – and they tired very quickly – you no longer existed and weren't worth a gob of spit. And they were weird. They kept to themselves. They touched each other. They kissed. The other kids whispered that they were lesbians. It was as if they weren't of this world and had only come down to it for a moment to make you understand that you would never be able to have them.

The strategy that Cristiano Zena had adopted with the female sex was to ignore them. To act tough, play the guy who minds his own business, the mystery man. But he had the impression that his method wasn't very effective.

'Have you missed the bus?' Fabiana asked him.

Cristiano lit a cigarette and nodded.

'Wow! You smoke!'

He shrugged.

'School will be over by the time you get there . . . ' Fabiana eyed him, then gave a little smile. 'You don't give a shit, do you? You don't give a shit about anything.'

'Exactly.'

'Do you want a lift?'

At this point Esmeralda, squirming as if she had nettle rash, lifted her visor and snorted: 'For Christ's sake, Fabiana! We'll get stopped with three on the scooter. Forget about it. What does he matter to you? We're late.'

Cristiano only caught snatches of their conversation.

He was wondering which of them he liked more. Esmeralda was dark-skinned, with eyes as black as drops of crude oil. She had straight, raven hair and thin, plum-coloured lips. Fabiana was the exact opposite. Pure blonde, with eyes as green as pond-water and large, bloodless lips. But in other respects they were strikingly similar. They were both thin and tall, with little snub noses, long necks, straight hair that fell halfway down their backs, and small breasts. They dressed alike. And each of them wore a silver ring embossed with a beautiful skull, and had the same piercings on the eyebrow, tongue and navel. Minardi claimed to know for a fact that they had one on their fannies too and that when they were alone they fixed a chain to the rings and walked around the house in tandem.

'Come on, Esme, who's going to stop us in this weather?' Fabiana said to her friend. 'Let's put him in the middle. We can squeeze up.'

'I'll walk,' he said, without realising what he was saying.

Now it was Esmeralda's turn. She gazed at him and then said mischievously: 'What's the matter, don't you like the idea of being in between us?'

There were stories going around the school that Esmeralda and Fabiana had threesomes with the older boys from the high school. Especially with one of them, a certain Marco Mattotti, nicknamed Tekken, a burly guy with a ponytail who was the regional Thai boxing champion. Whenever Tekken turned up in front of the school on his motorbike they would fawn all over him like cats on heat and kiss him on the lips.

But there was something phoney about that scene; it was like a show that was being deliberately put on to make their male classmates sick with envy and the female ones sour and bitchy.

Countless times Cristiano had wanked off imagining he was screwing them together. And the image was always the same. While he screwed one, the other kissed him. Then they would switch roles.

He tried to banish that image from his head.

What should he do?

'Okay. I'll come,' he said with a bored sigh.

Esmeralda cheered triumphantly: 'I win! I win the bet! I told you so! I get to copy your homework.'

'Huh, some bet. Talk about predictable!' Fabiana slammed down her visor.

'What?' Cristiano couldn't stop himself asking.

Esmeralda exulted: 'I said you were all talk. That you weren't really tough and you'd accept a ride on the scooter with us. We had a bet on it.'

'Congratulations. You won,' said Cristiano, and he bowed his head and trudged off, stabbed to the heart.

19

After picking up Danilo from the Bar Boomerang, Quattro Formaggi headed for Rino Zena's home.

The old Boxer disappeared under the two of them. Danilo's big buttocks bulged halfway out from the little saddle.

Danilo hated riding on the scooter with Quattro Formaggi, who drove like a maniac, went straight through any red lights he encountered, and to make matters worse never washed.

'Today we mount the ram on the tractor and then it'll be finished, right?' Danilo yelled in Quattro Formaggi's ear.

'Right.'

The day Danilo had read the article about the ram raid on the cash machine he had rushed round to Rino's house in great excitement.

He had found him with Quattro Formaggi, drinking grappa and roasting chestnuts on the resistor coils of an electric heater.

After reading him the article, Danilo had said: 'Don't you see what a brilliant idea it is? No guns. No safes to open. No complicated plans. A nice clean job. With style. You take the cash machine away, hide it somewhere, then open it in your own good time and bingo! Loads of money, clean and ready to use.'

Rino and Quattro Formaggi hadn't been greatly impressed. They had looked at him with a glazed expression in their eyes and nodded their heads.

Over the next few days Danilo had kept on at them about the ram raid and the beneficial effects it would have on their standard of living. And in the end the other two, having nothing to do all day, had begun to come round to his way of thinking and to draw up some semblance of a plan.

First they would have to get hold of a robust car to smash through the wall of the bank. Rino's Ducato, the only vehicle they possessed, would have crumpled up like a beer can.

Danilo had suggested, after some painstaking research in *Quattroruote*, that they buy a Pajero Sport 3.0. A monster with a hundred and seventy horsepower under its bonnet.

'And how much would this powerhouse cost?' Rino had asked.

'Well, if you want it new, without optionals – and we don't need optionals – about thirty-six thousand euros.'

Rino had laughed so much he had almost choked. 'Yeah. You think I'm going to smash a luxury car like that into a wall? Oh, and just as a matter of interest, who's going to give us the money to buy it, you?'

Danilo had said that his cousin's godfather was a second-hand car dealer and would give them a fantastic discount on a 1998 Pajero in perfect condition. All they would have to do was remortgage Rino's house. 'I can't do it with my house, you see – the deeds are in Teresa's name.'

Rino had leaped to his feet and pinned him to the wall, growling: 'Are you out of your mind? Do you expect me to run up debts with the bank for you and your knicker shop?'

Danilo, purple in the face, had gurgled: 'Well, let's steal one, then.'

Ah, that was a different matter.

There was the Grand Cherokee owned by Giorgino Longo, the son of the owner of the Bottegone dello Sport, which was just waiting to be stolen. A four-by-four the size of a small truck, with huge wheels, which the young man was always showing off in out-side the bar.

To Rino the idea seemed feasible, but the problem, when it came to venturing into the realm of crime, was always the same.

Cristiano.

Rino had to keep his nose clean. He was already under the super-vision of a social worker. If the police once caught him stepping out of line the judge would instantly deprive him of custody of his son. 'I could only be a lookout.'

'And I don't drive,' Danilo had added.

The two of them had turned towards Quattro Formaggi, smiling sadistically.

As usual, he would have to do everything. How strange – he was the village idiot, the imbecile, but he was the only one who knew how to cut ignition wires and steal a car without the slightest diffi-culty.

'I won't! I don't want to . . . ' he had managed to stammer. He had a number of bones to pick with those two. A friendship was only a friendship if there was equality. He would walk through fire for them, but they would never do the same for him. And they took advantage of him, because he was too good-natured and could never say no. But although these fine concepts were perfectly clear and distinct in Quattro Formaggi's mind, when the moment came to express them they got as tangled up in his mouth as a serpent's nest. So he had concluded, purple in the face, twisting his mouth and thumping his leg: 'I won't.'

But to persuade Quattro Formaggi to do even the most incredible things all it took was a little stratagem. Refusing to talk to him and treating him coldly.

Before three days were up, desperate to get back into his friends' good graces, Quattro Formaggi had agreed to steal the off-roader.

One moonless night, when a Champions League match was on TV, Danilo and Rino dropped him not far from the villa of the owner of the Bottegone dello Sport and agreed to meet him on a piece of waste ground near the river.

And amazingly, less than an hour later two powerful yellow head-lights lit up the weed-covered field and Quattro Formaggi stepped out of the four-by-four, jumping about like a madman, dancing a jig and spluttering: 'Well? Well? I'm good. Aren't I good? Admit it!' All three of them climbed into the Grand Cherokee to celebrate with a nice big bottle of grappa.

Fantastic! Black leather seats like the ones in the dentist's waiting room. An arm rest in the middle where you could put your elbow while you were driving and insert your plastic cups. A walnut dashboard. Hundreds of little lights and indicators. They touched it in awe, as if it were an alien spaceship.

While they were fiddling about they accidentally turned on the stereo and Sting launched into 'An Englishman in New York'. On this equipment, Rino observed, even that wanker Sting sounded almost passable. And as they went on pressing buttons a screen lit up, showing a little pulsing dot near two strips, one red and one blue.

'What the hell is that?' Rino asked.

'Don't you even know that, you ignoramus? It's the satnav! That dot is us and the blue line is the river and that line there is the highway. The computer even tells you which way to go. It talks: "Straight on, turn right, turn left, no that's wrong,"' Danilo explained in the tones of an expert.

Rino shook his head. 'What the fuck have we done to our brains if we need all this electronic crap to get from one place to another?' But then he started insisting that before they used the Grand Cherokee for the ram raid they ought to go on a trip round Italy. 'It'd be great . . . We could take Cristiano to Gardaland!'

'Isn't he a bit old for Gardaland?' Danilo objected.

'Fucking hell, I promised to take him there when he was only five years old . . . There's a pirate's ship. It'd be fun.'

'Yes, it would be fun,' Quattro Formaggi concurred.

'All we'd need to do is change the number plate, and . . .' Rino was explaining when the stereo suddenly fell silent and a voice with a posh Milanese accent interrupted him: 'Good evening! Could you tell me the name of your father's favourite dish?'

The three men gaped at each other.

'Tell me what your father's favourite dish is, please.'

The voice was coming out of the speakers.

Rino gazed at the others in amazement: 'Who the fuck is speaking?'

Danilo said: 'Don't worry. It must be the car computer.'

'The computer? Why does it want to know what my father's favourite dish is? My father's dead.'

'How the hell should I know?'

The voice said: 'It's the security question. I need the answer so that I can tell whether you are the owner of the vehicle or whether the owner has lent it to you. He hasn't notified us . . . Would you please tell me what your father's favourite dish is?'

'Whose father do you mean?' Danilo put his mouth right up against the speaker. 'Mine? My father was very fond of rabbit stew.'

Rino was puzzled. 'Can a computer really understand what we're saying?'

Danilo shrugged: 'That's the new technology for you . . . '

Rino cleared his throat: 'Hello, can you hear me?'

'Loud and clear. Your father's favourite dish, please?' the voice went on unperturbed.

Danilo cocked his head on one side and then resumed his conversation with the dashboard: 'Look, who are you? Are you the car computer?'

'I am an employee of Sicurcar, the car's satellite-linked security system. If you don't give me the right answer I shall be forced to transmit your position to the nearest police station.'

The three were speechless for a moment, then Quattro Formaggi said: 'You mean you're human?'

'This is the last time I shall ask you. Your father's favourite dish?'

They exchanged glances and all three of them shrugged.

'You try,' Rino whispered to Quattro Formaggi.

'I haven't got a father. He must mean yours.'

Rino had a stab: 'Risotto with mushrooms.'

'I'm sorry? Please speak clearly.'

'Ri-sot-to with mush-rooms.'

'That is the wrong answer. I'm sorry.'

'Wait . . . Wait . . . The father . . . is he the owner of the Bottegone dello Sport?' Rino hazarded.

The voice did not reply.

Quattro Formaggi leaped out of the four-by-four. 'He said he was going to call the police. Let's get out of here!'

So the three men, running in the darkness, abandoned the Grand Cherokee, climbed into the Ducato and fled.

About a kilometre down the highway they passed a police car coming in the opposite direction.

A few days later they found a rusty old tractor and decided to get it back into working order. That at least wouldn't talk.

20

Quattro Formaggi and Danilo had nearly reached Rino's house when they passed a beige Scarabeo with two girls aboard coming in the opposite direction.

Danilo didn't notice, but Quattro Formaggi felt in his heart a sharp, stabbing pain, which for an instant took his breath away.

Ramona.

The little blonde on the front seat was just like Ramona, the heroine of *Ramona's Big Lips*, a pornographic video which Quattro Formaggi had found in a rubbish bin.

Ramona lived in America and hitch-hiked. She got picked up by lots of men who fucked her in their cars or in the desert or in motels, and she was always kind and would screw as many as three or four men at the same time. Then she met a black motorcyclist who fucked her and beat her up, but Ramona was saved by the sheriff, who took her to jail, and there too all the prisoners fucked her. On her release she met Bob the lumberjack, who had a family that lived in the woods, and there she was given a very warm welcome: they gave her turkey for dinner and then, with his wife and son, they fucked in the kitchen and then on a boat in the middle of a lake, and they all lived happily ever after. Or at least Quattro Formaggi thought they did, because after the orgy on the boat the film ended.

Quattro Formaggi had seen that film so many times he knew all the dialogue by heart. And there was one part that was his particular favourite: where Ramona went into the woods with Bob the lumberjack and she smiled and took his cock in her hand and started stroking it . . .

That little blonde on the scooter was so much like Ramona that perhaps it was actually her. Even though Ramona was American and had far bigger tits.

He would see her riding around the village with her friend. And often he would end up following her. He was very good at spying on her without being noticed. He would watch her and then he would have dirty thoughts.

Why did his brain torment him like this?

He liked Liliana. The accounts clerk at Euroedil. She was a woman, not a young girl. Alone, like him. And she was kind. She would smile at him, ask him how he was doing. He only had to find the courage to ask her out to dinner, and he could do that . . .

But a deep, hollow voice that lived inside him whispered that Liliana wasn't like Ramona.

(*Did you see her with that boy with the motorbike?*)

It was evening. Quattro Formaggi had been in the public gardens and had just found a one-armed King Kong doll for his nativity scene when he had seen the little blonde arrive with a boy on a motorbike. Hiding behind a tree he had watched them snogging and then the boy had pulled it out and she had put her hand round it.

Up and down. Up and down.

That scene had lodged in his brain like a piece of shrapnel. At night he would wake up and see it. The little hand holding that stiff thing. And Quattro Formaggi, lying on his bed, couldn't help closing his eyes, pulling down his underpants and . . .

(*Up and down. Up and down. Up and down* . . .)

. . . he was Bob the lumberjack, and the little blonde and Ramona were holding his cock.

21

The Mahatma Gandhi Junior High School stood on an artificial hill about thirty metres high which dominated the plain. It was a box-like building with large windows, which on the rare sunny days would fill with light. A trim lawn covered the slopes, and a narrow road led up to a car park for the use of the disabled and the teaching staff. Behind the school was a sports complex with an Olympic-size swimming pool and a gym.

The school had been built on the outskirts of Murelle in the early Eighties as a collection point for all the pupils from the dozens of villages in the surrounding area. It had a population of seven hundred and fifty children divided into eight sections.

Cristiano Zena was sitting at the back of the class. From his desk he stared out at the rain-lashed volleyball court, the lawn strewn with rotting leaves and behind them, half-hidden in the mist, the concrete bastions of the shopping mall 'I Quattro Camini'.

He had managed to get in halfway through the first lesson. The first excuse that had come to his mind was that a frozen water pipe had burst at home and that since his father had gone out to work he'd had to wait for the plumber. The Italian mistress had pretended to believe him.

Lately Cristiano had noticed that the teachers no longer bothered him very much. And he knew the reason why.

A few months earlier all third-year students had had to complete a questionnaire in which they were asked which high school or other institution they were going to attend after the exam. Cristiano had put a big cross against the option of not continuing his education. And on the three lines provided for an explanation he had written:

> Because I don't want to study any more there's no point and I want to work with my father.

From that day on, as if by magic, he had suddenly become invisible, like Sue Storm of the Fantastic Four. Now the bastards rarely tested him in class and if he didn't go to school at all they didn't give a shit. When he had put that cross on the form they had mentally put another one on his forehead.

He spent the rest of the first lesson and the whole of the second with his chin on his desk thinking about those two bitches Fabiana Ponticelli and Esmeralda Guerra. He had fallen for it again. He hated them.

He must do something to pay them back. Like going out with Laura Re, a girl in 3D whom they loathed because she was even more beautiful than they were.

'Hey, what about the essay? Aren't you going to do it?' A whisper brought him back into class.

It was the boy who sat next to him. Colizzi. A pathetic little nerd whom the maths mistress had put with him because Cristiano used to lark about with Minardi.

Colizzi looked like an old man. He even moved like one. He kept his desk impeccably tidy. And he wrote with a fountain pen without ever making a blot. The things he valued most in life were the cartridges of light turquoise ink that he used for his Mont Blanc. He was such a weed that it wasn't even worth hitting him – as soon as you touched him he would drop down on the ground and behave like those cockroaches that pretend to be dead when you touch them.

'What the fuck do you want, Colizzi?'

The rest of the class were bent over their sheets of paper doing the history essay. The teacher was sitting at her desk reading *Gente*. You could have heard a pin drop.

'You'd better hurry up, there's only . . . ' Colizzi looked at his gigantic calculator watch ' . . . one hour six minutes to go. You haven't written a word.'

'What the fuck do you care?'

Colizzi retreated along his seat, like a crab into a crevice in the rocks. 'Oh . . . No . . . I just . . . '

'Okay. Don't waste time. You'd better get writing, it's late. No, wait, since you're a genius you've probably finished yours already: if you write mine too I'll give you a videogame.'

The crab's eyes showed a flicker of life and then Colizzi leaned down flat over his desk and whispered, wrinkling up his nose: 'You haven't *got* any videogames.'

'No, but I can go to the mall and steal one. Just tell me which one you want.'

Colizzi thought this over for a moment, nervously rubbing his mouth with his hand. 'But will you really give it to me? You won't double-cross me like you usually do?'

Cristiano put his hand on his heart: 'Trust me.'

'All right. But you'll have to copy it out. Otherwise she'll twig.'

'Of course.'

Colizzi started scribbling away. Cristiano looked for the first time at the title written on the blackboard.

> THE RISE OF NAZISM IN GERMANY IN THE THIRTIES.
> EXPLAIN ITS CAUSES AND EFFECTS.

He smiled. 'Forget it, Colizzi. I'll do it myself. Don't worry. I know this one.'

He was an expert on Nazism. His father talked to him about it every day.

He picked up his pen, took a deep breath and began to write.

22

Rino Zena had begun working for Euroedil in Bogognano in the mid-Eighties. On the death of Bocchiola the notary, Quattro Formaggi had been taken on, and in 2002 Danilo Aprea had arrived, having lost his job in the transport firm.

Euroedil was a construction business which had prospered during the Nineties thanks to some large state contracts, but since 2003 it had been going steadily downhill and its workforce had dwindled to a few employees. Only when he won bigger commissions did the owner call in Rino and his friends to do labouring work. This happened two or three times a year. And it would only tide them over for a few weeks.

For the rest of the time the three made do with whatever work they could find. They did small transporting jobs. Emptied cellars and cesspits. Delivered plants for a nursery. Painted walls. Mended roofs. That kind of thing, often arranged at the very last moment.

They were perennially hard up and could barely make it through to the end of the month. And while Danilo and Quattro Formaggi only had themselves to think about, Rino had Cristiano to support as well.

According to a recent survey, the area comprising Varrano and the surrounding villages had one of the highest per capita incomes in Italy. Thanks to a generation of small and medium-scale businessmen who had known how to exploit the region's resources and human capital, unemployment was practically non-existent.

Our heroes were probably the only citizens of Varrano with an income of less than six hundred euros a month.

But that morning Rino was pleased. At last a bit of well-paid work was in prospect. Euroedil had won a big contract to build a new BMW showroom and was looking for labourers.

The Ducato went through Euroedil's wide gateway and into a large area of beaten earth, which that day was nothing but a quagmire, surrounded by a high fence. On one side of the yard stood the lorries, the mechanical diggers and the bulldozers, on the other the workmen's and secretaries' cars and the Porsche Cayenne of Max Marchetta, the owner's son, who during the past year had taken over the running of the firm from his father.

In the middle of the yard was a prefabricated building which contained the offices and a meeting room. Next to it, a corrugated iron shed which served as a changing room for the workmen.

Rino parked next to a big yellow bulldozer and the three men got out of the van. The rain had stopped, but there was a cold, biting wind.

'We're going to have to get out with the digger in a moment. Can you move your van?' a black man in a hard hat said to Rino.

'Move it yourself!' Rino threw him the keys and the other man, taken by surprise, dropped them and had to fish them out of the mud.

'Isn't it amazing. They're even giving the orders now.' Rino smirked at Danilo as he set off towards the offices. 'I'm going to see Marchetta. What about you two?'

Quattro Formaggi and Danilo stopped. 'We'll wait for you here . . . '

Rino wiped his boots on the mat, opened the glass door of the offices and entered a small square room. The floor was covered with imitation parquet. A glass-fronted noticeboard hung on a wall next to a closed door. Two shabby armchairs and a table littered with building trade magazines stood in a corner. Opposite them was a desk covered with an incredible number of little wooden Pinocchios.

Behind a computer screen sat Rita Pirro. The secretary had always been there, at least in Rino's memories. In her youth she hadn't been bad looking, but age had robbed her of whatever beauty she'd had.

Her age was impossible to determine. She might have been fifty, might have been sixty. Long years of sitting in that windowless little room suffering the cold in winter and the heat in summer had shrivelled her up like a kipper. She was tall and thin, had a thick layer of foundation cream on her face and wore a pair of red-rimmed glasses with a string of pearls dangling down from them. Behind her back, stuck to the wall, were some faded photographs of three toddlers playing on a seashore thick with beach umbrellas. Her children, probably all married by now.

According to Rino, Rita Pirro had once been old Angelo Marchetta's mistress. 'A blow-job now and then. That kind of thing. Short and sweet. In the office, during the lunch hour, so as not to waste any time.'

'Hello, Zena,' said the woman, looking up from the screen and scrutinising him, before her fingers continued tapping on the keyboard.

For a moment Rino had an image of her giving a blow-job to that fat old letch Angelo Marchetta, and he smiled.

'Hello, beautiful. How are things?'

The secretary didn't even turn her head. 'Can't complain.'

What a strange woman. She had always treated him like dirt. As if she was the Duchess of York and it was only by some quirk of fate that she had ended up in that dump. Hadn't she ever looked in the mirror? Hadn't she ever stopped to think that all she had to live for was a collection of Pinocchios, some children who didn't give a shit about her, a husband who had died in a factory accident and that windowless little hole?

Rino approached her desk. 'Is Marchetta in?'

'Do you have an appointment?' asked the secretary, her eyes still on the screen.

'An appointment? Since when has anyone had to have an appointment to speak to Marchetta?'

'New orders.' Rita Pirro made a movement with her head, indicating Marchetta's door. 'I'll fix you one if you like.'

Rino placed his hands on the desk and said: 'Is this the dentist's? Will he clean my teeth for me as well?'

The secretary widened her mouth into a kind of smile. 'Very funny. Would next Friday suit you?'

Rino was astounded. 'Friday? That's a week away.'

'Exactly.'

'They'll have organised the team for the BMW showroom by then.'

'That's already closed.'

'What do you mean, it's already closed? You only won the contract the day before yesterday.'

At last she raised her eyes and stared at Rino. 'Do you think we mess about here? The team was formed that very same day. Work begins on Monday.'

'Why didn't you call me? You didn't call Danilo and Quattro Formaggi either.'

'You know I don't deal with those things.'

'Where's the team list?'

The secretary went back to her typing. 'Where it always is. On the noticeboard.'

Rino went over and scanned a sheet of paper with twenty names on it. All Africans or East Europeans, with just a couple of Italian master builders.

He rested one hand against the wall and closed his eyes. 'Couldn't you have called me? Told me? We've known each other for twenty years . . . '

'What have you ever done for me?' And she rearranged some of her Pinocchios.

He felt anger spreading throughout his body like a toxin.

Keep calm . . .

Yes, he must keep calm. Cool-headed. Serene. But how do you stay serene when, as regular as clockwork, people keep ramming a cucumber up your arse?

To keep calm he was going to have to let out a bit of shit. He needed to smash something. Set fire to that fucking hut. Take one of those Pinocchio dolls and . . .

Meanwhile the bluish veins on his forearms had swollen up under his skin till they looked like macaroni and his calves had started tingling as if he had nettle rash. He clenched his fists, digging his nails into his palms, and breathed in and out to release a little anger.

But he knew that it wouldn't be enough.

When he opened his eyes again he noticed that the list was signed at the bottom by Massimiliano Marchetta.

He smiled.

23

Max Marchetta was sitting at his desk and talking on his mobile phone, arguing with the Vodafone call centre.

He was having trouble in expressing his dissatisfaction owing to the AZ Whitestrips which he had applied to his teeth and which had to be left on for at least twenty minutes. 'I just don't undersh-tand . . . I keyed in the code but I got a different ringtone. And ish awful . . . '

He was a large young man of about thirty, with a dark com-plexion and small, turquoise eyes. Beneath his strawberry-shaped nose he had grown an impeccable D'Artagnan-style moustache, and under his fleshy lips he had a goatee beard. His black hair was slicked back with gel and reflected the neon lights on the ceiling. His hands were freshly manicured.

Max Marchetta was particular about his appearance.

'A businessman must always be elegant, because elegance is synonymous with efficiency and reliability.'

He couldn't remember whether this was a saying of some important person or a slogan from an advert. It didn't matter. They were words of wisdom.

Usually he wore a tailor-made pinstriped suit with matching waistcoat. That day, however, for a change, he was dressed in a double-breasted blue blazer and a blue-and-white striped shirt with a high, three-buttoned collar sealed by a dark tie with a knot as big as your fist.

The operator's voice, in a strong Sardinian accent, asked him which ringtone he wanted to download.

'"Toxic". By Britney Shpearsh. The one that goes . . . ' and he made an attempt at humming the refrain.

The operator interrupted him. 'No, I mean which code?'

Max Marchetta picked up the magazine and checked. 'Four three four one shix.'

There was a moment's silence and then: 'Number 43416 corresponds to "Era del cinghiale bianco", by Franco Battiato.'

'What do you mean? Why does it shay in this magazhine that "Toxic" is four three four one shix, then? Why does it shay that?'

'I don't know . . . Maybe the magazine got it wrong . . . '

'Oh, they got it wrong, did they? And who's going to give me back my three euros? Vodafone?' As he talked he sprayed out little drops of foam.

The operator was caught off guard. 'I hardly think it's Vodafone's fault if the magazine printed the code wrongly.'

'It's eashy to go around blaming other people! It's the Italiansh' national shport, isn't it? What do you people care if your clients loshe their money? And your tone ish very offensive.' Max picked up his pen and held it against his diary. 'What'sh your . . . '

He was on the point of demanding the operator's name to scare the shit out of him, but suddenly he found himself up in the air. The next moment he flew over the desk and crashed into a wall covered with framed photographs. A second later a copy of his degree certificate in Economics and Business Studies fell on his head.

Max thought the gas tank must have exploded and that the shock wave had hurled him out of his chair, but then he saw two paint-spattered boots, and at that very moment two burly arms covered with ugly tattoos lifted him up by his lapels and pinned him against the wall like a poster.

He spat out all the air that he had in his body and, with his diaphragm contracted, tried to breathe in but without succeeding, and made a sound like the gurgle of a blocked drain.

'You're short of air. A horrible feeling, isn't it? It's like the feeling you get when you reach the end of the month and don't know where the fuck you're going to find the money to pay your bills.'

Max couldn't hear the voice. A jet engine was roaring in his ears and all he could see was some streaks of light criss-crossing in front of his eyes. Like when he had been small and there had been a firework display at Ferragosto. His mouth was open and a whitening strip hung from his upper teeth.

If I don't breathe I'm going to die. That was the only thought his brain was capable of formulating.

'Calm down. The more you struggle the less you'll breathe. Don't be frightened, you're not going to die,' the voice now advised him.

At last the contraction of his diaphragm eased, Max's rib cage opened and a stream of air flowed down his windpipe and into his lungs.

He brayed like a donkey on heat and gradually started breathing again. And as his purple face returned to its natural colour he noticed that about twenty centimetres from his nose there was the smiling face of a skinhead.

Then he recognised it. His anal sphincter contracted to the diameter of a stick of macaroni.

It was Zena.

Rino Zena.

24

Rino Zena examined the terrified face of that pansy Max Marchetta. His moustaches had gone limp and looked like two rats' tails, his glistening, greasy quiff hung down over his forehead like a shed roof.

Rino couldn't make out what that piece of cellophane was that was hanging from his teeth.

He continued to hold him pinned to the wall with his left arm.

'Please . . . Please . . . I haven't done anything to you . . .' whimpered Marchetta desperately, waving his arms like a disco dancer.

'Well, I'm going to do something to you.' Rino raised his right arm and closed his fist. He took aim at the nose, anticipating the pleasure of hearing the septal cartilage crunch under his knuckles. But his fist remained suspended in the air.

Right next to that terror-stricken face hung a photograph. It had been taken in open country, on a windy day. The reeds with their plumes were bent over to one side. The sky was streaked with wispy clouds. In the centre was old Marchetta, in his younger days. He was short and round-faced. He was wearing a heavy, ankle-length overcoat, and holding his cloth cap down on his head with one hand and clasping his walking stick in the other. Around him stood five workmen in blue overalls. In a corner, slightly to one side, was Rino, sitting on the wheel of a tractor. He was thin and gaunt. At his feet sat Ritz, Marchetta's fox terrier. A thick pipe came out of the ground and ran across the field. Everyone was looking at the camera lens with very solemn expressions on their faces. Including the dog.

Still holding Max Marchetta fast, Rino grasped the picture and lifted it off its hook.

In one corner was the date '1988'. Nearly twenty years had passed.

Such a long time.

Then Rino looked again at the young businessman who stood there motionless, with his eyes screwed up and his arms in front of his face, whispering: 'Mercy. Mercy. Mercy.'

So this was the new owner of Euroedil. A guy who spent his days waxing his chest and looking at himself in the mirror at the gym and who as soon as anyone raised their fists started begging for mercy.

He grabbed him by the scruff of the neck and hurled him on the sofa.

25

Max Marchetta opened his eyes slowly, with the expression of a lobster that has been dangled over a cauldron of boiling water and then, by some inscrutable decree of fate, put back in the fishtank.

In the chair, on the other side of the desk, sat Rino. He had lit a cigarette and was looking straight through him as though he was facing a ghost. He was holding the photo. A very, very unpleasant feeling was forming inside Max Marchetta. He was going to remember this day for a long time, if he was still capable of remembering.

Zena had gone mad and was dangerous. How often had he read in the news about workers running amok and murdering their bosses? A few months earlier near Cuneo some workers had set fire to a young textile entrepreneur in the car park of his factory.

He peeked at the cigarette in Zena's mouth.

I don't want to be burned to death.

'Look at this photograph.' The psychopath tossed the plexiglass frame over to him. Max caught it. He looked at it and then sat motionless.

26

Rino Zena leaned back in his chair and focused on a corner of the ceiling. 'Eighteen years ago. A fucking eternity. I'm the thin one on the right. Sitting on the tractor. I still had a good head of hair then. Do you know how long it took us to build that water pipe? Three weeks. It was my first real job. One of those where you turn up at five in the morning and go home at dusk. On the twenty-eighth we'd get our pay cheque. Your father would hand one to each worker and every time he'd crack the same old joke: 'I'm paying you this month; I don't know if I will next month.' In hindsight it wasn't so very funny. But you could bet your life he would say those words. Just as you could bet your life you'd get your money on the twenty-eighth, even if the Third World War had broken out that very same day. Do you see that workman there, the shortest one? His name was Enrico Sartoretti; he died ten years ago. Lung cancer. Two months and he was gone. It was him who introduced me to your father. In those days there was only the shed where the changing rooms are now. And your father worked in a sort of glass booth. But you must remember that. I used to see you sometimes. You used to turn up in a red sports car. We must be about the same age, you and me. Anyway, to cut a long story short, your father took me on on trial the very day they started building the pipe that took the water out of the river and carried it to the power station. Twenty days to finish it. And there were six of us. In all my life I don't think I've ever worked so hard as I did in those three weeks. On the last day we worked till four in the morning. And fuck me if we didn't finish on time.'

What the hell has got into me? Rino asked himself. Why was he telling that son of a bitch all these things? And yet he felt that it was doing him good. He picked up a paperweight made from an old brick faced with a brass plaque, and turned it over in his hands.

'Your father cared about his workers. I don't mean he was like a father to us or any of that crap. If you didn't do your job properly you were out on your ear. No two ways about it. But if you didn't complain and you worked hard he respected you. If there was work, you could be sure he'd call you.

'One Christmas he turned up with panettoni and bottles of spumante and gave one to every other workman but none to me. I was upset. Then I thought I must have fucked something up and that he was angry with me. That job was important; if he sacked me I was in the shit. He called me into his office and said: "Did you see that? No panettone for you." I asked him if I'd done something wrong and he looked at me and said yes I bloody well had – I'd brought a son into the world without having the wherewithal to give him a decent life. I told him it was none of his business. He was beginning to piss me off. Who did he think he was to pass judgement on my life?

'But he burst out laughing. "Are you planning to bring him up in some ramshackle hut? The first thing is a house; everything else comes afterwards." And he told me to look out of the window. Well, there was nothing outside but a truck loaded with bricks. I didn't understand. "You see those bricks?" he said "They're for you. They were left over from the last job. If you use them sparingly you might even get two floors out of them." And using those bricks, working at weekends, I built my house.' Rino continued to turn the brick over in his hands. 'They were just like this one here. I don't expect your father has ever told you that story; he's not the type. And when the phone calls started getting less frequent I realised Euroedil must be in trouble. There are more building firms around now than there are dog turds. The last time I saw him was about six months ago, in the little park near Corso Vittorio. He was on a bench. His head was nodding and his hands were shaking. There was a Filipino who treated him like a baby. He didn't recognise me. I had to repeat my name three times. But in the end he understood. He smiled. And do you know what he said to me? He said there was no need to worry, you were there now. And Euroedil was in good hands. Can you believe that? In good hands.'

Rino slammed the brick on the table, splitting it in two, and Max Marchetta shrank even further back into the huge black leather armchair.

'You're a lucky man, you know. If I hadn't seen that photograph you'd be in an ambulance by this time, believe you me. But you got away with it, as you always will, because the world is made for people like you.' Rino smiled. 'The world is made to measure for nonentities. You're clever. You take the black slaves and those bastards from the East and you pay them peanuts. And they put up with it. Hunger's an ugly beast. And what about the guys who've worked their arses off for this firm? Sod them. You don't even waste a phone call on them. The truth is, you've got no respect for those sons of bitches who come to steal the bread from our mouths, or for us, or even for yourself. Look at you, you're a clown . . . A clown dressed up as a manager. If I'm not going to break every bone in your body it's only out of respect for your father. In the end, you see, it all comes down to respect.'

Rino got up from the chair, opened the door and left the office.

27

It took Max Marchetta about two minutes to get over the fright. His behaviour in such situations was much the same as that of a pilchard. After an attack, if it manages to survive, a pilchard starts swimming around again just as energetically as before.

Max stood up, smoothed down his suit with his fingers and straightened his hair. His hands were still shaking and his armpits felt as cold as if they had ice cubes under them.

He took a deep breath and wondered if the whitening strip he had swallowed when he had been rammed against the wall would be bad for his stomach. Should he ring his dentist? Or a gastro-enterologist?

How on earth had his father been able to stand working with such people? That psychopathic Nazi, along with all those other layabouts, had nearly been the ruin of Euroedil.

The niggers were different: they had respect. And he thanked his father's arteriosclerosis for enabling him to take up his rightful position and steer the ship back into safer waters where he could repair the leaks and drive out the parasites that had been infesting it.

At least Zena wouldn't show his face round there again. Something advised him not to mobilise lawyers and make official complaints, but to overlook what had occurred and keep out of his way.

But there was someone else who was going to have to pay. That stupid bitch of a secretary hadn't warned him of Zena's arrival, and hadn't even taken the trouble to call the police.

He lifted the telephone, pressed a button and said in a quavering voice: 'Mrs Pirro, could you come here, please?' He hung up and straightened the knot of his tie.

For weeks he had been looking for an excuse to get rid of the old bat. Well, she had presented him with one on a silver salver.

28

The Nazis originated in Germany in the early twentieth century. And they owe everything to Adolf Hitler who thought up the whole idea.

Adolf Hitler was a penniless painter but, he had a great dream of glory making Germany the strongest nation in the world and then conquering the whole of Europe. In order to do this he had to drive, out of Germany all the Jews who were polluting the Aryan race. The Jews had come and now they owned the factries and practised usury, forcing the Germans to work in the steel factories. The Aryan race was the strongest in the world, only: they needed a leader and Hitler knew he had to get power and take it by force and then send all the Jews to the concentration camps because, they were polluting the master race. He invented the sign of the swastika, which is the sign of the rising sun and he told the Germans that if they believed in him they would get rid of the politicians and then he would create an invincible army. And he did all this because together with Napoleon, he was the greatest man in history. Though really Hitler is greater than Napoleon;

today we need a new Hitler, to drive out of Italy all the niggers and the im migrants who steal work and to help real Italians to work. The niggers and the im migrants are creating a mafia in Italy: worse than that created by the Jews in the second world war. The trouble is nobody in Italy is patriotic any more.

The European community is wrong every nation is different and the Slavs must not be allowed to steal the Italians' jobs and women. Because the Italians, have always been the strongest just think of the ancient Romans and off Julius Caesar who conquered the world and brought civilization to the barbarians who were Germans too by the way.

People hate Nazism today because they pretend it's right to be open to different cultures. They always say that, but they don't really believe it themselves. The Arabs are worse than the Jews: look at what they do to women they treat them like slaves and make them go around dressed in black cloaks. And they should cut each others' throats in their own countries. They want to distroy us. They hate us. Because our culture is superior. We must fight back. Attack them with our army and exterminate them, like the Jews.

Cristiano paused for a moment. It was as if he had opened a tap and the words had gushed out. He hadn't said much about how the Nazis had seized power because he couldn't remember the dates. The essay was a bit on the short side, too, but there was only a quarter of an hour left before they had to hand their work in and he still had to make a fair copy.

29

While Rino was talking to Max Marchetta, Quattro Formaggi had slipped away from Danilo and gone to the personnel office.

He had looked in through the window. Sitting at her desk was Liliana Lotti.

For a while Quattro Formaggi stood there looking at her, knowing he himself was unobserved. She was a bit plump, but she was beautiful. Not at first sight. You had to look carefully and then you discovered that her beauty was hidden beneath her fat. She kept it covered as grasshoppers do with their colourful wings.

Besides, he and Liliana had a lot of things in common. They weren't married. They lived alone. And they both loved pizza (though her favourite was the Napolitana). She had a little dog. He had two turtles.

He often saw her at San Biagio, at the six o'clock mass. When they exchanged the sign of peace she would smile at him. And once, a few days before Christmas, he had met her in the high street carrying a lot of plastic bags.

'Corrado!' she had called out.

No one ever called him Corrado, so it had been a few moments before Quattro Formaggi had realised she was talking to him.

'How are you?'

He had straightened his glasses and thumped himself on the thigh. 'Very well, thank you.'

'I've been buying the usual presents for my relatives . . . ' Liliana had opened the bags, full of brightly coloured parcels. 'How about you? Are you giving any presents?'

Quattro Formaggi had shrugged.

'Look what I've bought . . . But this one's for me.' Out of one plastic bag she had taken a statuette of a fishmonger standing behind a market stall covered with octopus, mussels and silvery fish. 'This year I took my crib out of the cellar. And I thought it needed a new character.'

Quattro Formaggi had turned it over in his hands, astonished.

'Do you like it?'

'Yes. It's beautiful.' He wanted to tell her that he had a crib too, but supposing she asked to see it? He couldn't let her into the flat.

'Listen, why don't you take it? As a Christmas present from me. I know, I really should wrap it up . . . '

Quattro Formaggi had felt his face flush with embarrassment. 'I can't . . . '

'Please take it. I'd be so happy.'

In the end he had accepted it. He had put it beside one of the lakes in his crib. He considered it, together with the Barbapapa, the finest piece in the whole scene.

If now, for example, he were to enter the office and greet her, he was sure Liliana would be pleased. The problem was that he found it impossible to speak to her. As soon as he came anywhere near her the words dried up.

Quattro Formaggi gave himself a thump on the leg and a slap on the neck, summoned up his courage and grasped the handle of the door, but then he saw her answer the phone and start fiddling with a large envelope full of papers.

Some other time.

30

Danilo Aprea, leaning against the van, saw Rino come striding out of the prefabricated building. From his manner it was clear that he was furious. He must have found out that they had been dumped.

Danilo had known for a couple of days that Marchetta's son didn't want them, but had kept the news to himself.

He had heard it from Duccio, one of the old team, who had also been ditched.

But that job with Euroedil was a serious problem. It would have gone on for a month, if not longer. And Rino, who wasn't really that keen on the bank raid, would have dropped out as soon as he had the money in his pocket; and if he had dropped out, Quattro Formaggi would have followed suit.

It was madness to slog your guts out for others when you had a foolproof plan for making a million.

At the moment, however, Rino was too angry; this wasn't the time to discuss the raid with him. Like a pressure cooker: he needed to have his steam let out before you opened him up.

Danilo had a two-and-a-half litre bottle of grappa in his bag. The perfect extinguisher for spitting rages and similar complaints.

'Let's go. Come on. Get in.' Rino climbed into the Ducato and turned on the engine.

Danilo and Quattro Formaggi obeyed without a word.

The van moved off, raising a spray of mud, and shot out onto the road without stopping at the give-way line.

'What happened?' asked Quattro Formaggi hesitantly.

Rino stared at the road, his jaw quivering. 'We've finished with that dump.' Then he went on: 'I should have killed him, but . . . Why didn't I? What the fuck's got into me lately?'

' . . . for Cristiano's sake,' Quattro Formaggi prompted him.

Rino swallowed, squeezing the steering wheel as if he was trying to snap it. His eyes were glistening, as though he had put them too close to a flame.

'Yes, that's it. I held back for Cristiano's sake.'

Danilo realised that this was the moment to produce the extinguisher. He opened his battered old bag and pulled out the bottle.

'Surprise, surprise!' He unscrewed the top and waved the grappa in front of Rino's nose.

'If it wasn't for you two . . . ' Rino was overcome by emotion and couldn't finish the sentence. He opened his mouth and gulped in air. 'Give it here.' He took a good swig. 'Shit, what hooch! It tastes like turpentine. Where did you get it, the DIY store?'

The three of them passed it around in silence. None of them was thinking about where they were going. On either side, beyond the rows of skeletal trees, the fields of black earth ran by, with their rows of high-tension pylons resembling little Eiffel Towers.

Suddenly Rino started chuckling.

'What's so funny?' asked Quattro Formaggi.

'That prick Marchetta. He had some of those whitening strips on his teeth. Like the ones in the TV adverts. He swallowed one of them . . . '

All three of them starting roaring with laughter and thumping the dashboard of the van.

The alcohol was finally taking effect.

Rino dried away his tears. 'Hey, weren't we supposed to be finishing the work on your tractor?'

Danilo sat up abruptly. 'Damn right we were! The only thing missing is the ram.'

Rino switched on the radio, did a U-turn and headed back towards the village. 'Okay, but first we'll go and pick up Cristiano. We'll surprise him!'

31

We can be a great pure nation again like the ancient Romans where there'll be jobs for everyone and there won't be any communists who've destroyed the idea of the family, they don't believe in God and they've accepted abortion which is murder of the innocents and they want to give the vote to the immigrants.

THE END

Cristiano quickly re-read the essay.

It was good. Pretty damn good.

He took a clean sheet of paper and was about to start writing out the fair copy, when a doubt crossed his mind. He stopped. He read it through again more carefully.

No, he couldn't hand it in. That commie bitch his teacher would show it to the social worker.

Doubtfully he read it through yet again, gnawing at the end of his pen.

Why land yourself in the shit for the sake of a stupid essay? It's a pity, though, it was really very good.

He carefully folded the sheet of paper and slipped it into the pocket of his trousers.

'What's up?' asked Colizzi, who had handed in his own essay half an hour since and was doing a cryptic crossword.

'Nothing. I'm not handing it in.'

'You see? You should have let me do it for you.' said Colizzi.

Cristiano didn't even bother to reply. He rested his chin on the desk and looked out of the window. He was astonished.

On the other side of the lawn, where the downward slope began, were his father, Danilo and Quattro Formaggi. They were sitting on a bench, looking perfectly relaxed, with their legs stretched out in front of them, as they passed around a bottle of grappa.

Cristiano was about to wave to them, but restrained himself and glanced at the clock above the teacher's desk. Only seven minutes to go to the bell.

If only he had a mobile phone . . . He grabbed Colizzi's fingers and gently squeezed. 'Give me your mobile,' he whispered.

'I can't. Please, my mother checks it every evening. She'll kill me if I make a call.'

Cristiano squeezed a little harder. 'You'd better hand it over.'

Colizzi grimaced and stifled a yelp. 'Be quick, though. And call a TIM number if you can. I've got the Horizon special offer.'

Cristiano took the phone and rang his father. He saw him pat the pockets of his jacket and take out his own mobile.

'Hello?'

'Papa! What are you doing here?'

'When do you finish?' Rino turned towards the school, spotted

Cristiano behind the window and pointed him out to the other two, who started waving.

'In five minutes.'

'We'll be waiting for you.'

Cristiano burst out laughing.

Those idiots out there had started dancing. They were doing a conga round the bench.

32

The Ducato bumped along the little road dotted with puddles and white stones which followed the bank of the Forgese. Reeds and brambles scraped against the sides of the van.

The sky was grey, but the rain had stopped.

Cristiano Zena was squeezed in between his father, who had his feet up against the windscreen and was smoking as he gazed blankly at the road ahead, and Danilo, who was mechanically clicking his mobile on and off. Quattro Formaggi was driving.

When they hit the bottle too hard it was always Quattro Formaggi who drove. Today they had started drinking earlier than usual; usually they didn't reach that state till mid-afternoon.

Cristiano guessed there had been a problem at the construction firm. The previous day Rino had told him they were going to start a job, yet here they were . . .

But if they didn't volunteer any information it was better not to ask.

He looked at Quattro Formaggi. Alcohol had no effect on him. According to Rino it was because of the electric shock. Whatever the reason, Cristiano had never once seen him drunk.

He adored Quattro Formaggi.

With him you didn't need to speak to make yourself understood. And it wasn't true that he was stupid. If he didn't say much it was because the electricity had affected his speech. But he was attentive: he listened to everything that was said and made strange movements with his head as if he was conducting the conversation.

Cristiano would spend whole days with him. They would watch TV and ride around on the Boxer. Quattro Formaggi was a skilled mechanic and could get even the rustiest old banger working again. And if you needed anything or asked him for a lift, even if you wanted to go to the back of beyond, he never said no.

Sure, he was strange, with all those tics and his manias, like his thing about never letting anyone into his flat. Cristiano could have killed all the bastards who made fun of him. There were even rumours that he kept his mother's corpse in his home and claimed she was still alive so he could draw her pension. But that was bullshit.

Quattro Formaggi was an orphan.

Like me.

'What did you do at school today?' asked Danilo, interrupting Cristiano's thoughts.

'We wrote a history essay. Shall I read it to you?'

'Yes, let's hear it,' said Quattro Formaggi.

'Let's hear it,' echoed Danilo.

'Okay.' Cristiano took the sheet of paper out of his pocket and started reading. With all those ruts in the road he felt sick. He made an effort to get to the end. ' . . . like the ancient Romans where there'll be jobs for everyone and there won't be any communists who've destroyed the idea of the family, they don't believe in God and they've accepted abortion which is murder of the innocents and they want to give the vote to the im migrants. The end.' He looked up. 'Well, did you like it?'

Quattro Formaggi honked the horn enthusiastically.

Danilo was in raptures. 'Fantastic! Incredible! Especially the bit where you say we need a new Hitler to build concentration camps for the Slavs and Arabs. Those bastards steal our jobs. Top marks!'

Cristiano turned towards his father. 'What about you? Did you like it?'

Rino took a draw on his cigarette and didn't reply.

What's the matter with him now?

Half an hour earlier he had been capering about like a lunatic and now he was scowling.

Danilo patted Cristiano on the thigh. 'Of course he did. It's a brilliant essay. Nobody could help liking it. It's impossible.'

33

Rino Zena put his feet down on the floor and looked at Cristiano, then stubbed out his Diana Rossa in the overflowing ashtray. His migraine had risen like an acidic tide and swamped his brain. It was that shit Danilo had given him to drink.

He glared at his son. 'Are you out of your mind?'

Cristiano looked at Danilo in bewilderment. 'Why?'

'Did you hand that stuff in?'

Cristiano shook his head. 'No, I didn't. I'm not daft.'

'Bollocks. You handed it in. I know you too well. You're so full of yourself you thought you'd written a masterpiece. You can't understand, with that pea-sized brain of yours, what a fucking stupid thing you've done. Do you realize you're going to regret this day for the rest of your life?'

Cristiano's voice cracked: 'I didn't hand it in, I said! Are you deaf? I wrote it, then I put it in my pocket. End of story! Here it is.'

Breathe. Calm down. Maybe he's telling the truth. 'Did you show it to anyone?' he asked him, suppressing the urge to grab him by the hair and bang his head on the dashboard.

Cristiano gave him a hate-filled glare. 'No, I didn't.'

'You must have read it to your classmates. It's only natural.'

'I swear to God I didn't, for fuck's sake!'

Rino pointed his finger at him. 'Don't you dare use God's name to cover up your lies, Cristiano. Don't use His name. Or I'll kill you.'

34

He hated him when he was like this.

He didn't believe him. And he never would. Not even if the teacher materialised in front of him and told him Cristiano hadn't handed in the essay. Not even if God, the Madonna and all the saints came down from heaven. He would think they were all in it together. All conspiring against him.

What sort of father have I got?

Anyone with any guts had told him to his face that Rino was a fool, and Cristiano had flown at them like a wildcat. He had taken a lot of beatings in the course of his life defending a stupid dickhead. But they were right, a thousand times right. Cristiano felt a piercing pain below his breastbone. 'I haven't shown it to anyone.'

Rino shook his head and gave that infuriating little smirk of his. 'Come on, admit it. You did it without thinking, you didn't realise what you were doing, you were just showing off to your mates . . . "I'm a Nazi, I'm this, I'm that." Where's the harm in that? Come on, admit it. What's the problem?'

Cristiano couldn't take any more. 'No,' he shouted, 'I didn't do that! Fuck off! You're not going to get me to confess to things I didn't do. Anyway, I haven't *got* any friends. And do you know why? Because everyone thinks you're a weirdo. Just a pathetic weirdo . . . '

He was close to tears, but he would have torn his eyes out of their sockets rather than cry.

35

Rino Zena couldn't hear anything. A whirlpool of terror had sucked him down into darkness. He could already picture the social worker accompanied by two carabinieri waving Cristiano's essay in front of his face.

They would take him away. For ever.

And that couldn't happen, because without Cristiano he was nothing.

Rino swallowed hard and put his hands over his eyes. 'Where the fuck do you get these ideas?' He spoke quietly, breathing through his nose. 'How many times have I told you you've got to keep everything inside . . . you mustn't let anyone know what you think, or they'll use it against you. You and I are hanging by a thread, don't you realise that? And everyone's trying to break it. But they won't succeed. I'll always be with you and you'll always be with me. I'll help you and you'll help me. Don't you understand that you must never bare your throat? Think of tortoises, think of their shells. Always remember you've got be so strong that nobody can harm you.' He slammed his fist down on the dashboard so hard that the glove box shot open, spewing out paper.

'Why do you do this, papa? Why don't you believe me?' said Cristiano in a broken voice.

'Don't whine like that! Nobody's hurt you, have they? What are you, a little girl? Are you going to burst into tears?'

Danilo motioned to Cristiano not to react and to keep quiet, and tried to mediate: 'Come on now, Rino, he told you the truth. Your son doesn't tell lies. You know him.'

Rino rounded on him. 'You shut your face! Don't interfere! Do I interfere in the problems between you and that whore of a wife of yours? I'm talking to my son. So keep quiet.'

Danilo lowered his gaze.

Cristiano dried his eyes with his hands. Nobody dared to speak. Everyone sat in silence, and the only sound was the background noise of the river and of the branches brushing against the sides of the van.

36

They stopped in the yard of a disused sand-dredging works from the Seventies. Huge mounds of sand formed a semicircle round the rusty machinery.

Cristiano jumped out and ran towards the extraction tower.

He stopped by a tumbledown hut. Its windows were smashed and it was plastered with graffiti and drawings.

He wanted to go home on foot. It was a long way, but that didn't matter. Although the air was cold, it probably wouldn't rain for a while. The weather was changing. To the south the grey blanket of clouds had broken up, revealing patches of crystalline blue. A pair of cormorants flew overhead. The sound of the rain-swollen river could be heard in the distance.

He pulled his hoodie over his head.

In front of the hut were the charred remains of a bonfire. The metal skeleton of a chair. Tyres contorted by the heat. Some sandals. A gas cooker.

Cristiano took the essay out of his pocket and flicked on his cigarette lighter. He was about to put the flame to the paper when he heard behind him: 'Cristiano! Cristiano!'

His father was approaching. He wore a tartan woolly jacket with a plush lining. It was open and he only had a vest on underneath.

How come he never feels the cold?

He set light to a corner of the paper.

'Wait!' Rino took it out of his hand and blew on it, putting out the fire.

Cristiano lunged at him, trying to snatch it back. 'Give it to me. It's mine.'

His father took two steps backwards. 'Are you crazy? Why do you want to burn it?'

'So there won't be any evidence. And you'll be happy. There's always a chance burglars might break in during the night and steal it, isn't there? Or the police . . . Or the extraterrestrials . . . '

'No, don't burn it.'

'What do you care? You didn't even like it.' Cristiano ran off towards the river.

'Stop!'

'Leave me alone! I want to be on my own.'

'Wait!' His father caught up with him and grabbed him by the arm.

Cristiano tried to wriggle free, shouting: 'Let me go! Go away! Fuck off!'

Rino hugged him tightly and held his face against his chest. 'Listen to me for a moment. Then you can go if you want.'

'What do you want?'

Rino let go, and stroked his shaven skull. 'It's just that . . . Look . . . ' He was having difficulty in finding the words. Finally he lit a cigarette. ' . . . You must understand that if I get angry there's a reason . . . If you'd handed it in, that bitch of a teacher of yours would have immediately given it to that arsehole of a social worker and tomorrow we would have had them both on our doorstep waving your essay in our faces.'

'I'm not a fool and I didn't hand it in. I've told you that, but you don't believe me. What's the point?'

'Look, it's just that . . . I wanted to be sure.' Rino kicked at a rock and then, with a sigh, looked up at the clouds. 'I'm scared, Cristiano . . . Scared they'll split us up. That's what they want. If they split us up, I . . . '

He didn't finish the sentence. He squatted down and went on smoking his cigarette, holding it between his thumb and forefinger.

All Cristiano's anger melted away like the snow that had fallen that night. He felt an overwhelming urge to hug his father, but just said, with a lump in his throat: 'I'll never let you down. You must believe me, papa, when I tell you things.'

Rino looked at his son, then narrowed his eyes, with the stub between his lips, and said in a serious voice: 'I'll believe you if you can beat me.'

'What?' Cristiano didn't understand.

'I'll believe you if you can beat me to the top.' He pointed to the hill of sand in front of them.

'What the fuck has that got to do with it?'

'Never mind about that. Don't you realise what a fantastic opportunity this is for you? If you beat me I'll have to believe you for the rest of my life.'

Cristiano was trying not to laugh. 'What a load of bullshit . . . Typical . . . '

'What's the problem? You're young. Athletic. I'm an old man. Why shouldn't you win? Just think, if you beat me you'll be able to tell me that you heard Quattro Formaggi repeat "Thirty-Three Travellers from Trento" and I'll have no choice . . . You little bastard!'

Cristiano had suddenly sprinted off towards the hill of sand.

'This time I am going to beat you!' growled Cristiano, hurling himself at the steep side of the little mountain.

He took the first three steps and had to dig his hands into the sand to stop himself sliding back. All the sand was crumbling away. His father was below him, a couple of metres behind.

He had to win this time. He always lost against his father. At darts. At arm wrestling. At everything. Even at ping-pong, where

Cristiano knew he was an ace and his father was crap. He would get to eighteen or nineteen–six, and only two points away from trouncing him, then that bastard would start telling him he was tiring, that he was scared of winning – he would dazzle him with words and he wouldn't score another point and Rino would win.

Not this time. I'm going to beat you.

He imagined he was an enormous, climbing spider. The secret was to dig your feet and hands right in. The sand was cold and damp. The higher he climbed, the steeper the slope became, and it crumbled under his shoes.

He turned to check where his father was. He was getting closer. His face was contorted with the effort, but he wasn't slowing down.

The trouble was, every three steps Cristiano took forward he slipped another two back. The top wasn't far away, but it seemed impossible to reach.

'Go on, Cristiano! Go on . . . You can do it! Beat him!' Danilo and Quattro Formaggi cheered him on from below.

He put everything into it, shouting with the effort, and he was almost there, only a metre and a half from the top, he'd made it, he'd beaten him, when a clamp gripped his ankle. He was pulled down, together with a landslide of sand.

'It's not fair!' he shouted, as his father went straight over him as if he had caterpillar tracks. Cristiano tried to grab him by the seat of his pants, but his hand slipped and he nearly got a kick in the face.

And his father dug his hands into the summit of the hill, got to his knees and raised his arms to the sky as if he'd scaled K2, shouting: 'Victory! Victory!'

Cristiano lay there gasping, flat on the sand, half a metre from the top, while everything around him crumbled away.

'Hey . . . Come on up. You nearly made it. Never mind. After all, you did come second . . . you weren't last,' panted his father, bent double with the effort.

'It's not fair! You held me back.'

'What about you, then . . . starting before the word go? Is that . . . sporting?'

He was blue in the face. 'Jesus, I'm knackered . . . The cigarettes . . . Come on, give me that hand.'

Cristiano grasped his father's hand and allowed himself to be pulled up. He was sick with exhaustion.

'Well, you lost . . . But . . . you did well . . . I believe you.'

'You . . . bastard. I let you win . . . because you're an old man . . . That's the only reason you won . . . '

'Yes . . . And quite right too. You should always show respect to the elderly.' Rino put his arm round his shoulders.

Father and son sat on the top of the hill, looking down at the misty plain and the river, which at that point widened out into a big, sandy loop. The opposite bank was far away, lost in the haze, with only the bare tops of the poplars showing through, like the masts of ghost ships. Further downstream the river had overflowed its banks, flooding the fields. They could see the silhouette of the power station, the string of electricity pylons and the viaduct along which the motorway ran.

Rino broke the silence: 'It was a good essay. I liked it. What you said was right. Immigrants out, jobs for the Italians. That's right.'

Cristiano scooped up a handful of sand and made it into a ball. 'Sure, we don't even have the freedom to write what we think.'

Rino zipped up his jacket. 'Don't give me that crap about freedom. Everybody talks about freedom. Freedom here, freedom there. They fill their mouths with it. What good is freedom? If you're penniless and jobless you have all the freedom in the world, but you can't do a thing with it. You're free to go away if you want, you say. But where to? And how are you going to get there? Tramps are the freest people in the world, but they freeze to death on park benches. Freedom is a word that only serves to delude people. Do you know how many fools have died for freedom when they didn't even know what it was? Do you know who are the only people who really have freedom? The rich. They have freedom, all right . . . ' He mused in silence for a while, then put his hand on his son's arm. 'Do you want to see what my freedom looks like?'

Cristiano nodded.

Rino pulled out a pistol from behind his back. 'This young lady's last name is freedom and her first name is Magnum 44.'

Cristiano's jaw dropped. 'My God, it's beautiful.'

'It's a peach. Smith & Wesson. Short barrel. Chromium plated all over.' Rino held it in his hand approvingly. He pulled out the chamber, spun it round, then snapped it back into place.

'Let me touch it.'

Rino held it out to him butt first.

'Wow, it's heavy. Is this the gun that's used by . . . ?' Cristiano held it in both hands and aimed into the distance. 'What's his name? The detective in *The Enforcer*?'

'Dirty Harry. Only his has a long barrel. What do you think? Isn't it great?'

'It's incredible. What would have happened if I'd shot Castardin's dog with this?'

'You'd have blasted him out onto the road. This girl's an orphan, like you. Only she's lost her father as well as her mother. Her serial number has been erased.'

Cristiano closed one eye, held his arm out full length and tilted the gun over at an angle. 'How much did you pay for it?'

'Not much . . . '

'Why did you buy it? You've already got the Beretta . . . '

'That's enough questions! Aren't you going to ask me if you can try it out?'

Cristiano gazed at his father incredulously. 'Can I?'

'Yes. But mind the recoil. This gun's not like the other one. It's got a real kick. Release the safety catch. Hold it in both hands. Stay loose. Don't stiffen up or you'll hurt yourself. And keep it well away from your face.'

Cristiano obeyed. 'What shall I aim at?'

Rino looked around for a target. When he found one he smiled. 'Hit the bowl of macaroni. We'll give those two a heart attack,' he whispered in his ear.

Cristiano laughed.

On the other side of the yard Danilo and Quattro Formaggi were working on the old tractor. About five metres away, near a beaten-up old sofa, there was a plastic container full of rigatoni al ragù, a crate of beer and the now half-empty bottle of grappa. Danilo's picnic.

'Aim carefully, though. Don't hit them. Don't hit the bottle either, because if bits of glass go flying around . . . ' Rino said in a low voice.

Cristiano closed one eye and squinted with the other. He moved the sight till it framed the bowl. It was hard to keep the gun on target; it weighed a ton.

'If you don't shoot now your arms will start to ti . . . '

Cristiano pulled the trigger. There was a deafening bang, the bowl disintegrated as if it had been hit by a cruise missile, and rigatoni, splashes of ragù and fragments of plastic were scattered over a radius of ten metres.

Danilo and Quattro Formaggi jumped in the air with fright.

Cristiano and Rino laughed so much they rolled down the hill of sand while the other two, spattered from head to foot with rigatoni and ragù, stood there, cursing and swearing.

37

They took some calming down.

Danilo in particular was furious. They had stained his trousers; he would never get the grease out, even in the washing machine.

Cristiano knelt down and pleaded, with his arms round his feet. 'Please don't be cross, Danilo. It was only a joke. And you're such a nice guy . . . '

'Fuck you! You could have killed us! And that pasta had ragù! Ragù with carrots, celery and onions. Teresa only makes it once a month.'

Quattro Formaggi was walking quietly round the yard, picking up the rigatoni and putting them into a plastic bag.

Finally Rino had to promise that as soon as he earned some money he would treat them both to a pizza at the Vascello d'Oro.

They sat down on the sofa, each holding a beer. They passed round the plastic bag and fished out the rigatoni.

'How's the work on the tractor going?' asked Cristiano, trying to blow the sand off a piece of pasta.

'Quite well,' replied Danilo, after taking a swig from his bottle of beer. 'Quattro Formaggi says we only need to repair the clutch discs, then the engine should work perfectly.'

'And is the tractor strong enough to break through the wall?'

'Are you kidding? I've studied the problem carefully. The wall of the bank is made of such crappy little bricks you'd only have to fart and they'd come tumbling down.'

When they had finished their meal the three men sat on the sofa in a drunken stupor. Cristiano was getting impatient. It was cold, and next day Beppe Trecca, the social worker, was coming round for his regular visit and the house was in a mess.

'Can't we go, papa? It's Saturday tomorrow. Trecca's coming. We've got to tidy up.'

'Another five minutes. Why don't you run off and play?'

From the tone of his reply, Cristiano understood that he wouldn't move his arse off the sofa till nightfall.

'Shit!' he muttered, and started throwing stones at a fire-blackened barrel.

38

Quattro Formaggi lay on the battered old sofa, gazing at the clouds that swirled in the sky.

'Do you . . . do you know . . . Liliana?' he said, as his mouth twisted and his arm began to quiver.

Danilo, befuddled by the beer, was gazing into the void. He raised his head, but it fell back against the sofa. 'Who's she?' he muttered, without much interest.

She works . . . 'at Euroedil.'

'Who is she?'

In the accounts department. She has . . . 'black hair. Long. She's . . . ' *beautiful.*

Rino, who was lying nearby with his feet up on an empty gas cylinder, nodded. 'She works in accounts. I know her.'

'Oh, I know who you mean! That fat cow with three kilos of make-up plastered all over her face?' asked Danilo.

Quattro Formaggi nodded.

'Good old Liliana,' Rino said to himself, and put the empty bottle to his lips, searching for the last drops of grappa.

Quattro Formaggi, by now twitching all over with tics, could only manage to say: 'Well . . . Well . . . '

'Speak up! What?' Danilo goaded him.

'I'd like . . . I'd like to ask her out to dinner . . . ' and he swallowed something that was blocking his throat.

Danilo guffawed. 'She wouldn't go out with you even if . . . ' He pondered for a moment. 'No, I can't think of anything that would make her go out with someone like you.'

'Let him speak . . . ' Rino sighed.

Quattro Formaggi was encouraged. 'I'd like to . . . mar . . . ry her.'

Danilo belched and shook his head. 'What bullshit!'

'It's not bullshit. I want to marry her.'

'Do you like her?' asked Rino.

'Yes. A lot. And . . . ' Quattro Formaggi broke off.

Danilo, sprawled out like an albino gorilla, was shaking with laughter. 'Have you taken a good look at her? She's got a bum as big as Sardinia. And the worst thing is, she thinks she's Marilyn Monroe. Forget her. She's not for you.'

But Quattro Formaggi was undaunted. 'You're wrong. I can make her like me.'

Danilo nudged Rino. 'Well, go and tell her you want to marry her . . . But call me first. I want to be there to enjoy the show.'

Quattro Formaggi picked up a stone and threw it into the distance. 'I've got a plan.'

Danilo scratched his stomach. 'For what?'

'For getting to talk to her.'

'Let's hear it . . . '

Quattro Formaggi gave himself three thumps on the chest. 'She likes Rino.'

Rino looked up in surprise. 'Me?'

'Yes. She's always looking at you.'

'Really? I'd never noticed.'

Danilo didn't get it. 'Hang on a minute, if she likes Rino you're in the shit.'

Quattro Formaggi narrowed his eyes irritably. 'Let me speak.'

He turned to Rino: 'You invite her out to the restaurant. But you turn up with Danilo. And you don't talk to her, you only talk to Danilo – about football. Women hate football . . . '

'How would you know? Since when have you been an expert on women?' Danilo interrupted him yet again.

Quattro Formaggi ignored him. 'Then I appear . . . You go away and I stay with her.' He paused. 'What do you think, Rino?'

'Who pays for the meal?' Danilo asked.

'Me. I've saved up.'

'But what's in it for us?'

Quattro Formaggi looked around in bewilderment. He wasn't prepared for that question. He thumped himself hard on the leg. 'The pizza.'

Rino stood up and stretched. 'That's enough talk, let's go home. I'm not feeling too great. Cristiano, you can drive as far as the highway!'

39

Cristiano didn't feel like driving, but his father insisted: 'You need the practice. You're still having problems with the clutch. Don't argue, I've got a splitting headache.'

Cristiano had started driving a few months earlier. And he thought he was quite good at it. He wasn't very good at starting – when he released the clutch he couldn't control the accelerator, and the van would either stall or lurch jerkily forward – but once he got going it was fine.

With his father shouting in his ear, though, it was a nightmare. 'Look out! Change gear! Can't you hear the engine?'

But that day Rino had one of his headaches. They had been getting more and more frequent lately. He said it was like having a swarm of bees inside your skull. And he could hear the blood throbbing in his ears. Sometimes it would last all day and he would have to lie down in the dark, in silence, and the slightest noise would drive him wild. In such cases Cristiano had to stay in his bedroom.

When Danilo had advised him to see a doctor, Rino had given eloquent expression to his thoughts on the matter: 'If there's one thing doctors don't know the first fucking thing about it's the brain. They fire out theories off the tops of their heads. They stuff you with medicines which cost an arm and a leg and which fuck you up so badly you don't even have the strength to pull out your pecker and have a piss.'

Cristiano drove while the other three, still knocked out by the alcohol, lay slumped across each other, snoring. The sun had set, leaving pink streaks on the horizon, while the seagulls dived into the river.

When they reached the highway Quattro Formaggi took the wheel.

40

By the time they got home it was already dark.

Rino, without saying a word, set about washing the pile of dishes that had accumulated in the sink over the past two weeks and Cristiano started tidying up the sitting room.

Both of them hated the day of the social worker's visit.

They had dubbed it 'keeping-up-appearances day'. But what they hated even more was 'the day before keeping-up-appearances day', because they had to straighten up the whole of the ground floor. Not the first floor, because, in Rino's words, you only need to clean the parts where the bishop's going to walk.

This happened every other Saturday.

For the rest of the time the house was left to its own devices.

They used all the plates and forks till there were none left. They washed their clothes in Danilo's washing machine once a month and then hung them out to dry in the garage.

The sitting room wasn't hard to clean, being almost completely empty.

Cristiano cleared away the beer cans, the pizza boxes and the foil trays from the takeaway. They were everywhere. Even under the cupboards and the sofa. With the beer cans alone he filled a whole rubbish bag.

Then he gave the floor a token wiping-over with a cloth.

In the kitchen, while his father was rinsing the dishes, he removed from the fridge the remains of a piece of provolone that was green with mould, some rotten vegetables and some peach jam covered with white tufts. Then he cleaned the greasy table top with a damp cloth.

Athough Christmas was long since past, the Christmas tree, all withered up, still stood in the hall. Cristiano had decorated it with beer cans and stuck a little bottle of Campari Soda on the top.

It was time to chuck it out.

'I've finished!' he said to his father, wiping his brow.

'What food have we got?'

'Pasta and . . . ' he looked to see what was left in the fridge: 'some cheese spread.'

You squashed it down in your dish and dumped the partly drained pasta on top.

The good old stand-by.

He put the water on to boil.

After supper Cristiano lay down on the sofa to watch TV. It was nice there. The heater gave off a pleasant warmth. He loved to fall asleep like that, wrapped up in the tartan blanket.

His father stretched out on the lounger with a beer in one hand and the broomstick for changing channels in the other.

That evening Cristiano would have liked to watch *You Reap What You Sow*, the show where they played tricks on people (which even if they weren't genuine were funny anyway), but his eyelids were heavy, and without realising it he fell asleep.

41

Rino Zena hated television. The variety shows, the chat shows, the political programmes, the documentaries, the news bulletins, even the sport and the perennially inaccurate weather forecasts.

It had been different in the old days.

Television had been something else in his childhood. Two channels. No more, no less. State-run. There had been good programmes, made with passion. Things you looked forward to all week. *Pinocchio*, for example. A masterpiece. And what about those actors? Manfredi, one of the greats. Alberto Sordi, a genius. Totò, the best comedian in the world.

Now all that had changed.

Rino hated the presenters with their tinted hair and the half-naked dancing girls, and it made him cringe to see people willing to talk about their private lives in front of half the population of Italy. He despised those stupid pillocks who went on TV and burst into tears and told everyone how sad they were that their wives had left them.

He hated the hypocritical politeness of the presenters. He hated the phone-in games. The slapdash dance routines. He hated the comedians' corny jokes. And he loathed the impersonators and the impersonatees. He hated the politicians. He hated the TV films with their good cops, friendly carabinieri, funny priests and crime squads. He hated the spotty little kids who would give their back teeth to gain admission to that cheap-jack paradise. He hated the hundreds of semi-famous celebrities who wandered around like stray dogs begging for a place on a talk-show. He hated the experts who made money out of other people's tragedies.

They know everything. They know all about betrayal, poverty, the glut of road deaths on Saturday nights, the minds of murderers.

He hated it when they feigned indignation. When they licked each other's arses. He hated the quarrels that lasted about as long as a fart. He hated the appeals for African children when there were people in Italy who were starving. But what he hated most was the women. Bitches with breasts as round as grapefruit, swollen lips and made-to-measure reconstructed faces.

They always talk of equality, but what kind of equality is that? When the image they present is that of a bunch of brainless bimbos. They would sleep with some arsehole who had a bit of power just so they could get out of the house and be recognized. They would walk over their own mothers' bodies for a bit of success.

He hated every person in that little box, so much that he sometimes had to restrain himself from picking up the broomstick and smashing it to pieces.

I'd like to line you up one behind the other and shoot you. What's your crime? You lie to people. You're rotting the minds of millions of children. Showing them worlds that don't exist. You drive people to run up huge debts to buy a car. You're ruining Italy.

Yet Rino Zena couldn't stop watching television. He would sit glued to it all night. And in the daytime, when he was at home, he was always there on that lounger swearing at them.

Rino changed channels, then he turned and noticed that Cristiano was asleep.

His temples were beginning to throb, but he didn't feel like going to bed. For a moment he considered going round to Danilo's, but he decided against it. In the evening Danilo was a pain in the arse: he would start moaning about his wife and go on till he collapsed, felled by the grappa.

No, what I need is a fuck.

He put on his jacket and went out, with no clear destination in mind.

The van was nearly out of petrol. Those two thought it ran on water. They never contributed a penny. He found an all-night garage on the highway and put in his last ten euros. Now he didn't even have the money to buy a beer.

He replaced the nozzle and was about to get back into the van when a silver Mercedes with its headlights on full beam stopped two metres short of him. A female arm extended from the window on the driver's side. The hand clasped a fifty-euro note and a two-euro coin.

Rino drew nearer.

At the wheel was a slim woman with long blonde hair and a pair of oval glasses with blue lightweight frames. A microphone wire ran down from her ear across her cheek, ending beside her thin lips, which were painted dark red.

'Fifty euros,' she said to Rino, then carried on talking into the microphone. 'I don't think so . . . No, I really don't think so . . . You're wrong, you're missing the point, Carlo dear . . . '

Rino took the money, got back into the van and drove off.

42

Danilo Aprea lay in bed in the dark. His arms alongside his body. His face looking up at the ceiling. His green pyjamas with blue polka dots smelled of fabric softener. The sheets, too, were fresh and well ironed. He put out his hand on the side where Teresa used to sleep. It was cold and flat. He regretted changing the mattress. The new one, which had springs, was hard and unyielding. The old one had taken on the shapes of their bodies. On Teresa's side there had been a long S-shaped hollow, because she always slept on her side. With her back towards him and her face towards the wall.

The red digits of the radio alarm showed 23:17.

He was wide awake. And yet in front of the television he hadn't been able to keep his eyes open . . . There had been a documentary on the migration of whales. Nature documentaries had always been Teresa's passion. And her favourites were those about whales and dolphins. She loved cetaceans because, as she said, they had made such an effort to get out of the sea and then, once they had got onto the land, they had decided to go back again. Millions of years spent turning into four-legged animals and then millions of years to turn back into fish. Danilo didn't see what was so wonderful about that story. Teresa had explained to him: 'Because when you make a mistake, you must have the courage to retrace your steps.' Danilo had wondered if she was alluding to the two of them.

He could call her and tell her that there was a documentary about whales on TV.

He heard his wife's voice thanking him.

Don't mention it . . . Can I see you tomorrow?

(Why yes, of course.)

Shall we meet at the Rouge et Noir? I've got lots of news to tell you.

(Would four o'clock be okay?)

Four o'clock it is.

He switched on the bedside lamp, put on his glasses and eyed the telephone . . .

No. I promised.

. . . then picked up *The Da Vinci Code*, of which, in two years, he had read about twenty pages.

He got himself comfortable and read a page without really reading it. He looked up from the book and stared at the wall.

But this time he would be calling her about something important. She would be able to see the last quarter-of-an-hour of the documentary. There were killer whales in it too. He picked up the receiver and dialled the number, with bated breath. The phone rang and nobody answered.

Two more rings and I'll hang up.

One . . . two . . . three . . .

'Hello! Who is it?' Teresa's sleepy voice.

He didn't reply.

'Hello, who is it? Is that you, Danilo?'

He repressed the impulse to reply and ran his hand over his cheeks and mouth.

'Danilo, I know it's you. You mustn't ring me, don't you understand? I've turned off my mobile, but I can't unplug the landline. You know Piero's mother's not well. Every time you call you give him a turn. You've woken us up. Please stop it. I beg of you.' She stopped for a moment as though she didn't have the strength to go on. Danilo could hear her breathing heavily. But then she did go on, in a flat tone: 'I told you *I'd* ring *you*. If you keep doing this I won't ring you any more. I swear it.'

She hung up.

Danilo put down the receiver, closed the book, took off his glasses, lay them on the bedside table and turned out the light.

43

Ramona had just been released from jail. She wore a sleeveless top, a pair of skin-tight denim shorts and cowboy boots. She was hitch-hiking and Bob the lumberjack, dressed in a checked shirt and sitting at the wheel of a pickup, stopped.

'Where are you going?' he asked Ramona.

Quattro Formaggi, sitting in his underpants in front of his little TV, said together with the blonde: 'Wherever fortune takes me. What have you got to offer me?'

Bob smiled and let her in.

Quattro Formaggi reached out and pressed the fast-forward key on the video recorder.

The images on the screen began to flash by. The pickup came to the little house in the woods. Quick greetings. Lunch with turkey. And then everyone naked on the table, screwing. Darkness. Morning. Ramona woke up naked and went out into the yard.

Bob the lumberjack was chopping wood. Ramona undid his trousers and took his cock in her hand. Here Quattro Formaggi pressed PAUSE.

This was his favourite scene. He had watched it at least a thousand times and the quality of the pictures was terrible, the colours had all toned to red. He went into the kitchen and turned on the light.

The smell of the boiled cauliflower he had eaten two days before hung in the air, its purple remains still floating in a saucepan on the gas cooker. On the table were the dried-up carcase of a chicken and an empty Fanta bottle.

He took a dozen ice-cube moulds out of the freezer. He put them under the tap and dropped the cubes into a bucket, which he filled with five inches of water. He stood the bucket on the table, rolled up the right sleeve of his dressing gown and thrust in his hand.

A thousand needles pierced his flesh. But after a while the water began to seem boiling hot.

He knew from experience that it took at least ten minutes.

He gritted his teeth and waited.

When it seemed to him that enough time had passed, he took his red, frozen hand out of the bucket and dried it with a rag.

He pinched it.

Nothing.

He picked up a fork from the table and stuck it into his palm.

Nothing.

Holding his right arm up, he went back to the television and pressed PLAY.

He sat down, lowered his underpants and grasped his penis with his ice-stiffened hand.

He felt on his skin the cold fingers squeezing it hard.

That was just how it felt when a girl took your cock in her hand.

It was exactly how it felt.

Ramona's icy hand started going frantically up and down.

Quattro Formaggi parted his legs and opened his mouth. His head fell back and an incandescent pleasure exploded just below the back of his skull.

44

The Peace Warrior squat was a leather goods factory which had closed down in the early Seventies. The building had been occupied and rock concerts were often held there.

Six enormous concrete buildings all in a row, covered with graffiti and surrounded by a gravel yard. Tongues of flame and columns of black smoke poured out of a cluster of barrels. A thick fog had formed which dimmed the headlights of the cars into golden haloes. Deafening music came from inside.

Rino parked near a row of big choppers.

He got out of the van clutching a bottle of Johnny Walker Red Label, courtesy of the lady in the Mercedes. He set off, with two slits instead of eyes, towards the entrance.

A lot of young men, dressed as punks, American bikers or metalheads, massed in front of the social centre.

Rino pushed his way through the crowd. Some guys protested, but when they looked at him even the biggest and meanest fell silent and let him through. Despite the alcohol that dulled his senses Rino could almost smell their fear of him, as a wild animal can, and it felt great. It was like having a sign on your head: MAKE MY DAY: PISS ME OFF.

But that evening he wasn't looking for a fight. And it had been a mistake to drink all that whisky when he had such a headache.

He reached the doormen. Three arseholes with hair curled into thick, filthy, evil-smelling twists were holding shoeboxes full of banknotes.

One gaunt-faced guy with sunglasses asked him to make a contribution of his own choosing for the musicians. He clearly hadn't realized, in all the crush, who he was dealing with, and when he looked up and saw that shaven-headed, muscular, eyeless beast in front of him, he gave a nervous smile and stammered: 'No . . . You . . . I know . . . Go on in . . . Go on in . . . ' And waved him through.

Inside it was at least thirty degrees and the air was unbreathable. The effect of those thousand-odd bodies crammed into the place, heaving and surging like the sea. There was a horrible smell.

A disgusting mixture of marijuana, cigarettes, sweat and damp plaster.

At the other end of the room a wall of speakers was blasting out music at the audience. The band, distant dots lit up by red spotlights, were playing some dreadful crap, a mess of fuzzy guitars and drums. One poor idiot was screaming his head off and jumping about as if someone had rammed a hedgehog up his arse. A huge peace flag hung above the stage.

Rino slipped through the crowd and reached the side of the room, near the wall. There the pressure eased and there was a little room to breathe. The beams of the spotlights hanging from the ceiling didn't reach there and in the half-light you could see silhouettes sitting on the ground, red cigarette stubs, heads kissing, groups of people talking.

Stepping over legs and beer cans, Rino got to within thirty metres of the stage. The music here was so loud he couldn't hear himself think.

Now he could see the band. With their long hair, those wedges on their feet and their faces plastered with greasepaint, they looked like a poor imitation of an American heavy-metal group.

Below the stage he saw a tall, slim girl with short blonde hair, dancing.

She looks like Irina.

He leaned against a pillar, took a swig from his bottle and shut his eyes. His chin dropped onto his chest. The whole room swayed. He grabbed hold of the pillar to stop himself falling.

Irina had been tall and very slim. With small breasts and wonderful legs. Her legs and her neck were the best things about her. And, apart from her brain, the rest of her wasn't that bad either . . .

How he'd loved her! He remembered that if he went without seeing her for more than half a day he would get a pain in the stomach.

Where had it all gone wrong?

"I want an abortion . . . I'm too young, Rino. I want to live."

"You do and I'll kill you."

And his hand clenching into a fist.

I'm getting maudlin. I've had enough of this. I'm going.

Besides, in the state he was in, he would never be able to pull a girl. And he was feeling so miserable now that if he didn't get out of there he was going to start crying like a baby.

He took another swig of alcohol and stared blankly at the undulating, arm-waving sea of people excited by the deafening music.

I'm thirsty.

Opposite the point where he was standing, on the other side of the room, was a long table where they were selling beer and mineral water.

He still had some money in his pocket. But getting across that human carpet seemed to him an impossible task.

Among the people thronging around the drinks table was the blonde girl. Now he could see her more clearly.

It's her . . .

Rino recognised that slim model's body, that neck . . . And he thought he remembered that white dress which fell like a tube over her body, leaving her back exposed.

His heart leaped in his chest as if he'd seen a ghost. He gave an alcoholic belch, clutched at the pillar and leaned unsteadily against it, as if he had taken a punch in the face. His legs wouldn't support him.

Irina!

It can't be! What's she doing here? She's crazy. I told her if she ever came back I'd kill her.

And yet it was her. The same height. The same hair. The same way of moving.

He couldn't believe it. Not once in those twelve years had he considered the possibility of seeing her again.

One morning he had woken up with a hangover. Cristiano was crying in his cot. Irina wasn't there. Her things weren't there. She had left.

Why's she here now? She wants to take Cristiano away. Why else would she have come?

He felt a lump in his throat. He pushed through the crowd, heading for that blonde hair on the other side of the hall, clearing himself a path with his elbows. She was closer now. He could see her long hair and her bony shoulders. It was her. She didn't look a day older.

Now he only had to grab her wrist and whisper in her ear:

'Surprise, surprise! I've got you!' And drag her outside. She was only a few metres away.

His heart was beating frantically. He reached out and just at that moment Irina turned her head and . . .

Fuck!

. . . it was someone else.

Rino felt a strange emotion resembling disappointment. As if . . .

As if, nothing.

It wasn't her.

45

Cristiano woke up in front of the television. A man was cutting up a Coca-Cola can with a knife.

Cristiano got up and passed by the window. The van wasn't there.

He's gone out.

He peed in the kitchen sink. Then he turned on the tap and had a drink.

He went back into the living room, sat down in front of the TV and started to surf the channels, using the broomstick. On a regional channel he found Antonella, a pasty-faced redhead with an eagle tattoo on her shoulder, who was taking off her clothes and talking on the phone and grimacing a lot. It was a good ten minutes before she got around to removing her bra. At that rate it would be day-break before she got her knickers off. Besides, with all those numbers and written messages you couldn't see a thing.

Maybe he could have a wank.

He imagined the redhead coming into the living room. A skimpy blue top finished just above her navel, leaving the rest of her body bare. She wore pointed black shoes with high heels. Between her legs there was a little strip of blondish hair. She sat on a chair with her legs apart and a ray of sunlight from the window shone on her pussy, which was open like an oyster . . . And she was talking to him in a matter-of-fact tone about homework.

He could hear the breathy voice from the television repeating: 'Go on, call me . . . Call me . . . What are you waiting for?

Call me . . . Don't be shy. Call me.' In the background, behind
the voice, Eros Ramazzotti was singing 'I'm still hung up on you',
then this faded out and gave way to a mournful song performed
by a famous singer of yesteryear, whose name he didn't know,
and who was saying 'when you are here with me this room has
no walls, but only trees, countless trees, when you are here close
to me . . . '

Cristiano had heard a Frenchwoman sing that song on the radio,
in a voice so sweet and clear it made you feel like crying. She had
sung it in a normal voice, just as if she was at home singing to her
baby boy to lull him to sleep. Maybe that really had been what she
was doing. Maybe her husband had taped the song unknown to her
and had then told her she ought to make a record of it, and that
was how she had become famous.

He didn't know why, but the song reminded him of his mother.
He saw her sitting on his bed with her guitar, singing him a song.
She had straight blonde hair and looked like a girl who presented
A Special Family on Channel 2.

He had gone to Disco Boom to buy the CD, but when he'd found
himself in front of the sales assistant he had been too embarrassed
to ask him if he knew it. He didn't know the name of the singer or
the title of the song. And he could hardly start warbling 'when you
are here with me' to him . . .

His desire to have a wank had gone. He switched off the television and went upstairs to bed.

46

Rino Zena woke up in darkness, waving his arms about.

He was falling from an aeroplane. Below him there was a black
expanse of asphalt. Gasping for breath, he realised it had only been
a dream and it was over.

It was dark. He had a stale taste of whisky in his mouth; his
tongue had swollen up as if it had been stung by a wasp and he had
a splitting headache. From the smell of cigarettes and damp carpet
he understood that he was in his bedroom, lying on the mattress.

He reached out, groping for the light switch, and touched a body lying next to him. At first he thought it was Cristiano. Until a few years earlier he had let him sleep in his bed when he had nightmares.

He turned on the light, and when he finally succeeded in opening his eyes he saw the blonde from the concert. The one he had mistaken for Irina. She was sleeping with her arms outspread. Her mouth open. She was naked, apart from a bra pulled down to reveal two small breasts with small dark nipples the size of fifty-cent coins.

Looking more closely, he saw that she wasn't really a bit like Irina. She had the same milky-coloured skin, long legs and narrow hips, and a beautiful neck. But the face was different. This girl had a longer nose and a protruding chin. And she couldn't be more than twenty-five.

But how the hell did she get here?

Rino tried to think back to the concert. He remembered crossing the floor, certain that she was Irina, and realising that she wasn't.

But after that, nothing.

Darkness.

He must have brought her home.

He touched his cock. It was numb.

He had screwed her.

A confused image was fixed in his mind. Him on top and her underneath. His hands clutching her hair.

Rino was about to get up to go for a pee when he noticed that beside the mattress, on the blonde's side, there was a syringe, complete with needle, and all the other accoutrements of the perfect junkie.

Rino looked at the girl's arm. It was peppered with tiny coagulated holes surrounded by purple skin.

A fucking needle freak. And she shot up here, while I was asleep, with Cristiano in the other room.

Rino grabbed her by the neck, lifted her up off the mattress and put his hand between her buttocks as if he intended to penetrate her with his fingers, but instead hurled her like a sack of potatoes, and she opened her mouth and didn't even have time to wake up, scream, do anything at all, before she bounced off the door of the built-in wardrobe and found herself lying on the floor in a corner of the room.

'Jesus!' she screamed, coming to her senses, in terror. She put one arm round her neck and held the other out in front of her in an attempt to shield herself, then got on her hands and knees and started crawling round the room.

'Get out, you scum! You've been shooting up in my house!' Rino gave her a kick in the backside which lifted up her legs. The junkie ducked forward, rubbed her face on the carpet and found her nose two centimetres away from the pistol lying on the floor.

Rino, who was standing up, stark naked and as wild as a demon, dived to get it away from her, but she nimbly grabbed the weapon, held it in both hands and backed into the corner. 'Don't come any closer, you son of a bitch! I'll kill you, I swear I will.' She was breathing hard, her eyes wide open. Then she seemed to get her surroundings into focus: the flag with the swastika on the wall, the tattooed psychopath who wanted to kill her. 'You fucking Nazi, you're dead!' And she shot him.

'You stupid bitch! It's not loaded.' Rino shook his head. He opened his right arm, spread the fingers of his hand and moved towards her, but he stepped on the syringe and the needle stuck in the sole of his foot. He stifled a yell and started hopping about holding his foot in his hand.

The girl seized her chance and made a dash for the bedroom door.

Rino grabbed a glass ashtray full of cigarette stubs and hurled it at her like a frisbee. It hit her on the shoulder. She bent forward, dropped the pistol and managed to slip out.

47

Cristiano Zena was woken up by the frantic shrieks of a woman.

Papa's screwing one of his whor . . . Before he could finish the thought someone burst into the room screaming.

Cristiano screamed too. He turned on the light.

It was a naked, terrified woman who kept bumping into the walls like a swallow that had flown in through the window by mistake.

Rino entered the room, in the nude. He was clutching her clothes and handbag in one hand and her pointed boots in the other. His eyes were narrowed to slits and his jaw was quivering with rage.

He's going to kill her, thought Cristiano, and he clasped his head in his arms.

But instead Rino threw her clothes in her face. 'Get out of here, you bitch.'

The woman picked them up and wanted to make her escape, but was scared to go past him.

Finally, clutching her clothes in her arms, she summoned up the courage. She dashed towards the door, getting a kick in the backside from Rino as she passed. She tripped and fell headlong on the landing. Cristiano heard her stumble downstairs and slam the door.

His father went over to the window. 'Good. She won't be coming back.'

Cristiano curled up under the bedclothes. 'What happened?'

Rino came over the bed. 'Nothing. Just a tart. Go to sleep. Good night.' And he went back to his bedroom.

Saturday

48

There was no school on Saturday so he could sleep late.

It was eleven thirty when Cristiano Zena stuck his head out from under the bedclothes.

At one o'clock Trecca would be arriving. There was barely time to wash and have breakfast.

He was starving. He could have eaten a whole chicken – bones and all. At the thought his stomach started rumbling.

But he was going to have to make do with bread and jam.

He rubbed his eyes and, yawning, looked out of the window, and laughed as he thought of that poor girl who had fled from the house stark naked and with a footprint stamped on her buttock.

That afternoon he fancied going to look at the motorbikes in the showroom. Maybe he could ask Quattro Formaggi to give him a lift.

He got dressed and went downstairs. The television was tuned to MTV.

Rino was in the kitchen and was already set for the meeting with the social worker. Whenever he saw him dressed up as if he was going to a wedding Cristiano could hardly help laughing. He looked like a tailor's dummy. Light-blue shirt. Tie. Blue trousers. Low-heeled shoes with laces.

'Take a look at this!' His father pointed at the formica top of the dresser.

There was a sheet of greaseproof paper on which a dozen slices of mortadella were laid out, and on a plate a big wedge of fresh stracchino and a baguette. The smell of coffee hung in the air. And a pleasant warmth emerged from the oven door.

The mortadella and stracchino sandwich was in Cristiano's opinion the best sandwich in the world (closely followed by the one made with mozzarella and cured ham) and there was nothing better than eating it in the morning with caffè latte.

What had happened? This wasn't Christmas, nor his birthday.

'I did a bit of shopping. Tuck in.'

Cristiano didn't need telling twice. They ate in silence, relishing every mouthful. Rino held his sandwich well away from his chest for fear of staining his shirt.

49

Beppe Trecca was driving his Puma along the streets of Varrano and listening to a CD of dolphin noises mingled with piano music. He had bought it on a special offer at the service station because the sleeve notes said the music was suitable for yoga or for relaxing after a hard day's work, but he didn't find the squeaks of those animals in the least relaxing, especially after a sleepless night.

He turned off the stereo, stopped at the traffic light and, as he waited for it to change to green, opened his briefcase. Inside was a bottle of Ballantine's. He looked around, took a quick swig and put it back in the briefcase.

He started the car up again and, pitching his voice, declaimed: 'You see things as they are and say, "Why?" I dream things that never were and say, "Why not?"'

This saying of George Bernard Shaw which he had found in the *Big Book of Aphorisms* would make a perfect starting point for the discussion on 'Young people as a motor of change in society' which he had organised that afternoon for the voluntary workers of the parish.

He wasn't entirely sure of its relevance to the subject of the seminar, but it sounded good.

Beppe Trecca was thirty-five years old and hailed from Ariccia, a small town on the hills outside Rome. He had moved to Varrano after qualifying as a social worker.

He stood one metre seventy tall. Over the past few days he had lost weight, and being pretty slim of build, with those two kilos less looked as thin and spiky as a seahorse. His hair was a mass of blondish curls which defied even the strongest gels.

He was wearing a blue suit, a white shirt and a striped tie. Plus a pair of braces to keep up his trousers, which were a size too big.

He had dressed like this ever since he had read a book entitled *Jesus as Manager*.

This was a study by a certain Bob Briner, a brilliant American businessman who had made an extensive study of the Gospels in order to establish why Jesus, besides being the son of our Lord, had been such an outstanding manager. His launching of a major project, his selection of his staff (the twelve apostles), his rejection of all forms of corruption and his good relations with the people of Palestine had been the key factors in making him the greatest manager of all time.

This had given Trecca the idea that his own job required not a welfare approach but a managerial one, and consequently he had taken to dressing like a manager.

He took off his sunglasses and examined the shadows under his eyes in the mirror. He looked like a raccoon.

He knew that women used some stuff, a cream, to hide them; maybe he ought to get some.

Ida mustn't see him in that state. Though he was sure she wouldn't come to the discussion group that afternoon after what had happened between them.

Ida Montanari was the wife of Mario Lo Vino, the director of the Varrano health authority and possibly Beppe Trecca's best friend.

Possibly, because after what he had done to the poor guy Beppe wasn't sure he still had a right to call himself his friend.

He had fallen in love with his wife. No, fallen in love was an understatement, he'd gone nuts about her.

It wasn't like him. He was a guy who believed in values such as loyalty, fair play and friendship.

But it wasn't his fault if in the dreary world of voluntary work twenty-seven-year-old Ida stood out like a bird of paradise in a hen house.

It had all begun with an innocent friendship. They had met through Mario. When Beppe had arrived from Ariccia, depressed and demotivated, he had been welcomed into the Lo Vino household like a friend. He had discovered the pleasures of family life, of playing cards in the evening over a glass of wine. He had become like an uncle to Michele and Diana, their children. The previous summer he had even gone on holiday with them in the mountains. And it was there that he had discovered Ida's soul. She made him feel good and showed him life in all its better aspects. Above all, she cheered him up. There were days when they never stopped laughing.

And it had been she who had asked him to help her organise the parish's group of voluntary workers.

Everything, in short, had been fine. Until, three days before, God and Satan in person had joined forces to plan his ruin.

That evening, for no particular reason, the meeting with the disadvantaged parishioners had been cancelled and Beppe had found himself alone with Ida in the video-Internet room. Even Father Marcello, who had never left the rectory in the past fifteen years, had gone out for a pizza with the alcoholics group.

And here the Evil One had intervened, taking possession of his tongue and jaws and speaking instead of him. 'Ida, I've got a very interesting video about voluntary work in Ethiopia. I'd like to show it to you. It's really worth seeing. The guys down there seem to be doing an excellent job.'

Beppe Trecca, as he waited at the traffic light, started punching himself on the forehead. 'In front' punch 'of' punch 'the video' punch 'about the African children. Shame on you!'

He had to stop because alongside him two boys on a big scooter were looking at him dubiously.

He gave an embarrassed smile, lowered the window and said: 'Hi boys . . . It's nothing . . . Thoughts . . . Just thoughts . . . '

Ida had glanced at her watch and smiled. 'Mario and the children have gone to dinner at grandmother Eva's. Why not?'

'Damn you, grandmother Eva!' And with a squeal of tyres Beppe drove out onto the highway.

Beppe had put the cassette in the video recorder, which usually didn't work, but which that evening, God knows why, was in perfect working order, and the documentary had started.

On one side the two of them, next to each other, in the dark, sitting on an imitation leather sofa. On the other the children, their stomachs bloated with starvation and dysentery.

She had been sitting up straight with her legs crossed and her arms folded, but suddenly she had leaned back and, casually, laid her hand a few centimetres from his thigh. And he, continuing to stare at the television, slowly, imperceptibly, but as remorselessly as the roots of a wild fig tree, had opened his legs till he felt the knuckles of her hand brush against the flannel of his trousers.

He had turned and, with the determination of an Islamic suicide bomber, kissed her.

Forgetting Mario Lo Vino and the innocent Michele and Diana, forgetting all the evenings when he had been fed, welcomed, entertained like a friend – no, more than that, like a brother.

And what about her? What had she done? She had let herself be kissed. Or she had at first, anyway. Beppe still felt the touch of her lips on his. The taste of her xylitol chewing gum. That fleeting yet undeniable contact with her soft, liquid tongue.

But then Ida had recoiled, pushed him away and said, blushing: 'Are you out of your mind? What are you doing?' And she had stalked out indignantly, like a respectable young lady in a romantic novel.

The next day she hadn't come to the parish hall, nor had she the day after that.

During this time Beppe had suffered desperately, as never before in his life. And the pains were physical. Especially in his intestine. He had even had a recurrence of his spastic colitis.

He had discovered that he had been hiding his passion for Ida from himself as if it was some kind of venereal disease.

He had thought of confiding in his cousin Luisa. Of asking her for help. But he was too ashamed. And so – alone, confused, and without even the comfort of a friendly voice – he had suffered in silence, hoping that this sickness would pass of its own accord, that his body would immunise itself against the diabolical virus.

He hadn't succeeded. He had been unable to sleep and had started drinking in an attempt to forget. Impossible. He had cursed himself for behaving like that, but he had also kept telling himself that there had been tongue contact. This was true. Undeniable. As true as the fact that he had been born in Ariccia. If she really had been unwilling she wouldn't have let him stick his tongue in her mouth. Would she?

At five forty-three that morning he had sent her a text message. The text, which he had spent the whole night composing, was:

Forgive me. ☹

That was it. Simple. Precise. She, of course, hadn't replied.

The social worker stopped in front of Rino Zena's house, picked up his briefcase and got out of the Puma.

That's enough of that, though. Personal problems mustn't interfere with work, he told himself, skipping between the puddles so as not to dirty his shoes, and he was on the point of pressing the bell when his mobile vibrated twice.

A shock wave went through Trecca's body, as if someone had clapped the pads of an electrostimulator on his heart.

He stiffened, and took his mobile out of his pocket with bated breath. Next to the envelope symbol was the name IDA.

He closed his eyes, pressed the key and opened them again.

What for? It was wonderful.
Can we meet today?
You organise it. ☺

The little tart! So she *had* enjoyed it!

He clenched his teeth, bent his knees and, raising his fists in the air, said: 'Yesss!'

And he rang the bell.

50

'Terrible weather, isn't it, lads? Well, how's it going?' Beppe Trecca sat down beside Rino, put his briefcase on his lap and rubbed his hands contentedly.

'Very well. I'm winning,' replied Cristiano, throwing the dice and looking at him.

There was something strange about him. He was exuberant, yet since his last visit he seemed to have lost weight, like he'd been ill;

his eyes were sunken in his skull and had rings round them, as if he hadn't slept.

'Excellent! Excellent! You really like Monopoly, then, do you?'

Ever since Beppe had rebuked them for not playing together enough (play fosters the building of a closer and more confidential father–son relationship), they had put on this act every time he came to see them.

Rino threw the dice in his turn and gave a sarcastic smile. 'Yes, we really do. It's nice handling all this money.'

Cristiano was always shocked at how calm his father managed to keep during Trecca's visits. He was unrecognisable. He hated the man, and would gladly have run him over with his car, yet he glued a fake little smile onto his lips and replied as politely as an English gentleman. What a superhuman effort he must be making not to explode, not to grab him by the tie and nut him in the face . . . After a while, though, Cristiano would get worried because he could see him turning blue, swallowing air and gripping the edge of the table as if he wanted to break it, and he would have to think up some excuse to get rid of the social worker.

Beppe opened his briefcase and took out some printed sheets of paper. 'Rino, here's a questionnaire that I'd like you to fill in.'

'What is it?' said Rino suspiciously.

'The trouble with alcohol is that people who have problems with this social disease deny it. It's natural to the alcoholic to lie and to do everything he can to hide it, even from himself. And do you know why, Rino? Because of the stigma attached to the issues around the abuse of alcoholic substances. That's what contributes to the denial. You don't need me to tell you what serious damage alcohol does to your body. And what a bad effect the habit can have on family, working and social relationships.'

Cristiano was uneasy. This guy was just looking for an excuse to put him in a home. And separate him from his father. Two days earlier he had passed him on the main street and Trecca had only given him only the most cursory of greetings, as if he was hiding something. And now he'd produced this questionnaire. He seemed to be planning something.

The social worker smiled. 'Listen, Rino, I'm seriously consid-ering the possibility of having you attend a course I'm going to

give on the damage alcoholism does to society, so fill in this questionnaire with complete honesty. I know you're a heavy drinker,
you don't have to hide it from me. As a matter of fact, today we're
going to do something. I want you to make a symbolic gesture in
front of your son.' He opened his briefcase and took out a half-
empty bottle of Ballantine's. 'Cristiano, bring us two glasses, would
you?'

Cristiano hurried into the kitchen and returned with the glasses.

'Thank you.' Beppe poured two fingers of whisky into one glass
and gave it to Rino, then filled the other glass more than half full
and kept it for himself. 'This is the last glass of strong liquor you're
going to have till our next meeting. All right? That's a promise! Do
you understand?'

'Yes, I understand,' replied Rino, like a soldier answering his
captain.

The social worker raised his glass to the sky and knocked it back.
Rino did the same.

'Ahhhh . . . ' Trecca twisted his mouth and wiped it with the
back of his hand. Then he straightened his tie. 'Can I use your bathroom for a minute, lads?'

'Sure,' said Cristiano and Rino, relieved.

The social worker locked himself in the toilet.

'What's got into him? Did you see that? He finished a whole glass
of whisky . . . ' whispered Rino.

Cristiano shrugged. 'How should I know?'

51

Beppe Trecca locked himself in the toilet and washed his face.

He had talked to the Zenas without even knowing what he was
saying. He couldn't stop thinking about Ida's lips, as dark as black
cherries, about the cleavage that she always allowed her dresses to
reveal, and about those fawnlike eyes that made her look like Meg
Ryan. And above all, about where the hell they could meet.

He looked at himself in the mirror and shook his head.

I'm too pale. Maybe I need a spell under the sunlamp.

His flat was no good. Too risky. Nor was a hotel. Too sleazy.
What they needed was a special, romantic place . . .

He had a brainwave.

Of course! The camper van, the pride and joy of my cousin's husband.

He pulled out his mobile and wrote quickly:

> Great!
> See you tomorrow 10 pm
> Camp Bahamas

He was about to send the message when he had second thoughts
and tremulously added:

> I love you. ☺

52

That afternoon Cristiano Zena got on the bus and went for a ride.

He had no particular aim in mind and only ten euros in his
pocket, but he couldn't stay at home on Saturday.

After lunch he had tried to ring Quattro Formaggi to ask him if
he wanted to go and look at motorbikes, but his mobile was switched
off as usual.

Maybe he had gone to church.

When the doors of the bus wheezed open and Cristiano stepped
down onto the pavement it was only four o'clock, but night was
already falling over the plain. Between the sky and the earth all that
remained was a salmon-coloured strip. There was a biting east wind
and the cypresses along the central reservation of the highway were
all bent over to one side. The long advertising banners which hung
under the footbridge were flapping like the slack sails of a yacht.

Straight ahead of Cristiano lay a kilometre and a half of stores,
wholesale and retail outlets, self-service car washes, warehouses,
coloured lights, signs flashing up offers and discounts. There was
even a mosque.

To the left, behind the low roof of the Shoe Cathedral, among the clouds of smoke produced by itinerant vendors of sausages and roast pork, rose the imposing walls of the Quattro Camini shopping mall. A little further back stood the glass cube of Mediastore, and on the other side of the road the big Opel and General Motors showroom with its lines of new cars, and the wide open space of the second-hand car lot with its streamers proclaiming special offers. And the car park of the Multiplex cinema next to the little McDonald's.

In the middle of the roundabout, onto which two other long, straight roads converged, the old sculptor Callisto Arabuia had erected his latest creation, a huge bronze sculpture in the shape of a pandoro which went round and round spurting little jets of water into a basin.

Cristiano set off towards the mall. The four towers at the corners of the building could be seen, on a clear day, from kilometres away. They were said to be half a metre taller than the bell-tower of the cathedral in St Mark's Square in Venice. For the price of one euro you could go up in a lift to the top of Tower Two. From there you could see the Forgese snaking its way towards the sea, and all the tiny hamlets and villages that speckled the plain.

The mall was an immense rectangular building, bigger than an aircraft hangar, blue and devoid of windows, dating from the mid-Nineties.

That day, in honour of the month of discounts, the tops of the towers had been embellished with hot-air balloons decorated with yellow and blue segments and flaunting the slogan: BIG BARGAINS TO BE HAD AT THE QUATTRO CAMINI. All around the building was a large expanse of asphalt covered with thousands of cars.

The Quattro Camini attracted people from far and wide. It was the largest mall within a radius of a hundred kilometres. A hundred thousand square metres, distributed over three floors and two mezzanines. Plus an underground car park with a capacity of three thousand vehicles. The ground floor was given over to the Coral Reef hypermarket where those big bargains were to be had and you could take home a crate of beer for less than ten euros. The rest was occupied by shops. You could find everything your heart could possibly desire: a branch of the Monte dei Paschi bank, sales outlets of Vodafone and TIM, a post office, a nursery, the big clothes and shoe stores, three hairdressers, four pizzerias, a wine bar, a Chinese restaurant, an Irish pub, a games arcade, a pet shop, a gym, a medical testing centre and a solarium. The only thing it lacked was a bookshop.

In the centre of the first floor there was a large oval concourse adorned with a fountain in the form of a boat and a marble staircase leading up to the second floor. It had been intended by the architect as a surreal re-creation of Piazza di Spagna in Rome.

Cristiano walked across the car park, hunched up against the icy wind. There were huge crowds, it being the first day in the long month of special offers.

A long queue of vehicles was waiting at the automatic barriers of the car park and a river of people was pouring in through the doors. Families came out with trolleys piled high with goods; there were mothers with children bundled up like astronauts on pushchairs, gangs of teenagers on scooters weaving in and out between the cars, drivers quarrelling over parking places, coaches spewing out parties of old folk. In one corner of the car park there was a little funfair with dodgems and a shooting gallery.

The music blared out fuzzily from the loudspeakers next to the doors.

Cristiano looked behind the row of rubbish bins where Fabiana Ponticelli and Esmeralda Guerra usually hung around with their group in the summer and parked their scooters in the winter.

The Scarabeo with the smiley was there, chained to Tekken's motorbike.

His heart began to beat faster.

He looked at the motorbike. He hated to admit it, but that son of a bitch had a beautiful machine. He had changed the wheels and had racing ones put on, to make it easier to slalom through the traffic. Cristiano also noticed that the exhaust pipe wasn't the standard one. God only knew how much it had cost him to have it modified. But that wasn't a problem. His father was a big-shot at Biolumex, the light-bulb factory near San Rocco, so he had always been spoiled rotten.

Cristiano couldn't help seething with envy. But then he told himself that rich kids had it too easy and when the going got tough they started whimpering like girls.

Suppose there's an earthquake, for example, and he loses everything he owns, Tekken won't know what to do, he'll be so sad to be poor that he'll hang himself from the nearest tree. Whereas I won't lose a thing.

It would be cool if there was an earthquake.

He also found comfort in the idea that great men have always had to struggle through shit on their own. Just think of Eminem or Hitler or Christian Vieri.

He joined the crowd going into the mall.

Inside it was very warm. At the sides there were lots of girls dressed in miniskirts and jackets showering you with promotional flyers about telephone call rates and discounts on gyms and solariums. A cluster of people had formed around a man who was cutting carrots and courgettes with a plastic gadget.

As always Cristiano stopped outside Cellulandia, the mobile phone shop.

How he longed for a mobile.

He was probably the only pupil in the whole school who didn't have one.

'Aren't you proud to be different from all the others?' That had been his father's reply when he had pointed this out.

'No. I'm not proud. I want one too.'

He passed an electrical goods shop which was advertising fantastic offers on monitors and PCs. But he didn't stay long. He was jostled by shoulders and bellies, deafened by lipsticked mouths shouting in his ears, choked with clouds of perfume and aftershave, dazzled by tinted hair.

Why the hell had he come to this madhouse?

He reached the Electric Bear Pub and had a look round inside to see if Danilo was there.

The tables were dimly lit by soft lighting and surrounded by dark figures. The bar, too, was crowded with people perched on stools. Three plasma screens were showing a wrestling match. The music was deafening. And whenever anyone gave a tip the waiters rang a bell.

There was no sign of Danilo.

Cristiano went out and with the last three euros in his pocket bought a slice of pizza topped with salami and mushrooms. He decided to have a quick stroll around without stopping to look at the shop windows.

As the solid mass drifting along Gallery B dragged him with it, he nearly bumped right into Fabiana Ponticelli.

He just managed to dodge her. He heard Esmeralda saying: 'This way! This way!'

Two colourful imps darting through the crowd, uttering little squeals of joy. They jumped. They got shoved by people they came up against, and they shoved back in their turn. They got a lot of insults hurled at them, but didn't even hear. They seemed possessed by a crazy demon.

He followed them, trying to keep out of sight, yet never taking his eyes off them. Fabiana, quite suddenly, pointed at a clothes shop, and in gales of laughter she and Esmeralda plunged inside, hand in hand. Cristiano approached the window.

They took skirts, cardigans and T-shirts off the shelves, gave them the briefest of glances then rolled them up and dumped them back in a heap among the neat piles. But every now and then they would stop and look at the walls and the ceiling.

At first Cristiano couldn't make out what they were doing. Then the penny dropped.

The CCTV cameras.

When they were out of range of the cameras one of them would make a loud noise, attracting attention, and the other would quickly stuff the things in her bag.

He saw Fabiana enter a fitting room with her handbag while Esmeralda kept watch outside the curtain, pretending to try on a hat, and when a shop assistant came over, furious at the mess they had made, she put on a phoney smile and started asking her a lot of questions, leading her away towards a distant shelf.

Cristiano had no doubt that Fabiana, concealed in the fitting room, was busy with a pair of pliers, cutting the security tags off the clothes.

When she re-emerged, she made a sign to Esmeralda and calmly, with the bag bulging, they walked out of the shop and melted into the crowd.

They were good. Holy shit, were they good.

He was hopeless at stealing. He made every mistake in the book.

It took him ages to summon up the courage, and if the shop assistants never caught him it was only because they were too bloody thick. But he always ended up taking things that weren't any use. A pair of Adidases that were too small for him. Another time a PlayStation joypad which there was no point in having without the console.

The worst time had been when he had had the brilliant idea of stealing Strawberry, the ferret in the pet shop.

It had been love at first sight when he had seen that furry creature. It had a face like a mouse, the ears of a teddy bear and two ink-drops for eyes. A coat the colour of cappuccino and a tail like a paintbrush. It slept in a big cage, lying on a kind of hammock. A little notice said TAME. And Cristiano, unseen by the woman who owned the shop, had opened the cage and put his hand inside. Strawberry had let him stroke his stomach, and had grasped his thumb with his little paws and licked it with his rasp-like tongue.

Day after day he had gone to the shop to ask for information about how much he cost (an impossible price!), what he ate, where he crapped, whether he was good-tempered, whether he smelled, and finally the shopkeeper had said in exasperation: 'Either buy him or get lost'.

Cristiano, offended, had headed for the door, but before reaching it he had seen that the bitch was selling a packet of cat biscuits to a customer. He had opened the cage, grabbed Strawberry by the scruff of the neck and without further ado stuffed him in his trousers and legged it.

The ferret, after a few seconds, had started struggling, squirming and scratching as if someone was trying to kill it.

Meanwhile Cristiano was trying to walk nonchalantly along the mezzanine floor but the animal was tearing the skin off his thighs. Eventually he couldn't stand it any longer and started shouting out loud and hopping through the crowd like a thing possessed. He stuck his hand down his trousers while behind him a voice started shouting: 'Stop thief! Stop thief! He's stolen my ferret! Stop him!'

The shopkeeper was running after him among the astonished faces. Cristiano broke into a run. Then the ferret's little head popped out at the bottom of his trouser-leg, Cristiano shook his leg and the animal shot out, flew a couple of metres through the air and then bolted in the direction of the TIM shop, while Cristiano raced towards the exit.

After that traumatic experience he had sworn to himself that he would never shoplift again.

But in the meantime, where had those two girls got to?

He went on along the gallery, looking into the clothes shops and shoe shops.

Piazza di Spagna was crowded with people relaxing at the tables of the Wild Goose Chase Bar. There was a clown with a top hat and walking stick who for three euros would pose for photographs with children. And a bikini-clad blonde lying on a sunbed, her body covered with sticking plasters and coloured wires which made her buttocks quiver.

There they are.

They were sitting on the steps, engrossed in trying on the clothes they had just stolen.

Cristiano's first impulse was to just walk on by, but instead he kept going anxiously backwards and forwards, throwing furtive glances at them without their noticing his presence. He pretended to have an appointment with someone, looking up at the clock on the wall from time to time.

Another thirty seconds and I'm going.

When the thirty seconds had passed he decided to wait another twenty. And it was a good thing he did, because when the hand reached the eighteenth second he thought he heard Esmeralda call his name.

The music played by the clown was so loud he couldn't be absolutely sure.

Then the two of them beckoned him over.

Cristiano took his time sauntering up those four steps. Esmeraldo spread her arm, inviting him to sit down. 'How are you doing?'

The saliva had gone from Cristiano's mouth and he had difficulty in saying: 'I'm okay.'

Esmeralda put on a violet top over her blouse. 'How do I look?'
'Fine.'

'Only fine?' and then, to her friend: 'See? I told you it wouldn't suit me.' She took it off and dumped it on the ground.

Fabiana observed him for a moment with her pale blue eyes. 'What are you doing here?'

'Nothing . . . '

'Are you waiting for someone?'

'No . . . ' Then he remembered the act he had been putting on. He shrugged. 'Well, yes . . . But I was late getting here.'

Esmeralda pulled out of her bag a sweatshirt emblazoned with the S of Superman. 'Your girlfriend?'

Cristiano said a too hasty 'No!'

'There's nothing wrong with having a girlfriend, you know. Are you scared of girls?'

'No, why should I be?' With these two he always felt as if he was under interrogation. He added, to make himself clearer: 'I just haven't got a girlfriend, that's all.'

'What about Angela Baroni?'

'Angela Baroni?'

'She's always telling everyone how crazy she is about you . . . '

'But you don't even deign to look at her, poor girl. You're a hard-ass,' Fabiana mocked him.

Angela Baroni was in 3C. A little girl with long black hair. He had never noticed that she liked him.

'I don't fancy her,' he whispered awkwardly.

'Who *do* you fancy?'

Cristiano dug his fingernails into his arm. 'No one.'

Esmeralda rested her head on his shoulder. His whole body went stiff, as if someone had rammed a broomstick up his arse. He caught a sweet smell of shampoo which made his head spin. She purred in his ear: 'It's not possible. You, the handsomest hunk in the school, and you don't fancy anybody . . . ' and gave him the lightest of kisses on the neck.

And, although he was sure she was only taking the piss, it was a dizzying, disorientating sensation, which stunned him for a long, long moment, leaving him breathless and with gooseflesh all down his back.

'Hey, what's this? You get to kiss him and I don't?' And Fabiana kissed him full on the lips. Cristiano felt a second shock, perhaps even more violent than the first, as if he had been stabbed in the chest. An indescribable noise escaped his throat.

It had been all too brief, the contact with that soft flesh. Beautiful and painful. He stopped himself putting his fingers to his lips to see if some of that moistness had clung to them.

'What about us, then?'

'Don't you fancy us?'

Esmeralda picked up a Cossack hat made of phosphorescent green plush and plonked it on his head. Then she burst out laughing. 'It really suits you.'

Fabiana got out her lipstick and ran it over his lips.

By now Cristiano was so confused and disorientated he would have let the two girls give him a shampoo and set.

Esmeraldo took a pocket mirror out of her handbag. 'Look at yourself!'

Cristiano took the briefest of looks and cleaned his lips.

'Why don't we go to the games arcade?' Esmeralda said to her friend, and walked off towards the gallery.

Fabiana crossed her arms and pouted. 'Has anyone ever told you you're a real drag? Why don't you ever laugh? I reckon you take after your father.'

Cristiano stiffened. He didn't like talking about his father. 'Why?'

'Well, he looks so mean, with that shaven head and those tattoos . . . Hey, where did he get them, by the way?'

'What?'

'The tattoos.'

'I don't know . . . At the tattooist's.' Cristiano genuinely didn't know. Rino had had most of them done when he had been too small to remember, and the more recent ones in some place near Murelle.

'I know that. But where?'

'I've no idea. Why do you want to know?'

'I'd like to have one done.'

'Where?'

She smiled and shook her head. 'I'm not telling you.'

'Go on! Where?'

'In a secret place.'

'Oh go on, tell me.'

'You tell me where your father had his tattoos done, then.'

He put his hand on his heart. 'I don't know. I swear.'

'I could ask your father myself, you know. Do you think I'm scared? I wouldn't think twice about it.'

Cristiano shrugged. 'Go ahead and ask him, then.'

Fabiana stood up, grasped his hand and pulled him to his feet. 'Come on, let's go.'

The games arcade was full of young people. Some were from their school, but most were older.

It was an enormous room. There was a four-lane bowling alley, a game that involved throwing a ball into a basket, with a scoreboard recording each successful shot, cranes that picked up cuddly toys, and hundreds of videogames. The music was deafening. The place was full of Filipinos, Chinese and children jumping about on a platform trying to dance in time to the music, following the instructions of a videogame. Down at the other end was a second room, darker and less crowded than the first, with fruit machines all round the walls. In the middle were a dozen green billiard tables illuminated by low-hanging lights, with black figures armed with cues standing around them.

Cristiano had never been in there. In the first place because there was a notice saying you had to be eighteen to enter, secondly because he didn't know anybody, and thirdly because he was crap at billiards.

Fabiana rushed into the room, ignoring the age restriction, and Cristiano was about to follow, but he stopped in the doorway when he saw that Tekken was there.

Tekken was playing a doubles match and Esmeralda was doing her level best to put him off. She would knock the cue when he played a shot, tickle him under the arms or rub up against him. He pretended to be annoyed, but anyone could see he was loving it.

He was with two other boys. Memmo, a guy with a fancily trimmed goatee beard and a ponytail, and Nespola, who thought he looked like Robbie Williams but didn't.

Just then Esmeralda climbed up on the billiard table and Tekken fired a ball between her thighs, to the raucous guffaws of everyone present.

Cristiano closed his eyes and leaned against the wall. He couldn't breathe. He could still feel on his neck and mouth the pressure of Esmeralda and Fabiana's lips.

'What a pair of tarts . . . ' he whispered, resting his head against the wall.

His father was right – girls like that only liked rich guys. Like Tekken. Their motorbikes. Their money.

If you were poor, like he was, they just took the piss out of you.

He felt something acidic burning his stomach, as if he had drunk a bottle of bleach. He felt like throwing up.

A wild anger clouded his thoughts. His hands itched. He felt like going in there, picking up a billiard cue and smashing it over that bastard's head. But instead he turned and ran out, panting hard. He hated this place. The people. The shop windows full of useless things he couldn't buy.

He went into a kichenware shop, took a long knife out of a block of wood, hid it under his jacket and walked out into the car park, elbowing his way through the crowd.

He ran round behind the rubbish bins, pulled out the knife and slashed the saddle and punctured the tyres of Tekken's motorbike. He was about to dig a deep scratch across the petrol tank when he heard a voice behind his back shout: 'Hey! What the fuck are you doing?'

His heart leaped into his tonsils with fright.

He turned round. Sitting astride a big Ducati was a guy in a black helmet and a leather jacket. 'You little creep, I'm going to beat you to a pulp!' the biker shouted as he propped his motorbike on its stand.

Cristiano threw away the knife and ran off between the cars, while the guy shouted after him, 'You coward! It's no use you running away. I know who you are! You're at the junior high! We'll find you! We'll find you and when we do . . . '

He came out onto the highway and kept on running.

He couldn't believe he had been such a fool. In the space of a few seconds he had landed himself up to his neck in shit.

Of all the stupid things to do, he had chosen the most stupid one possible. Slashing Tekken's motorbike and getting caught in the act!

He kept one eye on the ground as he ran, trying to avoid the puddles. He had a stitch in his side and pressed his hand against it. The highway, the guardrail and the car headlights blurred over and reappeared at every step.

Below the hoarse wheeze of his breathing he kept hearing the threats of the black-clad biker: 'Where are you running to? I know who you are! I know you! We'll get you for this!'

He felt as if it was all a bad dream, as if all he had to do was stop, close his eyes and open them again and he would be back in that dark corner of the games arcade which smelled of sweat and deodorant.

He must have been out of his mind. He had stolen the knife and slashed the motorbike in a kind of hypnotic trance. As if he'd had a kind of blackout. When he had entered the kitchenware shop he hadn't even looked round to check if anyone was watching.

He didn't know how he could keep on running, with all that fear in his body. Soon Tekken's vengeance would come down on him with all its merciless, crushing force.

The guy was quite capable of killing him.

Once Cristiano had seen him get into a fight with a truck driver outside the bar.

The thing he remembered was his coolness in confronting a man who was twenty kilos heavier than him and had fists as big as shoulders of ham. Tekken had skipped about, swaying his hips like a merengue dancer. He was enjoying himself. As if he was training in the gym.

While the big ape swung his arms and hurled insults, Tekken had kicked him on the knee and the giant had collapsed on the ground. Then he had grabbed hold of his ear, jerked up his head and said, wagging his finger from side to side: 'You're nobody around here. So don't try to throw your weight around.'

And all this simply because the big brute had asked Tekken, without saying 'please', to move his motorbike so he could park his truck.

Just think what he'll do to me for destroying it . . .

His lungs were on fire and he had to slow down. He ran onto a bridge that passed over an irrigation canal and stopped, panting, in a bus shelter halfway across. The timetable and walls were plastered with coloured scrawls. The bench was caked with ketchup and with the remains of chips and rice croquettes. And the place reeked of urine. A dim neon light crackled on the ceiling.

He stood there, scanning the road for a sight of the bus.

By this time the biker would have told Tekken what had happened. *"Who the fuck was it?"*

"A fair-haired guy. From the junior high."

Fabiana and Esmeralda would have twigged at once that it had been him. *"We know him. His name's Cristiano Zena. He goes to our school."*

Those two bitches would never cover for him.

Meanwhile there was still no sign of the bus. And Tekken and his gang would certainly be on his trail by now. Cristiano hid in the narrow space between the shelter and the guardrail. He could hear the gurgling of the water that flowed in the canal some ten metres below the bridge.

He was just wondering whether to continue on foot when the yellow eyes of the bus appeared in the distance.

Thank God.

He emerged from behind the shelter, leaned out into the road and was on the point of raising his arm when three motorbikes overtook the bus on the right and dazzled him with their headlights. He stepped back and the bus flashed by without even slowing down. He saw the people sitting behind the windows and, immediately afterwards, the red rear lights.

It hadn't stopped. But the motorbikes had.

He tried to make a run for it, but a black Ducati swerved round and braked in front of him and Tekken, who was riding on the back, leaped on him.

Cristiano fell down in the mud and banged his shoulder hard. He tried to struggle, to kick, but Tekken had gripped him at the base of the biceps, pinning him down with an arm across his chest. With the other hand he grabbed him by the hair, pulled him up and slapped him full in the face with the back of his hand, knocking him back against the guardrail.

Cristiano's suprarenal glands were producing millions of molecules of adrenalin which prevented him, at least for the moment, from feeling any pain.

He jumped to his feet, trying to escape towards the road, but only managed to take a few steps before he fell down again.

Tekken had scythed his legs from under him with a kick.

Now Cristiano was gasping in the ice-cold mud, trying to get up, but his legs wouldn't respond.

He swore to himself that he wouldn't utter even the faintest groan.

Tekken put the heel of his shoe on Cristiano's hand and pressed and Cristiano gave a piercing shriek with what little air remained in his lungs.

'Why did you do it, eh? Why?' Tekken kept repeating to him. 'Tell me!' His voice was plaintive, incredulous, as if he was about to burst into tears.

Cristiano couldn't answer, because he had no answer to give, except that during those five minutes he had had some kind of brainstorm.

Tekken pressed harder and Cristiano felt an explosion of pain envelop his forearm and fingers.

'Why? Speak!'

On the one hand Cristiano wanted to plead for mercy, to beg him to stop, to say it hadn't been him, that they were wrong, that he had nothing to do with it; on the other hand he felt inside him a block as hard as stone which stopped him doing so. They could kill him if they liked, but he would never beg for mercy.

Tekken stepped back and Cristiano started crawling towards the shelter. Everything around him had got tangled up in a rainbow of colours, exhaust fumes, wheels and legs. His ears were buzzing and he could hear what the others on their motorbikes were saying.

He thought he could hear female voices.

Esmeralda and Fabiana.

They were there too. Another reason for not giving in.

Cristiano dragged himself under the bench of the bus shelter.

Maybe if I can get a little further in they won't find me.

It was a vain hope. Tekken grabbed him by the ankle and dragged him back. 'Well, what am I going to do with you?' He gave him a kick. 'Can you believe it, you guys? This little pillock has ruined my motorbike.' He sounded despairing, as if someone had just shot his mother. 'What am I going to do with him?'

Cristiano curled up, his knees against his chest. He couldn't stop shaking. He must react, get up, fight.

'Let's chuck him off the bridge,' suggested a voice.

A moment's silence, then Tekken decreed: 'Good thinking.'

Through a mist of confusion and pain Cristiano found the idea of dying like that, thrown off a bridge, almost beautiful, a liberation.

'Get hold of his legs.'

They grabbed his ankles. An iron hand tugged at one of his arms. He didn't resist.

He would be spotted next day by an old woman waiting for the bus, squashed like a cockroach on the concrete embankment of the canal. He felt sorry for his father.

He'll die of grief.

But when he suddenly sensed a dark abyss sucking him down, heard the sound of the water and felt the icy wind on his face, he realised that they had lifted him up and something inside him snapped. He opened his eyes wide and started struggling frantically and shouting, 'You bastards! You bastards! Sons of bitches! You'll pay for this! I'll kill you. I'll kill you all!'

But he couldn't break free. There seemed to be at least three of them holding him fast.

The blood went to his head. Below him was a black stream which gleamed silver each time a car passed by.

'Well, you little runt, do you want to die?'

'Fuck off!'

'Ooh, tough guy, are we?'

They pushed him further out.

'Fuck off, you bastards!'

He got a slap in the face which brought blood spurting out of his nose.

Tekken's voice: 'Listen to me very carefully. If you don't give me a thousand euros, on the nail, on Monday, I swear on the head of my mother that I'll kill you! And don't even think of running away, because I'll find you!' And then, to the others: 'Now let him go.'

They put him down on the ground.

The whole world seemed to be a whirl of lights and featureless faces.

Sitting there, slumped against the guardrail, Cristiano saw them start up their engines, turn round and ride off towards the village.

It was five minutes before he tried to move a muscle, and when he did so he discovered he had pissed himself.

53

When Cristiano Zena got home the lights were on.

Nothing was going right.

If his father saw him like this, with his trousers soaked in piss and covered with dirt, his jacket bloodstained and torn . . .

God knows what he'd do.

Cristiano limped across the yard, past the van and round to the back of the house. A concrete ramp led down to an underground garage with an aluminium rolling door. He lifted up a flower pot to find the key. He put it in the lock and, stifling a cry of pain, raised the door far enough for him to slip under it.

It was cold in the garage. He switched on the light, to reveal a room which smelt of damp and of the paint in the tins that stood on the long shelves. The pea-green walls and the yellow neon light made it look like a morgue. In the middle was an old ping-pong table covered with piles of newspapers, tyres and other junk which had accumulated over the years. A dusty, worm-eaten upright piano stood against one wall. Rino had always been evasive about its origins and why it was there. It had nothing to do with the two of them. And his father was the most tone-deaf person Cristiano had ever met. At the millionth time of asking, he had finally got a reply.

'It was your mother's.'

'What did she do with it?'

'She played it. She wanted to be a singer.'

'Was she any good?'

His father had been reluctant to admit it. 'She had a nice voice. But when it came down to it, it wasn't singing she enjoyed, but tarting herself up and going to piano bars and fooling around. I tried to sell it, but I could never find a buyer.'

So for a while Cristiano had taken to going down to the garage and trying to play it. But he was even less musical than his father.

Inside some boxes stacked up against a wall Cristiano found some old clothes. He took off his jacket and put on a moth-eaten cardigan and a pair of jeans. He washed his face in the basin and straightened his hair. He wished he had a mirror to check his appearance, but there wasn't any.

He locked up the garage and went back round to the front door.

The problem was his swollen lip. He also had grazes on his back and hands, and bruises on his leg, but those he could hide.

Another problem, which wasn't so much a problem as a disaster, was the thousand euros. Well, he would have to think about that later, think long and hard, because he didn't have the faintest idea how he was going to solve it.

Now he could only hope his father was asleep or already dead drunk, so that he could enter the house, slip past him as silently as a panther and steal upstairs into his bedroom.

He took a good, deep breath. He had another quick look at his clothes, then opened the front door and closed it behind him, trying not to make any noise.

In the living room only the lamp beside the television was on. The rest of the room was in semi-darkness.

His father was in his usual place, on the lounger; Cristiano could see his shaven head. Quattro Formaggi was with him, sitting on the sofa with his back to the door. Were they asleep? He waited for a while to hear if they were talking. He couldn't hear anything.

So far so good.

He tiptoed towards the stairs. Hardly daring to breathe, he put one foot on the first step and the other on the second, but he failed to notice a hammer and some pliers, which fell down with a clatter.

Cristiano gritted his teeth and looked up, and at the same moment he heard his father's hoarse voice: 'Who's there? Cristiano, is that you?'

He suppressed an oath and replied, trying to sound casual: 'Yes, it's me.'

'Hi!' Quattro Formaggi raised an arm.

'Hi.'

His father slowly turned his head, a mask which the television screen had painted light blue. 'Have you been at home, then?'

Cristiano, as stiff as a statue, gripped the banister. 'Yes.'

'I didn't see any light in your room.'

'I was asleep,' he improvised.

'Ah!'

Emergency over. Rino was so drunk he wasn't interested in what he was doing. He took another step.

'There should be some mortadella left. Could you bring it to me with some bread?' Rino went on.

'Can't you get it yourself?'

'No.'

'Oh come on. Is it such a big effort?'

'I'll get it for you,' Quattro Formaggi offered.

'No, you stay where you are. If a father asks his son for some mortadella, his son goes and gets the mortadella. That's the way it works. What's the point of having children, otherwise?' He had raised his voice. Either he was in one of his bad moods or he had a headache.

Cristiano came back down the stairs, muttering to himself, and went to fetch the mortadella. There was one single slice left in the desolate fridge.

Then he got the bread. Still hidden in the shadows, he approached his father.

But just as he was handing it to him, misfortune struck again. On the television some guy gave the right answer to the twenty-thousand euro question, whereupon two thousand million-volt light-bulbs lit up all at once, flooding the lounge with light.

Cristiano lowered his eyelids, and when he raised them again his father's expression had changed.

'What's the matter with your lip?'

'Nothing. What do you mean?' He covered it with his hands.

'And what are those scratches on your hands?'

'I fell over.'

'How?'

Out of the void of Cristiano's mind came the first, foolish lie. 'I slipped on the stairs. It's nothing,' he said, airily.

His father eyed him suspiciously. 'On the stairs? And you made such a mess of yourself? What did you do, fall all the way down?'

'Yes . . . I tripped over my shoelaces . . . '

'How the fuck did you do that? It looks like someone's punched you in the mouth . . . '

'No . . . I just fell down . . . '

'Bullshit.'

It was impossible to con his father. He had a special gift for spotting untruths. He used to say lies stank and he could smell them at a distance of a hundred metres. And he always saw through you. How he managed it Cristiano didn't know. He suspected it had something to do with that quiver of the jaw which he could never control when he was lying to him.

It was strange – with everyone else he was brilliant at lying. He could spin the most outrageous yarns with such self-assurance that nobody doubted him. But with his father it was different, he just couldn't do it, he felt those black eyes boring through him in search of the truth.

And at that moment Cristiano wasn't in the right frame of mind to stand up to an interrogation.

His legs were still trembling and his stomach was churning. A wise little voice told him that the only person who could get him out of that mess with the thousand euros was his father.

Fatally, he lowered his head and, almost in a whisper, confessed: 'It's not true. I didn't fall down. I had a fight . . . '

Rino sat in silence for a long time, breathing through his nose, then switched off the television. He swallowed saliva. 'And by the look of it you came off worst.'

Cristiano nodded.

He shouldn't have spoken, because he could feel that all the strength he had been using to stop himself crying was exhausted. Coils of barbed wire seemed to be wrapped round his throat.

He lifted up his sweatshirt to show his grazed back.

His father looked at him expressionlessly for a moment, then started rubbing his hands over his face like someone who's just heard that his whole family has been killed in a road accident.

Cristiano wished he hadn't told him the truth.

Rino Zena looked up at the ceiling and asked, very politely: 'Would you mind leaving us, Quattro Formaggi?' He breathed hard. 'I need to be alone with my son.'

He's going to give me a thrashing . . . thought Cristiano.

Quattro Formaggi got up without a word, put on his old over-coat, and, with an incomprehensible grimace at Cristiano, went out.

When the door was closed Rino stood up and switched on all the lights in the sitting room. Then he went over to Cristiano and examined his wounds and his mouth, as if he was checking a horse at the market.

'Does your back hurt?'

'A bit . . . '

'Can you bend down?'

Cristiano leaned forward. 'Yes.'

'It's not serious, then. What about your leg?'

'Yes, I can bend it.'

'Your hands?'

'They're okay.'

Rino paced silently round the room, then sat down on a chair. He lit a cigarette and stared at him. 'And how about you?'

'What do you mean?'

'Did you hurt him?' He only had to look his son in the eye for the answer. 'The hell you did!' He shook his head in despair. 'You . . . you don't know how to fight, do you?' It was a revelation. 'You really don't know how to.' He sounded half scandalized, half ashamed of himself. As if he had failed to teach his offspring to talk, or to walk. As if he had fathered a son with a fatal allergy to gluten and then forced him to gorge himself on bread.

'But . . . ' Cristiano tried to interrupt him, to explain exactly who Tekken was. But his father was in full flow.

'It's my fault. It's my fault.' Now he was walking round with his head in his hands like a penitent at Lourdes. 'He doesn't know how to defend himself. It's my fault. I'm a failure . . . '

God knows how long he would have gone on like this if Cristiano hadn't shouted, 'Papa! Papa!'

Rino stopped. 'What's up?'

'He's eighteen years old . . . and he's an expert at Thai boxing. He won the regional championships.'

His father looked at him blankly. 'Who is?'

'Tekken!'

'Who the fuck is Tekken?'

'The guy who beat me up.'

Rino grabbed him by the collar. His face was contorted, his nostrils flared, his mouth clamped shut. He raised his fist. Cristiano instinctively shielded his head with his arms. Rino held him there, hesitating, then gave him a shove, so that he fell back onto the sofa.

'You're a stupid little prick. You believe all that crap about martial arts experts being good at fighting. What have you learned about life? Where do you get all this bullshit from? Wait a minute, I know! You believe everything you see on TV and you try to be like them. That's it, isn't it? You watch those cartoons where people do kung fu and all that kind of crap and you think it's clever to act like Bruce Lee or some other Chinese moron, prancing about like an acrobat and shouting *ha* all the fucking time instead of fighting. You've got no idea! Do you know what it really takes to be good at fighting? Well, do you or don't you?'

Cristiano shook his head.

'It's so simple. Meanness. Meanness, Cristiano! All you have to do is be a son of a bitch and not give a shit about anyone. Even if you're up against Jesus Christ raging about in the temple, with steam coming out of his ears, if you know what you're doing you can knock him down like a skittle. You walk up behind him, you say, "Excuse me?", he turns round, you hit him in the face with an iron bar and he goes down, and then, if you feel like it, while he's on the ground you give him a kick in the teeth, and that's it. Amen. Or suppose some guy's fucking you around, jostling you and threatening you and trying to scare you by doing some of those kung fu moves, you know what you have to do? Nothing. You just stay where you are. Then,' he pointed one foot forward, 'you place your foot like this. And when he moves in closer you head-butt him on the nose. Like you were heading a football, using all the force of your neck and shoulders. Only make sure you hit him with this part here, or you'll hurt yourself.' He touched the top of his forehead. 'If you do it right, you won't feel a thing. You might be a bit sore the next day, but that's all. He'll go down and then it's the same routine – a kick in the teeth and bob's your uncle. I defy anyone to get up after that, even this jerk Tekker or whatever his name is . . . But you have to be decisive and you have to be mean, do you understand? Now come here.'

Cristiano looked at him. 'Why?'

'Just come here.'

Hesitantly, Cristiano obeyed.

'Head-butt me. Show me how you'd do it.'

'What?'

'I said head-butt me.'

Cristiano was incredulous. 'Me? You want *me* to head-butt *you*?'

His father seized his wrist. 'Who else? Get on with it, for fuck's sake.'

Cristiano tried to break away. 'No . . . Please . . . I don't want to . . . I can't.'

Rino gripped his arm more tightly. 'Now listen to me carefully. Nobody's going to beat you up ever again. Nobody in the whole wide world is going to even think about doing it. You're not a little fairy who lets himself be kicked around by the first pillock he meets. I wish I could help you – you don't know how much I wish I could – but I can't. You've got to fight your own battles. And there's only one way of doing that: you've got to become mean.' He felt his arm. 'You're too nice. You're soft. You're not angry enough. You're made of cotton wool. Where are your balls?' He shook him, as if he was a rag doll. 'So go ahead and nut me. Don't think about me being your father, don't think about anything, just think that you're going to hurt me and that I'm going to spend the rest of my days regretting that I once had the stupid idea of picking a fight with you. Don't you see that once you've whipped a couple of the bastards word will get round that you're a son of a bitch and nobody will ever bother you again? I'm doing it for your sake. If you can't head-butt me you'll never be able to do it to anyone else.' He pointed to his nose with both forefingers and said: 'So let me have it!'

There was no alternative. Cristiano knew it. He was going to have to give him that head-butt.

He pointed his foot forward, drew back his head, shut his eyes and jerked his head forwards. He hit his father on the bridge of the nose and heard a nasty sound, like that of teeth crunching on chicken bones. All he felt was a slight tingling in the middle of his forehead.

Rino took a step backwards, like a boxer who's taken an uppercut to the jaw, put his hand to his nose, stifled a yell and went purple in the face. When he took his hand away there were two trickles of blood coming out of his nostrils.

Cristiano embraced him. 'I'm sorry, papa, I'm sorry . . . '

Rino hugged him tightly, stroked his hair and said in a strangled voice: 'That's my boy! I think you've broken my nose.'

54

While Rino Zena was stuffing two bits of cotton wool up his nostrils, Cristiano sat on the toilet watching him, and reflected that the problem, all things considered, remained exactly the same as before.

Okay, he had learned to give a head-butt, but if after vandalising Tekken's motorbike he had gone on to give him a head-butt, the rest of the gang would have grabbed him and dragged him up and down the highway to their hearts' content.

But what he found most amazing was that his father hadn't asked him what the fight had been about. The question hadn't even crossed his mind.

All he cares about is that nobody hits his son.

To be honest, the beating he had taken had been richly deserved. Cristiano would have done exactly the same if someone had wrecked *his* motorbike.

He put his hand on his forehead.

What if I tell him about the thousand euros?

It would mean telling him the whole story. He just didn't know what to do.

'Are you ready?' said his father in a Donald Duck-like voice, as he dried his face.

'What for?'

Rino changed his T-shirt. 'What do you mean, what for? We're going to find your kick-boxing champion and show him what a big mistake he made when he beat you up.'

Cristiano felt like throwing up. It wasn't possible. 'You are joking, aren't you?'

'Certainly not. You must never let these things drag on. If someone hits you, you must hit back straight away. And, as the Bible says, seven times harder.'

'Do we really have do it right now?'

'Don't tell me you want to be thought of as someone who takes a beating and keeps his mouth shut . . . This kind of problem has to be dealt with immediately.'

Cristiano objected disconsolately: 'But he'll be with the others . . . '

Rino started jumping up and down like a boxer who's about to enter the ring. 'So much the better. They'll all see that nobody messes with Cristiano Zena.'

'But what if the others defend him?'

'Don't worry about that . . . I'll be with you.' A wild elation shone in his father's eyes.

'Suppose he reports me to the police . . . ? I'll be in the shit . . . '

His father went through into the sitting room without replying.

Cristiano followed, imploring him. 'Please, papa. You know Trecca . . . He's just looking for an excuse to put me into care.'

Rino went over to the stove, where there was a pile of firewood. He selected a piece about seventy centimetres long and swung it approvingly through the air like a baseball bat.

'Good! Now you're going to give him this prime piece of beechwood smack in the teeth.'

'I'm not coming, papa.' Cristiano shook his head dejectedly and threw himself on the sofa. 'You're always saying we mustn't do anything stupid. I'm staying at home . . . I'm not interested. You can go if you want to . . . You said I've got to solve my own problems . . . I will. Please put down that stick. You look stupid . . . '

'Listen to me. Do you think your father's a fool? Your father may not look like a thinker, but he is.' He tapped his temple with his finger. 'This brain still works pretty well, so you've got to do as I say. Relax. Don't worry. Leave everything to me.' He gripped his son's arms. 'He's eighteen and you're thirteen. He's an adult and you're a minor. He's the one who'll be in the shit. And he started it . . . The way I see it, you're simply sticking up for yourself. And afterwards, if he has any problem . . . ' he took the pistol out of the drawer in the dresser, 'we'll introduce him to this young lady here. One sight of her pointing right at his face would be enough.'

'But . . . '

'No buts!'

Rino picked up the bottle of grappa from the table, gulped down a quarter of it and uttered a kind of roar. 'Drink some of this. It'll give you courage.'

Cristiano took a swig. He felt the alcohol burning his guts and realised that Tekken was for it.

55

Three times, on the way to Varrano, Cristiano felt the urge to come clean, and three times he did no more than imagine his confession.

Papa, there's something I've got to tell you . . . . Look, I wrecked his motorbike . . . That's why he beat me up. I did a thousand euros' worth of damage to his bike, when he hadn't done anything to me.

It was the truth. Tekken had never touched him. He had picked on a lot of other people outside the school, but never him. He had never even spoken to him. Until that evening Tekken probably hadn't even known he existed.

When they caught up with him, Tekken would say Cristiano had wrecked his motorbike and his father would find out . . .

What a mess.

But when they got to the mall it was closed. The gates locked. The illuminations switched off. The towers black. The expanse of asphalt lashed by the rain, which had started dancing in the beams from the spotlights again. Tekken had even removed his motorbike.

Cristiano heaved a sigh of relief. 'He's not here. Let's go home.'

But the only reply was: 'Don't worry. I'll find him.'

They started driving round the village. The bar. The high street. The other main roads. It was only a quarter past nine, but there wasn't a soul to be seen.

His father drove in fits and starts, wrenched the gears, broke all the rules in the highway code. 'Where the fuck has he got to?'

'He's probably gone home. Why don't we just forget it? It's late.'

The streets were empty and the rain was drumming on the roof of the van.

They stopped at the side of the highway. Rino lit his umpteenth cigarette. 'What shall we do?' he asked.

'I don't know.'

His father sat in silence, touching his swollen nose.

'Come on, let's go home,' Cristiano advised him.

So they set off, but just to make quite sure, Rino decided to do one more circuit round the village. He passed the church, went along the residential streets with their rows of illuminated cottages with tidy gardens and with station wagons and four-by-fours parked outside, and then, finally, drove back out onto the deserted highway. Every hundred metres the streetlamps threw yellow rings on the asphalt and the windscreen wipers worked frantically to keep the glass dry.

Cristiano was about to tell him to head for the takeaway when he saw, on the other side of the highway, a black-clad figure pushing a motorbike in the rain.

Tekken.

His windproof jacket soaked. His tyres slashed. What a struggle he must be having. He was all alone on the highway . . . There wasn't even the risk of being seen, let alone of being caught by the police.

Tekken would shit himself with fright and withdraw his demand for the money. But Cristiano would have to be quick – jump out of the van and hit him with the club before he had time to react.

He counted up to three and then shouted, bouncing up and down on the seat: 'I saw him! Papa, I saw him!'

'Where? Where?' Rino roused himself from his lethargy.

'On the other side of the road. We just passed him. He's on foot. Turn round! Turn round!'

'Fantastic! You son of a bitch, we found you in the end!' shouted Rino, and without so much as a glance in the mirror he did a U-turn, with screeching tyres. 'Is he alone?'

'Yes. He's pushing a motorbike.'

'A motorbike?'

'Yes.'

Rino registered the information without any comment.

Cristiano felt his excitement rising and his breathing getting faster. He gripped the club. It was nice and heavy. All the saliva had gone from his mouth. 'What shall we do, papa?'

'First of all we'll switch off the lights so he won't notice we're behind him. When we get to within fifty metres you get out, creep up on him quietly so he doesn't hear you, then you call out his name, and when he turns round you give him just long enough to recognise you, then you hit him. Just once. If it's a good hit, that'll be enough. Then I'll come along and pick you up.'

'Where shall I hit him?'

Rino thought for a moment, then touched his jaw. 'Here.'

A car overtook them and lit up the motorbike's rear reflector.

'There he is. Go.' Rino stopped the Ducato.

Cristiano got out of the van, holding the club tightly. Now that son of a bitch would learn what it meant to mess with Cristiano Zena.

I'll smash your head in, you bastard.

He looked back. There were no cars in sight.

He started running, club in hand. The black figure of Tekken pushing the motorbike grew bigger at every step. The flat tyres flapped on the asphalt. When he was about ten metres away he slowed down abruptly and started tiptoeing forward till he was about a metre away from him.

Make it accurate, he said to himself.

He lifted the club and shouted: 'Tekken! Fuck you!'

Tekken turned his head and hadn't even had time to realise what was happening before Cristiano unleashed a blow straight at his temple which would have killed him or put him in a coma, if he hadn't, at the last moment, through instinct or through the habit of fighting, moved his head just far enough for the club to miss his cheekbone and land between his neck and collarbone.

Without so much as a groan Tekken let go of his motorbike, which fell on the ground, smashing a mirror. He teetered for a moment and then, as if in slow motion, put his hand on the place where he had been hit and, shocked and silent, fell back with a crash on top of his motorbike.

'You bastard! Leave me alone, okay? You don't know me, so leave me alone.' Cristiano raised the club again. 'If you don't leave me alone, I'll kill you.' He felt an overwhelming urge to hit him, to smash his fucking head in. 'You think you're special, but you're nobody.' He swallowed. 'You're nothing.'

Then he saw in Tekken's terrified eyes the belief that he was going to die and he realised that all his anger, as quickly as it had ignited every fibre of his being, had vanished. He had only had to look into his eyes and . . .

I was going to kill him.

. . . it had gone, as if someone had pulled out a plug and all his pent-up fury, like evaporating gas, had whooshed out of him. Now he felt nothing but nausea and a terrible weariness.

'Why? I've never done anything to you . . . I've never . . . ' stammered Tekken, with his hands raised.

At that moment the van pulled up behind Cristiano and the door opened.

'Get in! Get in, quick!' Rino beckoned to him.

Cristiano lowered his arm, dropped the club on the ground and jumped into the Ducato.

Sunday

56

The Frecce Tricolori were coming.

At two o'clock in the afternoon the three hundred and thirteenth display team of the Italian Air Force would circle in the skies above Murelle, painting them red, white and green.

At eight o'clock in the morning Danilo Aprea phoned Rino Zena in great excitement. 'What a show! The best pilots in the world. The pride of Italy. And I'm not just saying that because I saw them ten years ago . . . They're world-famous. And it's free.'

Rino asked Cristiano if he wanted to go and Cristiano said he did.

So it was settled.

They would go to see the Frecce.

Quattro Formaggi was called too, and since the display would be taking place above a big field they decided to have a picnic, with grilled sausages, bruschetta and wine.

57

Like a grey blanket, a layer of cloud had spread over the field where the Frecce Tricolori were to pass.

The plot of land, measuring several hectares, had been cordoned off with long ribbons of striped plastic. A few leafless trees rose up out of the mud like sad black aerials.

When our heroes reached the car park it was already occupied by hundreds of cars and minibuses. They weren't the only ones who had had the idea of a barbecue. All around, columns of smoke spiralled up from charcoal grills. There were also rows of vans with illuminated signs selling drinks and sandwiches, to the sound of electricity generators.

People sat on deckchairs and plastic stools, their feet in the mud and their noses in the air.

Quattro Formaggi parked alongside a big blue pickup.

A small family sat on the back, guzzling pizza, rice balls and chicken croquettes.

Rino Zena got out of the van and realised that he wasn't feeling at all well. His headache was still there, alive and pulsing. Sometimes, like an octopus, it hid in the crevices of his brain, but when he drank or smoked too much, it emerged angrily and extended its electric tentacles into his temples, his eye sockets, the back of his head, and down into his stomach.

I must give up drinking. I really must.

Maybe he should join Alcoholics Anonymous, or follow Trecca's advice – he must do something, anyway. Although the social services might take this as proof that he couldn't look after Cristiano.

Before going into rehab I must get married. Preferably to someone with a job.

There had been one woman Rino had once thought of marrying: Mariangela Santarelli, who owned a hairdressing salon in Marezzi, a hamlet near Varrano. Mariangela had three daughters (five, six and seven years old) and was a young widow. Her husband, who had owned a building supplies firm, had died of leukaemia after eight years of marriage.

The real reason why Rino had stayed with Mariangela was that she had looked after Cristiano when he went out at night. 'If three can sleep on it, I don't see why four can't,' the hairdresser used to say, leaning against the door frame, contemplating a double bed covered with children.

Rino, who hated spending the night with the women he screwed, would go and pick up Cristiano next morning and take him to kindergarten.

Then one day Rino and Mariangela had split up, because he wasn't a serious person and didn't want to marry her.

'I bet you never find another woman stupid enough to look after your son while you cheat on her!' she had said.

And she had won her bet.

Maybe I could ring her . . .

Though he doubted if Mariangela was still alone. She was an attractive woman with a steady income.

Cristiano came over to him, holding the plastic bag from the cash-and-carry. 'Papa, how are we going to make the fire for the sausages?'

Rino rubbed his sore eyes. 'I don't know. Look for some firewood, or ask someone if they'll give you some charcoal. I've got to lie down for a minute. Call me when the planes come.' He opened the rear doors of the Ducato and lay down on the floor.

Maybe he just needed a nap.

'How are you feeling?'

Rino half-opened one eye and saw Quattro Formaggi looking at him, his head cocked on one side.

'Not too good.'

'I wanted to ask you something.'

'Ask away.'

Quattro Formaggi lay down beside Rino and started scratching his cheek, then both of them stared in silence at the roof of the Ducato.

'Will you help me with Liliana?'

Rino yawned. 'You really like her, do you?'

'I think so . . . What do you think?'

'How would I know, Quattro? You're the one who's got to know.'

After their discussion by the riverside, Rino had made inquiries and found out that Liliana had been seeing a guy for over two years, but he hadn't yet found the strength to tell his friend.

'No, you know best about my affairs. You always save me. You helped me in the children's home. Remember . . . '

'For God's sake don't start going on about how I always save you . . . I've got a splitting headache.'

Undaunted, Quattro Formaggi reminded him of their time in the care home, when they had met. Back then he had still been plain Corrado Rumitz and had been teased, bullied, humiliated and bossed about by all the other kids, before the indifferent eyes of the priests.

And he had helped him. Perhaps because by protecting him he could show everyone that they had better keep away from Rino Zena and everything he owned, including the idiot. Yes, that was the truth of it.

Rino was fourteen years old and was sitting on a low wall outside the care home smoking a cigarette while three bastards stuffed a poor idiot into a rubbish bin and kicked it around the yard. Rino had thrown away his stub and knocked one of them down.

'You pick on him again and you'll have to reckon with me. Just imagine he has a label on him, saying "property of Rino Zena". Okay?'

From that day on they had left the idiot in peace.

That had been the beginning of their friendship, if it could be called that. Well, twenty years had passed and they were still there, side by side. So maybe it could.

'Will you help me, then, Rino?'

'Listen . . . That Liliana's not for the likes of . . . us. Haven't you seen the way she behaves? She's after men who bring a bit of money home. What have we got to offer her? Fuck all. You'd do better to forget all about her. Anyway, what would you do? You won't even let me into your flat – where would you take her?'

Quattro Formaggi grabbed his wrist. 'Has she got a boyfriend?'

'I don't know . . . '

'Tell me.'

'Okay. Yes, she has! Are you satisfied now? Now stop going on about it. It's over. Finished. I don't want to hear any more about it.'

Silence. Then, quietly, Quattro Formaggi said: 'Okay.'

58

Quattro Formaggi said, 'Okay.' And he lay there in silence, staring at the roof of the van, beside Rino.

To tell the truth, he too had heard that Liliana had a boyfriend, but he had been hoping God had decided to lend a hand and would make her quarrel with him.

Besides, Rino was right, he had nothing to offer a woman like that. But when the crib was finished, he too would have something to brag about. His house would become a museum.

It was strange, though: now that he knew he had no chance with Liliana he felt as if a weight had been taken off his shoulders.

Rino passed him the bottle of wine. 'Well, are we going to do this raid or not?'

Quattro Formaggi took a swig, then said: 'You decide.'

'Is the tractor ready?'

'Yes.'

'Well, it's worth a try. But if we can't knock the cash machine out of the wall first time, we give up. The police will be there in a flash.'

'All right. But when?'

'Tonight. Will you tell Danilo?'

'No, you tell him.'

'We'll tell him later. It'll be a nice surprise for him.'

Then they lay there in silence, passing the wine back and forth.

59

Danilo Aprea, sprawled in the wheelbarrow with a bottle in one hand and a raw sausage in the other, unaware that a few metres away Rino had decided that his plan would be carried out, looked in awe at the three hundred and thirteenth air display team as they made tricoloured trails above his head, to the applause of hundreds of people.

He was drunk and smiling inanely, and the only thought he managed to produce was:

Wow, they're good. They're really good.

Then, like a dopey camel, he lowered his gaze and saw Cristiano beside him silently watching the planes, and he succeeded in producing another thought:

If Laura was alive now, she would be sitting here between me and Cristiano.

THE NIGHT

It was getting dark so suddenly that Alice thought there must be a thunderstorm coming on. 'What a thick black cloud that is!' she said. 'And how fast it comes! Why, I do believe it's got wings!'

Lewis Carroll, *Through the Looking Glass*

60

The terror dance began at half past ten in the evening, when a stormy front that had been tangled up for days among the mountain peaks was freed by a Siberian airstream which pushed it southwards.

In less than ten minutes the half-moon that hung in the middle of a clear, starry sky was smothered by a blanket of dark, low clouds.

Darkness fell suddenly on the plain.

At ten forty-eight, thunder, lightning and gusts of wind marked the opening of a long night of storms.

Then it started to rain and just went on and on.

If the temperature had been only a couple of degrees lower it would have snowed, and the rest of this story might have taken a different course.

Streets emptied. Shutters came down. Thermostats were adjusted. Fires were lit. The satellite dishes on the roofs began to creak, the Milan–Inter derby started breaking up into squares and furious viewers reached for their telephones.

61

While the storm was raging over the Guerra home, Fabiana Ponticelli was lying on Esmeralda's bed in her knickers and bra, contemplating her feet, which she had up against the wall.

Maybe it was only the effect of the pot, but from that position they looked like two cod fillets.

So white, thin and long. And oh my God, those toes! So bony, and with such big gaps between them . . .

Just like her father's.

Ever since she was small she had always hoped she was the secret daughter of an American millionaire who would one day carry her off to live with him in Beverly Hills, but those feet were worth more than a thousand DNA tests.

The previous summer the Ponticellis had gone to the Valtour holiday village on Capo Rizzuto, and a cute but rather obnoxious boy from Florence had pointed out to her, on the beach, that her feet were identical to her father's.

Fabiana's consolation was that this was the only physical resemblance between her and her father, and that it could be hidden in her shoes.

Maybe I could put some nail varnish on them.

Esmeralda had a collection covering all the colours of the rainbow in the bathroom.

But the mere idea of sitting up, getting to her feet and going to look for the right one made her lose interest.

Meanwhile, on the radio, Bob Dylan started singing 'Knockin' on Heaven's Door'.

'I like this song . . . ' yawned Fabiana.

'It's a masterpiece,' said Esmeralda Guerra, who was sitting cross-legged on the desk. She too was in bra and knickers. With the smouldering end of her joint she was boring holes in the head of an old doll, producing a black, toxic smoke which mingled with that of the cigarettes and of the incense burning on the bedside table among piles of fashion magazines.

'Who's the singer?' Fabiana slowly turned her head and saw that the mute television screen was showing a heist film that she'd already seen, starring that famous actor . . .

Al . . . ? Al . . . ? Al something or other.

'Some famous guy. From the Eighties . . . My mother's got the record.'

'But what do the words mean?'

'*Evven* means paradise. *Dor,* door. The door of Paradise.'

'What about *nokkin*?'

Her friend threw the doll in the wastepaper basket and thought about it a little too long.

She doesn't know, Fabiana said to herself.

Esmeralda claimed to be practically a native speaker of English because she'd once been to California when she was small, but if you asked her the meaning of any word a little more complicated than *window* she never had a clue.

Let's see what crap she comes up with . . . 'Well? What does it mean?'

'It means knowing . . . knowing the door of Paradise.'

'And how does it go on?'

Esmeralda listened to the song with her eyes closed and then said, in a serious tone: 'He says that if you know the door of Paradise it's easy to find it. And when you find it you can take your mother with you, even though it's very dark . . . Something like that, anyway.'

Fabiana grabbed a pillow and propped it under her head. 'Jesus Christ, what a stupid song.'

If she ever opened a door and found herself looking at Paradise, complete with woolly clouds and fluttering angels, she doubted that she would go in. And certainly not with her mother.

Maybe I should put my head under the tap. Her eyes felt as swollen as grapes and her skull so heavy it seemed full of gravel. All because of that yellow limoncello and the pot supplied by one Manish Esposito, a friend of Esmeralda's mother who lived in a community of orange-clothed freaks near Santa Maria di Leuca.

Esmeralda yawned: 'Shall we have a bath?'

'What?'

'A bath. I've got a lovely lily-of-the-valley bath foam.'

It wasn't a bad idea. But what was the time? Fabiana looked at the big clock shaped like a Coca-Cola bottle that hung above the head of the bed.

Ten forty-five.

They had been shut up in that room for at least eight hours.

We're burying ourselves alive.

In the beginning it had seemed like an interesting project.

The Big Lock-Up.

That's what they had called it.

They would stay in the bedroom all Sunday, watching DVDs, smoking joints, drinking and eating.

Better on their own than with that bunch of zombies who hung around in the shopping mall and only woke up to have a fight. They had come to this decision after that idiot Tekken had nearly thrown Zena off the bridge.

God knows why he had slashed Tekken's motorbike like that . . . What was he trying to do? If she and Esmeralda hadn't interceded they really would have chucked him off.

Zena certainly had guts. But he was a difficult guy. Very touchy. You couldn't say anything to him.

She had been thinking about Cristiano Zena a bit too much lately. 'Well?'

Fabiana turned towards her friend. 'Well what?'

'Are we going to have this bath?'

'I can't, I've got to go home.'

She had promised the Turd – aka her father – that she would be home by ten thirty.

The next morning, at half past eight, skipping the first lesson at school, she had an appointment with the dentist for a check-up.

Fabiana calculated that even if she left straight away she would be late home. It took a good twenty minutes from there. So she might as well take her time.

Lucky she'd switched off her mobile.

The Turd would have just got back from . . .

Where was it he went?

. . . and not finding her at home had no doubt jammed her voice-mail with messages.

62

Rino had switched off the television and was staring at the rain that beat against the sitting room windows, trying to understand what had made him watch that film. He knew it by heart, he had seen it dozens of times, yet he hadn't been able to tear himself away from the screen.

Dog Day Afternoon. Starring Al Pacino. One of his two favourite actors, along with Robert De Niro. If Rino should ever happen to meet the pair of them in the street he would bow down before them and say, 'You're two of the greats, and you'll always have Rino Zena's respect.'

They succeeded in portraying the crummy lives of ordinary folk better than anyone else.

But that evening he shouldn't have watched the film. Al Pacino went into a bank to carry out a robbery and it turned into a blood-bath.

He had realised that the raid on the cash machine was a mistake. A terrible mistake that he would regret for the rest of his life.

And although reason suggested that the downpour was a stroke of luck (the streets would be deserted), his stomach told him that this film shown by Channel 4 exactly two hours before the raid was a God-sent sign that he should drop the whole idea.

Now he kept thinking about the plan and his mind was haunted by images of blood and death. Raids like this, seemingly foolproof and unambitious, were exactly the kind that suddenly turned into massacres.

Are you out of your mind . . . ?

How many reports had he read in the newspapers about service station robberies and car thefts that had ended in massacres? You could bet your life that as soon as they got there with the tractor, police would pop out from behind every corner.

Why did I let Danilo talk me into this? He doesn't know his arse from a hole in the ground.

If anything went wrong it meant prison. And a long sentence at that. A couple of years at the very least.

And if he went to jail, Cristiano would be put in a home or a foster family till he was eighteen.

How much money would there be in a cash machine, anyway? Splitting it three ways, too . . .

Peanuts.

He must bite the bullet, phone Danilo and tell him he was backing out.

He won't be happy.

When they had told Danilo, on the way home from the Frecce Tricolori air display, that the raid was on for that evening, he had almost burst into tears of joy.

But what does that matter to me?

It was a stupid plan, and the only reason he had listened to Danilo was that he had nothing to do all day. If Danilo really wanted, he could still do it with Quattro Formaggi. No, on second thoughts he couldn't do it with Quattro Formaggi either.

He'll just have to find someone else.

Lucky he was still in time to drop out.

But what if that presentiment had been nothing but fear? *What if I've lost my balls?*

He turned to look at Cristiano, curled up on the sofa fast asleep. *Maybe I have. So what?*

He was about to pick up the phone and call Danilo, but he changed his mind. It was better to wait for him to arrive with Quattro Formaggi and tell him to his face.

63

At the same moment when Rino Zena was being assailed by doubts, Danilo Aprea was sitting in front of the television and smiling.

What a stupid film he had been watching. A story where two crooks got trapped in the middle of a bank robbery. His own plan was perfect. There would be no people around, no weapons, no hostages or any crap like that.

He picked up the newspaper and, with his glasses on the tip of his nose, leafed through the pages of the property ads, reflecting that, if you had plenty of capital and a bit of intuition, there are a million ways of getting rich.

And since he was sure he had a natural instinct for business (he had predicted that the Quattro Camini would be a great success), he would soon have the cash to prove it to the rest of the world.

He had already drawn circles with his biro round at least five hot properties among the business premises for sale. All in shopping malls or in newbuild blocks near the bypass. Strategic points which would see immense commercial growth over the next few years.

After the shock of the euro, which had brought the country to its knees, there was bound to be an economic recovery.

The theory of flow and counterflow.

That was what Berlusconi said, anyway. And how could you not believe an industrialist of the north who was a self-made man and had become the richest person in Italy, despite everything the commie judges had done to thwart him?

And when the recovery came, Danilo would be there, ready and waiting, with his lingerie boutique.

Now the problem was that he couldn't imagine how many square metres it would take to set up a decent lingerie shop.

Would forty be enough? The important thing is to have a small back room you can use as a store and where you can put an armchair to relax in and a little fridge in case you get peckish . . .

And then, a crucial point, it would have to be tastefully decorated, but Danilo wasn't concerned about that. That was Teresa's territory. He wondered if his wife would like a shop in a mall . . .

You must be joking.

He was sure she would want one right in the centre, on the main street, to make the whole village green with envy. And, all things considered, she was right.

Eat your hearts out, you bastards. Look at the Apreas' boutique.

Danilo breathed in deeply, closed the newspaper and went over to the window.

The wind had snatched all the clothes off the clothesline on the balcony of the flat opposite, and they had blown onto the leafless branches of an apple tree. The streetlamp was swaying to and fro and the alley had turned into a torrent which was gushing out into the canal beside his house. Through the double-glazing he could hear the roar of the current held in by the banks of the canal.

So much the better. There'll be nobody around.

The display on the video recorder showed ten forty-five.

In a quarter of an hour Quattro Formaggi would be there.

He had lost track of time while looking at the small ads. He must get ready, and he'd better wrap up warm, or he'd catch pneumonia out in that downpour.

For too long his life had been parked in a dusty hangar; it was time to taxi it out onto the runway, ready for take-off.

Rino had told him the news on the way back from Murelle, and he had been so delighted he had almost burst into tears. Then, when he had got home, he had spent several hours sitting anxiously on the toilet, but now that the great moment had arrived he felt as calm as a samurai before a battle. Something told him that everything would go like clockwork, without a hitch.

He went over to the television and was about to turn it off when he saw a big painting on a green panel which occupied the whole screen.

They were showing the usual auction on Channel 35.

In the middle of the painting there was a clown, complete with top hat, lozenge-patterned tie and a round, cherry-red nose.

The clown was clinging like a climber to the peak of a mountain and stretching out his arm in an attempt to grasp an edelweiss which grew alone among the grey rocks.

The painter had succeeded in freezing the movement, like when you put a video recorder on pause.

It was easy to imagine the conclusion: the clown picks the flower and puts it to his nose to smell its scent.

But that wasn't all there was to the picture. Behind the figure that occupied the foreground there was a breathtaking sunset. It reminded Danilo of those summer evenings when he was a child and the sky was something different, as if the Eternal Father himself had painted it. The colour tones shaded and blended into each other as they do on the peace flag. From black to blue to violet to the orange of the distant valley, over which floated the ball of the sun, enveloped in white clouds like a bride in her veil. Above, where the night had already gained possession of the sky, some distant little stars were twinkling. But lower down, the plain, with its villages and roads and forests, was still bathed in the last rays of the sun.

Danilo knew nothing about art and had never wanted to own a painting. Pictures, to him, were just receptacles of dust and dust-mites. But this one was a real masterpiece.

You can keep your Mona Lisas and your Picassos. This is something else.

What he found most moving was the clown's expression.

Sad and . . . even Danilo himself couldn't describe it.

Stubborn?

No, not exactly.

Proud.

Yes, that was it. The proud clown had defied the mountain and all its dangers to get up there. Although he wasn't an expert climber, but just a poor clown. What an incredible effort it must have been, in those long, broken shoes. And just imagine the cold . . .

Why had he made all that effort? Of course, to pick a rare little flower to offer to the woman he loved, along with his heart.

He and that clown had a lot of things in common. He too had been treated like a bum, almost like a murderer, an alcoholic who was a public laughing stock, but tonight he would defy the mountain, he would risk his life just for the sake of picking a flower, the boutique to give to Teresa, the only woman he had ever loved.

Yes, he and that clown were sad and proud. Two misunderstood heroes.

The picture widened out to reveal a man at the side of the painting. His hair was flecked with grey, and he wore a blue blazer and a pink shirt with a white collar.

Danilo seized the remote control and turned up the volume.

'This painting is one of the magnificent series of clowns in the mountains by maestro Moreno Capobianco,' said the telesalesman, who spoke with a pronounced guttural R. 'But of the whole series, if I may say so, this is undoubtedly the most effective and accomplished, a consummate work of art, where the artist has given of his best and has most poignantly expressed the . . . how shall I put it . . . the titanic, timeless struggle between man and nature. The meaning is clear, even to the layman: the clown represents farce, which ranges beyond the confines of the world as we see it, to reach places where no one has ever gone. Travelling towards God and love, on a mystico-religious journey.'

Danilo was incredulous. The expert was saying, in more precise terms, the very things he had thought himself. He turned the volume up even higher.

'But, ladies and gentlemen, leaving aside the philosophical implications, let us look at concrete things: the magnificent landscape, the light, the refined phrasing, the confident brushwork . . . Capobianco's brushwork is so delicate that . . . Just imagine for a moment having a picture like this in your sitting room, in your hall, if I may say so, wherever you wish, this is an unrepeatable opp . . . '

Danilo glanced at the bare wall beside the door. A rectangle measuring one metre by two seemed to pulse out from the rest of the wall.

That's where it must go.

With a little halogen light just above it, it would be a knockout.

'Imagine making yourself a gift of this masterpiece . . . Imagine having it, owning it, being able to do what you want with it, and for a mere seven thousand five hundred euros! An investment, ladies and gentlemen, which in the space of five years will multiply seven or eight times over, never mind your unit trusts and ISAs . . . If you pass up this opportunity, I would almost . . . '

Danilo turned back towards the television and then, as if in a trance, picked up the telephone and dialled the number that was scrolling across the screen.

64

Quattro Formaggi, too, had absently watched *Dog Day Afternoon*, but hadn't made any connection between the film and the raid. Afterwards, growing bored, he had switched on the video recorder and started up *Ramona's Big Lips*.

He had fast-forwarded to the scene where she was fucking the moustachioed sheriff.

'Don't you know that only whores hitch-hike in this county?' he recited in the voice of the lawman. And then, in falsetto, imitating Ramona's female voice: 'No, I didn't know that, sheriff. All I know is I'll do anything to avoid going to jail.'

While he was performing the dialogue he squatted down on the floor and started building a new railway station with Lego.

The window, pushed by the wind, suddenly blew open, and a gust of rain spattered his face and toppled a big table lamp which, like a crippled spaceship, crashed down onto a cardboard bridge lined with cars, destroying it, and then plunged into a papier-mâché mountain on which herds of rhinoceros and blue smurfs were grazing and scattered them among the flocks of sheep and Tiny Toons that were advancing into the mouth of a canyon.

Quattro Formaggi rushed over to shut the window.

On closer inspection he saw that the wind had wrought further havoc. The troops of blue soldiers, snakes and galactic robots had fallen over and some of them were floating in a lake made out of a Danish biscuit tin.

He ran his fingers through his hair, making strange grimaces with his mouth.

He must tidy up at once. He couldn't do anything else while he knew that the crib was in such a mess.

'But I've got to go round to Danilo's. What am I going to do?' he said to himself, pinching his cheek.

A minute. It'll only take a minute.

What if Danilo rings me?

He switched off his mobile and started tidying up.

65

'Fabi, listen, I've had a brilliant idea!' Suddenly, as if someone had pressed PLAY on her remote control, Esmeralda woke up and jumped off the desk.

'What?'

'Let's play a trick on Carraccio.'

'What kind of trick?'

Esmeralda and Fabiana were sure Nuccia Carraccio, their maths mistress, hated them, because she resented the fact that they were pretty and she was a monster. And as well as never giving them good marks, they were sure she held black masses with Pozzolini, the PE teacher, against them.

'Listen, you know the fat boy?'

'Which fat boy?'

'The one in 2C.'

'Rinaldi.'

'That's him.'

Matteo Rinaldi was an unfortunate little lad. He suffered from a serious pituitary imbalance, and weighed a hundred and ten kilos at the age of twelve. In his fifth year at primary school he had won a certain notoriety by doing a testimonial for a campaign against child obesity promoted by the local council.

Fabiana stretched and yawned: 'Well, what about him?'

'Ravanelli said he was in the scouts with Rinaldi and that once Rinaldi crapped in a field. And out of curiosity he went to look at the turd . . . ' Esmeralda shook her head. 'You can't imagine the size . . . He said it was as big as . . . ' She struggled to remember.

' . . . as a packet of precooked polenta. You know what that's like, don't you?'

'No. I've never seen one. My mother usually makes it herself. What's it like? Does it taste good?'

'No, not really. You cut it into slices and heat it up in the oven. The home-made stuff's much better. Anyway . . . ' Esmeralda indicated the size with her hands and then added: 'He says it was really hard, like a torpedo.'

'So?'

'We must get Rinaldi to crap on the teacher's desk. On Wednesdays we have gym just before maths. During that lesson we could take him to the classroom and get him to climb up on the teacher's desk and crap.'

Fabiana laughed scornfully. 'What a stupid idea!'

Esmeralda looked at her in disappointment. 'Why?'

'How are you going to get Rinaldi to do it?'

Esmeralda hadn't thought about that. Their weapon, seduction, which bent practically all the males in the school to their will, had no effect on that sexless lump.

'What if we offered him cash? Or food?' hazarded Esmeralda.

'No, he's got pots of money. I suppose maybe if you gave him a blow-job . . . '

Esmeralda made a disgusted expression: 'Yuck . . . Not even if they killed me.'

Fabiana touched her kidneys with a grimace of pain. 'How much would you charge him for a blow-job?'

'There's no price!'

'A thousand euros?'

'Are you crazy? Too little.'

'Three thousand?'

She smiled. 'Three thousand. Well, I might consider it . . . '

It was their favourite game. They spent hours imagining giving hand-jobs and blow-jobs and letting themselves be sodomised by the ugliest guys they knew for money.

'Suppose you had to choose between Rinaldi and . . . ' Fabiana couldn't think of anyone more disgusting, but then had an inspiration: ' . . . the tobacconist in the shopping mall?'

'The one with the toupee stuck on with Bostik?'

'Yes!'

'I don't know . . . Neither of them.'

'If you don't do it, they'll kill your brother.'

'You bastard! That's not fair!'

'Yes it is! Yes it is!'

Esmeralda reflected for a moment. 'Well, if I think about it carefully, the tobacconist. At least he might throw in a few packets of fags.'

'You have to swallow, though.'

'Of course, I'd give him the full service . . . But can you imagine what it'd be like if we succeeded? Can you imagine Carraccio coming into class and finding a hot, steaming turd on her desk? As a personal monument, just for her . . . '

'She calls the carabinieri . . . '

'And the carabinieri have to requisition it.'

'Why?'

'It's evidence . . . '

'But they can't touch it, or they'll leave fingerprints.'

Esmeralda burst out laughing. 'And they take it to the, er . . . To the . . . Oh hell, what are they called?'

'Who?'

'The guys who analyse the evidence . . . You know . . . Them.' It was no good. It wouldn't come. Her head felt like it was full of foam rubber.

'I don't know . . . Who do they take it to?'

'Oh you know, those guys in the TV series.'

'Forensics?'

'That's it. And they do a DNA test and trace it back to Rinaldi.'

66

He had done it. He had phoned and bought *Climbing Clown*, the masterpiece by Moreno Capobianco.

No problem.

Danilo strolled contentedly round the room, looking at the wall where he would hang the painting.

Fantastic. You entered the room to be met by a climbing clown. It would give his apartment a touch of unique style and refinement. A painting of such quality would brighten up a catacomb.

Danilo was holding a glass of grappa.

He had sworn he wouldn't touch a drop till after the raid, but he couldn't very well not drink to a purchase like this. Perhaps he had been a little hasty in buying it, but with the guarantee of the money from the cash machine it had been a good decision.

'A *great* decision.' He raised his glass to the blank wall.

The young lady at the call centre had been extremely kind. She had congratulated him on his choice and had added that Capobianco's paintings were selling like hot cakes.

If I hadn't called right away I'd certainly have missed out on it.

Danilo had made a no-obligation appointment for the next day. One of their experts would bring the picture round to his home.

'Here's to a new life!' And he knocked back the grappa.

The young lady had assured him that he would be able to look at it for as long as he liked and then decide at his leisure. Danilo hadn't told her, but he had made up his mind to buy it the moment the figure of the clown had appeared on television.

That painting had spoken to him through the screen.

It was the baptism of Danilo Aprea's new life.

First the picture, and immediately afterwards the boutique for Teresa.

And everything would start over again.

67

The headlights of Beppe Trecca's Puma lit up a huge sign, in the shape of a banana, bearing the words CAMPEGGIO BAHAMAS.

Here we are.

The social worker, in a fever of excitement, emerged stooping from the metallised coupé, sheltering under a tiny umbrella, which the wind promptly turned inside out. He approached the gate, which was chained up. He pulled out of his raincoat pocket the bunch of keys for the camper belonging to Ernesto, his cousin's husband.

The key to the gate must be here too.

But he wasn't absolutely sure, because he had . . .

(stolen)

. . . borrowed them from the tray by the front door of his cousin Luisa's flat, without telling them.

Well, where's the harm? Tomorrow morning I'll put them back and no one will be any the wiser.

The idea of asking Ernesto if he could borrow his camper for the night hadn't even crossed his mind, for two reasons:

1) Luisa's husband was as curious as a monkey and would have discovered everything, and nobody in the whole world must know about him and Ida Lo Vino. If word got out, he was finished.

2) Ernesto never lent his camper to anyone. He'd sunk himself up to his neck in debt in order to buy it.

Beppe managed to find the key to the padlock, pushed the gate and drove his car into the campsite, leaving it open behind him.

The gravel yard on the banks of the Forgese was flooded. The inky-black river, which usually flowed thirty metres away, had engulfed the jetty and was lapping at the canoe shed. The palm trees, their leaves ragged from the winter, were battered by gusts of wind and rain. The roar of the swollen river was audible even through the window panes.

A worse night for a romantic rendezvous would be hard to imagine.

The campers and caravans were parked side by side.

Now which of the bloody things is Ernesto's?

Beppe remembered it was called something like Rimmel. Finally, right at the end of the row, he saw a big white beast with the name plate 'Rimor SuperDuca 688TC'.

There it is.

It was inside that vehicle that the dreadful act of betrayal would be performed. Yes, for as Beppe was well aware, what he was about to commit was a dastardly deed, an assault on the integrity of a family. Poor Mario really didn't deserve such treachery from his best friend.

(Forget the whole idea. Turn back. Mario welcomed you into his home like a brother. He loves his wife dearly and he trusts you.)

He parked the car, trying not to listen to the voice of his conscience.

(Ida would certainly be grateful to you, too.)
Beppe sighed, turning off the engine.
*I'm a shit. I know I am. I wish I could do it, but I can't . . .
Maybe I'll break it off after I've had her. But I can't go on living
like this, I must have her at least once.*

He got out of the car and walked round the camper, pulling a
blue trolley case along between the puddles.

After a couple of attempts the door opened, and with a mixture
of excitement and shame the social worker climbed the steps and
entered, as a flash of lightning bathed the dinette and the mini-sofa
in pale blue light.

68

Cristiano Zena was awoken by a clap of thunder so loud that for
a moment he thought a tanker had exploded on the highway.

He felt some cushions, the back of a seat, and realised he was
on the sofa. He had fallen asleep while they had been watching the
Al Pacino film.

It was pitch black. The rain was beating on the window panes
and the gate in the yard was rattling in the wind.

'Don't worry, Cri. It's only a power cut.'

Cristiano could barely make out the features of his father's face,
tinged red by the ash of his cigarette.

'There's one hell of a thunderstorm. Go to bed.'

'What's the time?'

'I don't know. About eleven thirty.'

Cristiano yawned. 'How are you going to get the tractor? The
riverside road will be a sea of mud.'

'Sure,' replied Rino calmly.

Cristiano was about to ask if he could go too, but checked himself. He knew what the answer would be. 'But isn't it late?' he asked,
finally.

'Maybe.'

'What's the matter? Don't you want to do it any more?'

His father breathed out through his nose. Silence. Then: 'No.'

'Why not?'

'I've had second thoughts.'

'Why?'

'It's too dangerous.'

Cristiano didn't know whether to be pleased or not. With the money they could have bought a lot of things, got a new car, had a better life, travelled. On the other hand the raid had always worried him a little. All in all, it was better like this. With hindsight, he had always sensed that his father's heart wasn't in it.

Cristiano sat up and crossed his legs. 'What are you going to say to Danilo?'

'I've got a headache. Go to bed.' Rino was beginning to get tetchy. As if his son was prodding at an open wound. Cristiano knew he should drop the matter, but it really irritated him that his father never kept his promises. Like when he'd said he would give him a PlayStation for Christmas.

'But you promised him.'

'Who cares?'

'Danilo will hate you.'

'No problem. He can do it with someone else if he likes. Not with me.'

'Yes, but you're their leader. They can't do it on their own, you know that. You can't let them down like this.' As he talked, Cristiano wondered why the hell he kept going on about it if he was pleased his father had decided to drop out.

Rino started to shout: 'Listen to me, you little brat. Get this into your head: I'm nobody's leader, least of all theirs. Besides, I've got a son, unlike them. I'm not risking that for a bit of loose change. End of discussion.'

The light came back on. The television started up again. In the kitchen the fridge started to buzz.

Cristiano screwed up his eyes. 'When are you going to tell him?'

Rino opened a can of beer and took a swig from it. Then, wiping his mouth with his arm, he replied: 'Now. When they get here. You go to bed. I don't want to quarrel in front of you. Move.'

Cristiano was on the point of retorting that it wasn't fair, that he'd always been present at their meetings and he ought to be present now, but he bit his tongue.

'Shit . . . ' He got up and went towards the stairs without saying goodnight.

You could hear everything upstairs anyway.

69

Inside the camper there was a horrible smell.

It wasn't just the damp, it was something much worse, something disgusting . . . Something to do with human excrement and chemical toilets.

Beppe Trecca groped around on the walls, searching for a light switch.

The previous summer he had ridden in this thing when they had taken a trip to the monastery of San Giovanni Rotondo, but he'd been car-sick all the way.

Finally, behind a cupboard, he found some switches and started to press them at random.

The neon lights on the ceiling and the spotlights over the sink lit up, spreading a cold light.

In front of him was a narrow space lined with wall units covered with beige formica, the day area with a little table and the sofa, and above the driver's cab the sleeping area with a double bed.

With one hand over his mouth he opened the toilet door. It was like getting a punch in the face. The social worker turned purple, dazed by the stink, and had to lean against a partition to stop himself collapsing on the light-blue carpet.

The smell, as solid as a wall, was both human and chemical at the same time. For a moment he thought his cousin's husband must have dissolved a dead animal in the acid, but then he saw some violet-coloured sludge in the bowl with some material floating in it which at first sight seemed organic, though of uncertain origin.

He pressed a big red button, hoping some pump might drain that pestilential pond, but it didn't. All he succeeded in doing was opening the port-hole, turning on a weary little fan and shutting the door.

The impact of the stench had been so strong that only now did he realise that the temperature in the camper was at least five degrees below zero and that the rain was beating down on it like a hammer on an anvil.

How did the heating work? But above all: did campers have any heating?

They should do.

He laid the trolley case on the table and unzipped it. He began to arrange on the little cooker a series of foil dishes containing chicken with bamboo shoots, spring rolls, won tons, sweet and sour pork and Cantonese rice. All bought from the Pagoda Incantata restaurant at the twentieth kilometre-mark on the highway. Then he took out a bottle of Falanghina which had cost him twelve euros, and another of melon vodka to give Ida the coup de grâce if she . . .

(What?)

Nothing.

He laid a red cloth on the little table, added some plastic plates and chopsticks and then lit some cedar-scented candles and a dozen sticks of incense, which began to send up spirals of white smoke.

That should cover the smell . . .

The mobile phone in his jacket pocket gave two beeps.

A message.

He took out the handset and read:

> Mario has come home unexpectedly.
> I'll wait till he's gone to bed then I'll join you.

70

It was eleven thirty and Fabiana Ponticelli couldn't believe she was still lying on Esmeralda's bed.

She was an hour late, but the thought of going out and doing twenty minutes on a scooter in the storm made her feel like weeping.

Besides, she couldn't stop thinking that next morning, before school, she had to see the dentist, who would find the piercing on her tongue.

What if I just said sod it and stayed here for the night? That way I'd miss the dentist too. What could happen?

In the first place the Turd would confiscate her scooter. The thing she cared about most in the world, and which enabled her to escape from Giardino Fiorito, the estate where her family lived.

Oh yes, he didn't just take things away, he *confiscated* them. And how he loved doing it.

'I'll confiscate your mobile!' 'I'll confiscate your bovver boots!' *I'll confiscate all the fun out of your life.*

How much did she hate him? She wished she could quantify it, she wished she had an instrument like the one for pressure, a hateometer, to measure the loathing she felt for her father. She'd melt it. She hated him as much as all the grains of sand on all the beaches of the world. No, more. As much as all the molecules of water in the sea. No, even more. The stars in the universe. Yes, that was it.

Well, he'd only take away my scooter for a week, or ten days at most.

She knew the reason she felt so anxious was that pot they had smoked. Lately she had noticed that joints, instead of making her giggly as they used to, turned her paranoid.

To keep this effect under control Fabiana had drunk half a bottle of limoncello.

The alcohol and the pot were two monsters that were fighting for supremacy over her mind. The marijuana monster was geometric. All sharp points, blades, hard edges. The limoncello monster was shapeless, slobbery and blind. And if you took them in the right proportions, the two monsters, instead of fighting, fused into a perfect hybrid which made you feel out of this world.

But now the monster had lost its spherical perfection and had got out its blades and sharp points (thanks to that last, damned joint) and kept jabbing them into her brain.

She breathed in deeply and blew the air out.

In these cases never think about your parents, school or a sodding visit to the dentist.

But if I don't go to the dentist the Turd will get suspicious. He'll start thinking I'm pregnant or something.

Why didn't Esmeralda ever get attacks of paranoia? She stuffed herself with joints and never had any side effects. It must be a genetic thing.

Drink. Drink, it'll do you good.

Fabiana took a swig from what was left of the warm limoncello and tried to think about something else, but without success. 'I'm so anxious . . . ' she said out loud, without meaning to.

Esmeralda, who was busy plucking hairs out of her eyebrows with tweezers, looked up. 'What?'

'I've got to go home.'

'Stay here for the night. Why do you want to go? Haven't you seen what it's like outside?' Esmeralda lit a cigarette.

'I can't. My parents will kill me if I don't go home.'

Esmeralda started burning her split ends with the lighted end. 'The truth is, you're not methodical. You don't tell your parents to fuck off often enough. It's just a question of regularity. You've got to be strict with yourself – even if you don't feel like it you must do it every day. Look at me. I tell my mother to fuck off every day of the week and we've settled all our conflicts.'

Fabiana didn't reply. It was stuffy in the room. What with the incense, the joints and the cigarettes, there was such a haze she could hardly see Esmeralda.

'Esme, open the window, I'm suffocating.'

Her friend, intent on her coiffuring, took no notice.

'Mrs Ponticelli, your daughter's got a little silver ball on her tongue.' That was what the dentist would say to her mother.

She had been clever, so far she had managed to hide the piercing. It hadn't been difficult. All you had to do was keep your mouth shut, avoid yawning, and above all, never laugh. There wasn't much to laugh about in her home anyway.

The problem had been getting used to having a nail through the middle of your tongue. And, to be honest, Fabiana still hadn't got used to it. She would keep twisting it around in her mouth and running it along her teeth, and by evening her tongue would be all swollen and her mouth sore.

When her mother found out she would make a melodramatic scene in front of the dentist, the patients, everyone. Her mother loved making a fool of herself in public. But that would be as far as it would go. The woman had about as much backbone as an earthworm.

You accepted the one on my eyebrow and the one on my navel.

Now, mama dear, you're just going to have to learn to live with another one. What's the big deal?

The real problem would come if she told the Turd. And since mama had no real personality, no individual life of her own, and was only an external organ of her husband, Fabiana was sure she would go and tell him.

But on reflection, there was a slight possibility that for once in her life the external organ would restrain the urge to confess all. And this solely and exclusively for sordid, utilitarian reasons.

Her father would bang on about it for the next twelve years, accusing her of not knowing how to bring up children. Anyway, who said the dentist would spill the beans?

'I bet you're freaking out about that piercing!' said Esmeralda.

How did that girl always know what she was thinking? Could she read her mind?

Fabiana looked at her friend, who was rolling another joint.

She tried to appear calm. 'No, I was thinking about something completely different.' But it was as if she had GOTCHA! written across her forehead in great big letters.

'What *were* you thinking about, then?'

'Nothing.'

'You were thinking about when the dentist goes to see your mother . . . "Mrs Ponticelli, your daughter's got a piercing in her tongue" . . .

How you love it when my parents give me a hard time! 'Oh come on, doctors have a professional obligation to respect their patients' privacy.'

Esmeralda raised her eyes from the cigarette paper and goggled at her. 'Are you crazy? The dentist?'

'It's true. They take an oath . . . I know they do . . . '

'Oh sure, the Xenophontic oath. Yeah, sure . . . Listen, take my advice . . . Don't go to the dentist's. Stay here. If I were you I wouldn't give a damn about the Turd and your mother . . . They boss you about, they treat you like an imbecile. Stand on your own two feet for once in your life.'

Fabiana got off the bed.

Esmeralda had given her the strength to go home. She started nervously searching for her clothes among the debris scattered on the floor.

'You know what I'm going to do? I'm going to take it out before I go to the dentist's.' She would have liked to add that she didn't like it anyway, in fact she loathed it, and that really it was just a nightmare, especially since someone had told her a piercing on your tongue gave you a tic, so that for the rest of your life you looked like a ruminating camel.

'That'd be a big mistake, I warn you . . . Remember what James said – if you take it out the hole will close up immediately.' Esmeralda sealed the joint with a deft flick of her tongue.

Fabiana put on her T-shirt. 'I'd just take it out during the check-up . . . '

Esmeralda lit the joint and blew out a white cloud. 'That's plenty long enough. The mucous membranes heal up instantly! And don't think I'm going to put it back in for you.'

Fabiana didn't reply. She finished dressing and glanced at her reflection in a long mirror framed by photos of Christina Aguilera and Johnny Depp. She had bloodshot eyes and dry lips, like Regan, the girl in *The Exorcist*. She ran her fingers through her hair and touched up her lipstick. 'Okay, I'm off.'

Esmeralda held out the joint to Fabiana. 'At least let's have a goodnight puff.'

'No, I'm too spaced out. I can hardly stand up. I'm going.'

'Oh come on, Fabi, you know it's bad luck to smoke a joint on your own,' said Esmeralda in the voice of a sad little child.

'I've got to go . . . '

She seized her hand. 'You're cross with me, aren't you, because of what I said about the dentist?'

'No, it's just that I've got to go.'

Esmeralda lowered her black eyes and then raised them again. 'I'm sorry, Fabi.'

'What for?'

'You know . . . It'll be all right, you'll see. The worst that can happen is that your mother will make a scene at the dentist's . . . Don't worry.'

Fabiana realised that her anger had evaporated. Esmeralda only had to look at her like that and she'd melt like a little idiot. 'Okay, but then I really must go.'

'I love you!' Esmeralda jumped to her feet, planted a kiss on her lips and hugged her tight and then said: 'But we've got to make this a good one. Pass me the bottle of Uliveto and a pen.'

71

That imbecile Quattro Formaggi was more than half an hour late.

Danilo paced around the room in galoshes, a blue windcheater, a scarf and a woolly hat, repeating over and over again like a cracked record: 'I don't believe it, I don't believe it! Where the hell has he got to?'

He had already tried calling him six times on his mobile but every time the fucking number had been unobtainable.

'What a stupid bastard . . . ' muttered Danilo, collapsing in a heap on the sofa. 'It's impossible to work with people like this. Turn on your mobile, you fool!'

He poured himself his fourth (was it his fourth or his fifth?) glass of grappa and tossed it back with a grimace.

Maybe he should call Rino and tell him Quattro Formaggi was behind schedule, that he must have got lost somewhere.

But Rino would hit the roof.

And this evening there was no room for rages.

They had to be a united, close-knit, focused team.

But how do you form a close-knit, focused team with a hysterical lunatic and the village idiot?

He was about to pour himself another glass, but decided against it. *I'd get drunk . . .*

He closed his eyes, trying to calm himself.

'He'll be here any minute. He'll be here any minute. He'll . . . ' he started repeating like a mantra. 'If he isn't here in a quarter of an hour I swear I'll kill him.' He forced himself to be silent and heard the fury of the storm swirling round the house and, below, the canal surging, swollen with water.

72

There, finished.

All the inhabitants of the crib were back on their feet and the bridge had been repaired. This made him feel much calmer. But that bridge had been worrying him for some time and sooner or later he was going to have to build a new one, bigger and stronger, with at least a three-lane road across it.

Quattro Formaggi put on his waterproof trousers and checked for the umpteenth time to see whether he'd missed anything.

The next morning, first of all he would tidy up the hill, and while he was about it he could make it into a mountain, a high, rocky one. He could go down to the river and get a few large stones from the beach and it would be perfect.

Lots of animals live on rocks.

The . . . He couldn't remember what they were called. *The what-do-you-call-ems. Those things with long horns that jump.*

'Steinbock,' he said, pulling on his rubber boots. He put on his balaclava and over it his green full-face helmet.

He picked up his yellow cape, but didn't put it on.

Danilo had told him not to wear it because it could be seen from kilometres away.

But who's going to be out in this weather?

He put it on.

He had no desire to go out. He would have been happy to stay at home, working on the crib.

Did they have to do the robbery that evening, of all evenings? In all that rain?

He turned off the television just as Ramona was coming out of the house stark naked, meeting Bob the lumberjack and saying to him: 'Get out your joystick and let's have some fun.'

'Snap out of it. Go,' he ordered himself. He put on his gloves and left the flat.

73

Cristiano Zena was in bed, buried under three layers of blankets, listening to the storm. If he closed his eyes he felt as if he was in a bunk on an ocean-going liner in the middle of a hurricane. The rain drummed against the window panes, and the frames creaked, pushed by the wind. A trickle of water was running down from the windowsill into the room and in one corner of the ceiling a dark patch had spread and every one, two, three, four, five seconds a drip fell making a loud PLIC.

He would have liked to get up and put a bucket there and roll up a cloth and lay it along the windowsill to stop the rain, but he was so sleepy . . .

74

Fabiana Ponticelli staggered out of Esmeralda's room. She stood in the hall in the half-light, trying to muster the strength to face the storm. The last joint had finished her off.

I'm going to throw up.

To her left, on a long dresser, she saw the silhouettes of four Chinese vases and for a moment she thought of vomiting in one of them.

Swaying and putting her hands on the walls lined with old Arabian carpets and shelves full of books, she advanced towards the exit. The front door, at the end of the hall, was illuminated by a patch of reddish light that came from the sitting room.

Please God, don't let Esmeralda's mother be there . . . If she sees me in this state . . .

Over the past year Serena Guerra had caught her in even more disastrous situations than this one, embracing the toilet bowl or comatose on the bed.

That time we dropped acid and . . .

But now, with the paranoia that had taken hold of her, Fabiana didn't think she was even capable of saying 'goodnight'.

Walk straight past, quickly, don't stop, don't look into the sitting room, open the door and go out.

She closed her rainproof jacket more tightly, put up the hood, took a breath and headed for the door as boldly as a hussar on parade, but when she was outside the sitting room door she took a quick glance inside.

Serena Guerra was lying on the floor on a coconut mat, leafing through a big book of photographs.

The room was lit by the weak glow of the fire that was dying on the hearth and by a dozen candles on a chest made of red wood. On an old sofa, muffled up in blankets and with a funny woollen hat on his head, little Mattia was sleeping with his mouth open.

Even in her present delicate mental and physical state, Fabiana couldn't help being flabbergasted for the millionth time at the resemblance between mother and daughter.

The first time she had seen Esmeralda and Serena together she had been lost for words. The same straight brown hair, the same oval face. Same eyes, same shaped lips, same everything. Except that Serena was an extra-small version of Esmeralda. There was a good ten centimetres' difference between them. On her arms and shoulders the mother was a trifle more muscular, she had a fairer complexion, a slightly irregular nose and gentler, more liquid eyes. A certain angularity in the daughter's features was, as it were, smoothed out in the mother.

Serena must be about forty but looked much younger. She could easily have passed for thirty.

Fabiana found her dress sense excellent. That evening she was wearing a pair of low-waisted Levi's, Texan boots and a coarse woollen cardigan with geometric patterns, and she had gathered her hair into a mass of little plaits.

A few days earlier, in a condition not dissimilar from her present one, Fabiana had met Esmeralda's mother and they had had a chat. Serena knew how to put you at your ease, she talked to you like an adult and listened to you. Only, that evening she'd looked at her for a little longer than usual and then asked her: 'Don't you think you two are overdoing the pot?'

Fabiana, like a dog that has just crapped on the carpet, had squatted down against the wall and with a smile that had nearly dislocated her jaw had said, in the falsest of tones: 'What? I'm sorry, I don't understand.'

'Don't you think you're overdoing the pot?'

She had opened her mouth and hoped that some meaningful sentiment would come out, but none had, so she had closed it again and shaken her head.

'I know . . . it's your business and I'm sure . . . well, I'm sure you're intelligent enough to keep it under control. But with pot it's easy to get carried away . . . Then it gets difficult to concentrate at school . . . Look, I'm sorry to be a bore . . . I don't usually do this.'

It's a terrible effort for her to say this to me, Fabiana had thought.

'I'm a bit worried, if you want to know the truth. It's impossible to talk to Esmeralda at the moment . . . She's always angry, as if I'd done something terrible to her. She answers me so aggressively, it frightens me . . . All I'm saying is that if you smoke too much pot you become isolated and the world begins to seem small and stifling . . . Maybe you should both try to get out more, not to keep to yourselves all the time, shut up in that . . . '

Fabiana had gazed at her open-mouthed in wonder, like a child watching a chameleon change colour.

The small, stifling world.

That was it. Esmeralda's mother had put her finger on a problem she had been aware of for some time, the reason she felt so dissatisfied.

A small, stifling world. Which you must escape from as soon as you finish school. You must go to America, Rome, Milan, wherever you like, but you've got to get away from this small, stifling village.

Why was that sensitive, beautiful creature standing in front of her Esmeralda's mother, not hers? Why was she so unfortunate as to be the daughter of a woman who was about as open-minded as a cloistered nun and who spent her whole life repeating the refrain that papa was having a hard time at work and that they must do all they could to make his life easier?

What about me? Don't I exist? No, as far as my mother is concerned I don't. Or rather, I exist because I'm part of the Ponticelli family, so I must be Good, Nice and Beautiful.

Isn't that a wonderful thing, a mother who tells you that if you get stoned out of your mind it's none of her business?

When her mother had discovered a minute quantity of marijuana in the pocket of her trousers, she had first pretended to have a fainting fit, then she'd taken her to speak to Beppe Trecca, the social worker, then she'd tried to send her to boarding school in Switzerland. And if it hadn't been for the tight-fistedness of the Turd, by this time she'd be locked away in some paramilitary college in Lugano.

And the most ridiculous thing of all, which really upset her, was that Esmeralda didn't realise how lucky she was to have a mother like that. She would answer her rudely on principle. Raise her eyes to the sky. Snort with exasperation.

For a moment, hidden in the shadow, Fabiana was uncertain whether to ask Serena to give her a lift home. But it was better to face the rain than show herself in that state.

With the furtive lightness of Eva Kant, Fabiana Ponticelli turned the key in the lock and went out into the storm.

75

Danilo was holding the receiver in two hands like an iron mace. 'How the hell *can* I keep calm, Rino? *You* tell *me*! That idiot has disappeared! We're way behind sche . . . '

'He'll be there. Keep calm! And behind what schedule, anyway? What difference does it make whether we get there a bit sooner or a bit later?' replied Rino, yawning.

Pure hydrochloric acid was bubbling inside the walls of Danilo Aprea's stomach. He made a superhuman effort not to start shouting so loud he would burst a blood vessel. He must keep calm. Very calm. He swallowed the bile that was stinging his oesophagus and piped: 'What do you mean, behind what schedule? Please, Rino, don't be like this . . . '

'Don't be like what? Have you seen what it's like outside? How are we going to get to the tractor? Swimming? Let's wait for the storm to ease off, then we'll see.'

Danilo inhaled and exhaled, puffing out his cheeks like Dizzy Gillespie.

'What are you doing? Having an asthma attack?' asked Rino.

'Nothing. Nothing. You're right. As always, you're right. We'll wait.'
Pure hatred.

It was that placid tone of Rino's, that air of a know-it-all God Almighty who remained calm even when the Martians were invading the Earth, that drove Danilo wild with rage. How he would have loved to plunge a dagger in his heart. A hundred, a thousand times, shouting: 'So you know everything, do you? Yes, you're perfectly right, you know everything!'

'That's the way. You've got to relax. I'll wait for you here, we need to talk.' And Rino hung up without even saying goodbye.

'Talk? Talk about what?' Danilo shouted. He seized the remote control and hurled it against the wall, smashing it to pieces, then started jumping up and down on it.

76

The dark sky was hammering down on Quattro Formaggi and his Boxer. Gusts of wind and rain buffeted him this way and that, and it was a struggle to keep the scooter on line.

The rush of the torrents that flowed down the roadside and the gurgle of the drains vomiting out streams of brown water merged into a fearful roar inside his helmet..

It was impossible to see anything and Quattro Formaggi was making his way towards Danilo's house from memory.

The wind had uprooted a row of trees from the pavement and thrown them into the middle of the road. A big pine had fallen on a car, smashing its windscreen.

What was this, the storm of the century?

The next day all the television news bulletins would talk of rivers in spate, floods, collapsed buildings, damage to agriculture, compensation. And while the downpour lashed the plain, a gang had carried off the cash machine from the Credito Italiano dell'Agricoltura.

As well as being rich we'll be in all the papers . . .

Over the past few days Quattro Formaggi had tried to imagine what he would do with all that money. The only idea he had come up with was buying some more clay to build a big castle and an electric train complete with points, level crossings and stations to link up the south and north of the crib. Journeys were very complicated now with all those mountains, lakes and rivers, and having a railway at their disposal would help the inhabitants of the crib no end.

What if I put in a . . .

What was the name of that box hanging from a wire which people who went skiing used for going up mountains? He didn't know, but it didn't matter. In the toyshop in the shopping mall he had seen a fantastic one. With two cabins made of green tin with black roofs, and skiers inside them and an electric motor that made it really work.

It could take people straight to Baby Jesus's cave instead of them having to go all that way on foot . . .

He was already imagining his ski lift going up and down when, beyond the rain-streaked visor of his helmet, there appeared in the distance a red gleam in the middle of the road.

It looked like the rear light of a scooter.

77

In the camper Beppe Trecca, sitting on the little sofa, had eaten the won tons, which with the cold had taken on the consistency of chewed-up Hubba Bubba. To warm himself up he had drunk a little melon vodka and wrapped himself in all the blankets he could find.

Let's face it, Ida will never come.

Mario had arrived home. She would have to wait till he went to sleep and then sneak out secretly. It was madness.

But if Ida was willing to take such a risk she must be madly in love with him. And that made him feel very good.

Certainly, it might be better to put it off to another day.

The social worker took a box of Xanax tablets out of the inside pocket of his jacket and held it close to the candle as if it was a magic amulet.

He had already taken two. Would a third make him as brain-dead as a lichen?

On the internet he had read that the usual effect of tranquillisers on sexual activity was to inhibit the orgasmic reflex, which might lead to a slowing down in the process of reaching a climax. This had various consequences, one of which was a significant improvement in the quality of intercourse for both the man and his partner, should there be a pre-existing tendency to rapid ejaculation.

And a pre-existing bloody tendency to rapid ejaculation had indeed afflicted Beppe since the far-off years of his adolescence. He had carried it with him through four miserable years of Sociology at the University of Rome.

Now, being a good manager of himself, he decided to assess the various effects that the taking of a further tablet might have.

He could only think of two, both of them unpleasant:

1) Despite the massive presence of benzodiazepine in his body he would still come in the time it took a sprinter to do the hundred metres.

2) He wouldn't be able to get it up at all.

He wasn't sure which of the two options he preferred.

He stroked his chin in the manner of Rodin's thinker. *Yes, perhaps not being able to have an erection would be preferable. I'd still look a twat, but not quite such a stupid one. And I might even find an excuse to back out. But if I come straight away she'll think I'm pathetic.*

Then a further possibility flashed through his mind: *Suppose I legged it? If I just wasn't here when she arrived?*

Disconsolate and undecided, he took another sip of vodka.

78

Fabiana Ponticelli, on the saddle of her scooter, was frozen stiff. The pudding-basin helmet on her head was completely useless. The rain got into her eyes and ran down her neck and froze the tip of her nose. Her ears had gone numb. In the attempt to see something she had tried putting on her sunglasses, but that had only made things worse. Her trousers were soaked and she was now beginning to feel her feet floating in her trainers.

Since leaving Esmeralda's house she hadn't passed a single car or human being.

Everything was closed. All the lights were out. The place was deserted. Fallen trees lay in the middle of the road. Cars had been crushed. Fabiana felt like the sole survivor of a catastrophe that had exterminated the human race.

But if it goes on like this the river will overflow and flood the road . . . so my appointment with the dentist will be cancelled. Great!

That thought was enough to put a little warmth back into her limbs and improve her mood.

And if I got flu as well . . . she said to herself, trying to zip her jacket up more tightly. *It would be the icing on the cake.*

That way she wouldn't have to go to school for a few days either.

At home. Without a care in the world. MTV. Charin doing the cooking . . . And Esme out of my hair for a while. Esmeralda hated going round to her house anyway. She said it was too neat and tidy and 'too much tidiness smacks of madness to me'. According to her the Ponticelli family was the classic perfect family where the father comes home from work, kills his wife and children and puts a bullet in his head.

She thinks she can say anything she likes to me.

Perhaps she ought to keep away from her for a while. She was beginning to get a bit fed up with her. She was a petty dictator. In order to be her friend she had changed her life. Because if you're with Esmeralda Guerra either you do what she wants or you don't exist. In order to be her friend she had stopped seeing Anna and Alessandra.

Maybe they're not very cool, but I used to enjoy hanging out with them.

And she had practically thrown her into Tekken's arms.

Esmeralda had slept with him a couple of times and had insisted that she do the same. She kept saying it had been a wonderful fuck, that she'd had three orgasms, one after the other, like she'd had a thousand men. But if it had been so divine, why, all of a sudden, had she stopped?

Simple: Tekken was about as romantic as a pig on a dunghill. He had screwed Esmeralda and then given her the boot. And she had been devastated. Hence her eagerness for Fabiana to sleep with him too. That way at least both of them would have been deflowered and dumped.

The only time Fabiana had been on a date with Tekken they had gone to the cinema and his hands had been all over her. And while he was taking her home they had stopped at the public gardens and he had pulled out his erect cock, as proud as could be, and had practically forced her to give him a hand-job twenty metres from the newsagent's kiosk. And if she hadn't threatened to scream he would have screwed her there in the gardens, in front of everyone.

The deafening roar of a broken exhaust pipe made her jump. Fabiana turned her head and saw in the outside lane a man, covered in a yellow cape and a full-face helmet, on the saddle of an old green Boxer.

So I'm not alone in the world. I've seen that scooter somewhere before . . .

It only took her a moment to connect it with that tramp-like guy who looked as if he was breakdancing when he walked, and whom she had often seen with Cristiano Zena's father.

But where was he going in this weather?

79

Impossible!

It couldn't be true.

The little blonde who was a dead ringer for Ramona!

That was her scooter. Her yellow sticker. Her helmet.

What was she doing out in this downpour?

And yet it was definitely her, in the flesh, dripping wet.

Quattro Formaggi could see her in the public gardens, that summer night, standing there with her hand around . . .

Up and down. Up . . .

The vision of that little girl holding the biker's cock in her hand blinded him and evoked a guttural moan. A thrill of pleasure ran up his spine, jumping from one vertebra to another, and Quattro Formaggi suddenly felt his arms and legs go as limp as a jellyfish's tentacles and had to grip the handlebar tightly to stay in the saddle.

Ramona comes out of the house and says to the lumberjack with a smile: "Get out your little joystick and let's have some fun."

Up and down. Up . . .

Quattro Formaggi felt his blood seething as it circulated in his ears, his bowels, between his legs.

He gave himself a few thumps on the thigh. Then he put his hand under his windcheater and dug his fingernails into his ribs.

'You whore. You damned whore,' he grunted, enclosed within his helmet. 'Why? Why do you like doing these things? Why don't you leave me in peace?'

She did it against him. To make him feel bad.

(Go on! Stop her.) The voice of Bob the lumberjack spoke out, powerful and decisive. *(Go on, what are you waiting for?)*

I can't.

(You'll never have another opportunity like this. Don't you realise what a stroke of luck it is? She'll be happy to do it to you as well.)

No, she won't.

(Yes, she will.)

I can't. I can't do it.

(You're just a poor fool, an idiot, a cre . . .)

Quattro Formaggi shut his eyes, trying not to listen. He was breathing with his mouth open and the visor of his helmet was misted over.

(Her hands will be cold and wet. And she'll smile.)

No. I can't . . .   What if she doesn't want to?

(Of course she'll want to. Look, let's say this. If she takes the bypass, it means she doesn't want to. But if she takes the road through the woods, that settles it . . .)

He was right. The road through the woods was deserted. If she didn't want to be stopped she would never take it, so if she did go that way, it would mean . . .

(Bravo! You finally understood.)

. . . she wanted to, so he would stop her.

He didn't know how, but he would stop her.

80

The tramp was now travelling at the same speed as her, behind her but on the wrong side of the road. At one point Fabiana Ponticelli had seen him thumping himself on the leg.

Better accelerate.

With that clapped-out scooter the loony wouldn't have much chance of keeping up with her.

Fabiana turned the throttle and gradually drew away from him.

She must be careful – at that speed if she saw a rut she wouldn't have time to brake. She looked in the rear-view mirror.

The Boxer was still behind her. But further back.

She gave a sigh and realised that she had hardly breathed since the guy had materialised alongside her.

81

Sleep had eventually prevailed over the Zena family.

Cristiano had collapsed after a desperate struggle to stay awake until Danilo and Quattro Formaggi arrived, and downstairs Rino was snoring in front of the TV, which was still on.

82

Beppe Trecca, too, with three Xanaxes and half a bottle of melon vodka inside him, was snoring, with his forehead resting on the table between the foil dishes of the Chinese meal.

83

'I could have found anyone I liked to join me on this job, Rino Zena, my friend. Who do you think you are? Do you think you're the only person who can do it? And what was that you said? "We must talk." What the fuck have we got to talk about? Has somebody made you our leader? I'm the leader, till I see any proof to the contrary. Do you know how many better men than you I could have found if I'd wanted?' Danilo Aprea was talking out loud, gesticulating and raising his shoulders. 'Who thought up the plan? Who did all the work? Who spent a month sitting opposite the bank watching every movement? Who found the tractor? Me! Me! And me! I did it all! I'm going to make you both rich. I . . . ' He was addressing the sofa, as if Rino and Quattro Formaggi were sitting on it. 'Shall I be honest, really brutally honest? No beating about the bush? I should have had fifty per cent and you two twenty-five. That would have been fair. But since I'm a gentleman, a great gentleman . . . ' He looked at the bottle of grappa on the table. He needed another drop. He raised it.

Empty.

After the phone conversation with Rino he had told himself a drop would help to soothe his anger and he had drained the whole bottle without even realising it.

I'm fine. Nothing to worry about. There's no problem. He shook his head like a cocker spaniel after its bath. *I'll be better in a minute.*

He took three unsteady paces. In fact he was a bit tipsy, but as soon as Quattro Formaggi arrived he would leave, and outside, in the wind and rain, he would recover in no time.

84

(She turned her head. Don't you see that she's calling you? You stupid fool) Bob explained to him.

Why did she accelerate, then?

Quattro Formaggi decelerated even more, though still keeping close enough not to lose sight of the scooter.

(Turn off your headlight. She'll think you've taken another road.)

He would be able to catch up with her again immediately. The Boxer's engine was souped up, it had an expansion exhaust and when he took up an aerodynamic position, on a downward slope, he could do as much as eighty kilometres an hour.

The little blonde would soon reach the fork.

It was up to her. If she took the road through the woods he would stop her.

Please take the bypass. Please.

(You fool.)

85

Fabiana Ponticelli looked in the rear-view mirror.

The Boxer's headlight wasn't there any more. The tramp must have turned off down another road.

A classic case of pot-induced paranoia.

My God, though, what a fright he gave me.

Meanwhile in front of her the road, with the rain beating down on it, widened out and a hundred metres further on divided into two.

To the left was the narrow road that passed through the San Rocco woods and led straight home, to the right you went onto the bypass, which ran all the way round the hill, and which was wide and brightly lit but never-ending.

She heard her father's voice. Like Little Red Riding Hood's mother, he was saying:

(Fabiana, remember, never go along the road through the woods at night.)

Yes, maybe I'd better take the bypass. I'm soaked to the skin as it is anyway.

But at the last moment she changed her mind – *in this weather the big bad wolf will stay in his lair* – and swerved sharply, taking the little road that burrowed into the woods.

86

When Quattro Formaggi had seen Ramona heading decisively towards the bypass his heart had filled with disappointment and happiness.

You see? I told you she doesn't want me. Now leave me alone.

But then, at the last moment, as if the Eternal Father himself had commanded the girl to take the road through the woods, she had swerved.

(Now you've got no more excuses.)

But how was he going to stop her? He couldn't very well just go up and say, 'Excuse me, would you mind stopping, please?' . . .

I'm shy.

(If you don't stop her you're a coward. You'll regret it for the rest of your life. She's dying for you to do it.)

This was true, but he had to think. He must try to find a way of stopping her and asking her.

(If you don't get moving you'll never catch her.)

Quattro Formaggi began to accelerate.

87

The trees bent down over the narrow road, stretching out their branches as if they were trying to grab Fabiana Ponticelli.

The rain, under the roof of foliage, was not so heavy, and there was a smell of wet earth and rotting vegetation.

The Scarabeo's headlight threw a weak cone of light on the leaf-strewn, muddy asphalt.

The girl rode, following, with intense concentration, the white line in the middle of the road. The game was to keep the wheels on the line, because there were bottomless pits on either side and if she went off the white she would go hurtling down for the rest of her life.

But suddenly the road curved sharply, following the line of the hill, and Fabiana failed to keep the tyre on the white line.

You'd be dead. Okay, the first time doesn't count. You don't fall into the pit till your third mistake.

She was so absorbed in the game that she didn't notice that behind her, fifty metres back, a Boxer was following her.

88

Now he knew what to do.

Quattro Formaggi had racked his brains, and finally Bob the lumberjack had come to his aid. A brilliant idea, as if by magic, had materialised in his brain.

He turned on the headlight and accelerated. The engine began to roar in protest and gradually the Boxer gathered speed.

The little red dot of the Scarabeo's rear light drew nearer at every bend. After about two hundred metres, if he remembered the road correctly, the descent would begin and at that point he would overtake her.

89

Fabiana Ponticelli, riding on the centre line, concentrating all her attention on not falling into a bottomless pit, almost fell off the saddle when out of the darkness, hunched up like a vulture on its perch, emerged the loony on the Boxer. He held his head at the level of the handlebars and his elbows splayed like wings.

The girl clutched the handlebars and stiffened.

Before she even had time to decide whether to speed up or slow down, he overtook her, charging on down the slope at a maniacal speed. She saw him take the bend leaning steeply over to one side, without braking.

Fabiana shut her eyes, certain she was going to hear the sound of a crash, but when she opened them again there was only a curtain of white smoke and the roar of the now distant exhaust pipe.

He's completely crazy, that guy.

What on earth was he doing? Did he want to get himself killed? Who did he think he was – Valentino Rossi?

She couldn't make out whether he was interested in her or if he was just a poor lunatic who liked racing in storms.

90

After overtaking her, Quattro Formaggi had nearly crashed into the guardrail. He had done well – when he was already practically down on the ground he had stuck out one leg and with a kick had managed to straighten up, but now, after taking another three bends at the risk of breaking his neck, he decided to slow down. Another bend like that, on the slippery asphalt, and he would be a goner.

He pulled the brake levers gently, not trusting the drums, especially now that they were full of water. The front shock absorber started juddering like a pneumatic drill and the back wheel began thrashing about like a fish caught on a hook.

He came to a stop fifty metres further on, at a point where the road through the woods widened out into a layby with a concrete electricity hut.

Quattro Formaggi quickly dismounted from the Boxer and laid it down on the asphalt, taking care not to turn off the engine, right in the middle of the road. He took off his gloves and lay face down on the ground, arms and legs outspread.

91

Fabiana Ponticelli rounded the last bend and entered the long descent that ran straight down the hill to the plain. She was almost there. She had to go past the service station and turn along a road that cut across the fields for about a kilometre, and she would be home. In her mind she was already in bed under the duvet, she had already had a boiling hot shower and what was left of the strudel in the oven. The rain and the cold wind had washed away her torpor, so if she did happen to find her parents still awake she wouldn't start giggling like an idiot.

I could tell them I was late because my scooter broke down and there was no one around. And that the battery of my mobile had run down. I coul . . .

She didn't finish the thought because she saw in front of her a red glow in the middle of the road. As she got nearer she noticed that there was also a pool of white light on the asphalt. She slowed down and heard the metallic gurgle of the exhaust of the loony's scooter, and realised at once that the idiot had crashed on the final slope.

92

(Keep still.
Motionless.
You're a scorpion-fish waiting for the minnow.)
There she is. I can see her.
(Keep still! Don't move.
Let her be.
Let her come closer.
If you move you'll ruin everything.
Dead.)
Sure, boss. Stone dead. Deader than the dead themselves.

93

Jesus, he had crashed all right.

He was on the ground, lying full length, beside the scooter, and wasn't moving. Fabiana Ponticelli passed by and didn't stop.

He must be dead. At that speed, on that ancient scooter . . .

She didn't know what to do. Or rather, she knew very well what she should do, but she didn't like the idea of it at all. She was soaked to the skin, half frozen and almost home.

(You can tell a person's quality from whether they help people in trouble.)

That's what papa would have said.

If Esmeralda was in my shoes . . .

Only she wasn't Esmeralda, though for the past six months she had been trying to be. *She* helped other people, even tramps who thought they were Valentino Rossi.

She puffed out her cheeks resignedly, turned her scooter round and went back.

94

Danilo Aprea was ringing Quattro Formaggi at thirty-second intervals and as soon as the odious recorded voice replied, saying 'The number you are calling is not . . . ,' he would hang up with a curse.

He was certain by now that, like the bonehead he was, he had forgotten all about the bank raid.

'It's possible. Oh yes, it's perfectly possible. He's capable of anything,' said Danilo, taking a swig from a bottle of Cynar that he had found at the back of a cupboard in the kitchen.

That bitter awareness was the result of years of friendship with Quattro Formaggi, and in particular of the famous 'Belladonna question', after which he had refused to see him for three months.

About a year earlier Danilo had found a job at the villa of the Avvocato Ettore Belladonna, but to do it properly he had needed help. Between Rino and Quattro Formaggi he had chosen Quattro Formaggi, because Rino wanted fifty per cent. A demand which, in Danilo's humble opinion, was ridiculous, given that he had found the job. He had offered Quattro Formaggi thirty-five per cent of the fee and he, without any argument, had accepted. The job involved repairing a crack in the villa's septic tank. It had been emptied a few days earlier by a specialised firm, but when Danilo had climbed down into it he had almost fainted from the stink.

In order to be able to work he had poured some eau de cologne onto his handkerchief and tied it over his face. When he had finished filling the crack with quick-drying cement, as agreed, he had given two tugs on the rope to alert Quattro Formaggi, but the top end had fallen into the tank. Danilo had shouted himself hoarse calling him. But there was no reply. He had gone away. All he could see from down there was the circular eye of the manhole and the blue sky with clouds scudding across it like a flock of fucking sheep.

Danilo couldn't sit down without putting his buttocks in the muck. It was hotter than the devil's arsehole in there and the air stank of rotten cheese.

Suddenly a little boy's face had appeared. Ten or eleven years old. A tuft of blond hair and a nice innocent smile. It must be René, the Avvocato Belladonna's son. René had waved to him and then, although Danilo implored him not to, had closed the manhole, burying him alive.

Quattro Formaggi, two hours later, had reopened it and pulled out a hysterical creature covered in excrement who bore a distant resemblance to his workmate Danilo Aprea.

The fool had apologised, saying, 'I went away for a moment,' *a moment*, that was what he'd said, 'to buy a slice of pizza because I was starving. I've brought you a piece with potato and rosemary, your favourite.'

Danilo had snatched the pizza out of his hands and jumped up and down on it with his shit-soaked boots.

'That's the kind of people I have to work with!' he said and took another swig of Cynar, grimacing like a little boy who has been forced to drink cod-liver oil.

95

Through the visor of his crash helmet Quattro Formaggi saw the long legs of the minnow approaching.

Come here, little fish.

It took one step and then stopped. But it was a well-brought-up little fish and would never leave a man lying injured, perhaps dead, on the road.

'Sir . . . ? Sir? Are you hurt?'

(Dead.)

'Sir, can you hear me?'

Three more three steps. It was less than three metres away.

If I make a sudden lunge . . .

(Wait!)

He had never been so close to that girl. The blood pulsed in his temples. His muscles were charged with enough electrical power to bend an iron bar. And, as if by magic, his twitches and tics had disappeared.

The minnow crouched down and looked at him uncertainly.

'Sir, would you like me to call an ambulance?'

Hidden behind the helmet, a dreamy smile spread on Quattro Formaggi's lips, revealing his big yellow teeth.

96

'Can you hear me? If you can't talk, move something . . . your arm . . . ' asked Fabiana Ponticelli.

Christ, he's really dead . . .

The scooter on the ground, in the middle of the road, with the wheel still spinning, illuminated the white exhaust fumes and the form of the motionless man.

A quick thought ran through her mind: how come he had crashed here, where the road was straight? He must have skidded in a puddle, or got a puncture and hit his head.

But he's wearing a crash helmet . . .

She took another hesitant step and stopped. It didn't make sense. She didn't know exactly what, but something was screaming at her not to go any closer. Not to touch him. As if what lay there on the road was not a poor devil who'd had an accident, but a scorpion.

I'm going to call an ambulance.

97

(Stop her! She's making a phone call.)

98

Fabiana Ponticelli didn't even have time to press the on-switch of her mobile before she felt the earth disappear from under her feet and found herself falling, open-mouthed, and she landed, hitting the asphalt with her chin, hip and knee.

She didn't understand what had happened and thought she had just slipped over and tried to get up again, but she realised that something was preventing her from rising.

When she saw a dark hand round her ankle, her heart, like a hydrant, burst in her chest and she gave a strangled little cry.

It's a trap! He's not hurt at all!

Fabiana tried to break free, but fear had snatched away the air she needed for breathing. Gasping, she tried to get up on her arms, to crawl away somehow, but all she managed to do was graze the palms of her hands and her elbows on the asphalt. Then she started kicking out with her free leg. She struck the man on the back and on the helmet, but to no avail. He lay there on the ground clutching her ankle; he took the kicks like a sack of potatoes and he didn't let go, the bastard, he didn't let go.

Kick him on the hand.

So she did.

Once, twice, three times, and at last she felt his grip slackening. Another kick right on those thick fingers and she was free.

She leaped to her feet, but the man threw himself at her with all his weight, tackling her round the hips like a rugby player and bringing her down again.

Fabiana, at this point, started writhing about as if she was having an epileptic fit, screaming, hitting out wildly, but most of her punches either missed altogether or landed on his helmet without hurting him. 'Let me go! You bastard, let me go!'

'No, don't scream! Don't scream, please! I don't want to hurt you!' She thought she could hear the muffled voice of the man in the helmet.

'Let me go, you piece of shit!' Fabiana looked around. If only she'd had a stick, a stone, anything, but she was surrounded by asphalt and nothing else, so she bent double and, with all the strength in her body, stretched out her arm towards the Boxer lying in the middle of the road.

Dragging herself along on her elbows, she managed to grab hold of the rear-view mirror and started pulling to get free of the man's grip, but the mirror, with its whole supporting rod, snapped off.

Fabiana turned and, screaming, jabbed it into his shoulder.

The man gave a yelp and lashed out with his elbow, hitting her full on the nose. The cartilage of her nasal septum broke with a crunching sound and at first she felt nothing, but her neck jerked back with a horrible CRACK and then a dense liquid began to flow out of her nostrils, mingling with the tears and rain.

She opened her mouth, spitting out streams of blood and trying to gulp in air.

99

(*What have you done?*)

I swear I didn't mean to hurt her . . .

Quattro Formaggi got up on his knees, pulled the mirror out of his shoulder and threw it on the ground.

The pain had clouded his vision. When he could see again he realised that Ramona was wheezing with her mouth open and spitting blood, her face a mask of terror.

He was about to take off his helmet but then . . .

(*She mustn't see you.*)

. . . thought better of it. He took his torch out of his pocket and switched it on. He pointed it at her.

She's in a bad way. She can't breathe.

'Wait . . . Wait, I'll help you . . . '

Ramona was bent over on the ground, but when he tried to touch her she got to her feet and started staggering, bent double, trying to breathe. A horrible noise was coming out of her mouth.

Quattro Formaggi put his hands into his crash helmet and started biting his fingers.

100

She had fallen into darkness and she was dying.

If her lungs didn't start working she would suffocate, of that she was certain.

Fabiana Ponticelli could still think and she knew she must calm down, because the more agitated she got the more oxygen she would consume. She stopped, with her mouth open, waiting for some miracle to start her lungs working again. And the miracle, which was not in fact a miracle but merely her paralysed diaphragm relaxing, did happen, and her rib cage started expanding and contracting of its own accord, without her having to think about it.

A thin thread of icy air was sucked into her windpipe and from there through her bronchial tubes into her compressed lungs, like when you open a vacuum-packed bag of coffee.

She started spluttering and gulping air and coughing violently, not caring about the light that was dazzling her and the man who was standing behind her.

The sounds around her had amalgamated and she felt as if she had an aeroplane's jet engine throbbing in her head, but despite this noise she could hear the man repeating over and over again like a cracked record: 'Please forgive me! I didn't mean to hurt you! I'm sorry, let me look at you.'

He's coming closer.

Fabiana straightened up and tried to run away, but as soon as she moved her head she was overcome by the pain, as if someone had inserted a blade between her collarbone and neck. With her eyes closed she hobbled towards the middle of the road, raising her arm and hoping someone would pass by.

Now! Now her saviour must arrive. This was the perfect moment.

He must get out of a car and shoot that bastard in the stomach, so she could just faint in peace.

101

Quattro Formaggi watched Ramona take a few steps, her body all twisted and her arm raised as if she wanted to call a taxi, then he saw her trip over the Scarabeo and fall down with her arms and legs splayed out like Wile E Coyote.

Poor thing, she must have hurt herself.

But there was something he couldn't understand. On the one hand he so pitied her, he was sorry, but on the other hand he enjoyed seeing her suffer. It was an agreeable sensation. He felt like a lion and could have fought anyone. His cock was stiffening and pressed against his belly.

Clutching his wounded shoulder he approached the girl, who was still lying on the ground and moving her legs and head like a pale water dragon.

102

Fabiana Ponticelli hadn't seen her scooter, and had banged into it and fallen over.

Her shoulder must have come out of its socket. That shoulder she had dislocated on a skiing holiday at Andalo. Her father had told her a million times she ought to have it fixed, 'otherwise what's the point in my paying for insurance against accidents? It's a simple operation, you'll be as right as rain in two days. If you don't, it might slip out again in unpleasant circumstances.'

Un . . . pleas . . . circum . . . stances, her brain repeated as she tried to get to her feet.

It was a pain far worse than that in her nose. An electric current was flowing through the muscles of her arm and shoulder, coiling them up like a rope.

Why don't I faint?

(Because you've got to put it back in.)

Stopping herself from retching, with her left hand she took hold of her right arm, just below the armpit, and pulled.

Nothing happened.

Again.

She pulled the arm again, but harder and downwards, and as if by magic the electric current switched off and, incredibly, for the first time since she had decided to stop and help the bastard a feeling of wellbeing spread through her body.

Good girl. Well done. Now you're okay. You can do it. Wait till he comes near.

Through her closed eyelids she could see the light that shone on her.

Wait.

103

Quattro Formaggi went over, grabbed her by the arm and dragged her towards the side of the road. She seemed to have fainted, but now and then she opened her eyelids a little to see what was happening.

He managed to pull her as far as the guardrail and had stopped for breath, when, with a sudden twist, she lashed out and kicked him between the legs.

Quattro Formaggi jumped backwards as if an invisible being had pushed him away, and clutched at his groin, then a yellow stream of bile came out of his crash helmet and as he vomited he realised that the little bitch had got to her feet and was running away.

104

The man in the helmet caught up with her and slapped her across the face with the back of his hand, making her do an ungainly half-pirouette, and Fabiana Ponticelli flew backwards, as stiff as a mannequin, banged her left hip against the guardrail, landed first with her cheekbone and then with the rest of her body on a carpet of plastic bags, paper and wet leaves, while her ankles rapped against the concrete base of the metal barrier.

She knew she must get up again, at once, and that she must start running and get away because it was clear that the man in the helmet was going to do something to her, something very nasty, yet her body refused to obey her. It had curled up into a ball of its own accord. Her hands had gripped her knees and her head had come to rest against her shoulder.

(At least open your eyes. Look to see where he is.) Her father's voice.

I can't.

(Let him do what he wants! Better to be raped than raped and beaten to death) said Esmeralda, not mincing her words, as usual.

Esme's right, papa. He'll rape me and he'll leave me here.

Yet inside her there was a stronger, more stubborn part which urged her not to give in. Because it wasn't right.

She started crying, in silence, sobbing convulsively, cursing herself for having stopped. If she'd known what a bastard he was she would have ridden her scooter straight over him.

A metallic noise brought her back to reality.

What's he doing?

But she had two black eyes, and even if she opened them she was submerged in darkness and couldn't see a thing, but she could still hear, and what she heard gave her a little hope.

The guy was messing about with her scooter.

He only wants to steal the Scarabeo.

He had beaten her up to steal a stupid scooter.

All he'd have had to do was ask.

Take it. It's all yours. Just don't hurt me.

She must just wait. Lie there quiet and calm. And it would all pass.

105

Quattro Formaggi picked up the Scarabeo and pushed it towards the electricity hut.

When he had seen Ramona spin round, bang into the guardrail and fall head first over it onto the ground he had been very alarmed.

Had he killed her with a slap across the face? Was that possible?

He had looked at her carefully and seen that she was still breathing, curled up in the rain. Defenceless and as wet as a tadpole when you take it out of the water.

(Now she's yours. You can do what you want with her. But you must take her into the wood, so that if anyone passes by . . .)

He hid the Scarabeo and the Boxer behind the electricity hut, then went to check whether anyone driving past would be able to see them.

106

How strange, despite the blood that was blocking her nostrils Fabiana Ponticelli thought she could smell mushrooms.

Not cooked mushrooms. But the fresh ones you take out of the wet earth with two fingers, careful not to break them.

This is the mushroom place.

She remembered that it was from that very spot, from that layby, that they used to start out on the chanterelle walk when she was small. They would leave the old Saab with its patched-up roof beside the electricity hut and set off into the wood in search of chanterelles . . .

She saw herself as a little girl, with her brother Vincenzo in his pushchair, her mother with her long hair gathered into a ponytail, like in that photograph that hung in the hall, her father still sporting a moustache and herself in her little red parka and woollen hat . . . All together they would get out of the car, holding baskets for the mushrooms, and papa would grab her under the armpits and, hop-la, whisk her over the guardrail and she would say: 'I can do it on my own' and would climb up onto that long metal strip (she seemed to see all four of them walk by without looking at her, as you do when you pass a dead dog on the road), then they would enter the wood and her father would stop them: 'The one who finds the most is the winner.'

In risotto, chanterelles are better than porcini.

Mama made a risotto a few days ago. But it was with porcini. No, it . . .

A noise.

So he didn't go away.

Fabiana opened one swollen eye. A light. The man in the helmet was in the middle of the road with the torch in his hand, and was running backwards and forwards.

(Fabi, you must get away.)

She just had to find the strength to stand up, but now she really didn't think she could do it. The pain seemed to be circulating from one side of her body to the other, through her bones, her muscles and her guts, and every now and then it stopped and dug in its claws.

The wood is big and dark and you can hide.

If she had been well, if that bastard had played fair and not laid a trap for her, he would never have been able to catch her.

I won the cross-country race three years running.

Fabiana the rocket. That's what they called me . . . The rocket.

(If you get up now and go into the wood you'll become invisible.)

(GET UP!)

(GET UP!)

She clenched her teeth and fists and slowly got up onto her knees, her right arm completely numb. There seemed to be fragments of glass in her ankle.

(GET UP!)

With her eyes closed she stood up, without even looking to see where the bastard was, and set off towards the wood, towards the darkness that would hide and protect her. The pain in the meantime had moved to her face, it didn't leave her for a single step, and . . .

It's just a matter of gritting your teeth.

. . . each time she inhaled the cold air it was like getting another slap across the face . . .

I must look a mess. But it'll pass. You go back to normal. I saw on TV a woman who'd had an operation . . .

She couldn't see a thing, but there was no danger because God would help her to find her way and not to trip over and not to fall down and to find a hole to disappear into.

She was safe, she was in the wood. The branches whipped her jacket and the thorns tried to stop her, but now she was far away, alone, in the darkness, she was walking over a lot of stones, of rocks, of tree trunks, and not falling down, and this was God.

107

Danilo Aprea was asleep, sitting in front of the television. He looked like the statue of the pharaoh Chephren. In one hand the empty Cynar bottle, in the other his mobile phone.

108

About eight kilometres away from Danilo's flat, Rino Zena woke up in his old camouflage sleeping bag. An atomic bomb had exploded in his skull. He opened his eyelids: the television looked like a painter's palette and a group of dickheads were blathering about pensions and workers' rights.

It was very late. Those two would never come now.

Rino pulled the sleeping bag over his nose and thought that old Quattro Formaggi was a genius. He had switched off his mobile and that was that.

'Thanks, Quattro.' He yawned, then he turned over on his side and closed his eyes.

109

Perfect. Nobody will see the scooters now.

Quattro Formaggi turned happily towards Ramona and . . .

Where is she?

. . . she had gone.

He must be mistaken, it was too dark. He started walking faster and faster, then running, towards the point where she'd fallen.

'Where are you?' he groaned in despair.

He ran back and forth along the layby and kept returning incredulously to the guardrail, where Ramona had been until thirty seconds before. He gazed for a long time at the black mass of vegetation which loomed over the road. No, she couldn't have gone into that tangle of brambles.

(Go and see. What are you waiting for? Where else can she have gone?)

He stepped over the guardrail and entered the wood, lighting his way with the torch.

Before he had gone ten metres he saw her. He leaned against a tree trunk and heaved a sigh of relief.

She was there, walking through the trees with her arms stretched out in front of her and her eyes closed, as if she was playing blind man's buff.

Quattro Formaggi moved towards her, careful not to make a noise, pointing his torch at the ground. He stretched out his hand and was about to touch her on the shoulder, but then he stopped to look at her.

She had guts. None of those other little tarts would have gone into the woods on their own. And they would have just lain there on the ground, crying their eyes out. This one never gave up.

"Come on, let's chuck him in the river!"

Quattro Formaggi was twelve years old and was being dragged along the dry part of the river bed on a carpet of sharp pebbles. They had caught him. They had stubbed out a cigarette on his neck, kicked him and thrown stones at him. Then two of them had grabbed him by the legs and were pulling him towards the water, but he wouldn't give up – he clutched at the rocks, at the branches whitened by the river, at the reeds. Silently, gritting his teeth: he wouldn't surrender. He too had shut his eyes and refused to give up, but he had been picked up bodily and dumped in the water and carried away by the current.

We're two of a kind.

Quattro Formaggi hurled her to the ground.

110

Fabiana Ponticelli fell right on a branch, which bent under the weight of her body and then with a loud crack snapped, tearing her jacket and cardigan and grazing her side. A sharp pain twisted its tentacles round her ribs.

So I'm not invisible. And God isn't here, or if he is, he's just standing by and watching.

She felt a weight on her stomach. It took a few seconds to realise that the bastard was sitting on top of her.

He grabbed her wrist and she didn't put up any resistance.

Something warm and soft on the palm of her hand. She couldn't make out what it was.

(Well what do you think it is?) Esmeralda's voice. *(Do it. What are you waiting for?)*

Crying, Fabiana began to move her hand up and down.

111

(See? She did it like a shot, you fool.)

Quattro Formaggi panted as he watched Ramona's little hand. She was wearing a ring with a silver skull, which was going up and down, slowly. Breathtaking.

He closed his eyes and leaned sideways against a tree trunk, waiting for it to stiffen.

He didn't understand. This was the most beautiful thing in the world, so why was it still so limp? He tightened his buttocks and gritted his teeth, trying to arouse it, but without success.

No, it wasn't possible, now that Ramona was finally doing it to him . . .

'Slower. Slower, please . . . ' Quattro Formaggi raised a trembling fist in the air and thumped himself on the chest.

He knew he could come almost instantly. But it was as if that thing didn't belong to him. A dead appendage. This was the exact opposite of what he had expected. The warm hand, and his body cold and unfeeling. Why did it work when he did it himself, but not like this?

(It's her fault. It's this little tart's fault.)

He grabbed her by the hair and muttered to her desperately: 'Slower. Slower. Please . . . '

112

It was never going to stiffen.

Fabiana Ponticelli felt as if hours had passed, but it was still as limp as a dead slug. It seemed to be melting in her hand, like a lump of butter.

'Slower. Slower. Please . . . '

She would gladly have obliged, but if she went any slower . . .

'No, squeeze it. Hard. Very hard. Pull it.'

She didn't understand, first slow and now . . . But she obeyed.

Eventually she stopped, feeling frustrated and scared and guilty, and she realised that the bastard was crying.

'Calm down, relax, or you won't make it . . . ' she said, hardly realizing what she was saying. 'Just wait, you'll see, . . . '

But the man angrily snatched away her hand and started frantically undoing her belt, her trousers. He pulled down her panties . . .

Fabiana's heart began to race. She opened her mouth and dug her fingers into the cold earth.

(Okay, this is it. Don't worry. It's nothing. Keep still.) It was her mother's voice. Like the time when they had put stitches in her forehead after she had fallen off her bicycle, and at the hospital . . .

(Just let him do what he wants and it'll soon be over.)

She felt him fumble between her legs, then he grabbed her by the hair, with a yell.

Away. Think of something. Something nice, distant. Away. Think of Milan. Of when you'll be in Milan, at university. In the little flat you've rented. It's small. One room for me. Another for Esme. Yes, Esme too. Posters. Books on the table. A computer. There'll be the usual mess. Tidiness is important in a small flat. The fridge, of course, will be empty. With me and Esme, what do you expect? But the door leads out onto a balcony full of sun and flow . . .

113

The mobile phone, on the ground, lit up and vibrated, and off went the polyphonic version of Verdi's *Va' pensiero*.

Rino Zena opened his eyes slowly and took a few seconds to realise that his mobile was ringing on the floor.

He yawned and with a weary movement picked up the phone, certain that it was that pain in the arse Danilo again, but instead on the display he saw the words: 4 FORM.

He answered, yawning: 'Did you stay at home?'

But the only reply was the sound of uncontrollable sobbing.

'Quattro Formaggi?'

He heard him sniff and start blubbing again. He couldn't be at home because there was the sound of rain.

'What's going on?'

At the other end Quattro Formaggi went on crying bitterly.

'Speak! What's the matter?'

After a while he heard him stammer out, between sobs, some confused words: 'Oh my God . . . Oh my God . . . Come here . . . Hurry.'

Rino got to his feet. 'Where? Tell me where!'

Quattro Formaggi sobbed and didn't speak.

'Stop crying! Listen to me. Tell me where you are.' Rino was beginning to lose his temper. 'Pull yourself together and for Christ's sake tell me where the fuck you are.'

114

Danilo Aprea woke up with such a start that he dropped his mobile on the floor and started screaming.

He had been dreaming that he was holding a tennis racket which had suddenly turned into a rattlesnake.

My mobile!

He sprang up to answer it, but had to sit down again. The room was swaying. The wooziness hadn't passed.

He reached out and picked up the mobile off the floor. He squinted, trying in vain to get the display into focus, certain that it was that imbecile Quattro Formaggi.

'Hello? Where have you been?'

'It's Rino.'

'Rino . . . ' There was a taste of dead rat in his mouth.

'Quattro Formaggi has had an accident. Something's happened to him. He was crying like a baby. I'm going to see him.'

Danilo massaged his temples and shook his head: no, no. Rino was bullshitting him. 'What's happened to him?'

'I don't know.'

'Why was he crying? I don't understand. I just don't understand.'

Surely you guys can think up a better story than that.

'Didn't you hear what I said?'

Danilo massaged his stomach. 'So? What are you saying? That you want to put the raid off?'

'Exactly.'

'Till when?'

Now he'll say he doesn't know.

'Do you understand that Quattro Formaggi has had an accident?'

An explosion of pain in his bowels deprived him of the strength to answer this insult to his intelligence. He felt as if a cork had popped in his stomach. Just like when you shake champagne. Only instead of champagne it was foaming rage which tasted of Cynar.

He felt like smashing everything. Kicking in the television, hacking down the walls with a pickaxe, blowing up the house, leading in a squadron of stealth bombers to flatten Varrano and the whole fucking plain, dropping an H-bomb on Italy.

He couldn't contain himself: 'Yes, I understand! Oh, I understand, don't worry! I'm not stupid! And do you want to know something? It serves him right, he deserves it. I told him to come round here. I even invited him for a meal. I told him to come round and have some spaghetti al pomodoro and then we could go together. And did he come? Did he hell. If he had done he wouldn't have had any accident. But you guys never listen to me! I'm just a fool and you two are the brains.' A wise little voice advised him to stop, but he took no notice. It was so wonderful to get it all off his chest. He started nodding his head like a pigeon. 'Anyway, I knew. I knew very well.'

'What did you know?'

'I understand. I'm not a fool, you know! You guys don't want to do it. Admit it. It's so simple. All this crap about an accident . . . "We're too scared to do it, we're shitting ourselves," why don't you just come out and say it? It's not a problem. Don't worry. It's human. I've known for a long time. You're scared shitless, not only of doing the bank raid, but of actually having some money, of changing your shitty little lives, of not being failures for all eternity.' While Danilo was venting his rage and disappointment the danger light started winking in his brain, but he ignored that too. For once in his life he had loosened the reins of the rearing stallion within him and he couldn't care less if that lying bastard Rino Zena was pissed off. Indeed, he added for good measure: 'The fact is, you like things the way they are. You're a pair of losers, content to wallow like pigs in your own unhappiness . . . How I pity that poor kid Cristiano . . . I . . . '

'You've been drinking, you scumbag!' Rino interrupted him.

Danilo stiffened, lengthened his neck and swelled out his chest and, as indignant as if he'd been accused of pissing in the sink, replied in an offended tone: 'Are you crazy? What are you talking about?'

'If we're two pigs that wallow in shit, what are you? The alcoholic son of a bitch who ought to be our leader?'

'But . . . ' Danilo tried to reply, to slap him down, but what had happened to his anger? To his desire to smash everything? They had faded away, along with his words and his courage.

His Adam's apple moved in his throat.

'The truth is, Danilo my friend, that you're just a paranoid, self-centred drunk who doesn't give a shit about anything or anyone else. If Quattro Formaggi has an accident you couldn't care less. In fact, you think it's a lie. You make me sick. You sit there on your own, thinking about your stupid boutique, your fantasies of being a great man. You're just a pathetic little jerk who feels sorry for himself because he's been dumped by a woman who was tired of swallowing the shit of a bastard who . . . '

Killed her daughter. Go on, say it, thought Danilo.

. . . ruined her life. Your wife was right to leave you. She was dead right. And I'll give you a piece of advice. You try once more, just once more, telling me how to bring up my son and . . . Let me be, Danilo. Let me be. Keep well away from me. Don't push your luck.'

115

'Let me be, Danilo. Let me be. Keep well away from me. Don't push your luck.' Rino Zena hung up, shaking his head, lit a cigarette and went out of the house. 'What a piece of shit . . . '

His hands were itching. If he hadn't been in such a hurry to find Quattro Formaggi he would gladly have dropped round on dear old Danilo Aprea to have it out with him.

But what's the quickest way to the San Rocco woods?

In the end Quattro Formaggi had managed, in between sobs, to stammer out that he was in the San Rocco woods. Near an electricity hut.

Why did he go all the way up there?

Rino was getting into the van when suddenly his head started spinning, he felt weak, he thought he was fainting, the cigarette dropped from his lips, his knees sagged and he fell to the ground.

What the hell's happening to me?

He tried to get up but he was too dizzy. He lay there for a long time, in the pouring rain, to get his strength back. His hands were trembling and his heart was pounding in his chest.

When he felt a bit better he climbed into the Ducato and drove out through the gate. The pain in his head was so acute that he couldn't decide whether to take the highway and then the road that ran along the river or to go up the narrow road through the woods near the bypass.

116

Danilo Aprea was paralysed, with the phone glued to his ear.

Rino Zena had threatened him. And a threat from that crazy Nazi was no laughing matter. That guy would kill you without so much as a second thought.

And above all, he never forgot.

Once when some poor bastard had pushed in front of him the thug had broken three of his ribs. Not immediately, though – six months later. All that time he had nursed his grudge and when one day he had happened to meet him in a pub he had first knocked him down with a beer glass and then kicked him in the ribs.

Suddenly he felt his bowels pulsing and his anal sphincter contracting and relaxing. He dropped the phone and rushed into the bathroom. He unleashed a stream of diarrhoea and sat there on the toilet with his elbows on his knees and his hands supporting his feverish forehead.

He was in a bad enough mess already, without getting death threats from Rino Zena.

'Well, if you want to kill me, go ahead and do it. What can I say . . . ' he murmured. 'I was only trying to make you guys rich . . . '

Another nightmare appeared in his mind. The next day at noon the TV salespeople would be coming round to bring him the painting of the climbing clown.

'What am I going to say to them? "I'm sorry, I haven't got any money. I don't want the picture any more. I made a mistake,"' he recited, sitting astride the bidet.

He couldn't let that masterpiece slip through his fingers so easily.

'Anyway, I'm not scared of you, Rino Zena, my friend. I don't give a shit about you . . . ' He curled his lip, baring his teeth like an angry wolf, and gargled with the throat mixture. 'Don't fuck with me, do you hear? You've got to be very wary about fucking with Danilo Aprea!'

He went back into the sitting room in his underpants and windcheater. A treacherous leer had formed beneath his moustache. He started cackling with laughter. 'Who's the drunkard?

I'm the drunkard, am I? Well, what are you then, Rino Zena? A pathetic alcoholic Nazi? A failure? A piece of human trash? Which? You decide. Which name would you like to be known by? Take your pick.' Then he started nodding his head and went on: 'You and me are finished. I'm not scared of you. Why don't you come round here so I can . . . ' he couldn't think of the word ' . . . knock your block off. You're going to regret the mistake you've made, regret it bitterly. Hah! You don't understand who you're dealing with!' He flopped back down on the sofa and concluded, raising his index finger towards the ceiling: 'Don't fuck with Danilo Aprea! I must get myself a T-shirt made, with that slogan across the chest.'

117

Beppe Trecca was sure Ida wouldn't come now.

So much the better.

He had spent a hellish evening cooped up in that stinking camper. At least it would serve as a lesson to him – it would teach him not to fool around with his best friend's wife.

Anyway, that was it, he must go home, get into bed and forget about this mad infatuation with Ida Lo Vino. It was only a temptation that was burning his soul and would bring him eternal damnation.

I got carried away.

He must write her a nice text message explaining that their relationship couldn't continue, for everyone's sake.

But how shall I put it?

"I apologise for pressing my attentions on you"? "Let's call the whole thing off"?

No. Too cowardly. He would meet her the next day and make her see reason. Reminding her that she had children, and a husband who loved her, and that it was right that they say goodbye.

Yes, that was a test of character which would reconcile him with his conscience and with God.

But outside a car horn hooted.

Beppe dashed to the window and saw two yellow headlights in the rain.

It's her! She's here. Now I'll speak to her.

Give yourself the once-over, though . . .

He was about to go into the bathroom to look in the mirror when he remembered what was in there.

He adjusted his tie, peering at his reflection in the rain-streaked window, and ran his fingers through his hair. Then he started jumping up and down, bending his head to the left and right and loosening up his arms, like a boxer who has just climbed into the ring.

I must find the right way of putting it, so I don't hurt her. But he didn't think he could even talk, he felt so excited. His stomach was tight and he had no saliva.

My breath must be bad enough to kill a rhinoceros.

With trembling hands he took out the little box of mints that he kept in his pocket, tipped the whole lot in his mouth and then started crushing them with his teeth, recalling a statement once made by Loris Reggiani, the great motorcycling champion: 'I've spent most of my life on a racing bike, knowing that I would achieve the best results if I could control my emotions and my potential.'

So go for it. Don't worry. You can do it.

He opened the door of the camper, breathing deeply in and out.

Ida Lo Vino rushed in, soaking wet. 'What's happening? Is this the biblical flood?' she said, removing her sopping raincoat.

Beppe would have liked to answer her, to say anything at all, but his vocal cords had been paralysed at the sight of her standing there in front of him.

Christ, is she beautiful.

Even shrouded in the clouds of incense she was a goddess. She wore a knee-length skirt, black high-heeled shoes and a peach-coloured jacket.

And she's come because of you.

'Brr, it's cold,' she said, rubbing her arms.

All Beppe could do was pick up the bottle of melon vodka and pass it to her.

She gave him a quizzical look. 'Aren't you going to give me a glass?'

'I'm sorry . . . You're . . . ' *perfectly right.* He took a wine glass from the table and passed it to her.

She poured herself two fingers of alcohol, looking around.

'Small. But well organised.' She wrinkled up her nose. 'You've lit some incense. There's a funny smell . . . '

It was like being inside a tin drum, with the noise the rain was making on the roof. He shouted: 'Yes, there is.'

He would have liked to ask her how she had managed to come without arousing Mario's suspicions, but he didn't.

Ida tossed off the vodka. 'Mmm, a bit of warmth. I needed that.'

She seemed even more tense and embarrassed than him. 'I'm dying for a pee. Is there a bathroom in here?'

He pointed to the door and wanted to tell her not to open it, that it was hell in there and that maybe she had better . . . But the paralysis of his vocal capabilities persisted.

'I won't be a minute.' Ida opened the door and locked herself in.

The social worker, in dismay, clapped his hand to his forehead.

118

The river had broken its banks and flooded the fields and soon the narrow strip of asphalt along which Rino Zena's van was speeding would be swamped. The headlights of the Ducato slid over the water-covered fields.

The worn blades of the windscreen wipers struggled to keep the screen clear, and on the inside the glass was misted up.

Rino wiped it with his hand and kept wondering why on earth Quattro Formaggi had gone into the woods. And why was he crying like that? Was there really something to worry about? Or was this just another crazy idea produced by that rotten brain?

Trying to penetrate the contorted mechanisms of Quattro Formaggi's mind was a task Rino had long since given up. Getting electrocuted at the weir hadn't helped, but even before that he hadn't been in such wonderful shape. He hadn't had all those tics and he hadn't walked with a limp, but he was already as daft as a brush.

He remembered him in the children's home. He would do crazy things like playing tennis for hours without a ball or a racket against an imaginary opponent called Aurelio.

He passed the pump of the deserted Agip filling station. From this point the road climbed up the hill, which was covered with woodland.

The headlights made the teeming raindrops glisten, but couldn't cut through the foliage at the sides of the road.

On the phone Quattro Formaggi had whimpered that he was in a layby where there was an electricity hut.

Shortly before the uphill road began to bend Rino saw a long layby on the left. At the end, near the guardrail, was a concrete hut daubed with coloured graffiti.

This is it.

Rino pulled in, turned off the engine, opened the tool drawer, took out the torch with the headband and switched it on.

No sign of life. Maybe this wasn't the right hut. He was about to return to the van when something gleamed behind the cabin. He went over and saw the Boxer and a Scarabeo leaned up against each other.

Whose is the other scooter?

Then he understood.

Some bastard who had nothing better to do than fuck other people around must have met Quattro Formaggi on the road.

There had been times in the past when they had surrounded him, shoved him around, amused themselves by making him dance and sing. They picked on him because he didn't react.

'You bastards. If you've hurt him I'll kill you.' Rino pulled his pistol out of his belt. He returned to the van, got out the bullets and loaded it, feeling the anger warming his blood.

He pointed the light towards the trees.

119

Danilo Aprea had lain down on the bed in his underpants and wind-cheater, and was looking at the ceiling, gasping for air.

I feel like shit.

His armpits were ice-cold. His feet boiling hot. His guts twisted in knots. And there was a worrying pain in his chest. The classic twinge that comes just before a heart attack. The sharp claw of a falcon digging in between your ventricles.

'Now watch me burst a vein. That'll be the end of me. And you'll all be happy,' and he gave a belch that tasted of grappa.

He wished he could turn off the television, which was blaring in the sitting room. The voices of Bruno Vespa and those other arseholes blathering on about deficits, taxes and inflation made him feel terribly sick. But he was afraid of dozing off and dying in his sleep.

What a fool he'd been to drink that Cynar.

Do liqueurs have a sell-by date?

And then as soon as he closed his eyes he felt like he was falling into a bottomless pit which would take him right down to the fiery centre of the Earth.

He had to think. Though in that state and with Bruno Vespa yammering away in the other room it was really hard.

The first thing to consider was that the cash machine plan, as originally conceived, was dead in the water. The second was that he had finished for good with Rino and Quattro Formaggi.

'But, as the proverb says, better alone than in bad company,' he mumbled, putting one hand on his chest.

He must revive the plan of the raid. Without them. It was the best thing his mind had produced since the day he had been born. It shouldn't just be dropped. The great thing about the plan was that you could do it any time. Any night. All you needed was the right mates, not a couple of cowards.

He would find some real professionals with whom he could start from scratch. At that moment he didn't know who they were, or how he was going to find them, but next day, with a clear head, he would certainly think of something.

'Albanians. Guys with balls,' he said, panting. 'Rino, my friend, you just don't understand me. What a pity. What a great pity. You don't realise who you're dealing with. If you want to stop Danilo Aprea you've got to blast him with a bazooka.'

The pale blue brushstrokes of the television, through the doorway, were painting the ceiling above the bed. It was strange, but in between the light-blue patches there seemed to emerge a dark patch with a human form.

'Is that you, my friend?' he asked, looking at the ceiling.

(Sure it's me.)

The climbing clown was looking down at him, stuck to the ceiling like Spiderman.

'I was right to tell Rino where to go, wasn't I? They mustn't fuck with me, they just don't understand. The only thing I'm sorry about is that tomorrow those people are bringing the picture and I won't have the money. That I really am sorry about.' He fumbled about on the floor for the bottle of Cynar but couldn't find it. 'Don't worry, though . . . Trust me . . . I'm not chucking my life down the pan.' He was addressing the clown above his head. 'I won't leave you. I'm not like some people I could mention. I swear, I swear on the head of . . . '

Laura.

' . . . Teresa, the most important thing in my life, that you'll be here, in this flat. Tomorrow. I'll sell everything I own if I have to.'

Suddenly a lump of pain burst like a bubble under his sternum. He touched his eyes, his cheeks. He was crying and he hadn't noticed.

'I'm not well,' he sobbed. 'What should I do? Tell me. Please tell me.'

(Ring her. She's the only person who understands you.) The clown smiled down at him from the ceiling.

'No, it's not true . . . She left me . . . It wasn't my fault that Laura died. I know she thinks it was . . . '

(Tell her you're giving up drink, as from tomorrow.)

Danilo knew there wasn't any clown up there on the ceiling, that it was only a shadow cast by the television in the sitting room. Yet it really seemed to be talking to him.

'Let's not kid ourselves, I'll never manage it.' Another bubble of pain burst under his Adam's apple.

(Yes you will. If she comes back to you and helps you you'll certainly manage it . . . Tell her about the boutique. She'll come back, you'll see.)

Danilo raised his head a little and narrowed his eyes: 'Now? Shall I call her now?

(Yes, now.)

'What if she's angry?'

(Why should she be angry?)

'It's too late. I promised not to call her at night.'

(It's never too late to tell the truth. To tell someone you love them. Tell her what you're doing for her. That you'll climb the great mountain just for her. That's the kind of thing women like to hear. Tell her about the boutique. You'll see, you'll see . . .)

Danilo lifted his head off the cushion and everything started spinning. He took a deep breath, groped for the switch and turned on the bedside lamp. The light stabbed his retinas. He put one hand over his eyes and with the other picked up the phone on the bedside table. 'I'll call her mobile, though.' He dialled Teresa's number.

The number was not obtainable.

'There's no answer, you see?'

(Call her landline.)

Now that *would* be a stupid thing to do. Especially at this time of night, when that shit of a tyre dealer would be there. And yet he had to do it, he had to hear Teresa's voice, the only thing that would do him any good at that moment.

(Do it. If he answers, you can hang up, can't you?)

That's true . . .

Besides, this time it was different. It was to tell her he was going to put everything right. Seriously. He was at the end of the tunnel, and if he didn't change he was finished. And she would understand. Teresa would understand how much he was suffering and she would come back home and he, next morning, would wake to find her curled up beside him wearing her eye-mask to keep out the light.

(What are you waiting for?)

His index finger slipped onto the keypad, and with surprising speed for his mental condition he tapped out her number.

120

He mistook it first for a dog, then for a wild boar and finally for a gorilla.

Rino took three steps backwards and instinctively pointed his gun at it, but as soon as the torchlight illuminated it he realised it was a human being.

There on all fours in the middle of the wood, beside the crash

helmet. Soaking wet. Black hair plastered down over the skull . . .
On one shoulder a hole from which blood was oozing. Hands
immersed in the mud.

'Quattro Formaggi? What happened to you?'

At first he didn't even seem to hear, but then slowly he raised his
head towards the light.

Rino instinctively put his hand over his mouth.

The eyes were wide open, two holes sunken in their orbits, and
the jaw hung down idiotically.

'What have they done to you?'

The face, etched by the shadows, was reduced to a skull. It was
as if something inside Quattro Formaggi's mind had short-circuited,
as happens in some mental patients after a lobotomy. It didn't even
seem to be him.

'Where are they? Where the fuck are they?' Rino started pointing
the gun around, sure they were there, hiding somewhere, in the darkness. 'Come on out, you bastards. Fight someone your own size!'
Then he bent down, still pointing the gun forward, and grabbed
Quattro Formaggi by the arm and tried to pull him up, but he seemed
to be rooted to the earth. 'Come on! Get up. We've got to get out
of here.' Finally, making a tremendous effort, he got him on his feet.
'I'm here. Don't worry.' He was about to start dragging him along
when he noticed that his cock was sticking out of his trousers.

'What the f . . . '

'I didn't mean to. I didn't mean to. I didn't do it on purpose,'
stammered Quattro Formaggi and he started crying. 'I'm sorry.'

Rino felt as if someone had ripped open his belly with a knife
and simultaneously rammed a sock down his throat.

He let go of Quattro Formaggi, who slumped down on the ground.
He took two steps backwards and realised he'd been wrong. Terribly
wrong.

*The Scarabeo belongs to that girl . . . The one that goes to
Cristiano's school . . . The sticker with the face on it.*

He was overwhelmed by the chilling awareness that Quattro
Formaggi had finally exploded. And done something really terrible.

Because Rino knew that the fairy tale the locals always repeated,
that Quattro Formaggi wouldn't hurt a fly, was as big a load of
bullshit as the idea that the government was going to cut taxes.

Every day there was someone who would go out of their way to make fun of him in some way or other, who would mimic him, give him less soup in the canteen, make him feel like a fool, but he would never lose his temper, he would smile, and everyone would say Quattro Formaggi was above all that.

Above it my arse!

That half-smile he gave after someone had imitated him and called him a spastic wasn't a sign that Quattro Formaggi was a saint, but that the insult had hit home, had pierced a sensitive part, and the pain went to swell a part of his brain where something tainted, twisted, was pulsing away. And some day, sooner or later, that festering thing would wake up.

A million times Rino had thought this, and a million times he had hoped he was wrong.

He had to summon up all his strength to be able to speak to him. It was as if he had been punched in the stomach. 'What have you done? What the hell have you done?' He turned on the leaf-strewn ground and walked a few steps, and the yellow beam of the torch on his brow slid over Fabiana's body lying in the middle of the path. Her head smashed in by a rock.

'A girl . . . You've killed a girl.'

121

The phone kept on ringing.

I'm going to hang up . . .

(No. Wait at least another fi . . .)

'Hallo?'

Danilo Aprea puffed out air and started breathing normally again. His mouth was dry and his tongue felt numb. 'Teresa, it's me.'

An instant of silence that never seemed to end.

'What is it, Danilo?' The tone of her voice conveyed not anger, but something worse, which made Danilo immediately curse himself for ringing her. It conveyed hopelessness and resignation. She was like a peasant who has accepted her inexorable destiny that now and then a fox will get into her henhouse and devour the chickens.

'Listen. I need to talk to you.'

'You're drunk.'

He tried to sound offended, almost outraged, at this base accusation: 'Why do you say that?'

'I can tell by your voice.'

'You're wrong. I haven't touched a drop. It's not right, you always thinking . . . '

'You promised you wouldn't call me . . . Do you know what time it is?'

'It's late, I know, but this is important, I'm not being stupid, or I'd never have called you. It's very important. Liste . . . '

Teresa interrupted him. 'No, Danilo, you listen to me. I can't unplug the phone, Piero's mother is seriously ill in hospital, and you know it.'

Shit, I'd forgotten about that.

'You know that very well, Danilo. Every time the phone rings our hearts are in our mouths. Piero's in the other room. He'll have realised it's you. You must leave me in peace. How can I make you underst . . . '

He managed to interrupt her: 'I'm sorry, Teresa. I'm sorry. You're right. Forgive me. But I've got a wonderful surprise for our future. Something you really must hear about . . . '

Now it was she who interrupted him: 'What future are you talking about? It's you who must listen to me. And you'd better listen very carefully. So pin back your ears.' She took a deep breath: 'I'm pregnant, Danilo. I'm expecting a baby with Piero. I'm in my third month now. You must come to terms with it. I don't want to come back to you, I don't love you. I love Piero. Laura's dead, Danilo. We must come to terms with that. I want to be happy and Piero makes me happy. I want to build a new family. And you keep pestering me, phoning me in the middle of the night! I'll be forced to go to the police. And if that's not enough I'll go away, I'll disappear. If you love me, as you keep saying you do, you must leave me in peace. So I beg you, I implore you, leave us in peace. If you won't do it for me, do it for yourself. Forget me. Start living again. Goodbye.'

CLICK.

122

She's dead.

At least five minutes had passed since Ida had locked herself in the toilet.

Maybe she had fainted from the stink.

Beppe Trecca, worried, put his ear to the door. He couldn't hear a thing, what with the drumming of the rain and the howling of the wind that was shaking the camper.

He had prepared a clear, simple speech, to make her understand that their relationship was a mistake.

He cleared his throat. 'Ida . . . ? Ida, are you there?'

The door opened and Ida Lo Vino came out, as pale as a ghost.

He gulped. 'Was there a bit of a stink?'

She nodded, and then said, 'Beppe, I love you. I love you madly.' And she stuck her tongue in his mouth.

123

'What the fuck have you done? You psychopathic, murdering son of a bitch!' Rino shouted, and he shook Quattro Formaggi by the arm. 'You've killed a girl! You've gone out of your mind, you fool . . . ' He slapped him across the face so hard he heard the bones in his hand crack.

Quattro Formaggi crashed to the ground and started sobbing convulsively.

'Don't cry, you bastard. Don't cry or I'll kill you.' Rino raised his head like a coyote howling to the moon, gnashed his teeth as he massaged his aching hand, then he kicked him hard in the ribs.

Quattro Formaggi rolled over in the mud, coughing.

'You smashed her head in with a rock.' Another kick. 'Do you realise what you've done, you scumbag?' Another kick.

'I didn't . . . mean to. I swear I . . . didn't mean to. I'm sorry,' whimpered Quattro Formaggi, shaking his head despairingly. 'I don't know . . . myself . . . why I did it.'

'Oh, you don't know, don't you? Well, I don't know either. You lousy fucking rapist . . . ' He grabbed him by the hair and thrust the gun barrel against his eye. 'Now I'm going to kill you.'

'Yes, kill me! Kill me. I deserve it . . . ' Quattro Formaggi moaned.

A violent red fury had seized Rino Zena's brain and swollen his muscles and tightened the tendons of his index finger as he squeezed the trigger of the pistol, and he knew he must calm down now, at once, or he would blow the bastard's head off.

He slammed the sole of his foot into the other man's face. Quattro Formaggi spewed out a stream of blood and then curled up in a ball, with his arms over his head.

Breathing hard, Rino stuck his pistol under his belt, picked up an enormous branch with both hands and smashed it against the trunk.

It wasn't enough. He still had too much rage inside him.

He put both arms round a rock, which must have weighed at least fifty kilos, to hurl it God knows where. He heaved it up out of the mud with a roar, but suddenly fell silent.

The rock slipped out of his hands.

The world around him broke up into hundreds of coloured fragments like a shattering pane of glass, and a vice as heavy as a mass of white-hot lead crushed his skull. Two drills bored into his temples, and all the extremities of his body started tingling.

He froze like that, with his knees bent, his trunk leaning forward like a sumo wrestler, his eyes bulging, and he realised that never until this moment had he had the faintest idea of what a headache really was.

He lost his balance and fell down stiff on the ground.

124

It was ten minutes since Teresa had given him the news that she was pregnant, but Danilo Aprea was still there, sitting on the edge of his bed.

He knew he should at best burst into tears, at worst jump out of the window and end it all.

If only I had the guts to kill myself. What a shit you'd feel, Teresa dear . . . Wouldn't it be great! You'd be racked with remorse for the rest of your life.

The problem was that he lived on the second floor. And with his luck he'd probably end up in a wheelchair.

He must do something, though. Maybe he could just go away. Fly off to some distant land. Go and live in India. No, he didn't fancy India. It was filthy. And full of flies.

But if he went on thinking about this kind of thing all night till morning, till daybreak, till the sun returned, this night, the shittiest night in a shitty life, would pass. Because Danilo knew that if he stopped keeping his brain occupied he might do something stupid, something he would bitterly regret.

He looked up at the ceiling. The clown was still there. Hanging in a corner where the glow of the television didn't reach.

(Poor woman, I wonder what she imagines, in her fantasies . . . That this wonderful news will hit you so hard you'll hang yourself from the chandelier? You think she'd be racked with remorse? Don't kid yourself – she'd be happy. She'd be rid of you. That's what she's hoping for. Well, she's mistaken. If anyone wants to get rid of you they'll have to blast you with a bazooka.)

Danilo would have liked to smile, but his lips had got stuck together. So he started shaking his head.

She was so naïve, Teresa. She just didn't understand. He had always known it would happen sooner or later.

She's forgotten about Laura. She thinks she can replace her with another child.

'Well done.' He clapped his hands. 'Well done, what a clever girl you are!'

(But this doesn't change your plans by one centimetre. Teresa isn't really interested in that nattily dressed tyre dealer. Let's be honest, he's been useful to her because he's got a bit of cash and he's got her pregnant. Period. But when you come along with the boutique and some real money, she'll come back to you.)

'Ah, who wants her anyway?' he muttered, with a sniff.

(Do the raid on your own. You don't need anyone else. Do it at once. Now.)

Danilo looked at the clown. 'You're right. Of course, I can do it on my own, why didn't I think of that before?'

Outside, the storm continued to rage over the deserted village. He didn't even need the tractor. A car would do just as well.

And he still had a car. It was in the garage, unused since the day of Laura's funeral. He'd had several opportunities to sell it, but had never done so. And why was that? Not because he thought he might decide to drive again one day, nor because it was the vehicle in which the angel of his life had gone to heaven. No. Not for that reason. But because he would need it to do the raid on his own.

'It all fits.'

So the fact that Rino and Quattro Formaggi had let him down was part of a grander plan that God had organised specially for him.

(All the money will be yours. You won't have to share it with anyone.)

He would be really rich, and to hell with everyone else. And Teresa would come crawling back to him with her tail between her legs.

'I'm sorry, Teresa. You've forgotten Laura. You said you loved the tyre dealer. That you wanted a child with him. Stay with him, then,' he said, jabbing his finger as if she was standing there in front of him, and feeling the first glimmer of pleasure he had felt in several hours.

He knew what he had to do.

He got up and staggered into the bathroom to stick two fingers down his throat.

125

When Rino Zena had pointed the gun at his face, Quattro Formaggi had known for certain that he loved life.

He had repeated 'Kill me, kill me' to show Rino that he felt guilty, not because he really wanted it; deep inside, more than ever before, he had wanted to live.

To live. To live after killing. To live regardless. To live with the burden of guilt. To live in a prison for the rest of his life. To live beaten and despised till the end of his days.

It didn't matter how, but to live.

And even when he had felt the cold steel of the gun against his nose he had known Rino wouldn't shoot him and that, as usual, he would sort everything out.

He just had to wait till his anger subsided.

He had curled up in a ball, and it was right, he deserved them, sure he deserved those kicks, even though it was Ramona's own fault if she had died. If she hadn't taken the road through the woods none of this would have happened.

From the ground, with his head hidden between his arms, he had seen the black silhouette of Rino storm about and pick up a branch and smash it against a tree trunk. And then, like a giant with an eye of light in the middle of his forehead, lift a huge rock and, as he was lifting it, suddenly freeze. For a moment Quattro Formaggi had thought he must have strained his back, but then Rino had fallen on the ground, quite stiff.

And he had lain there motionless. Not saying a word, not uttering a cry.

He had been lying like that for at least five minutes.

He went over to him, ready to run for it if he got up.

Rino's eyes were open and there was a strange expression on his face that Quattro Formaggi couldn't describe. As if he was waiting for an answer.

'Rino, can you hear me?' he asked, shaking him.

His teeth were clenched and white foam was trickling down from the corner of his mouth.

Quattro Formaggi knew nothing about medicine, but something very serious must have happened to him. That thing that happens in your brain, leaving you virtually dead.

A coma.

'Rino! What's the matter? Are you in a coma?'

No response.

He slapped his face, but Rino did nothing. He just lay there with a quizzical expression on his face.

He slapped him again, harder.

Still no reaction.

He took the gun out of Rino's belt, weighed it in his hand and put it against the other man's forehead, imitating his deep voice: 'You lousy fucking rapist, now I'm going to kill you.' Then he started sticking the barrel into a nostril, into his mouth, and smearing the drool over his chin.

When he tired of this he stood there for a while, his mind a blank, rubbing his bruised ribs and thumping himself on the thigh with the pistol butt.

126

Fireflies danced in front of Rino Zena's eyes. He could also see the raindrops, as heavy as mercury, falling on his face.

The rest was a tingling feeling, like ants crawling over his skin.

His legs. His arms. His stomach. His mouth.

Like a bag of skin, full of ants.

He couldn't remember where he was, but if he concentrated hard he could hear, too: the sound of his own breathing, the storm among the trees.

A kind of violet cloud was covering him, hiding the fireflies.

That was it, he was in the wood. And the patch where the cloud was lighter must be Quattro Formaggi.

"*Help me,*" he said. But his mouth didn't move, nor did his tongue, and the words didn't emerge from his lips, yet they echoed in his ears like a desperate scream of terror.

He felt something on his cheek. A slap, maybe. Or a caress. But it was far away. As if his head was stuffed with wool. Coarse wool. The dark green wool of the blankets in the children's home.

He was surprised he could still think.

Little thoughts. One after another. Violet thoughts immersed in an infinite blackness.

'Rino! What's the matter? Are you in a coma?'

His heart started beating more loudly. Quattro Formaggi's words, like sharp arrows, pierced through the violet, which closed again after their passage, and reached him.

"*I don't know,*" he replied, aware of not having spoken.

'You lousy fucking rapist, now I'm going to kill you.' More arrows pierced the haze. But this time Rino didn't understand what they meant.

If only he could move one finger . . .

A finger full of ants.

He made an effort, trying to move his hand. Perhaps he had moved it, but in this state he had no way of knowing.

'Are you dead?' Quattro Formaggi asked him.

The finger. Move that damned finger.

He must make Quattro Formaggi understand that he had to take him to hospital at once.

Move the finger. Go on.

He ordered all the ants to converge from every part of his body into the finger and lift it.

But they didn't obey, and suddenly the mist thickened and his body started to jerk and quiver as it was dragged into the violet which shaded into black.

A blazing fire exploded in the middle of his chest, sucking the air out of his lungs.

Rino implored God to help him, to pull him out of that black hole, and so as suddenly as they had arrived the spasms ceased and he found himself alone, in a calm without light.

127

Quattro Formaggi saw Rino writhing about and struggling against an invisible force that had caught him and was trying to carry him away. Rino waved his legs and arms and rolled his eyes, and his back arched like a bow; he twisted his mouth and shook his head, and the light on his forehead crazily slashed the woods with a thousand golden blades.

Frightened and shocked, Quattro Formaggi tried to help him, to throw himself across him so as to hold down his arms, but he got a blow in the face and a kick, so he retreated in dismay.

Tugging at his hair, he prayed it would soon be over. It was a terrible sight.

The invisible force was now pushing harder and arching Rino's back as if it wanted to break it, but an instant later it left him, and he lay there, limp in the mud. The torch had gone out too.

It's gone because it's taken Rino's soul.

His best friend was dead. The only person who had loved him. He had come here to help him, and God . . .

(who should have taken you, you dirty murdering rapist)

 . . . had taken his life as he lifted a rock.

He crouched down beside Rino.

What now? What must I do?

Normally it was Rino who answered these questions. He always knew what to do.

Quattro Formaggi sat down and patted him on the shoulder. 'Amen'. And he crossed himself.

He died for me. God wanted someone in exchange for Ramona's death and Rino sacrificed himself.

(They'll find him and think it was him that killed her. You'll be in the clear.)

Quattro Formaggi smiled with relief. Then he got up, tucked his cock back into his underpants, retrieved his torch and crash helmet, stuck the gun in his trousers and went back to Ramona.

He slipped the skull ring off her finger and limped away towards the road.

128

The aluminium doors of the lift drew apart and Danilo Aprea, wrapped up in warm clothes, came out into the hall of the apartment block.

 He leaned against the jamb of the lift with his eyes reduced to two slits.

The hall was a long room panelled with slats of dark wood. On the floor, polished marble. To the left, the porter's lodge with a little television and a pile of bills. To the right, the stairs. Beyond the glass doors the raindrops danced on the sodden doormat and lashed the geraniums in their flowerpots.

Danilo had vomited up three litres of alcohol and drunk a whole pot of coffee. Now he felt a bit better. His drunkenness hadn't passed, but at least he didn't feel sick any more.

He staggered over to a concealed door in the wooden panelling, opened it and without even switching on the lights went down a short flight of steps, found the handle and threw open the door of the communal garage. He breathed in.

The same smell of damp and petrol.

He hadn't been in there since 12th July 2001.

He steeled himself and pressed the light switch.

The neon tubes flickered and lit up a long underground garage where two rows of cars were parked.

Danilo walked across it, the sound of his footsteps echoing against the concrete walls.

The Alfa Romeo was covered with a grey tarpaulin.

He put his hand on the bonnet. On contact a shiver ran up his forearm, giving him gooseflesh.

Don't think about it.

He took a deep breath and lifted the tarpaulin.

For an instant he imagined his daughter sitting on the little green child seat, laughing. He banished the vision from his mind.

It was because of that seat that Laura Aprea had died.

'The damned buckle wouldn't open. It got stuck,' he had repeated to everyone till he was exhausted. To Teresa, to the policemen, to the whole world.

On 9th July 2001 Danilo had asked for a day off work and had taken his daughter to the doctor for a check-up. Usually it was Teresa who looked after these things, but that day she'd had some business to sort out with the notary's mother.

'Everything's fine,' the doctor had said, giving Laura an affectionate pat on the bottom as she chuckled and wriggled, stark naked on the couch. 'This little bundle's in perfect health.'

'This isn't a little bundle. It's a little rascal, isn't it?' Danilo had said to his daughter, grinning from ear to ear. And while the doctor washed his hands he had buried his face in the little girl's tummy, making a lot of rude noises. Laura had started chuckling. 'And where are those little mozzarellas? There they are!' And he had affectionately nibbled those plump little legs that he loved to bits.

After the check-up they had gone to the cash-and-carry.

It was no easy task doing the shopping with Laura sitting in the trolley singing 'I love teatime with to-to-to-to-tomatoes.'

Then they had got back into the car. Danilo had put the plastic bags on the back seat and had strapped the child into her seat and said to her: 'Now we're going to see mama.'

They had driven off.

Danilo Aprea was working for a freight firm as a night-watchman at the time and he knew that sooner or later there were going to be cuts in staff. And there was a good chance that he would be among the unlucky ones.

He drove along the highway, which was unusually empty for the time of day, trying to think of a job he might be able to find at short notice, even a temporary one, perhaps at Euroedil, a building firm where they often needed labourers.

Suddenly he had noticed that there was a smell of green apples in the car. Not real green apples, but the synthetic green-apple scent of the anti-dandruff shampoo.

'I mistook it for the scent of the Arbre Magique,' he had explained afterwards to his wife.

'How could you? The deodorant is forest pine and the shampoo is green apples. They're not the same thing!' she had cried in despair, her eyes puffy with weeping.

'You're right. But I didn't understand at first. I don't know why . . . '

Danilo had turned round and seen that Laura's little red T-shirt and blue trousers were all smeared with green liquid.

'Laura, what have you done?' Danilo had seen the overturned plastic bag and the capless bottle of shampoo on the soap-spattered seat.

Then – he remembered it as if it had happened that very day – he had heard a sucking noise, a strangled croak, and had looked at his daughter.

The little girl's mouth was wide open and her blue eyes, popping out of their orbits, were red. She was struggling desperately, but the safety belts of the child seat were doing their job and keeping her pinned down like a condemned prisoner in the electric chair.

She can't breathe. The cap! She's swallowed the cap!

Danilo had gripped the wheel and, without looking, had swerved sharply and darted, with a squeal of tyres, towards the edge of the road, just missing the front of a lorry, which had started honking furiously.

The Alfa Romeo had stopped in the emergency lane of the highway in a cloud of white smoke. Danilo had leaped out, tripped over, scrambled to his feet and with his heart thumping against his chest had grabbed the handle of the rear door with both hands.

'Here I am! Here I am! Papa's coming . . . ' he had gasped, and had grabbed the safety buckle of the child seat to free his daughter, who was flailing about with her little hands and legs, hitting him on the face and the chest.

But the incredible thing was that the bloody buckle wouldn't open, it had two huge orange buttons which you just had to push together, something he had done a hundred times, always opening it perfectly, a German buckle designed by the finest engineers in the world, because everyone knows the Germans are the finest engineers in the world, which had passed the most stringent safety tests, been certified by an international commission and been given the $C\epsilon$, and yet that damned buckle wouldn't open.

It simply wouldn't open.

Danilo had told himself to keep calm, not to panic, that the buckle would open in a moment, but Laura's desperate expression and strangled sobs made him lose his head, he felt like tearing at the straps with his teeth, but he had to keep calm. So he had closed his eyes so as not to see his little girl dying and had continued to push, fumble and pull while his daughter suffocated, but it was no good. He had tried to slip her out of the seat, without success, and then had grabbed the whole damned contraption, shouting, but there were the car's seat belts that were wrapped round the plastic frame.

I must get hold of her feet. I must get hold of her feet and shake her . . .

But how, if he couldn't get her free?

Then, inhaling the smell of green apples, he had stuck his big fingers into the mouth of his daughter, who was now struggling less, suddenly weaker and tired, and had searched for the cap that was stuck right down in her windpipe. With his fingertips he had felt her little tongue, her epiglottis, her tonsils, but not the cap.

Now Laura was no longer moving. Her little head lolled on her chest and her arms hung down by the sides of the seat.

Yes, he knew what he had to do. Why hadn't he thought of it earlier? He must pierce her throat, so that the air . . . but what with?

He had shouted and pleaded, 'Help, help me, a little girl, my daughter, is dying . . . ' and he had squeezed between the two front seats, he, a great hulk of a man weighing over a hundred kilos jammed between the two seats, with the gear lever sticking into his breast-bone and his arms reaching out towards the glove box in the dashboard. The middle finger of his right hand had succeeded in reaching the button and the door had come open and spewed out bits of paper, brochures, maps and a Bic pen which had rolled under the seat.

He had groped about, gasping, on the mat and at last had got hold of the pen and holding it like a bradawl had turned and raised his right arm, ready to . . .

She's dead.

The Bic had fallen from his hand.

Laura Aprea, lifeless, sat in the child seat, her blue eyes staring, her little arms outspread, her mouth wide open . . .

A year after the accident, when his life had gone completely down the pan, Danilo had come across this short item in a newspaper:

> Routine tests of child car seats carried out in 2002 have revealed that certain buckles, made by the Rausberg company in 2000 and 2001, and used by some manufacturers of child car seats, do not always close correctly, even if they make a distinctly audible click. If the two metal tongues are inserted obliquely the belt may not be properly fixed on one side or the other and the buckle may not open, to the detriment of the child's safety. The following child car seats have defective buckles: Boulgom, Chicco, Fair/Wavo, Kiddy and Storchenmühle. You are therefore advised to check the date of manufacture of the child car seat in your possession and should it have been produced in the period 2000–2001 to return it to the manufacturers, who have undertaken to replace it promptly.

129

Rino's van was parked in the middle of the layby.

Quattro Formaggi climbed over the guardrail and looked at it for a while, scratching his beard with one hand and holding his wounded shoulder with the other.

He must make sure that passers-by would notice it.

He could call the police and say he had discovered a murder, then he would be famous. He would appear on television.

No, I can't do that.

He was a friend of Rino's and they would immediately think he was involved too.

He started slapping himself on the forehead, repeating through clenched teeth: 'Think! Think! Think, you rotten brain.'

If he switched on the headlights everyone would see the Ducato. But the battery would go flat in less than an hour.

He opened the door, turned the radio on full blast and left the door open, so that the little internal light would stay on.

As he was walking round to retrieve the Boxer the radio began playing The Police's *So Lonely*.

He started nodding his head and then, spinning round and round, opened his arms to the rain, feeling a euphoric joy swell his chest.

Alive! Alive! I'm alive!

He had killed and he was alive. And nobody would ever know.

He wheeled out the Boxer, mounted it and donned his crash helmet. He couldn't move his left arm and found it a struggle to start the engine. After a couple of coughs the engine started turning and producing white smoke.

'That's the way, baby.' He stroked the headlamp and, singing 'So lonely, so lonely . . . ' headed for home, pushed by the wind and rain.

130

While Beppe Trecca and Ida Lo Vino were inside the camper the storm raged over Camp Bahamas.

Above the gate the big banana-shaped sign flapped about like a spinnaker. One of the four steel cables that held it in place snapped with a CRACK that was lost in the howling winds.

131

Danilo Aprea screwed up the tarpaulin and put it on the ground. He approached the driver's door and instinctively put his hands in his pockets.

Where are the keys?

When he remembered where they were he had to lean against the window to stop himself falling over.

'No, it's not possible. It's not possible,' he said, shaking his head. Then he put his hands over his face. 'What a fool I am . . . What a fool . . . '

He had thrown them in the canal on the day Laura had been buried, swearing that he would never drive that car again.

What now?

He couldn't give up just because of a fucking bunch of keys. He wasn't going to let such a stupid problem stop him.

'If you want to stop Danilo Aprea you've got to blast him with a bazooka,' he exclaimed, noting how firm and resolute his voice sounded. 'Anyway, all I have to do is go upstairs and get the duplicate keys.'

He went upstairs and set about opening all the drawers, searching in every cupboard, rummaging in every box, in every bloody corner.

They had gone. Vanished into thin air.

He was a meticulous man. He never lost anything. 'Every thing has its place and every place has its thing,' was his motto.

So the keys must be there, hidden somewhere. But he had no idea where else to look for them.

He was hot and tired and had a terrible headache. He staggered through the flat, which looked as if a herd of buffalo had just charged through it, and flopped down exhausted, with his legs apart, in the armchair.

Unless . . .

He jumped to his feet as if the cushion had caught fire.

What if that cow Teresa, on the advice of the tyre dealer, had pinched them?

But why?

The tyre dealer had a Lexus. What would he want with his old Alfa?

Maybe he didn't have any special reason. Just did it out of spite. Or perhaps it was Teresa, worried I might drive again.

But it could have been Rino too – he could have stolen them when he'd come round to do his washing. Or that young scoundrel Cristiano. And why rule out that halfwit Quattro Formaggi?

Everyone coveted his car. You could just imagine what it would be like when he had the painting of the climbing clown in his sitting room! An object of such value would have them all trying to steal it . . .

The first thing I must do tomorrow is put in a steel-clad door with multiple locks.

But in the meantime he was keyless.

I'm very tired. Perhaps I'd better call it off for this evening . . .

But he knew himself too well – if he backed out now he would never have the courage to do the raid on his own the next day. And then he would be forced to share the loot with somebody else.

No. It's out of the question.

Only he felt drained and his eyelids were drooping.

He must give himself a boost. And there was only one way he knew of doing that. He shuffled into the kitchen, yawning. He ransacked the cupboards and discovered, among all the other junk, a bottle of Borghetti coffee liqueur.

He took a swig and immediately felt better.

(Instead of standing here like an idiot, go and see if anyone has left the keys in their car in the garage.)

This brilliant idea could only have come from the clown on the bedroom ceiling.

'That's right! You're a genius!'

If there existed a plan of destiny that the course of his life should change that night, he would certainly find a car open.

132

In the first place he wasn't suffering.

That was one good thing.

Also, he didn't think he was dead.

That was another good thing.

There had been one immense instant, when the fluorescent cloud had been suddenly swallowed up by the blackness, during which Rino had been sure that his story had come to an end.

Now, however, the violet had returned.

Nobody had actually certified that he wasn't dead. But Rino had always believed in heaven and hell, and this place was neither the one nor the other. Of that he was certain. He was aware of still being inside his own body.

He could think. And to think is to live.

And although he wasn't suffering greatly, he was aware of a distant fire, a far-off pain and the ants running through his veins, but he also thought he could hear from a thousand kilometres away The Police singing and the rain falling on the leaves, dripping in silver drops on the branches, trickling down the bark of the trees and soaking the earth.

He was blind. Insentient. Paralysed. And yet, strangely, he could hear.

When he had come to, the darkness had been less intense, shading gradually into a phosphorescent violet, and suddenly millions of ants had been there. They covered the plain as far as the horizon. They were big, like the ones that appear in the wheatfields in August. With shiny heads and antennae.

Rino couldn't make out whether they were outside or inside him. And whether that desert over which they were crawling was him.

He sensed that there was another reality just behind the violet cloud which enveloped him. The reality from which he had fallen.

The woods. The rain.

He saw himself in the woods with the rock in his hands, Quattro Formaggi, the dead girl.

That was where he must get back to.

He thought he was still there, and he was sure Quattro Formaggi had gone to get help.

133

Danilo Aprea, holding the bottle of Borghetti coffee liqueur in one hand, had checked the cars in the garage. One by one.

All locked.

In that bloody condominium everyone lived in terror of having their cars stolen. And you could bet your life they had burglar alarms and all the latest security gadgets installed.

He had thought of smashing a window and putting the ignition leads together, like you see people doing in films.

But he was no good at that kind of thing. He would still be there at daybreak trying to get the dashboard open.

If only Quattro Formaggi was here . . .

Danilo gnashed his teeth like a rabid dog and shouted, white in the face with rage: 'Fuck you! Fuck the whole lot of you! You won't stop me. Do you hear? You won't stop me. You're doing everything you can to stop me, but you won't succeed. No! No! And no! I'm going to do this raid.' He kicked the door of a Mini Cooper, hurting his foot like mad.

He hopped around, cursing and swearing, and when the pain eased he raised the bottle of Borghetti coffee liqueur, gulped down a third of it and staggered towards the garage door.

134

In his trouser pocket he had his mobile phone.

When Rino Zena thought of the mobile he saw it appear huge, as if projected onto the violet sky.

It wasn't a photograph of a mobile phone, but a drawing done with a big black marker pen. The numbers written in a childish hand, and where the display should have been, a circle with a smile and eyes. He could have gazed at it for ever.

But now he must get his mobile out of his trouser pocket . . .

He must speak to the ants and explain to them what they had to do.

135

Danilo stood on the parapet of the canal, hands on hips, gazing blankly at the raindrops.

In the dim light shed by the lamp-post on the little footbridge they seemed like silver threads, which dissolved on the brownish surface of the canal.

The pebble shores and the greater part of the pillars under the bridge had been engulfed by the rising waters. If the rain kept coming down like this, by morning the flood would be over the dykes.

Danilo was soaked through to his pants. His cheeks and chin frozen and the lenses of his glasses streaked with rain.

It had taken just fifty metres, the distance from his home to there, out in that downpour, to reduce him to a sopping rag.

A polystyrene box, the kind that is used for packing fish, raced along through the waves, bobbing up and down, like a raft in the rapids of the Colorado River, and disappeared under the bridge.

Trying to ignore an icy trickle that was running down his back, Danilo closed his eyes and tried to remember where, five years ago, he had thrown the keys.

About here.

On the 12th of July five years ago . . . It was boiling hot and the mosquitoes were driving me mad.

After Laura's funeral he had sent Teresa home with her mother and had taken the Alfa and stopped at a bar where he had drunk the first glass of grappa of his life and for good measure had bought a whole bottle, then he had gone to a car accessories shop, bought a tarpaulin and returned home. He had parked the car in the garage, covered it with the tarpaulin and gone down to the canal.

That day it had looked very different. There had been no rain for a long time and the canal had shrunk to a stinking stream, infested with insects, which flowed slowly among carcases of scooters, skeletons of washing machines and bog arum in bloom.

Danilo had looked at the greenish water. Then he had taken the car keys out of his pocket and hurled them with all his might into the canal. The bunch had sailed over the stream and the sandy, reed-covered bank, hit the dyke and fallen back onto the foreshore, disappearing among some big concrete blocks embedded in the dry mud.

This he remembered well, because for a moment he had thought he had better go down and throw the keys in the water in case the old men, who sometimes came to fish from the bridge, should find them and then go and steal his car. But he hadn't done it.

Anyone would have thought that it was mathematically impossible for them still to be there – the current must have carried them away and by this time they would be out in the depths of the sea. But that was in ordinary circumstances. The circumstances in which Danilo found himself were not ordinary; this was his life, and if destiny had decided that he should find them, find them he would.

He ran along the canal, crossed the little brick bridge and went back along to the point where he remembered the keys falling.

He looked down. It wasn't a very big drop. Two or three metres. If he lowered himself down with his arms the jump wasn't impossible.

The problem would come later, when he had to get out.

Twenty metres downstream there was a tree trunk sticking out of the water.

From there I can climb up onto the road.

Danilo took off his glasses and put them in his jacket pocket.

He climbed up on the parapet, took out the chain with the Padre Pio medallion, kissed it and lowered himself down from the edge.

Now he only had to drop down.

It's just a question of finding the courage.

But even if he couldn't find the courage, he'd never be able to pull himself up again with the mere strength of his arms, so . . .

He took a deep breath and let himself go.

He landed up to his waist in water. It was so cold he didn't even have the strength to cry out. A billion needles pierced his flesh and he was immediately caught by the strong current. He had to cling with both hands to some weeds that grew in the cracks between the bricks of the dyke to stop himself being swept away.

He couldn't even rest his feet on the bed, such was the strength of the current. And the weeds, although they were tough, wouldn't support his weight for long.

He started searching for the keys on the bed of the torrent. He let go with one hand and the river pushed him under.

He drank a lot of water which tasted of earth.

He put his head up and started spluttering and then, gasping for breath, started groping around on the bed again. He felt with his fingertips the edges of the concrete blocks covered with algae and the slippery stems of the water plants. It was difficult to move his fingers, which were numb with cold.

They're not here. How could they be? Only a fool like me could have thought that after five years . . .

The branch he was clinging to, without warning, came away from the wall. Danilo felt the current seize him, started thrashing about with his arms and legs like a drowning dog, trying to resist, but it was impossible, so in desperation he tried to grab hold of the concrete blocks, but they were slippery. His knuckles knocked against a steel rod sticking out of the mud. He managed to catch hold of it and hung there, amid the eddies and the deafening roar of the water, like a great big tuna fish caught on a hook.

He knew he couldn't hold on for long – the cold was unbearable and the current was pulling him – but if he let go he would be swept away and would be dashed against the sluicegate a kilometre downstream.

What the hell am I doing?

Suddenly, like a sleepwalker who wakes up to find himself on a ledge on the fifth floor of an apartment block, he was terrified to see what a mess he'd landed himself in. Only suicidal madness could have brought him from the cosy warmth of home to the swirling eddies of a canal in spate.

He exploded into a fusillade of unrepeatable blasphemies which would have damned him for all eternity if he hadn't already been long since doomed, he was sure, to the fires of hell.

He was almost exhausted, he tried to resist, to cling on to the steel rod, but by now only his nose was sticking out of the water, like a shark's fin. He was about to give up when he realised that there was something around the rod, something like a metal ring.

He touched it.

No! It wasn't possible!

In his excitement he almost let go.

The keys!

I've found the keys!

My keys.

All three of them. The one for the car, the one for the front door and the one for the roll-down shutters of the garage.

What an incredible stroke of luck!

No, it was blasphemous to call it luck. It was a miracle. A fully fledged miracle.

When he'd thrown them the keys had hit the dyke, and as they fell the ring that held them together had dropped over the steel re-inforcing rod.

It was a bit like that game in the funfair where if you throw a quoit over a bottle you win a cuddly toy. But he hadn't taken aim. He hadn't even seen the rod.

This meant that God, fate, chance, or whoever it was, had wanted it to happen. What were the odds against such a thing happening? Ten billion to one.

Those keys had remained there, all those years, immersed in the water and mud, waiting for him to go and retrieve them.

Half-drowned and nearly frozen to death, Danilo Aprea felt a sensation of warmth in the middle of his chest which heated him up and banished any doubt or fear about what he was doing, just as a red-hot furnace instantly turns a piece of paper to ashes.

Up there in heaven there was someone who was helping him.

He slipped the keys off the rod and gripped them tightly, digging them into the palm of his hand. Then, confident that he would find a way of getting out of that river, he took a deep breath, shut his mouth, held his nose and let go.

136

The three rusty cables supporting the big banana strained like the rigging of a sailing ship in a northerly gale.

About thirty metres away from the sign, in the Rimor SuperDuca 688TC, Beppe Trecca and Ida Lo Vino were going at it hammer and tongs.

The social worker was lying on his back in the sleeping compartment above the driver's cabin, and sitting astride him, in a cramped version of the 'candlesnuffer' position, Ida was pounding and panting and massaging her small white breasts which spilled out of her black lace bra.

Deafened by the noise of the rain, the thunder and Ida's head bumping against the camper's padded ceiling, Beppe breathed in and out, with his best friend's wife impaled on his penis, and engaged in a battle against his sympathetic nervous system, which had decided to make him have an orgasm in the space of a few seconds. He felt it rise inexorably up through his spinal cord, sink its teeth into his thighs and converge angrily on his pelvis, contracting his muscles.

He must get Ida to slow down, to stop for a moment – just a moment would be enough – because if she went on like this he wouldn't be able to hold out much longer . . .

He grabbed her by the waist, trying to lift her up and take it out of her, but she misinterpreted the gesture, clung to him tightly and, still pumping away, whispered in his left ear: 'Yes . . . Yes . . . You don't know how often I've imagined this moment. Shaft me!'

Okay, so that didn't work. He'd have to find some way of delaying the orgasm on his own – distract himself, think of something disgusting, repugnant, which would calm him down. All he needed was a moment and it would pass.

He imagined he was humping Father Marcello. That hideous creature, pitted with smallpox and ravaged by psoriasis, who lived in the rectory. He imagined he was penetrating the flaccid, hairy buttocks of the priest from the Italian Marches.

That did indeed help a little. But as soon as he saw, in the half-light cast by the reading lamp, Ida's pleasure-distorted face and noticed how, as if in a trance, she was putting her forefinger between her wet lips and passing it over her tongue, he couldn't resist, he tried to think of something more depressing, he thought of Cortés's *noche triste* and the gruesome massacre of the Aztec people, but it wasn't enough, he came anyway, in silence.

He couldn't tell which was greater, the pleasure or the disappointment. He stifled a cry and hoped he could stay erect long enough for her to come too.

He gritted his teeth, as poker-faced as a Prussian infantryman.

'Beppe . . . Beppe . . . Oh my God, I'm going to come . . . I'm coming! I'm coming!' Ida moaned, digging her fingernails into his shoulders.

At that very same moment, outside, a gust of wind gave the coup de grâce to the camp sign, the cables snapped and the banana broke free of its moorings and took flight, whirling like a boomerang across the car park, skimmed over the soft drinks kiosk, over a few caravans and sliced into the right-hand side of the camper.

Beppe yelled, clutched hold of Ida and thought a bomb had gone off. Mario Lo Vino had discovered them and put an explosive device under the camper. But then he noticed that one wall was split, having been opened like a can of tuna by half a yellow banana, complete with brown stem, which was peeping in between the dinette and the kitchen area.

The sign must have hit a critical point in the camper's structure because the roof came away from the side with a sinister groan and the wind, howling through the gap, ripped it off and carried it away.

The two poor lovers, wet and naked, clung together in terror on what was left of the sleeping compartment.

137

On the way home Quattro Formaggi hadn't met a soul. This hadn't surprised him, it was a special night.

His night.

Nearly five kilometres of flooded streets, fallen trees and billboards torn down by the storm. In Piazza Bologna the great luminous display showing the temperature and the time of day, on top of the General Insurance building, had blown off and was dangling from an electric wire; there wasn't a single police car or fire engine about.

Quattro Formaggi stopped outside Mediastore, chained his scooter to the usual post and limped towards the narrow steps that led down to his basement flat. He opened the door and closed it behind him, leaned against it, opening his mouth, and despite the pain in his shoulder, where Ramona had stabbed him with the mirror, he began to weep with joy, shaking his head.

He looked at his hands.

Those hands had killed.

Quattro Formaggi gulped and a lustful shiver gripped his thighs and tightened his groin. His legs sagged and wouldn't support him, and he had to grab hold of the bolt of the lock to stop himself falling.

He kicked off his shoes and undressed, throwing everything on the floor as if his clothes burned his skin.

He shut his eyes and saw the girl's hand holding his cock, on her finger the silver skull ring. He searched for it in his trouser pocket and when he found it squeezed it hard between his hands and then swallowed it.

138

Rino Zena, the Great General of the Ants, had drawn up his army of insects in a million battalions.

The ants were good and obedient and would do anything he told them to do.

Listen to me!

The ants, under the violet sky, stood to attention and billions of black eyes looked at him.

I want you all to go into my right arm.

His arm – at least as he saw it – was a long black tunnel which widened out into a sort of piazza from which five small blind tunnels led off.

The ants piled up inside it, one on top of the other, and completely filled it, right down to the end, to the very tips of the fingers.

And now if you all move together, in the right way, my arm will move and my hand will pick up the mobile phone.

Well done ants, you're doing a great job.

139

Danilo Aprea had returned to the garage, he was shivering all over and his teeth were chattering. The cold had got into the very marrow of his bones.

'My God it's cold! I'm freezing!' he kept repeating, trying to open the door of his Alfa Romeo.

At last the half-rusted key entered the lock.

Danilo held his breath, closed his eyes, turned and, as if by magic, the knob of the door lock rose.

'Yes! Yes! Yes!' He started doing pirouettes with his arms in the air like a flamenco dancer, then he got into the car and stripped off his soaking wet clothes, socks and shoes and was left naked.

He needed something to wrap himself up in at once, or he'd die of cold.

He looked to see if there was anything on the back seat that he could put over himself . . .

That tartan blanket Teresa used to use for picnics.

. . . but couldn't see anything. What he did find was the bottle of grappa he had bought on the way back from the funeral. It was still half full.

'Just what I need!' He gulped it down in such a frenzy he almost choked himself. The alcohol went through his oesophagus and warmed his guts.

That's better. Much better.

But it wasn't enough. He needed something to wear, but he didn't want to go up to the flat.

Finally he stripped the black-and-white check plush covers off the front seats and put them on, one over the other. He stuck his head through the hole for the headrest and his hands out between the laces at each side.

'Perfect.'

But it still wasn't enough. He needed to switch on the car and turn the heating up to maximum.

He put on his glasses, inserted the key in the ignition and turned.

Not a tremor, not a lurch, from the starter.

The battery was flat.

What did you expect after all this time?

He put his hands on the steering wheel and gazed in a stupor at the bottle of Arbre Magique scented with forest pine.

It was really strange that the car hadn't started.

Something didn't add up. How come God had made him find the keys but hadn't recharged the battery?

He took another sip of grappa and, rubbing his arms, began to reflect on the nature of the two miracles.

As a matter of fact, if you thought about it, they were two very different phenomena.

That the key ring should have caught on the steel rod was highly unlikely – more unlikely than winning the first prize in the lottery. But there was a chance of it happening. A pretty remote one, admittedly, but there was a chance.

If the battery had recharged itself, it would have been a mega-miracle, like the Madonna of Civitavecchia weeping blood or Jesus Christ multiplying the loaves and fishes.

A real marvel which, if the Church had come to hear about it, would have turned that garage into a place of worship.

Danilo was sure the Lord was helping him, but not to the extent of performing an out-and-out miracle which broke the laws of physics. The finding of the keys was definitely a miracle, but – so to speak – a second-class one, whereas the battery's recharging itself would have been a first-class one, almost on a par with an apparition of the Madonna.

'Fair's fair! What you've done is enough for me, Lord. Don't worry, I'll see to the battery,' said Danilo, and at that very moment the garage door rolled up. The dazzling light of two tungsten headlamps lit up the whole place as bright as day.

Danilo tried to disappear under the dashboard.

Now who's this, for fuck's sake?

A big silver four-by-four with smoke-grey windows and golden wheel rims cruised past and parked in the space next to his.

It's that stupid little moneybags Niccolò Donazzan. His parents have bought him a car worth fifty thousand euros. He's probably coming back from the disco stoned out of his mind.

What the hell did his parents think they were doing?

Danilo looked at his watch. It was full of water and the hands had stopped. He must hurry, the first commuters would be leaving home soon.

Niccolò Donazzan got out of the four-by-four wearing a black bandanna, a buckskin jacket with fringes and, attached to his belt, some tatters of denim.

At the same moment the other door opened and out came a dumpy girl with straw-coloured hair braided into two plaits à la Pippi Longstocking. Some huge, very dark shades were wrapped round her face. She wore a violet coat with a fur-lined hood and trousers so baggy the crotch sagged down to her knees.

He saw his young neighbour unceremoniously grab the girl by the arms and dump her on the bonnet of the Alfa.

'What the f . . . ?' Danilo clapped his hand over his mouth.

Donazzan leaped on the bonnet himself and started kissing her passionately, like he was trying to rip her tongue out of her mouth.

Danilo, hidden below the dashboard, cursed and swore.

What now?

Those two randy little bastards meant to screw on his bonnet. Young Donazzan was tugging at the zip in the girl's trousers. She was banging her head against the glass, squirming and moaning, though the boy had hardly touched her yet. Either she was epileptic or she was so spaced out she thought she was acting in a porno film.

Donazzan tried to calm her down: 'Pannocchietta, if you keep wriggling about I won't be able to undo your trousers . . . '

Danilo straightened up and shouted: 'That's enough, you two! I'm going to tell your father!'

When he heard that voice explode in the silence the boy popped up in the air like a champagne cork and fell off the bonnet.

Pannocchietta gave a querulous squeal and jumped off the car too.

They clung together, frightened and guilty, trying to make out who had spoken.

'Did you hear what I said? I'm going to tell your father. And I'm going to bring it up at the next residents' meeting.'

At last the two saw that the head of a large man dressed like Fred Flintstone was sticking out of the window of the Alfa Romeo.

It took Niccolò Donazzan a few moments to realise that it was Aprea, the guy from the second floor. He was so terrified by the threat to involve his father that he didn't even wonder why Aprea was sitting in his car at three o'clock in the morning dressed like that.

'I'm sorry . . . We didn't know you were there. Or . . . ' he stuttered.

'Or what, son?'

'Or I wouldn't have done it. I swear! I'm terribly sorry.'

'Okay.' Danilo assumed a contented expression. 'Give me your jacket. I'll give it back to you tomorrow.'

'My jacket? But it's an Avirex original . . . It was a present from . . . ' The boy was evidently very attached to his horrendous biker jacket.

'Do you have a hearing problem? Your jacket! And cut the chat. Do you want me to go and see your father?'

'But . . . '

'But nothing. And give me your trousers and boots too.'

Donazzan hesitated.

'Give them to him, go on. Can't you see what a state he's in? He's out of his mind, he looks mad enough to carry out a massacre,' interposed the girl, quite calmly. She had recovered well from the fright and had lit herself a cigarette.

'She's right. Can't you see what a state I'm in? You'd better listen to your girlfriend.'

She corrected him, puffing out a cloud of smoke: 'I'm not his girlfriend.'

In the meantime the boy had taken off his boots and trousers.

'Give them to me. Quick.' Danilo reached out of the window and took them. 'And now you've got to push the car. My battery's flat.'

Niccolò Donazzan said to Pannocchietta: 'Come on, help me. His battery's flat.'

The girl slouched reluctantly round to the boot: 'What a drag!'

The two of them started pushing the car towards the garage door.

Danilo waited till they were going fast enough, released the clutch and went into second. The engine lurched three times and fired in a cloud of white smoke.

Those two kids, too, Danilo said to himself as he drove out of the garage, *were angels sent by the Lord.*

140

The ants were moving his arm, but in the effort thousands of them were dying and being carried out of the cave and replaced by others that arrived from distant regions of his body.

Rino Zena couldn't understand why they were sacrificing themselves to help him.

The ones inside his hand moved together, with coordination, so as to enable his fingers to bend and grasp the mobile phone in his trouser pocket.

Well done . . . Well done, little ones.

Now call Cristiano. Please . . .

Rino tried to imagine his thumb pressing the green key twice.

141

In the Zena household the phone didn't often ring.

And after a certain hour it never did.

A couple of times Danilo Aprea, during one of his fits of missing Teresa, had called after eleven o'clock at night in search of a friendly voice. Rino had listened and had then explained to him that if he ever tried phoning him again at that hour he would make him swallow his teeth.

But that night, after months of silence, the phone started ringing.

The sound took a full three minutes to wake Cristiano, who was asleep upstairs.

He was having a bad dream. He was very warm and had soaked the sheets in sweat, as if he had a fever. He lifted his head and noticed that the gale showed no sign of abating. The broken shutter was knocking against the window. The gate outside was rattling in the wind.

His mouth was parched.

The ham.

He reached out and picked up the bottle off the floor, and as he drank he noticed that the phone was ringing downstairs.

Why doesn't papa answer it?

He flapped the blankets to disperse some of the heat from inside the bed and then, since the phone kept on ringing, with a yawn he thumped twice on the thin wall that divided his bedroom from his father's and in a sleepy voice shouted: 'Papa! Papa! The phone! Can't you hear?'

No reply.

Just for a change he was drunk, and when he was drunk a herd of wild gnu could charge through his bedroom and he wouldn't notice.

Cristiano stuck his head under the pillow and in less than a minute the phone stopped ringing.

142

After the banana had turned the camper into a coupé, the storm had lifted up the cushions, the crockery, the Chinese food and everything else and dumped them in the car park.

Beppe Trecca and Ida Lo Vino lay locked in each other's arms, naked and trembling, on the roofless sleeping compartment. Over their heads the sky twisted and howled, and the clouds, as huge as mountains, were lit up by thousands of electric flashes.

At the boathouse a rubber dinghy rose up from the ground and whirled out into the middle of the swollen river.

'Beppe, what's happening?' Ida shouted, trying to make herself heard above the noise of the storm.

'I don't know. We've got to get out of here. Let's go down this way,' he replied, and eventually, hand in hand, they succeeded in picking their way through the remains of the camper and retrieving their clothes, which were scattered across the car park.

They took refuge in the Puma.

Luckily Beppe had his gym bag in the car. He put on his track suit, she a T-shirt and his bathrobe.

He wanted to tell her that he loved her more than he had ever loved anyone and that he felt as if he had been born again and that he would do anything in the world to keep her, but instead he just held her tight and they sat watching the storm finish sweeping away the campsite.

Then she stroked his neck. 'Beppe, it took me a while to understand it but now I'm sure. I love you. And I don't feel guilty about what we did tonight.'

Automatically Beppe said: 'What do we do now? What about your husband?'

She shook her head. 'I don't know . . . I'm so confused. I only know I love you. I love you very much.'

'I love you too, Ida.'

143

'The river's wide. On the other side a speeding car that leaves a trail of smoke and me. And this green and lovely world, so indifferent, unreal . . . ' sang Danilo Aprea at the wheel of his Alfa Romeo, going through the storm.

What a great feeling, to be driving again.

What a pleasure to hold the steering wheel in your hands and feel the warm blast from the radiator on your feet. The petrol gauge indicated half-full. In the stereo was a cassette of Bruno Lauzi's greatest hits.

Why on earth did I ever give up driving?

He no longer felt cold, his mind seemed to have cleared and his sadness had suddenly vanished, to be replaced by an alcoholic euphoria.

Danilo turned the radio up higher: ' . . . because everything has changed and its arms no longer open to one like me who hungers for something rare and new.'

'The Eagle' had always been his favourite song.

He found himself thinking about the trip he'd taken with Teresa in autumn 1995. How often they had listened to that record. And sung along with it.

Back then he'd had an Autobianchi A112 with a white roof.

He and Teresa had just got engaged. And they'd decided to go and spend three days at Riccione. How young Teresa had been then. How old would she have been?

Eighteen, nineteen.

She was slim. Since then she had put on a bit of weight, but she still had a good figure.

What a holiday! Three days making love in a room in a small hotel. And they weren't married, either. They got married soon afterwards. Teresa's parents hadn't come to the wedding. They didn't want their daughter to get married so young, especially not to a man who was out of work.

'But Teresa took no notice of them. She wanted to marry me,' said Danilo with a proud smile.

She had kept calm even on the day she'd given birth to Laura. She had told the obstetrician: 'Let my husband in. I want to hold his hand.'

'My husband,' said Danilo out loud. And he repeated it: 'My husband.'

144

Why hadn't he thought of it?

The ants couldn't speak for him.

It had been wrong to make so many of them die for that pointless phone call.

Rino Zena, imprisoned in his own body, didn't even know if the ants had really moved his arm, pushed the right key. And now, besides, he couldn't hear anything. The rain had disappeared. Quite suddenly. And that violet sky, towards the horizon, was covering over with bluish clouds.

It's too silent. Perhaps I've been buried alive.

"Every creature on Earth is alone when it dies," his mother always used to say.

But she was wrong: when you die the ants are there to keep you company.

They were standing in straight rows and were looking at him in silence. They only moved their antennae. He could feel billions of little eyes on him.

Please, little ants, try again. One more phone call, that's all. Please.

145

While Cristiano Zena, with his head under his pillow, tried to rock himself to sleep by moving his backside, some fragments of a dream came up to the surface from the depths of his subconscious and a knot of sadness blocked his throat.

He couldn't remember why, but in the dream he was in despair (perhaps because of something he didn't know how to do) and had decided to kill himself.

He was in the bathroom of the school gym, though it looked a bit different. In the first place it was a thousand times bigger and secondly it had lots of showers, all of which were spraying out hot water and steam. In the middle of the room was a bath tub, one of those old-fashioned ones with animal-like legs, and Cristiano was in it with the water up to his shoulders.

He had to commit suicide and he had to be quick – if anyone came in and caught him in the nude he'd look stupid. His classmates would soon be coming. He could hear them in the gym, playing basketball. Voices calling to each other. The ball rebounding from the backboard.

He was holding in his hand one of those old cut-throat razors, with a square, rusty blade. Slowly, without any fear, he had opened the veins in his wrists, but no blood had come out.

It's always like that when you cut yourself, a moment passes and then the blood starts to flow, but this time at least a minute had gone by.

So Cristiano had inspected the wound and out of the edges some ants had emerged, each with a bit of green leaf in its mouth.

And then he had woken up.

He hoped it wasn't one of those episodic nightmares which start again as soon as you fall sleep.

The telephone started ringing again.

So it wasn't a wrong number . . .

'What a fucking nuisance!' He got out of bed, snorting with exasperation, and went out onto the dark landing in his vest and pants. It was freezing cold and all the warmth in his body was immediately dispersed.

He opened the door of his father's room and fumbled for the light switch.

'Papa, can't you he . . . '

The bed was empty.

He's downstairs.

If he couldn't hear the phone, half a metre from his ear, he must be absolutely smashed.

146

Danilo Aprea could have gone on driving for ever. How wonderful it would be to leave behind you that thunderstorm and that grey land infested with snakes and scorpions and head south.

Down to Calabria. To Sicily. And from there further down. To Africa. Further and further down. The deserts. The savannahs. The Nile. The crocodiles. The blacks. The elephants. South Africa. Down to . . . What was it called? Cape Horn? There he would stop. On the southernmost tip of Africa, looking out in silence at the ocean.

' . . . rare and new that I'll never get from you. A moving car is enough to make me ask if I'm alive,' sang Bruno Lauzi. Danilo started beating the time on the dashboard.

In South Africa he would make a new start. *In those under-*

developed countries all you need is a bit of initiative and you'll have a thriving business in no time. And he would find a young woman, a woman much younger than him, and have a baby with her.

Then he would call Teresa. 'Hi, it's Danilo, I'm in South Africa, I just wanted to let you know I'm not dead, on the contrary I'm in the best of health and I've had a baby with a girl . . . ' he recited, pushing down the accelerator. The hand of the speedometer reached a hundred and forty km/h. The streetlamps flashed by on either side in a long trail of sodium.

He turned onto the flyover that led to the bank.

147

While the phone kept on ringing, Cristiano Zena went downstairs, cursing his father for a drunken fool.

It was dark and the television, which was on, spread a pale blue glow over a segment of the room. Inside the screen was a guy with a grey fringe and a big moustache who was drawing graphs.

The lounger was empty. The blanket screwed up into a heap. The heater off.

Where is he?

Running towards the phone, he passed the window just as an electric vein was printed on the dark blue sky, lighting up the highway and the yard as bright as day.

The van's not there.

That was why he wasn't answering.

So all his talk had been a load of hot air. 'I'm not going on the raid . . . I'm this, I'm that . . . ' And then he'd gone along anyway. It was strange, though. His father never changed his mind. Maybe he'd just gone out to find another tart.

Typical! It's probably him on the phone, the idiot.

Cristiano clumsily hurdled the folding chair and landed with one foot inside a pizza box while the other hit a bottle of beer and sent it rolling across the floor. A slice of ham got stuck to his heel. He picked up the handset and yelled into the microphone: 'Hallo! Papa?'

A clap of thunder deafened him, rattling the windows.

Cristiano put his finger in his free ear. 'Hallo? Hallo? Papa, is that you?'

Silence.

'Hallo? Hallo?'

Tekken!

His guts tightened in a spasm of pain and his scrotum shrunk between his legs as fear crept through his veins.

It was him, Tekken. Without a doubt. He wanted revenge.

He had waited for his father to go out before coming after him.

He took a deep breath and growled: 'Tekken, is that you? I know it's you! Speak, you bastard! What's the matter, haven't you got the guts? Answer me!'

The rain, quite suddenly, as if the sky had been ripped apart, started beating against the window panes and at the same moment the television went off and Cristiano found himself in the dark.

Don't worry. It's only a power cut.

'Is that you, Tekken? Admit it! It's you!' he repeated, without the same conviction as before.

He peeled the ham off his sole with his finger, squatted down shivering on the sofa and sat there in silence with the receiver pressed to his ear, waiting for the CLICK of Tekken hanging up.

148

Rino Zena thought he could hear Cristiano's voice.

But it was so far away that it might be only his imagination.

If only he could speak to him. If the ants had succeeded in moving his arm, perhaps they could move his lips, his jaws and his tongue and make him speak.

No, that was too difficult for insects.

The problem now was those big black clouds on the horizon which were covering the violet sky and which were bringing darkness back over him, the desert of stones and the ants.

Yes, he must try.

149

Danilo Aprea came off the flyover and turned down Via Enrico Fermi, singing at the top of his voice: 'And its arms no longer open to one like me who hungers for something rare and new that I'll never get from you . . . '

The bank was there. Right in front of the car.

Danilo kissed the Padre Pio medallion, sat back in his seat and aimed straight at the cash machine.

' . . . A moving car is enough to make me ask if I'm alive . . . ' he yelled along with Bruno Lauzi.

The right wheel hit the kerb at a hundred and sixty kilometres an hour and broke away from the axle and the car capsized and rolled over and over and crashed into an enormous concrete flower-pot which had been put there by the newly elected local council to stop cars entering what they called the historic centre.

Danilo dived through the windscreen, flew over the flowerpot and landed face-first on a bicycle rack.

He lay there with his arms outspread, but then slowly, as if he had been resuscitated, he got up and started staggering about in the middle of the little pedestrian precinct.

Where his face had been there was a mask of raw flesh and glass. With his only working eye he saw a greenish glow.

The bank.

I hit it.

He saw the cash machine spewing out money like a slot machine gone mad. But instead of coins there were green banknotes as big as hearth rugs.

I'm rich.

He knelt down to pick them up and spat out a lump of blood, mucous and teeth.

I don't believe it. I'm dying . . .

If he had been capable of laughing he would have.

How absurd life is . . .

If he had remembered to fasten his seat belt he wouldn't have dived through the windscreen and perhaps he would have lived, but now Laura . . . Laura was . . .

He fell down and death took him on the ground, in the rain, as he laughed and moved his fingers, gathering his money.

150

Beppe Trecca was driving along with his heart full of emotion. In front of him were the red tail lights of Ida's homeward-bound Opel.

He kept shaking his head incredulously. First making love to Ida, then the camper being wrecked and them, like the heroes of an adventure film, coming out alive . . . It had been incredible.

Now it was hard, very hard, to accept not being able to spend the rest of the night together, not seeing the dawn light as they lay in each other's arms.

In thirty-five years of life he had never known sexual intercourse be so intense and . . .

Mystical? Yes, mystical.

He smiled happily.

"Beppe . . . Beppe . . . Oh my God, I'm going to come . . . I'm coming! I'm coming!" he had heard her moan just before the camper was seized by the tempest like the house in *The Wizard of Oz.*

'You put on a great show,' he congratulated himself.

And that embrace in the midst of the fury of the elements had sealed a union that would not end like that, with a simple fuck. Before they had parted Ida had hugged him tightly and had started crying and then said to him: 'Beppe, do you really want me?'

'Yes, I really do.'

'Even with the children?'

'Yes, of course.'

'Then let's go through with it. Let's talk to Mario and tell him everything.'

For the first time in his life Beppe Trecca had not hesitated. 'All right. I'll speak to him.'

His mobile phone started ringing.

Ida.

He replied immediately.

'Beppe, darling, this is where I turn off. You sleep for both of us – I won't be able to. I'll be thinking about you all the time till I see you again. I can still feel you inside me.'

The social worker gulped. 'And I won't be happy till I can kiss your lips again.'

'Can I call you tomorrow?'

'Of course.'

'I love you.'

'Not as much as I love you.'

As Ida's car winked its indicator and turned off onto the sliproad for Varrano, Beppe Trecca declaimed in a melodramatic tone: 'Mario, there's something I've got to tell you. I've fallen in love with your wife. She loves me too. I know . . . It's hard, but these things can always happen in life. I'm terribly sorry. But the force of love is greater than anything else. Two soulmates have found each other, so please set us free.'

Pleased with his little speech, he pressed the CD button and started singing along with Bryan Ferry: 'More than this . . . '

151

He could just imagine him, that bastard Tekken, cackling away with his friends. Cristiano Zena couldn't see what was so funny.

From tomorrow I'm going to have to watch my step. He curled up on the sofa and grasped his big toes with one hand. *Tekken will be out for revenge.*

A clap of thunder exploded directly overhead and, with a strange stereo effect, he heard it croak through the earpiece of the telephone.

Cristiano opened his mouth and clamped his hand over it to stop himself screaming with fear.

He's here! He's near here! He called to find out if I was alone.

He dropped the phone and rushed over to check the door. He gave the key several turns in the lock and put on the safety chain.

The windows!

He lowered all the shutters, including those of the kitchen and the bathroom, and went back to the telephone, groping his way along in total darkness.

He picked up the receiver from where it lay on the cushions of the sofa. The line was still open. 'Tekken, you bastard . . . I know you're here . . . I'm not an idiot. You'd better keep away from the house . . . '

Will he have seen that the van's not here?

' . . . if you don't want me to wake my father. Do you hear, you bastard?' He closed his eyes and listened again. For a while he could only hear his own suppressed breathing, but then he thought he could hear something else. He pressed the receiver to his ear and held his breath.

What is it?

The wind, something rustling and rain on leaves, the sound rain makes when it falls on a tree . . .

He's just outside here.

The saliva had gone from his mouth. His guts had contracted like a dry floorcloth.

But there was something else. Something barely audible. Heavy breathing. Someone with asthma. Someone who was hurt. Someone who was . . .

. . . *wanking.*

Cristiano grimaced and shouted angrily: 'Who the hell are you? Some kind of maniac? Answer me, you bastard! You bastard!'

"I'm shitting myself with fear," he would have liked to add.

Why don't you just hang up? Go on! Pull out the plug from the wall. Check that the door's locked and go back to bed.

Then the voice of a dead man calling his name.

152

'Cri . . . stia . . . no . . . ' said the ants.

Rino Zena's tongue was a solid, black mass of swarming insects. And his lips, and also his teeth, his jaw and his palate, were covered with ants advancing in orderly fashion, moving like members of a vast ballet troupe, dying to enable him to speak to his son.

153

'Papa?' yelled Cristiano Zena, and as he shouted he understood that the ram raid on the cash machine had gone wrong and he imagined his father riddled with bullets and dripping with blood, pursued by police cars, and at the roadside murmuring his name into his mobile phone. 'Papa . . . ' but he couldn't go on. Someone must have sucked all the air out of the room and he was suffocating. With what little breath was left in his lungs he sighed: 'Papa? Papa, what's happened? Are you hurt? Papa! Papa?'

The television suddenly came back on at full blast. On the screen there appeared the man with the fringe and the big bushy moustache, drawing a curve and yelling obsessively: 'The variables x, y, z . . . '

154

Why couldn't he hear anything any more?

Rino Zena wasn't sure the ants had managed to pronounce Cristiano's name, or even that they had managed to phone him.

There were few of them left alive now.

He wondered if they could still do it.

155

Cristiano Zena pleaded into the microphone, while the storm wrapped itself around the house as if it was trying to suffocate it: 'Papa! Papa! Answer me, please, please! Where are you?'

He waited, but he got no reply.

He felt like shouting, like smashing everything to pieces.

Calm. Keep calm. He bent his head back and breathed in, and then said: 'Papa, listen to me, please. Tell me where you are. Just tell me where you are and I'll come.'

Nothing.

His father didn't reply and Cristiano felt the rock that was obstructing his throat melt and flow down into his chest like hot lava and . . .

You're not going to start crying!

. . . he put his hand over his mouth and held back the tears.

Why don't you answer me, you bastard?

He waited for a long time, for hours it seemed, but every now and again he couldn't help repeating: 'Papa, papa . . . ?'

(You know why he doesn't answer you.)

No, I don't.

(Yes you do . . .)

I don't! Fuck off.

(It's true.)

No! No!

(He's . . .)

HE'S DEAD. ALL RIGHT. HE'S DEAD.

That was why he wasn't answering any more.

He had gone. Gone away. For ever.

It was what he had always known would happen, because God is an arsehole and sooner or later takes everything away from you.

156

What if this is hell?

Rino Zena was among the ants inside the huge cavern that was his mouth.

157

He takes everything away from you. Everything . . . sighed Cristiano Zena, and his legs would no longer support him and he slumped down onto the floor and there in front of the television screen he opened his mouth and let out a mute scream and he repeated to himself that this was a very important moment, a moment he would remember for the rest of his life, the exact, precise moment when his father had died, and he had heard him die over the telephone, so he must print it all on his memory, every thing, every detail, nothing must escape him of that moment, the most terrible moment in his life: the rain, the thunder and lightning, the pizza al prosciutto under his foot, the mustachioed guy on TV and that house which he would leave. And the darkness. He would certainly remember that darkness which surrounded him on every side.

Sniffing, he said, almost in a whisper: 'Please papa! Answer me! Answer me . . . Where are you? You can't do this to me . . . It's not fair.' He sat down on the sofa, put his elbows on his knees, wiped his nose with the back of his hand and started squeezing his head and sobbing: 'If you don't tell me where you are . . . what can I do . . . what can I do . . . there's nothing I can do . . . Please, God . . . Please . . . Help me. Please God, help me. I've never asked you for anything . . . Anything.'

158

'San Rocco . . . Agip . . . p . . . '

159

Cristiano jumped to his feet and shouted: 'I'm coming, papa! I'm coming! I'll come straight away! Don't worry. I'll be there in a minute! Leave it to me.' To make quite sure, he waited a little longer, then he put down the receiver and started pacing backwards and forwards in the sitting room, unable to decide what to do.

Right . . . Right . . . Think, Cristiano. Think. He held his head between his hands. *Right . . . The Agip service station. Where the hell is the Agip service station at San Rocco? But which service station? The one on the sliproad? Or the one just before San Rocco? Isn't that Esso? Yes, it's Esso.*

He stopped and started slapping himself on the cheek. *Remember. Remember. Remember. Come on. Come on. Come on.*

No, he just couldn't remember, but it didn't matter, he would find it somehow.

He bounded upstairs, three steps at a time. He dashed into his room and started getting dressed and talking out loud: 'Wait a minute . . . Wait a minute . . . There's no Agip petrol station at San Rocco . . . The only one is the one after the bypass. Near the woods. The one with the carwash. Perfect! I've got it!' He put on his trousers. 'Quick! Quick! Quick! I'm coming, papa! But where are my shoes?'

He ransacked the room. He lifted up the bed and he saw them. As he sat on the floor putting them on, he stopped and began shaking his head.

But how the hell am I going to get there?

It was an incredibly long way.

He remembered that while he was going to bed his father had told him he was waiting for Danilo and Quattro Formaggi.

How did they get here, then?

On the Boxer.

Perfect!

He rushed downstairs, tripped over his shoelaces and flew down the second flight. He got up off the floor and . . .

I'm not hurt, I'm not hurt.

. . . put on his windcheater and limped out of the house.

160

161

Where was the Boxer?

Cristiano had searched all over the yard and had even gone down to the lamppost at the side of the highway where Quattro Formaggi usually left it, but the fucking scooter wasn't there.

So Quattro Formaggi didn't come. Maybe Papa went to pick them up. I don't understand.

How could he get to San Rocco now?

Two minutes out in that deluge had been enough to drench him from head to foot. The water was coming from the sky in buckets, and when a flash of forked lightning fell Cristiano saw the clouds catch fire overhead.

He went out onto the highway, having made up his mind to go on foot, but after twenty metres he stopped and came back again.

Where am I going? It's too far.

He had no idea how many kilometres it was to the Agip petrol station.

What about hitch-hiking?

(Forget it. There's not a single car on the roads.)

The bus?

(No buses after eleven o'clock.)

He slapped himself on the forehead with the palm of his hand.

He must call Quattro Formaggi or Danilo. *Of course!* Why hadn't he thought of it before?

He ran to the front door, gripped the handle and turned, but nothing happened. With a sinking feeling, he searched in his pockets for the keys.

They weren't there.

He had left them indoors.

And I closed the shutters too.

He picked up a flowerpot and hurled it at the door and then, for good measure, kicked the steps and started jumping up and down in the rain, howling and cursing the fact that he wasn't yet fourteen and didn't have a scooter of his own.

If I had a scooter, I'd already be . . .

(Stop it! Think!)

He wanted to, but he couldn't. As soon as one thought appeared in his mind it was erased by another.

If only he'd repaired the Renault . . . I could have driven it.

(Yes, but he didn't. So . . .)

His head was whirling. He could only imagine himself on a scooter speeding towards his father.

Cristiano closed his eyes, threw his head back and opened his mouth.

The bicycle!

What a fool he was! There was the bicycle in the garage.

He ran round to the back of the house, lifted a flowerpot and picked up the key. He put it in the lock and wrenched up the rolling door so violently he could have given himself a hernia. He switched on the long neon light and the bicycle, a green-and-grey mountain bike, was there, hanging by its wheel from a hook.

His father had given it to him six months earlier. He had won it with fuel points. But Cristiano hated pedal bikes, he only liked motorbikes. And it had remained hanging there, with the transparent plastic still covering the saddle and handlebars.

Cristiano stood on an old radio and took it down. It was covered in dust and its tyres had gone down quite a bit. For a moment he hesitated, wondering whether to look for the pump.

There's no time.

He hoisted the bike onto his shoulders and carried it out onto the road, then he took a run-up, jumped on and started pedalling for all he was worth.

162

As the Puma slid through the rain as silently as a torpedo, Beppe Trecca sang at the top of his voice: 'More than this . . . There is nothing . . . ' He wagged his head in time with the windscreen wipers.

His knowledge of English was pretty basic, but he understood what the great Bryan Ferry was saying.

More than this there is nothing.

It was absolutely true. What more could he want? Ida Lo Vino was crazy about him and he about her. And that was a truth, like the fact that that night it had seemed as if the end of the world had come.

There was so much joy and love in the social worker's heart that next day he was personally going to clear up the sky and make the sun shine again.

I feel like a god.

He remembered the camper. The banana.

Ernesto would have a fit when he saw what had happened to his motor home.

But he's so cautious, he's bound to have an insurance policy that covers natural disasters. And anyway, quite frankly, who gives a damn about such material things?

He felt like dancing. For a while he had attended a samba course organised by the local council and had discovered the pleasures of the ballroom.

Ida likes dancing too.

But this called for something with a bit more beat. He took the CD box out of the pocket in the door and looked for something more lively. He didn't have much, to be honest. Supertramp, the Eagles, Pino Daniele, Venditti, Rod Stewart. Then in the last compartment he found a Donna Summer compilation and put it in the stereo.

Perfect.

He turned the volume right up.

The singer started screaming: 'Hot stuff. I need hot stuff.' And Beppe joined in.

Hot stuff. I need hot stuff.

'You must be a little raver, then, like Ida,' Beppe chuckled.

Who would ever have thought Ida was such a sex-bomb? Even in his wildest fantasies he had never imagined that the coordinator of voluntary activities, that quiet, retiring woman, that loving mother, had so much fire inside her.

A thrill of pleasure ran up into his neck and ignited his spinal nerves.

What about me? I held out like the Alamo. Not a hint of a wilt. As steady as a rock.

It must have been those three Xanaxes and the melon vodka that had enabled him to stop himself coming immediately.

Different music. He needed different music. He took out Donna Summer, picked up the box and was putting in a Rod Stewart CD when suddenly he heard a bang on the front of the car and for a split second something dark slid over the right-hand side of the windscreen.

Beppe let out a yell and, without even thinking, rammed his foot down on the brake and the car skidded across the wet asphalt like a crazed surfboard and came to rest on the roadside verge, half a metre away from the trunk of a poplar.

Beppe, terrified, with his arms stiff and his hands glued to the wheel, heaved a sigh of relief.

Phew!

A little further to one side and he'd have crashed into that tree.

What had happened?

He had hit something.

A tree trunk. A dog. Or a cat. Or maybe a seagull.

The place was full of those big birds that had abandoned the seas for the inland rubbish dumps. It must have been dazzled by the headlights.

He switched off the radio, unfastened his seat belt and got out of the car with a plastic bag from the Esselunga supermarket over his head. He walked round the front of the Puma and with clenched fists exclaimed: 'Noooo! Sod it!'

I'd only just had the bodywork repaired.

The right side, above the front wheel, was dented, and there were bumps on the bonnet too. The right windscreen wiper was bent.

What did I hit – a brown bear? Will the insurance cover something like this? he wondered, getting hurriedly back into the car.

He shut the door and selected first gear, then changed his mind, put it into reverse and started driving backwards.

I want to have a look, just out of curiosity . . .

He travelled less than fifty metres and then braked. The white light of the reversing lights had fallen on something brown curled up on the edge of the asphalt.

There it is!

A dog! A damned dog.

He reversed three more metres and noticed that the dog was wearing a pair of trainers with the Nike ticks on their soles.

163

He must have done about ten kilometres and he still hadn't reached the turning for San Rocco.

Maybe it's been blocked off. Or perhaps I didn't see it and I've come too far.

Cristiano Zena was pedalling in the middle of the deserted highway. The dim light produced by the dynamo barely lit up a couple of metres of road in front of the wheel.

He was shivering with cold, but inside his jacket he was boiling. The rain was stinging his eyes, the back of his head and his ankles were frozen and he had lost all feeling in his chin and ears.

He had been a fool not to pump up the tyres. It was costing him three times the effort. If he didn't find the turning soon he was sure his legs would give out.

Now and then, for an instant, the electric glow from a flash of lightning would light up the storm-battered fields as bright as day.

Since he had spoken to his father on the phone more than half an hour must have passed.

If only I had a motorbike . . . I'd be there by now.

It was incredible, whatever he did his brain always returned to motorbikes.

An articulated lorry with a German number plate came up behind him, immense and silent like a humpback whale. It honked its horn and emitted a yellowish glare.

Cristiano dived in towards the side of the road.

The HGV went past very close, drenching him from head to foot.

While he was still recovering from the fright he saw up ahead a blue sign proclaiming: SAN ROCCO 1000 METRES.

So the turning did exist and he was near to it!

Though his fingers were stuck to the handlebar and his nose was an icicle, he stood up from the saddle, leaned forward, gritted his teeth, and with his muscles flooded with lactic acid pushed on the pedals, which were as stiff as rusty cogwheels, and shouted: 'Go, Pantani! Go!' Finally he took the turning at full speed and found himself, leaning over steeply to the side, in a puddle just around the bend. The wheels lost their grip and the bicycle skidded as if on a sheet of ice.

When he opened his eyes again he was lying on the ground. He got up and checked what he'd done to himself. He had grazed the palm of one of his hands, his jeans were torn at the knee and the sole of one shoe had been pared away by the asphalt, but apart from that he was all right.

He straightened up the handlebar and set off again.

164

I've hit a man.

Beppe Trecca, with his head turned back over his shoulders, continued to gaze through the rear window at the bundle on the road. His heart was pounding and his armpits were as cold as ice.

(Go and see.)

It wasn't my fault. I was driving very slowly.

(Go and see.)

The idiot must have crossed the road without looking.

(And you were putting the CD into the stereo.)

A second. It only took me a second . . .

(Go and see!)

If he's . . .

(Go and see!!)

He must be hurt. Maybe he's not too badly injured, though.

(GO!!!)

He ran his tongue over his teeth in his dry mouth and said: 'Okay, I'm going.'

165

The road to San Rocco was narrower and had no reflectors at the sides.

Cristiano, with his head down, was pedalling and following the white line painted on the asphalt. The wind had dropped and the rain fell so straight and fine that, in the feeble light from the bicycle's lamp, it resembled the silvery hair of a witch.

He didn't want to look up. Hidden in the darkness that surrounded him there might be castles haunted by skeletons, alien spaceships standing in the wilderness, chained giants.

When he finally did raise his head he saw a luminous dot which grew into a yellow patch and then turned into a sign, in the middle of which a black patch formed and became a dog-like creature, with six legs and with fire coming out of its mouth.

The Agip service station.

166

The man was lying at the edge of the road, curled up, as if he was asleep in bed.

Beppe Trecca walked around him, his left hand pressed to his lips. His tracksuit was already soaking wet and his hair drooped over his forehead like a mass of blond fusilli.

He's black.

One of the many Africans who worked in the local factories, or more likely one of the countless illegal immigrants.

The man wore a heavy beige jacket, and underneath it a coloured tunic from which protruded two long black legs and two enormous basketball shoes. Beside him lay a big red rucksack.

Senegalese, I should think.

His face wasn't visible. His head was tucked into his chest. His hair was short and flecked with grey.

Breathe deeply, the social worker told himself. *And take a look at him, to see who he is.*

He felt like throwing up. He breathed in several times through his nose, then at last found the strength to bend down over the body. He reached out, stopped for a moment with his hand five centimetres from the man's shoulder, then gave a gentle push, and the man rolled over on the asphalt.

His face was round. His forehead broad. His eyes closed. Well shaven. About forty years old.

I've never seen him before. I don't think so, anyway.

Beppe often met Africans in the course of his work. In the factories. In the centre for hospitality and orientation. Or when he went to visit them in the dormitory houses.

What now?

He tried shaking him and then stammered: 'Can you hear me? Can you hear me? Can you hear my voice?' but the man neither replied nor moved.

What now?

The only thing his mind was capable of producing was that fatuous question.

What now?

He felt bewildered, so confused that he didn't even notice the rain and the wind.

What if he's . . . ?

He couldn't even bring himself to finish the sentence.

That word was too terrifying for him even to think of it.

No! He can't be.

He tugged at his arm.

If he was . . . Beppe's life would be over.

His first thought was for Ida. If he went to prison all his plans for a life with her would be destroyed. There would be lawyers, court cases, police . . . *But Ida and I must . . .* He couldn't breathe. *It wasn't my fault. It was an accident.*

Why did I get out that CD?

Two yellow headlights appeared out of the darkness and dazzled him.

This is it.

Beppe Trecca, bent over the body, raised his arm and shielded his eyes.

167

'Papa! Papa! Rino! Rino!' shouted Cristiano Zena, with the crossbar of the bicycle between his legs.

The huge yellow canopy of the filling station cast a cold light on the pumps and on the pools of rainbow-coloured fuel oil.

His father wasn't there. Nor was the van. There was nobody there.

Not once along the way had it crossed his mind that when he got to the filling station his father might not be there.

The panic that had lain hidden in the coils of his guts, and that had only made itself felt when instilling in him the doubt that the turning for San Rocco might have been closed off, now invaded his head and blocked his throat.

'You said . . . the Agip . . . And I'm here. I know . . . I've been a long time, but it was a long way. You . . . said . . . the Agip. Where are you?' he moaned, running his fingers through his wet hair.

He took another turn around the carwash and the cashier's booth.

Go and look further on.

He started pedalling again, but barely two hundred metres from the petrol station the road began to rise gradually and went into the wood.

The light of the bicycle lamp fell on the black tree trunks that lined the roadside.

I don't like this place. He can't be here.

Perhaps the van had been parked before the petrol station and he hadn't seen it as he had gone by.

He was about to turn his bike round when something stopped him. Music, so faint as to be almost imperceptible. It mingled with the rain that lashed the road and the foliage of the trees and with the rustle of the wheels as they turned on the asphalt.

He stopped, with his guts twisting tight and an unpleasant tingling at the back of his neck.

Elisa.

The singer. He knew her.

Elisa singing: 'Listen to me . . . Now I can cry. I know I need you . . . We are light that . . . Like a sun and a star . . . '

He thought he could make out, on the other side of the road, a square silhouette which gradually took on the shape of a van. The rain was drumming on its bodywork. A dim glow tinged the glass of the window covered with raindrops.

The Ducato!

The music was coming from its radio.

Cristiano couldn't even feel glad, he was so scared.

What if it wasn't his father in the van, but someone else?

Don't be a wimp.

He got off his bike and laid it on the ground as quietly as possible. He tried to swallow, but the saliva had gone from his mouth.

Shit, I'm terrified.

His frozen feet slopped in his shoes as he moved closer. He was less than a metre from the van. He stretched out his hand and felt the bumper. It was dented. And the indicator light was broken.

It was their van all right.

Two steps, grab the handle and . . . I can't.

His legs wouldn't support him and his arms were so tired . . .

If I open the door . . .

All that came afterwards was dripping with blood and soaked with death.

I'm going to call someone . . .

With a sudden lunge he grabbed the handle, opened the driver's door and sprang back, ready to dodge the attack of a murderer.

There's nobody here.

The red display of the car radio on the dashboard lit up the driver's seat. He switched it off. He saw the key in the ignition. Underneath the passenger's seat was the toolbox. He opened it. He took out a long torch. He switched it on. Then he picked up the hammer, got out of the van and opened the big rear door.

But there was nothing in there either, except for a bag of cement, a couple of planks, a plastic bag containing the remains of the picnic, and the wheelbarrow.

Pointing the torch beam at the ground he checked the whole of the layby. Two rubbish bins, a notice saying DANGER OF FIRE, and an electricity hut.

No, there was nothing else.

168

Beppe Trecca was kneeling by the African, awaiting his fate.

The car, which was black with alloy wheels, stopped in front of him with its headlights full on, illuminating the road and the rain.

Beppe couldn't see who was inside.

It looked like an Audi or a Mercedes.

Finally the window lit up and rolled down.

Sitting at the wheel was a man of about fifty. He wore a camel-coloured jacket and a light-blue polo neck sweater. A thick black beard grew almost up to his cheekbones. His hair was slicked back with gel. He had a cigarette in his mouth. He stubbed it out in the ashtray, then moved over towards the passenger's window and, raising one eyebrow, looked out. 'Has he gone?'

Beppe raised his head, stared at him uncomprehendingly and stammered: 'What?'

The man pointed at the body with his chin: 'Is he dead?'

'I don't know . . . I think . . . '

'Did you hit him?'

' . . . Yes, I think so.'

'Is he a nigger?'

Beppe nodded.

'Well, what are you waiting for?' asked the man, as if he was enquiring when the next bus was due.

'What?'

'What are you waiting for? Why don't you just get out of here?'

The social worker couldn't manage to reply. He opened his mouth and closed it again as if a ghost had just stuffed a spoonful of shit down his throat.

The man stroked his beard. 'Has anyone else come past?'

Beppe shook his head.

'Well get moving, then, what are you waiting for?' He glanced at his watch. 'Well, I must be off. Bye, then. Good luck.'

The window rose and the Audi, or whatever it was, vanished as suddenly as it had appeared.

169

Cristiano Zena went out into the middle of the road, with the faint hope that someone would pass by.

How was it possible that this fucking road, which was a constant stream of cars, bicycles and motorbikes in the daytime, could be so deserted at night, as if there were monsters in the woods?

'Papa! Papa! Where are you?' he shouted at length towards the woods. 'Answer me!' His voice died away against the dense vegetation.

I wouldn't go into that wood even if . . .

But, now that he thought of it, the background noise he had heard during the phone call had been that of rain falling among trees.

What if he's in there?

He walked over to the guardrail. There was a gap between the metal strips from where a little path began and threaded its way through the weeds and brambles. Plastic bags, bottles, a condom, an old car seat among the moss-covered rocks. He pointed the torch ahead. Black trunks and a tangle of branches dripping with water.

He took one step, stopped and then started jumping up and down, trying to shake off his fear.

'Why do you do this to me? You bastard! I was in bed . . . If this is a joke . . . ' he muttered between his teeth.

He stood there, rooted to the beginning of the path, shifting the weight of his body from one foot to the other. Then he breathed in deeply and, raising the hammer, took one step and the mud sucked in his shoe, took another and it wrapped round his ankles. He set off down the path and the trees seemed to be waiting for him, stretching out their branches towards him (*Come! Come!*) and anyone might be there in the darkness, ready to leap out from behind a tree trunk and hit him from behind.

He had only gone a few metres but he already felt as if he was a thousand kilometres from the road. The rainwater dripping off leaves and running down tree trunks. The moss soaked with water. The air saturated with water, earth and rotten wood.

He imagined a pack of wolves with eyes as red as molten lava appearing out of the darkness.

His right hand held the hammer aloft, ready to strike anyone who appeared in front of him, while his left hand shone the torch around frenetically.

Sabre-thrusts of light flashed on the big jagged rocks, on the branches, on the trickles of water that dug rivulets in the mud, and on a pair of black boots.

Cristiano screamed, took two steps backwards, tripped over a branch and fell down on his back. He got up again and, with a hand that wouldn't stop shaking, shone the beam of the torch on the boots, the paint-splashed boots, on the cape, grey with an orange reflector strip, that his father used when he worked, on his shaven head immersed in the slime, on his hand and on his mobile phone which lay in a puddle.

170

Beppe Trecca was still kneeling in the rain, beside the corpse, and continued to ask himself: *What are you waiting for?*

The man in the Audi had made it quite clear that he would have driven on if he had been in his shoes.

But that man wasn't him. He wasn't a hit-and-run driver. He helped other people, he didn't abandon them.

(Just call the police and an ambulance. That's all you have to do.)

Why? To ruin my life? If this poor bugger had been injured, or dying, I'd have rushed him to hospital. But like this?

He dried his face with the palm of his hand; he was trembling and his teeth wouldn't stop chattering. He shook the African again. There was no response.

He's dead. That's it. Say it. He's dead.

And so . . . So there was nothing to be done.

Why couldn't he go back in time? Just a little way, just half an hour, to the moment before he had taken out the Rod Stewart CD?

The dreadful idea that there was no way of putting things right, that no one was capable of granting this simple wish, filled him with terror.

(Get a grip on yourself! Accept responsibility for what you've done.)

But what would it change? Nothing. It wouldn't bring him back to life. And I'd be up to my neck in shit.

So one unfortunate life had been snuffed out and another would be ruined for ever.

'There's no sense in it. No sense at all,' he whimpered, with his hands over his face. 'It's not fair. I don't deserve this. I can't do it, just now, when . . . '

Snap out of it! Move. Get into the car and drive away before anyone passes. As the man said: "What are you waiting for?"

Beppe Trecca stood up and, hanging his head, got back into the Puma.

171

Cristiano had imagined a thousand different ways in which his father might be killed (stabbed in a fight or crushed in the wreckage of the Ducato or falling off the scaffolding of a new apartment block).

And he had always imagined that they would give him the news at school. The headmaster calling him: "There's been an accident . . . I'm terribly sorry . . . "

"You don't give a damn, you arsehole," he would answer, and he wouldn't cry. Then he would set fire to their house and sail away on a merchant ship and never return to that fucking place again.

He had never thought he would die in the mud, like an animal.

Or that it would happen so soon.

But it's fair enough.

It all added up. He had started by taking his mother away and now he was taking his father away.

I mustn't cry, though.

He longed to pull him out of the mud. He longed to hug him, but he was paralysed. As if he had been bitten by a cobra. He opened his mouth and tried to spit out the thing that was stopping him breathing.

He kept looking at him because he couldn't believe it, he just couldn't believe it, that that dead man there was Rino Zena, his father.

Finally Cristiano took a step forward. The cone of light from the torch lit up a segment of forehead immersed in the grey slime, the nose, the eyes splashed with earth. The foam at the side of the mouth.

He took the torch between his teeth and with both hands grabbed hold of his father's wrist, trying to pull him up.

Rino Zena's helpless body bent slowly over and leaned sideways against a big rock covered with moss. His head drooped onto his chest and his arms opened out like the wings of a dead pigeon. The rainwater trickled down his forehead and over his earth-clogged eyebrows.

Cristiano put his ear to his father's chest. He couldn't hear a thing. All other sounds were drowned out by the pulsing of the blood in his eardrums and the rustle of the rain falling on the trees.

He knelt there, drying his face with his hand, not knowing what to do, then, after a moment's hesitation, he raised his father's head and pulled up one of his eyelids with his forefinger, revealing a glassy eye like that of a stuffed animal.

He picked up the mobile phone from the puddle. He tried switching it on. It didn't work. He put it in his pocket.

His father couldn't just lie there in a heap like that.

He grabbed hold of his shoulders and tried to sit him up. But he wouldn't stay put. Cristiano straightened him up, but as soon as he let go he slowly flopped down again.

In the end he bored a stick into the ground and propped it under his armpit.

What on earth did he come here for? Why did he leave the van and go into the wood?

He must have had some kind of turn. He'd had a headache all day. He must have got into the van, perhaps intending to go to hospital.

Does this road lead to the hospital?

He had no idea.

But he had been too ill and hadn't made it, and had got out of the van and gone to die in the wood.

Like a wolf.

When wolves are sick they leave the pack and go off on their own to die.

'Why didn't you wake me, you bastard?' he asked him, and kicked the stick, whereupon his father slid back into the mud.

He had to get him out of there. The only way was to grab him by the feet and drag him down to the road.

He got hold of his ankles and started to pull, but immediately let go again as if he'd had an electric shock.

For a moment he had thought a tremor had passed through his father's legs.

Cristiano dropped the torch, knelt on the ground and started frantically feeling his thighs, arms and chest and shaking his head, which lolled from one side to the other.

Was it just my imagination?

He put his hands on his chest, trying to push and repeat 'One, two, three', as he had seen them do on *ER*.

He didn't know how to do it or what the purpose of it was, but he went on doing it for a long time, with no discernible effect except that the muscles of his arms became as hard as marble.

He couldn't go on; he was wet through and frozen stiff. Suddenly all the accumulated tiredness and anxiety crushed him and he collapsed on his father's chest.

He must sleep. Just for a short while. Five minutes.

Then he would take him to the van.

He curled up on the ground beside the corpse. The cold was relentless. He hugged himself, squeezed his arms against his chest to stop the shivers, rubbed his shoulders trying to warm himself up.

He took the mobile phone out of his pocket, but it didn't come on.

Perhaps I could leave him here.

Better in a wood than in a fucking graveyard, with a bunch of strangers . . .

He would decay into compost. No priests, churches, funerals.

The torch, on the ground, painted a luminous oval on a carpet of dead leaves, of twigs, on a tree stump where a cluster of long-stemmed mushrooms grew and on his father's hand.

Cristiano remembered one time when Rino, halfway across a

bridge, had pulled the car over to the side of the road and jumped up onto the parapet. Down below ran the river, flowing between the rocks that protruded from the eddies.

Then he had started walking along, holding his arms out on either side like the acrobats in the circus.

Cristiano had got out of the car and started following his father on the pavement. He didn't know what to do. The only thing he could think of doing was to walk along beside him.

Cars passed by on the road, but nobody stopped.

Without looking at him, Rino had said: 'If you're hoping some-body will stop and talk me into getting down, forget it. Those things only happen in films.' He had looked at Cristiano. 'Don't tell me you're scared I'll fall!'

Cristiano had nodded. He was tempted to grab him by the foot and pull him down, but what if he accidentally knocked him down into the river?

'I can't fall.'

'Why not?'

'Because I know the secret of how not to fall.'

'What is it?'

'Do you think I'm going to tell a snotty-nosed little kid like you? You'll have to find out for yourself. I did.'

'Come on, papa, please, tell me!' Cristiano had protested. His stomach ached as if he had eaten too much ice cream.

'No, you tell me something. If I fall and die, will you go to my grave and pray for your father?'

'Yes. Every day.'

'And will you bring me flowers?'

'Sure.'

'Who'll give you the money to buy them?'

Cristiano had thought for a moment. 'Quattro Formaggi.'

'Some hope . . . He hasn't got a penny . . . '

'I'll take them from the other graves, then.'

Rino had burst out laughing and jumped down from the parapet. Cristiano had felt his stomach ache disappear. Then his father had picked him up and hoisted him over his shoulder like a sack. 'Don't you dare. I'll be watching you from heaven. I won't miss a thing from up there . . . '

On the way home Cristiano had asked a million questions about life and death. Discovering the secret of how not to fall off the bridge had suddenly become the most important thing in the world for him. And with an eight-year-old child's persistence he had kept pestering his father till one morning, while they were sitting on the sofa, Rino had given in. 'You want to know the secret? I'll tell you, but you mustn't tell anyone else. Do you promise?'

'I promise.'

'It's simple: I'm not scared of dying. Only people who are scared get killed doing stupid things like walking on a bridge. If you don't give a damn about dying you can be sure you won't fall. Death picks on the faint-hearted. Anyway, I can't die. Not until the Lord decides I must, anyway. Don't worry, the Lord doesn't want me to leave you alone. You and I are as one. I've got you and you've got me. There's nobody else. So God will never separate us.'

Cristiano, curled up in the mud, took hold of his father's hand and sighed: 'Why did you take him, then? Explain to me, why?'

172

Beppe Trecca was still sitting in the Puma at the side of the road, watching the windscreen wipers do their best to dry the glass.

He couldn't bring himself to drive on.

He was thinking of his mother.

"Don't worry about me, Giuseppe. Go. Go . . . " Such had been Evelina Trecca's words to him, from her bed in a ward of the Gemelli hospital in Rome.

He had sat there beside her, hardly able to recognise her, she was so withered up . . . The cancer was sucking her away.

'Mama, you know if you'd prefer me not to go, I won't. It's no problem. I don't mind,' he had said in a low voice, squeezing her bony hand.

Evelina had sighed, with her eyes closed. 'What's the point in your staying here? With all the poison they put into my veins I can't keep my eyes open. I sleep all day long. Don't worry about me, Giuseppe. Go. Go . . . Enjoy yourself a bit, while you can.'

'Mama, are you sure?'

'Go . . . Go . . . '

And he had gone. Five days. Just long enough to go and see Giulia Savaglia in Sharm-el-Sheikh and come back.

He had met Giulia Savaglia at university and now she was working as a group leader in a tourist village, and she had so warmly invited him to pay her a visit that Beppe had thought . . .

On his third day at the Coral Bay she had explained what he was to her.

How had she put it? *"A special person. A dear friend."*

That same day his mother had died. She had died without her son holding her hand. And she had probably wondered where he had gone after the twenty-five years they had spent together without ever parting. She had died alone.

Beppe Trecca hadn't forgiven himself.

He had shut himself up in his mother's flat at Ariccia, depressed and grief-stricken, not wanting to see anyone. His plans of becoming a sociologist, of applying for a job as a university lecturer, had gone to the devil. Doped up on antidepressants, he had vegetated for a year, and the only things he had succeeded in doing, apart from putting on ten kilos, had been going to church and praying for his mother's soul and taking a diploma in social work without even opening a book.

And the twentieth time that his cousin Luisa had told him there was a vacancy for a social worker in Varrano, he, in exasperation, had applied.

"Don't worry about me, Giuseppe. Go. Go . . . "

I left you to die alone. Forgive me. I ran away. And it wasn't because of Giulia Savaglia, it was because I knew you were going and I didn't have the strength to stay beside you and watch you die.

Suddenly, like a dazed boxer who gets a bucketful of water thrown in his face, Beppe Trecca realised the monstrosity of what he was doing.

Sobbing, he jumped out of the car, ran over to the African, who was lying where he had left him, seized him by the shoulders and said: 'Don't worry. I'll take you to hospital.' He started dragging him towards the car, but stopped, panting, and laid the body on the ground to regain his breath. He took two steps backwards, then like a madman grabbed him by the lapel of his jacket and started shaking him. 'Why do you have to ruin my life? Why did you step out in front of me? What do you want from me? It's not fair! It's not fair! I . . . I haven't done anything to you.' He froze, as if he had no more strength in his arms. The dead man's face a few centimetres from his own.

He looked peaceful. As if he was having a lovely dream.

No, I can't do it.

I wish I could, but I can't.

The realisation that he didn't have the guts to put that man in his car and take him to hospital made him burst into floods of tears. He opened his mouth and, sobbing convulsively, addressed the Eternal Father. 'Please, help me. What must I do? What must I do? Tell me! I can't do it. Give me the strength. I didn't do it on purpose. I didn't see him . . . Please, God, help me.' He started walking around the corpse, then put his hands over his eyes and implored: 'You who can do anything, do it. Perform a miracle. Bring him back to life. I didn't mean to kill him. It was an accident. I swear to you that if you save his life I'll give up everything . . . I'll give up the only beautiful thing in my life . . . If you save him I promise I'll . . . ' He hesitated for a moment. ' . . . I'll give up Ida. I'll never see her again. I swear to you.'

He dropped to his knees and knelt there, motionless, with his head bowed, no longer crying.

173

Cristiano Zena opened his eyes again.

He must have dozed off.

I must get papa home.

It took him a few seconds to realise that the dark thing slowly moving in front of his nose was his father's forefinger.

Wait. Don't move.

It must be another hallucination, like the tremor he had felt earlier when he had taken hold of his legs.

Cristiano slowly raised his head.

No, he hadn't been mistaken. It was moving. Only slightly, but it was moving.

He couldn't restrain himself, he let out a whoop and grasped his father's hand.

The thumb, the forefinger, the ring finger . . . were bending, as if trying to squeeze an invisible ball.

Rino Zena started twisting his mouth and blinking his eyes, and a trickle of white foam emerged from the corner of his mouth.

Cristiano shook him by the shoulders. 'Papa! Papa! Papa! It's me!'

His father started coughing and opened his eyes.

It was too much. Cristiano, in the dark, lost all control; the torch slipped out of his hand, he hugged him and, sobbing, thumped him on the chest. 'You bastard, you bastard. I knew you couldn't die. You can't die . . . You can't leave me . . . I'll kill you . . . I'll kill you, I swear it . . . '

He picked up the torch and shone it in his face. 'Papa, can you hear me? Give me a sign if you can hear me . . . Squeeze my hand if you can't talk . . . '

Suddenly a ten-thousand volt electric shock seemed to go through his father's body, and Rino opened his eyes again, rolled them upwards and started trembling, grinding his teeth and shaking his legs and arms and head as if he was possessed by the devil.

It all lasted less than twenty seconds and then, quite suddenly, the convulsions left him.

Cristiano gave him several slaps on the face, trying to revive him, but it was no good . . .

He wasn't dead, though. His chest was rising and falling.

He must rush to the hospital at once, call an ambulance, doctors . . .

Quick! What are you waiting for?

Cristiano got up and dashed towards the road, but he had only gone a few steps when he tripped, the torch flew out of his hands and he found himself in darkness lying on top of something . . .

He reached out and touched it, trying make out what it was. It was soft, wet and covered with wool and cloth and it had . . .

Hair!

He jumped to his feet as if he'd been snatched by an invisible hand and, backing away, put his hands in front of his mouth and shouted: 'Jesus Christ! Jesus Christ! Jesus Christ!'

He picked up the torch and with a trembling hand shone it down on . . .

Fabiana!

With her eyes open. Her mouth open. Her arms open. Her legs open. Her jacket open. Her blouse open. Her head open.

A gash began from her hairline, ran down her rain-spattered forehead and split one of her eyebrows in two. Her piercing hung from a strip of pink flesh. Her hair was soaked in blood and earth. Her eyes staring. Her bra torn. Her bosom, breastbone and stomach covered with some reddish stuff. Her trousers pulled down to her knees. Her legs scratched. Her violet panties torn.

His guts churning, Cristiano backed away and opened his mouth, trying to gulp down air, but a wave of warm stuff came up and he puked out a stream of sour liquid and then, groaning, fled into the wood, but after a few dozen metres he fell to his knees and, clutching a tree trunk, tried to vomit again but without success.

He wiped his mouth with the back of his hand and told himself he hadn't seen anything, that it was only a nightmare and that he must pull himself together, get out, out of there, and everything would be all right again.

'Pull yourself together. Now you're going to go away, very calmly.'

He must go out onto the road, pick up his bicycle, ride home and get back into bed.

I can do it.

So why couldn't he get to his feet, why did he keep seeing Fabiana's eyebrow split in two and that strip of flesh with the ring hanging from it and those blue eyes flooded with rainwater?

The secret was not to think, to give yourself simple orders and to carry them out one by one.

Now get up.

He breathed in and, using the tree trunk as a support, got to his feet.

Now go out onto the road.

He stood up and although his legs seemed to belong to someone else he started to walk, holding his arms out in front of him, through the dark vegetation. And at last he came out onto the road. He climbed over the guardrail and started running down the slope, forgetting his bicycle. Suddenly the wood was lit up by a beam of light.

Stop them.

He stood in the middle of the road and raised his arms, but at the last moment, when the car's headlights were about to light him up, an impulse made him dodge sideways and jump behind the guardrail before he could be seen.

Lying in the stream that flowed along the roadside he wondered why he hadn't stopped that car.

174

Beppe Trecca got back into his car, sniffling.

The Lord hadn't performed the miracle, but he hadn't given him the courage to take the man to hospital either.

The social worker turned the heating right up, pushed down the clutch, selected first gear, glanced in the mirror and nearly dropped dead on the spot.

The African was standing there peering in at him through the rear window.

175

Stop it. Stop thinking.

He must get his father and carry him away and stop wondering what the hell had happened in that wood. Cristiano Zena returned to the van, banishing the vision of Fabiana dead. He climbed into the back and started rubbing his body with a piece of cloth to relieve the cold that had penetrated his bones.

He hauled out the wheelbarrow and went into the wood.

176

'What happened? I can't remember anything.' The African was sitting next to Beppe Trecca, who was driving along at twenty kilometres an hour with an expression of terror on his face.

He couldn't even look at him, he was so terrified. This guy sitting beside him had come back, like Lazarus, from the realms of the dead.

Beppe was so shaken that he couldn't even feel happy.

(You asked for a miracle and the miracle happened.)

But how can it be? A miracle? Happening to me? What sense does it make? Why has God helped a pathetic little jerk like me?

(The will of Our Lord is inscrutable.)

How often he had uttered this platitude to get himself out of difficult situations. Now he understood its meaning to the full.

The social worker plucked up courage and, without turning, managed to stammer out: 'How are you feeling?'

The man massaged his neck. 'My head hurts a bit and I've got a pain here, in my side. I must have fallen over. I don't know what happened, I can't remember anything . . . ' He was confused. 'I was about to run across the road and then everything went blank. I woke up on the ground with your car nearby. Thank you, friend.'

Beppe opened his eyes wide. 'What for?'

'For stopping to help me.'

He doesn't even realize that I knocked him down.

A sense of wellbeing relaxed his abdominal muscles and the social worker knew that God was with him and that he might have been too hard on himself.

He glanced at the African. He didn't seem to be badly hurt. 'Would you like me to take you to hospital?'

The African shook his head and became as agitated as if Beppe had suggested calling in at the local branch of the Northern League. 'No! No! I'm fine. It's nothing. Could you drop me at the next crossroads, please?'

He hasn't got a residence permit.

'Perhaps you ought to see a doctor.'

'It's nothing, friend.'

'May I at least ask you what your name is?'

The black man seemed to hesitate for a moment about whether to tell him or not, but then said: 'Antoine. My name's Antoine.' He pointed to the road. 'Here, drop me here, please. This is fine. This is where I wanted to get to.'

Beppe stopped the car and looked around. There was a crossroads with a winking traffic light, and, all around, a wasteland.

At the end of the plain, beyond the factories and the electricity pylons, a faint glow had stolen a piece of sky from the night.

'Here? Are you sure?'

'Yes, yes. This is fine, friend. Stop here. Thank you very much.' Antoine opened the car door and was about to get out when he stopped and stared at him. Beppe saw shining in those big brown eyes the mystery of the Trinity. 'Can I ask you something?'

Beppe Trecca gulped. 'Yes, of course.'

The African opened his rucksack, took out a bunch of socks made of a spongy white material and held them out to him. 'Do you want them, friend? They're pure cotton. A hundred per cent. I'll give you a good price. Five euros. Only five euros.'

177

Cristiano Zena, with his chest right up against the steering wheel, was driving the van downhill round the hairpin bends.

The Ducato's engine, in second gear, was howling.

Cristiano knew that he ought to change gear, but until the bends finished he wasn't going to take that risk.

Dawn had come at last and the rain had eased off a bit. The headlights projected two ovals onto the road, which was strewn with earth and puddles and with branches that brushed against the underside of the Ducato.

Cristiano glanced back. Lying on the floor, side by side, were Rino Zena and the corpse of Fabiana Ponticelli.

Fabiana's body was swarming with evidence. He was an expert on these things, he had seen loads of TV detective films, and it's well known that if you look under the victim's fingernails you find the skin of the . . .

There was a sort of CLICK in Cristiano's mind, a momentary blackout.

. . . and there were bound to be millions of other clues, and it wouldn't take the police five minutes to find out . . .

(What?)

Nothing.

178

Beppe Trecca, with three packets of socks in his hand, entered his studio flat. He undressed in silence and took a boiling hot shower, his mind a total blank. He put on his pyjamas and lowered the shutters. Outside the rain had stopped and the day had taken possession of the world. The sparrows on the cypresses were timidly beginning to chirp, as if to say: 'Wasn't that a terrible night? It's over and life can start again.'

Beppe stuffed his earplugs into his ears and slipped under the blankets.

179

Cristiano Zena turned off the woodland road and found himself just outside Varrano.

He had almost made it. He had to drive through the village and take the highway. He turned down a wide, tree-lined avenue and decided that it was time to change up. He glanced at the lever of the worn-out gears. He grasped it and was about to go into third when he heard his father's dark voice saying:

(The clutch. Are you going to push that bloody clutch or aren't you?)

He pressed down the pedal and got into third at the first attempt.

When he looked outside again he noticed that at the end of the avenue there was a glow which tinged the tops of the plane trees blue and orange.

The police!

His heart missed a beat and he instinctively slammed on the brakes. The van came to an abrupt halt with a screech of brakes and then started moving forward in fits and starts for ten metres before stalling in the middle of the road.

Cristiano clung to the steering wheel without breathing. Then he closed his eyes and clenched his teeth.

What now?

He opened his eyes again and saw some men in phosphorescent yellow uniforms stretching long tapes from one side of the avenue to the other. Right beside them was a police car and a lorry with flashing orange lights.

A policeman came towards him, waving his signalling disc.

Cristiano tried to swallow, but couldn't. He kept his head down, because he didn't want the policeman to see how young he was.

Quick!

He turned the key and the Ducato started lurching forward, pushed by the starter.

The policeman had stopped fifty metres away and was telling him to turn back.

Now then . . .

(Push down that bloody clutch!)

He puffed out his cheeks in exasperation, stretched out his leg and with the tip of his toe pressed down the pedal.

Good.

(Now put it into neutral. It's the middle one.)

After several attempts he decided that he had found neutral. He turned the key again and this time the engine fired. He selected first gear and gradually released the clutch. The van moved, he pulled the wheel round and turned back.

On the highway he passed long articulated lorries with foreign number plates advancing one behind the other like a caravan of elephants. The sky had turned dark grey and to the east a thin strip of light was beginning to brighten the plain. The outline of the house seemed to emerge like a black bunker from the mist that enveloped the fields and the road.

He parked the van, switched off the engine and got out. He opened the rear doors.

His father had fallen on top of Fabiana's corpse and under the bicycle. His head lay in the middle of the remains of the barbecue and a Peroni beer label had got stuck to his cheek.

Cristiano climbed in and checked to see if his heart was still beating. He was alive. He got hold of his feet and pulled him out of the van, taking care not to knock his head against anything. He slid him down into the wheelbarrow again. Then he closed the doors and wheeled him towards the house, but when he reached the door he remembered that he didn't have the keys. He found them in one of Rino's trouser pockets. He opened the door.

After several attempts he managed to hoist him onto his shoulders and slowly, bending under sixty-eight kilos, he went up the stairs. Exhausted, without a trace of strength left, he laid his father on the bed.

Now he had to undress him, but that was something he knew how to do. How many hundreds of times in the past had his father had to be put to bed pissed out of his mind?

180

If there was one thing Dr Furlan was crazy about it was ziti alla genovese.

Put three kilos of onions into a large saucepan, add celery, carrots and a piece of lean veal and simmer all day over a low flame.

The onion gradually turns into a dark, delicious-smelling sauce, which you pour over the ziti together with a generous handful of grated parmesan and a few leaves of basil.

Fantastic.

Dr Furlan's wife made it extra tasty by adding a little bacon fat. And she cooked it for so long that nothing was left of the veal but the memory.

The problem was that Andrea Furlan, after losing the basketball final at the club, had returned home at midnight howling with hunger, had opened the fridge and wolfed down half a casserole of the stuff without even heating it up, and then, not content with that, had added three slices of a pie filled with endives, olives and capers, and two sausages.

In that state he had collapsed into bed. He had woken up three hours later for his shift in the ambulance.

Now, as he sat between Paolo Ristori, the driver, and nurse Sperti, he could feel the onions and sausages trying to climb their way back up his digestive system. He felt terribly sick and his stomach was as tight as a basketball.

What he would really have liked to do was get into the back and take a five-minute nap on the stretcher while those two fools bickered with each other.

With a disgusted grimace on his face, Furlan observed Ristori.

The driver was chewing gum and flashing his lights obsessively at a lorry full of pigs which wouldn't get out of the outside lane. He thought he was Michael Schumacher. On the pretext that he had to get around quickly he drove like a maniac.

'So anyway he crapped in his pants . . . ' said Michela Sperti, a blonde girl muffled up in her orange uniform. Underneath her jumpsuit (Paolo had seen her once in a bikini at the local swimming pool and had had a shock) she was a mass of muscles so precise and well-defined they looked like so many fishes piled up one on top of the other. Her enthusiasm for body-building had cost her her tits and her menstrual cycle.

Ristori gave her a quick glance. 'Are you telling me your boyfriend crapped in his pants during the preliminary rounds of Mr Olympia?'

'Yes. While he was on the platform doing the poses.'

'No . . . please . . . ' stammered Andrea, and putting his hand in front of his mouth he gave an onion-flavoured belch that almost knocked him out.

'Well, if you stuff yourself with Guttalax three hours before the competition . . . ' Michela started biting her fingernails.

'Why the hell did he do that?' asked Ristori.

'He was three hundred grams overweight. He would have been excluded from his category. The idiot had drunk half a bottle of Ferrarelle mineral water that morning. He went to the sauna, he sweated like a pig, but it was no good, he didn't lose half a gram. So he realised his intestine must be full. And he purged himself, but it took effect just when he was doing a front double bicep.'

Furlan saw the house and pointed to it: 'Slow down! Slow down! This is the place. Stop.'

'Okay, boss.' Ristori flicked the indicator and swerved abruptly, entering the front yard of the Zenas' house at full speed, skidding on the gravel and stopping half a metre short of a Ducato van.

Michela rounded on him furiously. 'You bastard! The next time you do a sudden turn like that I swear I'll punch you on the nose.'

'Ooh! Who are you, then? Shanna the She-Devil?'

Furlan took his first-aid case and got out of the ambulance. The fresh air made him immediately feel better. He went towards the front entrance of the house. The door was open.

Ristori with the stretcher and Sperti with the oxygen cylinder followed him into the house, shoving each other aside like two teenagers.

The doctor found himself in a large room. A table covered with beer cans. Some white plastic chairs.

What a dump.

In the half-light he could just make out a figure sitting on a folding chair.

Furlan went over and saw that it was a tall, thin, stork-like boy who was looking at them blankly. He wore a long orange bathrobe and a pair of baggy underpants. He was pale and had dark rings around his swollen, bloodshot eyes. When he saw them enter he did nothing but open his mouth.

He's either high or in shock.

'Was it you who called 118?' Ristori asked the boy.

He nodded and pointed to the stairs.

'You look a bit strange. Are you all right?' nurse Sperti asked him.

'Yes,' the boy said, as if in slow motion.

Furlan looked around. 'Where is he?'

'Upstairs,' said the boy.

Furlan dashed up and in the first room found a shaven-headed man covered in tattoos lying on a mattress. He was squeezed into a pair of flannel pyjamas with blue and white stripes.

As he opened his case Furlan took a quick glance around the room. Heaps of dirty washing. Shoes. Big boxes. Hanging on one wall was a large flag with a black swastika.

He stopped himself flying into a rage. This wasn't the first and it wouldn't be the last bloody Nazi skinhead he'd happened to help while doing this job. *How I hate these bastards . . .*

He bent over and grasped the man's wrist. 'Sir? Sir? Sir, can you hear me?'

No response.

Furlan got out his stethoscope. The heart was beating. And the rhythm was regular. He took a pencil out of his jacket pocket and pricked the guy's forearm with the point.

The man didn't show any reaction.

He turned towards the boy, who was leaning against the door-post, gazing at him listlessly.

'Who is he? Your father?'

The boy nodded.

'How long has he been in this state?'

The boy shrugged. 'I don't know. I woke up and found him like that.'

'What did he do last night?'

'Nothing. He went to bed.'

'Was he drinking? There are a lot of beer cans here.'

'No.'

'Does he take drugs?'

'No.'

'Please tell me the truth. Does he take drugs?'

'No.'

'Did he take any medicine?'

'No, I don't think so.'

'Is he suffering from anything? Illnesses?'

'No . . . ' Cristiano hesitated, then added: 'Headaches.'

'Does he take anything for them?'

'No.'

Furlan couldn't make up his mind whether the boy was lying.

It's not your problem, he said to himself, as he always did in such cases.

The doctor said to Ristori, pointing to the boy: 'Take him outside, please.'

He untied his tunic. Then he lifted the man's eyelids and with the help of his torch examined his pupils. One was dilated, the other contracted.

Ten to one a brain haemorrhage.

The Nazi, in his misfortune, was lucky: the Sacred Heart Hospital in San Rocco had opened a new intensive care unit barely a year earlier and the guy might even live to tell the tale.

'Let's ventilate him, pack him up and deliver him,' he said to nurse Sperti, who quickly put the endotracheal tube down the patient's throat. He in the meantime cannulated his forearm.

They put him on the stretcher.

And carried him away.

181

In later years Cristiano Zena remembered the moment when they carried his father away on a stretcher as the one that changed his life.

More than when he had pedalled through the rain believing that the turning for San Rocco had been closed off, more than when he had found his father lying dead in the mud, more than when he had seen Fabiana Ponticelli's corpse.

The world changed and his life became more important, worthy of having its story told, when he saw old baldy's head disappear into the ambulance.

AFTER

They've entered your name in a big game.

Edoardo Bennato, 'Quando sarai grande'

Monday

182

In the early hours of the morning the storm which had raged all night over the plain moved out to sea, where it worked off what was left of its anger by sinking a couple of fishing boats and then, tired and enfeebled, died off the Balkan coast.

The eight o'clock television news barely mentioned the storm and the fact that the Forgese was in spate, because during the night a well-known TV presenter had been kidnapped on the outskirts of Turin.

A watery sun spread its rays over the grey, sodden countryside, and the inhabitants of the plain, like crabs after the passing of the backwash, stuck their heads out of the holes where they had taken shelter and, like little accountants, began to assess the damage.

Trees and billboards blown down. A few old farmhouses stripped of their roofs. Landslides. Flooded roads.

The habitués of the Café Rouge et Noir thronged round the marble counter and looked at the glass display where the famous croissants filled with white chocolate were kept. They were there. And if the croissants were there it meant that life was going on.

The front page of the local paper was occupied by a photograph of the waterlogged fields taken from a helicopter. The Forgese had broken its banks a few kilometres upstream of Murelle and had overflowed, swamping factories and farms. In one vineyard a group of Albanians sleeping in a cellar had narrowly escaped drowning. A boy in a canoe had rescued an entire family.

Luckily nobody had been hurt apart from one Danilo Aprea, forty-five years old, who, either through drunkenness or through falling asleep at the wheel, had lost control of his car and crashed at high speed into a wall in Via Enrico Fermi, Varrano, and been killed.

183

Professor Brolli was bent over a table in the bar of the Sacred Heart Hospital, quietly drinking a cappuccino and watching the pale sun melt like a knob of butter in the centre of the grey sky.

He had a short torso, a disproportionately high neck and long, gangly limbs.

His curious physical conformation had earned him many nick-names: flamingo, grissino, goofy, vulture (undoubtedly the most apposite given the almost total absence of hair on his head and the fact that he often operated on near-corpses). But the only nickname he liked was 'Carla'. After Carla Fracci. They called him that because of the almost balletic grace and precision with which he handled a scalpel.

Enrico Brolli had been born in Syracuse in 1950, and now, at the age of fifty-six, was head neurosurgeon at the Sacred Heart.

He was tired. For four hours he had had his hands inside the skull of a poor devil who had been brought in with a brain haem-orrhage. They had got to him in the nick of time. Half an hour more and he would have had it.

While he was finishing his cappuccino he thought of his wife Marilena, who was probably already waiting for him outside the hospital.

He was free for the rest of the day and they had arranged to meet up to go and buy a new fridge for their house in the moun-tains.

Brolli was exhausted, but the idea of strolling through the shop-ping mall with his wife and then going to have a picnic in the country, with the dogs, appealed to him.

He and Marilena loved the same little pleasures. Going for walks with Totò and Camilla, their two labradors, sleeping in the after-noon, having an early supper and staying at home, on the sofa, watching films on DVD. Over the years Enrico had smoothed away his rough edges till he and Marilena were like two cogs in a single mechanism.

In the mall he also wanted to buy some osso bucco to cook with saffron risotto, then drop in at the video rental shop to hire a copy of *Taxi Driver*.

Before the operation, the sight of the patient's gaunt face and shaven head and all those tattoos had reminded him of Robert De Niro in *Taxi Driver*, and he would have been prepared to bet that the poor devil's condition was the result of a fight. But then, on opening his skull, he had discovered a subarachnoid haemorrhage due to the bursting of an aneurysm, probably of congenital origin.

He joined the scrum of nurses around the cash desk, rummaging in his corduroy trousers for some small change. In the pocket of his white coat his mobile started vibrating.

Marilena.

He took it out and looked at the display.

No, it was from inside the hospital.

'Yes? Hallo? What is it?' he grunted.

'Professor, this is Antonietta . . . '

It was the second-floor nurse.

'What's the matter?'

'The son of the patient you just operated on is here . . . '

'And?'

'He wants to know how his father is.'

'Get Cammarano to speak to him. I'm on my way out. My wife . . . '

The nurse hesitated for a moment. 'He's thirteen years old. And as far as I can tell from the documents he has no other relatives.'

'You want me to do it?'

'He's in the second-floor waiting room.'

'Have you told him anything?'

'No.'

'Hasn't he got anyone – friends, perhaps – that I could speak to?'

'He said there are only two friends of his father's. He's tried ringing them, but he can't get a reply from either of them.'

'I'll be right up. In the meantime, try calling them yourself. If you can't get hold of them, call the carabinieri.' He hung up and paid for his cappuccino.

184

Quattro Formaggi woke up immersed in a lake of pain.

He lifted one eyelid and a ray of light blinded him. He closed it again. He heard the sparrows twittering too loudly in the yard. He put his fingers in his ears, but the movement gave him a sharp twinge that took his breath away. He was overwhelmed by the pain. When he finally succeeded in opening one eye he recognised the dingy wallpaper of his bedroom. He was pretty sure he had fallen asleep beside the crib, so during the night he must have put himself to bed, which he didn't remember doing. He was finding it difficult to breathe. As if he had a cold. He touched his blocked-up nose and realized that it wasn't mucus but congealed blood. His beard and moustache, too, were encrusted with blood.

Now he noticed that in addition to pain there was thirst. His tongue was so swollen it seemed too big for his mouth. But in order to drink he would have to get up.

He jumped to his feet and almost passed out with the pain.

Finally, struggling along on his knees, he set off towards the bathroom. 'Oh . . . Oh . . . Rino . . . Rino . . . You hit me . . . You hit me really hard . . . '

He grabbed hold of the basin, pulled himself up and looked in the mirror. For a moment he didn't recognise himself. That monster couldn't be him.

His chest was covered with big bruises, but what fascinated Quattro Formaggi was his shoulder, which was as swollen and bloody as a Florentine steak.

He hadn't got that from Rino. That was Ramona's work. He pressed his finger on the wound and tears of pain ran down his cheeks.

So it was all true. It wasn't a dream. His body told the truth.

The girl. The woods. The cock in the hand. The rock on the head. The beating. All true.

He put his face up against the mirror, so that the tip of his nose touched the glass, and started spitting mucus and blood.

185

Cristiano Zena was sitting in the waiting room of the intensive care department. He had his head against the drinks machine and was trying desperately to keep his eyes open.

He had arrived on the first bus and a nurse, after asking him a stream of questions, had told him to wait there. Professor Brolli would come and speak to him. He had the shivers and was so tired . . . his eyelids were drooping and his head was lolling, but he mustn't fall asleep.

The nurse hadn't recognised him, but he remembered her well. She was the one who did the night shift.

Cristiano had already been in that hospital two years before, when they had removed his appendix. The operation had gone well, but he'd spent three days in a room next to an old man who had lots of tubes coming out of his chest.

It was impossible to sleep because every ten minutes the old man had a fit of coughing, it seemed that his lungs were full of pebbles. His eyes would bulge and he would start slapping his hands on the mattress, as if he was dying. He never spoke, not even when his son went to see him with his wife and his two grandchildren. They would ask him a lot of questions but he never answered. Not even with a nod of the head.

As he sat on that chair, waiting to find out if his father was alive, Cristiano remembered that during the second night, while he was dozing immersed in the yellowish gloom of the ward, the old man, quite suddenly, had spoken in a hoarse voice: 'Boy?'

'Yes?'

'Listen to me. Don't smoke. It's too horrible a death.' He spoke staring at the ceiling.

'I don't smoke,' Cristiano had defended himself.

'Well, don't ever start. Do you hear?'

'Yes.'

'Good boy.'

When the next day Cristiano had woken up, the old man wasn't there. He had died, and the strange thing was that he hadn't made a sound in passing away.

Now, as he felt the drinks machine vibrating against his temple, Cristiano said to himself that he was going to smoke a cigarette and to hell with the old man, but instead he took his father's mobile phone out of his pocket. He had dried it under the jet of warm air in the hospital bathroom and it had come back to life. For the umpteenth time he dialled Danilo's number. It was unobtainable. He tried Quattro Formaggi. His phone, too, was switched off.

186

As he walked along the corridor of the second floor Professor Brolli thought about the young shaven-headed man covered with tattoos who he had operated on. When he had opened his skull and aspirated the blood he had discovered that the brain haemorrhage, fortunately, had not affected the areas that controlled his breathing, so the patient could inhale and exhale for himself, but in other respects his brain was out of order, and it was impossible to say if or when it would start working again.

In the difficult economic situation in which the hospital found itself, cases like this were real disasters. Comatose patients required the constant attention of the medical staff and monopolised the machines that were necessary for maintaining their vital functions. In that state, moreover, the patient always suffered a general lowering of his immune defences, with secondary infective complications. But that was all part of his work.

Enrico Brolli had chosen this profession and this particular specialisation in the full knowledge of what he was getting himself into. His father had been a doctor before him. What Brolli hadn't given much thought to, during his six years at university, was the fact that *afterwards* you had to speak to the patient's family.

He was nearly sixty now and had three grown-up children (Francesco, the youngest, had decided to study medicine) but he still hadn't developed the doctor's proverbial bluntness in telling the plain truth, yet neither was he very good at sugaring the pill. When he tried to do so he would start stammering and get confused, which only made things worse.

After a career of over thirty years nothing had changed. Every time he had to break some bad news to a patient's family he felt his heart sink in the very same way. But that morning he faced an even more thankless task. Explaining to a thirteen-year-old boy, who was alone in the world, that his father IKEA in a coma.

He peered into the deserted waiting room.

The boy was sitting half-asleep on a plastic chair. His head resting against the drinks machine. His eyes fixed on the floor.

No! No, I can't do it . . . Brolli turned round and walked quickly back towards the lift. *Cammarano can tell him. Cammarano is young and decisive.*

But he stopped and looked out of the window. Hundreds of starlings were forming a black funnel which lengthened out against the white clouds.

He steeled himself and entered the waiting room.

187

Beppe Trecca woke up screaming 'The vow!' He gasped for breath as if someone had been holding his head under water. With feverish, bloodshot eyes he looked around in bewilderment. It took him a few seconds to understand that he was at home in bed.

He saw the face of an African staring in at him through the rear window of the Puma, brandishing a packet of spongy white socks.

What a nightmare that was!

The social worker lifted his head off the pillow. Daylight filtered between the slats of the shutters. He was soaked in sweat and he felt the goose-feather duvet weighing down on him as if he was buried under a ton of earth. In his mouth he still had the revolting taste of the melon vodka. He reached out and switched on the bedside lamp. He screwed up his eyes and they seemed to burn.

I've got a temperature.

He sat up. The room started spinning. Caught in a whirlpool, they all circled past him – Foppe the IKEA chest of drawers, the Mivar portable television, the poster of a tropical beach, the little bookcase crammed with paperback classics and the *Library of*

Knowledge, the table, a packet of spongy white socks, the silver frame enclosing the photograph of his mother, the . . .

A packet of socks?

Trecca gave an acidic burp and sat gazing at them, his body stiff under the duvet. He saw the whole night again as if in a film. The camper, Ida, the sex, the banana, Rod Stewart, him in the rain beside the corpse of the dead African and . . .

Beppe Trecca slapped his boiling forehead.

. . . The vow!

Please, God . . . I swear to you that if you save his life I'll give up everything . . . I'll give up the only beautiful thing in my life . . . If you save him I promise I'll give up Ida. I'll never see her again. I swear.

He had asked God, and God had given.

The African had returned from the realms of the dead thanks to his prayer. Beppe Trecca, that night, had witnessed a miracle.

He picked up the bible that he kept on his bedside table and quickly leafed through it. And he read, struggling to focus on the words:

> . . . So they took away the stone. Then Jesus raised his eyes and said, 'Father, thank you for listening to me. I know that you always listen to me, but I said this for the good of the people around me, so that they will believe that you sent me.' And having said this, he called out in a loud voice: 'Lazarus, come forth!' And the dead man came forth, with his feet and hands wrapped in bandages and his face covered in a shroud. Jesus said to them: 'Untie him and let him go.'

It's identical!

But at what a cost!

I'll give up Ida.

That was what he had said. So . . .

So I'll never see her again. I made a vow.

His head fell back heavily and he seemed to be sucked back down into the black hole.

He had given away his heart in exchange for a life.

I'll give up the only beautiful thing in my life . . .

With a grimace of terror on his face he clutched the sheet, as panic smashed into him like a wave hitting a sandcastle.

188

From the doorway of the waiting room a tall, thin doctor was looking at him.

Who does he remind me of?

Cristiano Zena had to think for a few seconds, then it came to him. He was a dead ringer for Bernard, the vulture in *Popeye*.

After clearing his throat, the doctor spoke: 'Are you Cristiano, the son of Rino Zena?'

He nodded.

The professor sat down, all bent over, on a plastic seat facing him.

His legs were even longer than Quattro Formaggi's, and Cristiano noticed that he was wearing odd socks. Both were blue, but one was smooth, the other ribbed.

He felt an instinctive surge of affection for this man, which he immediately repressed.

'I'm Enrico Brolli, the surgeon who operated on your father, and . . . ' He tailed off and started reading a folder which he held in his hand, scratching the back of his head.

Cristiano stood up. 'He's dead. Why don't you tell me straight out?'

The doctor looked at him with his small head cocked on one side, as dogs sometimes do. 'Who told you he's dead?'

'I won't start crying. Just tell me, so I can go.'

Brolli jumped to his feet and put his hand on the boy's shoulder. 'Come with me. Let's go and see him.'

189

Quattro Formaggi, under the shower, raised his arms, then lowered them again and looked at his hands.

Those hands had picked up a rock and smashed a girl's head in.

The boiling hot water of the shower turned to ice-cold rain and he felt on his fingertips the rough surface of the stone and the spongy texture of the moss and he felt again the vibration on contact with the forehead of that . . .

His head whirled, he fell against the tiles and let himself slip down them like a damp cloth.

190

Rino Zena was lying on a bed, with a turban of white gauze wrapped round his head. A lamp over the headboard formed a luminous oval and his serene face seemed to hover above the pillow like that of a ghost. The rest of his body was hidden under a light-green sheet. All around was an amphitheatre of monitors and electronic gadgets which emitted lights and beeps.

Cristiano Zena and Enrico Brolli were standing a couple of metres from the bed.

'Is he asleep?'

The doctor shook his head: 'No. He's in a coma.'

'But he's snoring!'

Brolli couldn't help smiling. 'Sometimes people in comas snore.'

'He's in a coma?' Cristiano turned for a second to look at him, as if he hadn't understood.

'Go closer, if you like.'

He saw him take two steps forward, hesitantly, as if the bed contained an anaesthetised lion, and then grasp the headboard. 'When will he wake up?'

'I don't know. But it usually takes a couple of weeks at least.'

They stood in silence.

It seemed as if the boy hadn't heard. He stood stiffly, clutching the headboard as if he was afraid of falling. Brolli didn't know how to explain the situation to him. He moved closer to him. 'Your father had an aneurysm. He'd probably had it since birth.'

'What's an aneu . . . ?' asked Cristiano without turning.

'An aneurysm is a small swelling of the artery. A sort of little bag full of blood which isn't elastic like the other blood vessels, and in time it can burst. Your father's burst last night and the blood got into the sub . . . let's say it got in between the brain and the skull, and penetrated the brain itself.'

'What happens then?'

'The blood compresses the brain and creates a chemical imbalance . . . '

'And what did you do to him?'

'We removed the blood and closed the artery.'

'And now?'

'He's in a coma.'

'In a coma . . . ' Cristiano repeated.

Brolli was about to stretch out his hand and put it on his shoulder. But he checked himself. This boy didn't seem to want comfort. His eyes were dry and he was exhausted. 'Your father can't wake up. He looks as if he's sleeping, but he's not. Fortunately he can breathe on his own and he doesn't need to be helped by a machine. That bottle hanging upside down,' he pointed to the drip by the bed, 'serves to feed him; later we'll put a tube into him to take the food straight to his stomach. His brain has suffered very serious damage and now is devoting all its resources to repairing itself. All its other functions, such as eating, drinking and speaking, have been suspended. For the moment . . . '

'But did the vein burst because he did something strange?' Cristiano's voice sounded shrill.

The doctor raised an eyebrow. 'What do you mean, strange?'

'I don't know . . . ' The boy fell silent, but then added: 'I found him like that . . . '

Brolli wondered whether the boy might have made his father angry that evening and now felt responsible. He tried to reassure him. 'He might even have been asleep when the haemorrhage occurred. He had a pretty extensive aneurysm. Did he ever have check-ups? Has he ever had a CAT scan?'

The boy shook his head: 'No. He hated doctors.'

Brolli raised the volume of his voice: 'Don't talk in the past tense. He's not dead. He's alive. His heart is still beating, the blood is circulating in his veins.'

'If I speak to him will he hear me?'

The doctor sighed. 'I don't think so. Until he gives some sign of regaining consciousness such as opening his eyes . . . I don't honestly think so. But perhaps I'm wrong . . . It's a mystery to us too, you know. Anyway, if you want to speak to him you can.'

The boy shrugged. 'I don't want to now.'

Brolli went over to the window. He saw his wife's car standing in the road. He knew why Cristiano didn't want to talk to his father. He felt abandoned.

Dr Davide Brolli, Enrico Brolli's father, had woken up at seven o'clock every day of his life. Exactly half an hour later he would have his coffee. At eight on the dot he would go out, walk down one flight of stairs and enter his surgery, where he would see patients till five to one. At one o'clock he was at home for the beginning of the television news. He ate on his own in front of the television. From one thirty to ten past two he would rest. At ten past two he would go back to the surgery. He would come home at eight. He would have supper and check his children's homework. At nine o'clock he would go to bed.

This happened every day of the year, excluding Sundays. On Sundays he would go to mass, buy the pastries and listen to the football on the radio.

Sometimes, when he had a doubt about an essay or a translation from Latin, little Enrico would go out of the flat, with his exercise book in his hand, and walk down to his father's surgery.

To reach it he had to thread his way along the corridor full of crying babies, prams and mothers. He hated all those little brats because his father considered them his own children. He had often heard him say, 'It's as if he was my own son.'

And Enrico couldn't make out whether his father treated him like those children or treated those children like him.

When Enrico was thirteen Davide Brolli started taking him along on his night calls. He would get him out of bed at any hour of the night and drive him in a blue Giulietta across the dark countryside searching for a farmhouse where there was a child with a temperature. Enrico would lie in the back, wrapped up in a blanket, and sleep.

When they arrived, his father would get out with his black bag and he would stay in the car. If they finished after five o'clock they would stop at the baker's and have a hot croissant, straight out of the oven.

They would sit, as night melted into day, on a wooden bench just by the door of the bakery. Inside there were lots of men covered in flour who transported huge trays of bread and cakes.

'What's it like?' his father would ask.

'Delicious.'

'They make really special ones here.' And he would stroke his head.

Even today Enrico Brolli still wondered why his father had taken him with him at night. For years he had wanted to ask him, but had never had the courage. And now that he felt ready to ask him his father wasn't there any more.

Perhaps for the croissants. His other children didn't like them.

His father had died nearly ten years ago. His intestine had been devoured by cancer. During his last days of life he could hardly speak any more and was doped up on morphine. With a pen he kept writing prescriptions on the sheet. Prescriptions of medicines for flu, scarlet fever and diarrhoea.

Two days before he died, in a fleeting moment of lucidity, the paediatrician had looked at his son, squeezed his wrist tightly and whispered: 'God comes down hardest on those who are weakest. You're a doctor and you need to know this. It's important, Enrico. Evil is attracted by the poorest and the weakest. When God strikes, he strikes the weakest.'

Enrico Brolli glanced at the boy standing by his father, shook his head and went out of the room.

191

Beppe Trecca, sitting at the living room table with a thermometer under his arm, took a sip of Vicks MediNite, which didn't remove the taste of the melon vodka. He gave a disgusted grimace and frowned at his Nokia mobile, which lay in front of him. On the display was a little envelope and beside it the word: IDA.

Can I read it?

He had promised the Eternal Father that he wouldn't speak to her or see her, so, theoretically, if he read a text message he wouldn't be breaking his vow. It was better not to do it, though. He must accept that Ida Lo Vino was a thing of the past, forget her and clear her out of his system.

Like a drug addict.

Cold turkey. And perhaps it would pass.

He would suffer like hell. But that suffering was the coin with which he would repay his debt to the Lord.

And this suffering will make me a better man.

He imagined himself as a kind of movie hero who committed a crime and who as a result of a vow to God became a man of peace, a superior being who devoted his life to the poor and the downtrodden.

There was a Robert De Niro film . . .

He couldn't remember the title, but it was about a knight who killed an innocent man. Afterwards he repented, and as a penance he dragged his weapons and armour, on the end of a rope, through the forests of Brazil and up a high mountain, and then became a priest, helping the Amazonian Indians.

He must do the same.

He picked up his mobile, turned his head away, stretched out his arm as if they were going to amputate it and, clenching his teeth, deleted Ida Lo Vino from his life.

192

'It's me. Cristiano. Papa, listen to me! I'm here beside you. I'm holding your hand. You're in hospital. You've had an accident. The doctor said you're in a coma but that you'll wake up in a few weeks. Now you're repairing your brain because you've had a thingummy . . . A haemorrhage. You needn't worry. I've seen to everything else. Nobody will find anything. I'm good at these things, you know that. So you just stay here and repair yourself and I'll look after everything else. Don't worry. I've tried calling Quattro Formaggi and Danilo, but they don't reply.' Cristiano peered at his father's face, searching for a movement, a twitch of the eyelid, an infinitesimal grimace that might show that he was listening. He looked around, to check once more that no one was there, then stretched out his arm and pressed his forefinger on his father's left eye, first gently, then harder. Nothing. He didn't react. 'Listen to me. I can only come here for a short time every day. So now I'm going home and I'll be back tomorrow.' He was about to get up, but stopped. He put his lips close to his father's ear and whispered: 'I know you can't hear me, but I'll tell you anyway. I told everyone you fell into the coma at home while you were asleep, so . . . ' *nobody will think it was you.*

Cristiano put his hand over his mouth. His stomach had suddenly contracted like a vacuum-packed plastic bag. He sniffed and rubbed his eyes to stop himself crying. Then he got up and left the intensive care ward.

193

Quattro Formaggi was sitting in front of the crib.

He'd had a good wash, had put on his bath robe and then had popped in his mouth all the medicines he had found in the house: three aspirins, two Ibuprofens, one paracetamol, one Sennakot and one effervescent Alka-Seltzer. He had smeared a whole tube of Anusol over his chest and shoulder.

Now he felt better, except that the more he looked at the nativity

scene, spread right across the room, the more he noticed how wrong
it all was. He didn't know exactly why, but it was. Not because of
the soldiers, all the statuettes and dolls, all the cars, or the little
Baby Jesus stuck to the manger. He had botched the world. The
mountains. The rivers. The lakes. They were all badly positioned,
without any order or meaning.

He closed his eyes and felt as if he was levitating from the chair.
He saw a huge valley of red earth which stretched as far as the walls
of the room, and mountains of immensely tall rocks that towered
up to the ceiling. And rivers. Streams. Waterfalls.

And in the centre of the valley he saw the naked body of Ramona.

A dead giant. The girl's corpse surrounded by the soldiers, the
shepherds, the miniature cars. On her small breasts, spiders and
iguanas and sheep. On her dark nipples, little green crocodiles.
Among her pubic hairs, dinosaurs and soldiers and shepherds, and
inside, inside the cavern, the Baby Jesus.

He thought he was falling, opened his eyes and frantically clutched
at the chair. He bent his bruised arm and felt as if a rotating blade
was slicing it in two. He let out a scream of pain.

He waited for the pain to pass before getting to his feet.

Now he knew what he had to do.

He had to go back to the wood, take the little blonde's body and
put it in the crib.

That was why he had killed her.

And God would help him.

194

Beppe Trecca was holding the thermometer in his hands.

*Thirty-seven point five. Must be flu. These things mustn't be under-
estimated, if you don't nip them in the bud they can drag on for
months.*

Better to take a day off work. That would give him a chance to
devise a strategic plan for keeping his vow. He would have to keep
his mobile switched off, and as soon as he recovered from the flu he
would change his number. Then he would have to stop organising

the meetings in the parish hall. And at the office he would have to avoid Mario Lo Vino as much as possible. Of course, Ida knew where he lived, so he would have to move house too. Though in a small village like that they might bump into each other anywhere. Perhaps it would be wiser to rent a flat in some neighbouring village and keep out of the centre of Varrano.

In short, he would have to live barricaded in a bunker, with no job and no friends. A nightmare.

He couldn't do it. There was nothing else for it but to go away. *For a while.*

Long enough for Ida to understand that the former Beppe Trecca, the one who had said he would take her even with the children, no longer existed. Had been the passing dream of a single night.

Keep away until she hates me.

That was the worst thing of all. Worse than the pain of not seeing her again.

Ida would think he was a shit, a despicable person. A disgusting individual who dishonoured her in a camper, made a thousand promises and then ran away like a snivelling coward.

If only I could explain the truth to her.

Perhaps he should confess all to his cousin Luisa and ask her to tell Ida. That at least would alleviate the pain a little. And Ida, who was a sensitive, God-fearing woman, would certainly understand and silently love and respect him for the rest of her days.

No, he couldn't. The value of that damned vow lay precisely there, in that torment. Being mistaken for a monster and not being able to do anything to clear his name. If he eliminated that suffering he would be breaking his promise.

Besides, if he told Luisa about the miracle he would have to tell her about the camper too.

No, it's out of the question. Her husband would kill me.

His mobile phone started ringing.

The social worker looked in terror at the handset vibrating on the table.

I didn't switch it off.

It's her.

His heart started fluttering inside his ribcage like a canary that has just seen a cat. He opened his mouth and tried to gulp down air. A wave of heat swept through him. And it wasn't the fever, but the passion that was burning him. The mere thought of being able to hear that sweet voice made his head spin, and nothing else had any meaning.

Ida, I love you!

He wished he could throw the window open and shout it to the world. But he couldn't.

That bloody African.

He put his hands over his face and through the gap between his fingers peered at the display of the mobile. It wasn't Ida's number. Not even that of her landline. But what if she was calling from another phone?

He hesitated for a moment, then answered: 'Yes? Who is it?'

'Hallo. This is Lance Corporal Mastrocola, calling from the carabinieri station in Varrano. I'd like to speak to Trecca Giuseppe.'

They've found the camper!

Beppe swallowed hard and whispered: 'Speaking.'

'Are you responsible for . . . ' Silence. ' . . . Zena Cristiano?'

For a moment the name meant nothing to him. Then he remembered. 'Yes. Certainly. I'm responsible for him.'

'We need your help. His father has had a serious accident and is now in the Sacred Heart Hospital in San Rocco. His son is there. Could you go to him?'

'But what happened?'

'I'm afraid I don't know. The hospital notified us and we've called you. Can you go? Apparently the minor has no family apart from his father.'

'Well, actually, I . . . I've got a bit of a temperature.' Then he said: 'Never mind. I'll go right away.'

'Good. Could you drop by at our office for the relevant documents?'

'Yes, of course. Goodbye. And thank you . . . ' Beppe hung up and stood there absorbing the news.

He couldn't leave the poor kid on his own.

He took two aspirins and began to get dressed.

195

If Fabiana Ponticelli hadn't decided to go through the San Rocco woods she would have had to make a long, tortuous detour to get back to Giardino Fiorito, the estate where she had lived for fourteen years with her family.

It was nearly six kilometres away from Varrano. You had to get onto the bypass, then take the provincial road for Marzio and after a couple of kilometres turn left in the direction of the motorway. After driving for another two kilometres between warehouses, factories and DIY stores, you would suddenly see in front of you, encircled with walls like a medieval citadel, the exclusive community of Giardino Fiorito.

Two hundred cottages (*ranchos*), built in the early Nineties in an improbable Mexican-Mediterranean style by the celebrated architect Massimiliano Malerba. Blue woodwork, rounded forms and earth-coloured plaster, vaguely reminiscent of the Indian adobes. Half a hectare of garden for each plot. Plus a shop and a sports club with three tennis courts and an Olympic-sized swimming pool. Three entrances manned twenty-four hours a day by private guards in blue uniforms. And halogen floodlights all round the enclosing walls.

The stuck-up inhabitants of the estate were not greatly loved by the people who lived alongside them. Giardino Fiorito had been dubbed 'Escape from New York', an allusion to the John Carpenter film in which the Big Apple, cut off from the world by huge concrete bastions, had been turned into a maximum security prison where all the criminals of America were dumped.

Until the day before, a huge oak tree, more than twenty metres high, had towered over rancho 36, where the Ponticelli family lived. Its green umbrella had arched over Via dei Ciclamini. Its trunk was so thick that three people linking hands could barely embrace it.

The tree had stood there since the days when there had been nothing here but swamps inhabited by snakes and mosquitoes. It had come unscathed through campaigns of deforestation and drainage, it had survived the concrete vice of the village, but not the *phytophotra ramorum*, a parasitic fungus of Canadian origin which had colonised its trunk like tooth decay, turning the solid wood into a spongy, friable substance.

That night the storm had dealt the death blow to the ancient tree, which had come crashing down on the Ponticellis' garage.

If its fibre had not been infected by the mycosis perhaps the oak would have resisted the storm as it had always done in the past and would not have reduced the garage to a heap of rubble, and Alessio Ponticelli would have discovered immediately that his daughter Fabiana had not returned home the night before.

Fabiana's father was a perfect representative of the community of Giardino Fiorito. An entrepreneur and a fine figure of a man. One metre eighty centimetres tall. Forty-two years old. Greying hair and white teeth. Married to Paoletta Nardelli, the former Miss Eleganza Trentino 1987. A good father. He frequented the club and detested politics. And, the most important thing, his money was clean and smelled of sweat. He had made it by creating out of nothing Goldgarden, a firm specialising in products for the garden, with a catalogue ranging from aluminium gazebos to reinforced concrete fountains.

On the night of his daughter's death Alessio Ponticelli had been stuck in Brindisi. The flight that was due to bring him home had been cancelled because of the bad weather.

He had informed his wife, eaten a too-salty pizza and spent the night at the Western Hotel. He had returned home on the first flight the next morning.

The drive to Giardino Fiorito had taken him the best part of two hours. They had diverted the road right out to Centuri. The Sarca bridge had been damaged by the floods and the highway swamped by the waters of the river.

When Alessio Ponticelli stopped his BMW SUV outside his home he thought he must have got the wrong rancho. A green jungle had grown up outside their cottage. It took him a few moments to grasp that it was the foliage of the great oak.

He got out of the car with the sensation that the earth was clinging to the soles of his shoes, pushed through the leaves and branches and saw to his horror that there was nothing left of his garage but rubble. His Bottega Veneta briefcase fell from his hand and he stared at the Jaguar which was as flat as a pancake, the remains of the ping-pong table, and the John Deere compact tractor, which he hadn't even started to pay for, reduced to a mass of twisted metal.

He remained where he was, frozen. There was an unnatural silence. Then he turned and saw that Renato Barretta, the owner of rancho 35, was walking towards him. He was holding a rake over his shoulder like a halberd and wore tracksuit trousers and a grey quilted jacket. He shook his head as he approached: 'What a smash! I had a real shock when I saw it this morning.' And then, proudly: 'I've already called the management and the fire brigade, don't worry. Lucky there was no one at home . . . '

Alessio looked at the house. At least that had been spared. The shutters of his bedroom window were down.

She's asleep.

Certainly his wife was still asleep, doped up on sleeping tablets and with earplugs in her ears. She hadn't noticed a thing.

But surely Fabiana must have heard it.

196

Quattro Formaggi, on the saddle of the Boxer, was climbing back up round the hairpin bends of the San Rocco woods.

A fire burned in his shoulder. Every rut that he crossed was agony. But that, too, was a sign that God was with him.

Just like the holes in Padre Pio's hands.

Through his helmet he could hear the sparrows twittering away merrily.

The sun, which had pushed its way between the clouds, was threading its rays through the vegetation, dappling the ground with patches of light. On the branches the wet leaves glittered like diamonds. During the night the rain had dug streams in the earth which were still pouring mud onto the road.

Quattro Formaggi had no plan for taking the girl's body home. He couldn't just pick up the corpse and load it onto the scooter. But God would tell him what to do.

He was excited. Soon he would see Ramona again and be able to touch her and have a better look at her. He feared that the blow he had given her with the stone might have disfigured her. But he would find a remedy for that too.

He stopped in the layby and dismounted from the scooter. He took off his crash helmet. And he filled his lungs with that fresh, damp air.

A car passed . . .

Look out!

. . . and he turned away so that he couldn't be recognized.

If the police caught him he would be sent to prison for the rest of his days. The idea terrified him. There were a lot of bad people in there. He reached the edge of the road and was about to put his foot on the earth, but he stopped with his leg suspended in mid-air.

Something wasn't right.

The van . . . Where's the van?

He turned back in bewilderment and looked around. This was the place . . . He was sure of it.

He felt his skin freeze and an icy hand grab his scrotum.

He plunged into the woods. He went a dozen metres and started thumping himself on the leg. He turned round and round in circles, incredulous.

Rino's body wasn't there, nor was Ramona's.

Where are they?

In panic he turned back, then he ran forward . . .

Maybe they're a bit further on.

Pushing his way through the brambles, he began to circle round, to step over rotten tree trunks, to climb over rocks, to blunder wildly about in the wood, as everything blurred into patches of light and shade.

No . . . You can't do this to me . . . You can't.

197

At the wheel of his Puma, Beppe Trecca watched the highway unrol between the flooded fields like a strip of liquorice. He moved up behind an HGV transporting some huge metal pipes. He turned to look at Cristiano Zena, who was sleeping beside him with his hood over his head.

Poor kid.

Trecca had found him at the hospital, disorientated and apathetic, as if his father was already dead. He could hardly walk in a straight line and had had to be helped down the stairs. As soon as he had got into the car he had fallen asleep.

The doctor had explained to the social worker that Rino Zena was in a critical condition and that it was impossible to predict how and when he would come out of the coma. But even if he woke up soon, and without any damage, he would still have to undergo a period of rehabilitation to complete his recovery.

It'll be six months at least. And who's going to look after this poor little bastard?

He flicked the indicator and overtook the lorry.

Cristiano didn't even have a mother, and there was no question of those crazy friends of Rino's being able to look after him.

Beppe knew he ought to call the juvenile magistrate to put him in the picture. But he knew what the response would be – to dispatch Cristiano immediately to a foster-family or a care home.

I can wait a couple of days. Till we see what happens to Rino. That way Cristiano will be able to be near his father.

Beppe could go and stay at their house.

His eyes lit up.

I'm a genius! Ida will never find me there.

In the background the radio was playing a song that he knew. He turned up the volume. A hoarse voice sang: 'Maybe tomorrow I'll find my way home . . . '

Maybe tomorrow I'll find my way home.

Yes, maybe he would.

198

Or was it possible that he had dreamed it all? And that Ramona had never existed? Or only existed in films?

But if that was so, why did he have those pains, those bruises, that wound in his shoulder?

Why were Rino and Ramona's bodies no longer there?

Someone's stolen them.

'What use are they to you, you bastards? Tell me. What use are they to you?' Quattro Formaggi, on his knees, wept and pummelled the ground. Then, like an actress in a third-rate soap opera, he raised his head towards the tangle of black branches that imprisoned the sky and spoke to the Eternal Father: 'Where have you put them? Tell me. Please . . . At least tell me if it was real. You can't do this to me . . . It was you who helped me.' His head dropped down and he started sobbing, 'It's not fair . . . It's not fair . . . '

(You've got the ring.)

He saw himself slipping the silver skull ring off Ramona's finger, and then . . .

I swallowed it. I went back home and I swallowed it.

He put his hand on his stomach. It was inside there. He could feel it burning inside him like red-hot embers.

(Go home.)

He hobbled out of the woods as fast as he could, picked up the Boxer and rode off in a cloud of smoke.

If only he had been a bit calmer, if only he had stopped to think, he would have remembered that Fabiana Ponticelli's scooter was lying behind the electricity hut.

199

At the police station an officer explained to Alessio Ponticelli that before you could register a person as missing at least twenty-four hours had to pass. Especially if it was a teenager.

Every year at least three thousand investigations into missing minors are initiated, but eighty per cent of them end after a few hours with the child returning home.

The officer asked him a lot of questions: if there were problems in the family, if the girl had a boyfriend, if she hung about with any strange people, if she had ever expressed a desire to travel, if she was rebellious, if she took drugs and if she had ever run away from home before.

To all these questions Alessio Ponticelli replied no, no, and again no.

The police had recently acquired the services of a support psychologist, who was extremely useful in such cases, and if he wished . . .

Alessio Ponticelli dashed out of the police station and began to retrace the route from Esmeralda Guerra's house to Giardino Fiorito.

First he went the long way round, following the bypass. He drove at twenty kilometres an hour, cursing and swearing and repeating all the while: 'Why did I ever buy her the scooter? It's all my fault. She hadn't even passed her exams!' Then, as if he was talking to his wife: 'It's all your fault for insisting that we buy it for her . . . '

He couldn't believe the stupid woman had stuffed herself with tranquillizers and gone to bed without waiting for Fabiana to come home. With all those stories on the news about Moroccans and Albanians raping girls on every street corner. Not to mention the kidnappings.

'You'll pay for this, so help me God . . . ' He had left his wife at home in case there was a phone call.

He decided to try the road through the San Rocco woods. Though it was unthinkable that his daughter would have gone that way. He had told her a thousand times not to.

He drove up the hill, round the hairpin bends. He went through the woods and out the other side. But then he decided to turn back. He parked the BMW in a layby where there was an electricity hut and got out of the car.

For the rest of his days Alessio Ponticelli wondered what had made him stop in that precise spot, but could never find an answer. According to some American research, certain animals can smell pain. Pain has a distinctive odour, strong and pungent, like the pheromones of insects. A stench which sticks to things for a very long time. And perhaps he, somehow, had smelled the pain that his daughter had felt before she perished.

At all events, when Alessio Ponticelli saw his daughter's scooter lying on the ground behind the electricity hut, something inside him withered and died. And he knew for certain that Fabiana was no longer of this world.

He listened to the gasps of his own irregular breathing. The universe broke up into a series of disconnected thoughts, and, descending over them, the grief that would accompany him, like a faithful dog, for the rest of his life.

200

Quattro Formaggi sat on the toilet and, with a series of thunder-claps and spurts, unleashed a spray of fetid diarrhoea. Then, with pain and satisfaction, he felt something as hard as a stone pass through his rectum.

There it is!

He started squeezing and gasping as if he was in labour, and at last pushed out something that fell with a TING on the porcelain.

He got up and looked into the bowl.

The sides were encrusted with limescale and a dark mess. Below, the pitch-black sludge reflected his pale face.

The light bulb that hung naked from the ceiling, behind him, cre-ated a luminous halo around his head like that of a saint in a reli-gious painting.

He dipped his hand into his shit and took it out again clenched into a fist. He held it under the tap and finally opened his fingers.

A big silver skull ring lay in the middle of his palm. Triumphantly he began to rinse it. 'There it is. You see? I wasn't mistaken, was I? I did kill her, and this is the proof.'

He smiled, opened his mouth and swallowed it again.

Now he must find out what had happened to the bodies of the little blonde and Rino.

201

"I could ask your father myself, you know. Do you think I'm scared? I wouldn't think twice about it." So Fabiana had said to him in the shopping mall.

That had been on Saturday. In the evening he and Rino had gone looking for Tekken and had then returned home. On Sunday they had been together all day.

There was no time for them to meet and get to know each other.

" . . . I wouldn't think twice about it."

If she wouldn't think twice, it was because she already knew him, Cristiano reasoned.

They had gone to screw in the woods because they didn't want to be seen.

In the rain? At that time of night?

And then he'd had the haemorrhage and had gone into a coma. And she . . .

Cristiano rubbed his feet against each other. The cold that he felt in his bones wouldn't go away despite the boiling hot shower and the layer of blankets under which he was buried.

Trecca had stationed himself downstairs and was watching the television with the volume turned right up. The broken shutter banged in the wind and the alarm clock kept winking. Everything had changed, yet that damned clock continued to show the time and that shutter kept banging, as though nothing had happened.

Cristiano put his head under the pillow.

And my father hit her on the head with the stone.

He just couldn't understand why.

Because she told him she was going to tell everyone about it – that he was screwing her. She's under age. They quarrelled and he lost his temper and killed her.

No, that was bullshit. It wasn't possible.

There must be another reason.

'That's enough,' he said, hugging his legs. 'Now I must sleep. I mustn't think about it.'

He closed his eyes and remembered a book he had found lying on the bench in the bus shelter, when he was ten years old. It was dog-eared and the pages were yellowed, as if it had been read and re-read a million times. The title was printed in red letters in the centre of a nondescript grey cover: *Mary Rebels.*

The first page was occupied by a black-and-white illustration. In the middle was a little girl with big round glasses, plaits and an apron below which protruded two legs as thin as twigs. On the right a portly priest with slicked-back hair, a double chin and a sharp-edged ruler in his hand, on the left a plump woman with her hair tied back in a bun and an unpleasant turned-up nose. The story was about Mary, the little girl in glasses, who was an orphan (her rich parents had been killed in a railway accident) and lived in an immense English house (she had to use a bicycle to get from the kitchen to her bedroom) with the unpleasant woman and the portly priest, who acted as her tutor and rapped her on the knuckles whenever she gave a wrong answer. The two of them stole all the money from her inheritance and were now the owners of the house, which was in a ramshackle state and had a leaky roof. Mary was alone, without even a dog for a friend. Whenever the two of them left her any time to herself, she would go and explore the garden, which had turned into a jungle.

One day she was playing in a little temple, overgrown with wild roses and ivy, which stood on an island in the middle of a small dark lake. She saw something moving. A mouse, she thought. She went closer and saw two little men and a tiny woman grazing a cow which was two centimetres high.

They were Lilliputians who had been brought to England by a certain Gulliver when he had returned from his travels to unknown lands. They had managed to escape and lived in that little temple in the middle of the pond.

Mary caught one and put him in a shoebox. And in time she became his friend.

It was a wonderful book. Cristiano kept it hidden in a cupboard. How he would have loved to have a Lilliputian to talk to at that moment; he would have carried him in his jacket pocket . . .

Rino's mobile phone started ringing.

Cristiano, who had almost dropped off to sleep, jumped.

Who was it?

(This is Dr Brolli. I'm sorry to tell you your father has died.)

He got out of bed and took the mobile out of his trouser pocket. 'Who is it?' Silence. 'Who is it?'

'Rino . . . '

'Quattro Formaggi! Where have you been? You never answered your phone! What happened to you? I've been worried.'

'Cristiano?'

'Why didn't you answer? I called you a million times. What have you been doing?'

'I haven't been doing anything.'

'But what about last night? What happened?'

'I was ill.'

Cristiano lowered his voice. 'And what about the bank raid? Did you do it?'

'No, not me. I stayed at home . . . Is Rino there?'

He must break it to him gently. Rino was his only real friend. 'Papa's not very well. He had a haemorrhage in the head.'

'Is it serious?'

'Fairly. But he should be better soon.'

'How did it happen?'

Cristiano was about to tell him the whole story when he remembered that you must never talk over the phone. Someone might be listening. 'Last night. I was asleep and this thing happened and he went into a coma. Now he's in the hospital at San Rocco.'

Quattro Formaggi said nothing.

'Hey, are you still there?'

'Yes.' His voice broke with emotion. 'How is he now?'

He repeated: 'He's in a coma. It's as if he was asleep, but he can't wake up.'

'And when will it end?'

'The doctor says he doesn't know. Maybe in a week, maybe in two years . . . Maybe he'll die.'

'What are you going to do now?'

'For the moment I'm going to stay here.' Cristiano lowered his voice to a whisper: 'Trecca's here! He's moved in.'

'Trecca? The social worker?'

'Yes. He's been very kind. He said he's going to stay for a week. But you and I can still meet.'

'Listen, is it possible to go and see Rino?'

'Yes. Only at certain times, though. Why don't you come round here? We could go and see him together.'

'I can't . . . '

'Oh, go on.' He wanted to say that he needed him, but as usual he kept it to himself.

'I'm not well, Cri. How about tomorrow?'

'All right. I won't be going to school for the next few days anyway.'

'But how . . . how did you find out about Rino last night?'

'Oh, I just went into his bedroom and found him in a coma.'

A pause, then: 'I see. Okay. Bye, then.'

'See you tomorrow?'

'See you tomorrow.'

Cristiano was about to hang up, but he couldn't restrain himself. 'Quattro? Quattro Formaggi?'

'Yes? What's up?'

'Listen, I know that if papa doesn't wake up immediately they're going to send me to a home. They'll never let me stay here on my own. I was wondering . . . ' He hesitated. ' . . . could I come and stay at your place? I know you never want to let anyone in there . . . But I'd be good, if you could just give me a corner I could sleep there. You know I'm not any trouble. Just till papa . . . '

'I don't think so. You know what they think about me.'

A coil of pain wrapped around Cristiano's windpipe. 'Yes, I know. They're bastards. You're not crazy. You're the best person in the world. Could I stay with Danilo, then?'

'Yes. Maybe.'

'I've called him lots of times but he doesn't reply, either on his mobile or at home. Have you spoken to him?'

'No.'

'Oh well. See you tomorrow, then.'

I've got so many things to tell you.

'See you tomorrow.'

202

Giovanni Pagani, a lanky and rather slow-witted young man, was sitting on a low wall outside the Sacred Heart Hospital. He had recently bought a jacket identical to that used by the Canadian explorer Jan Roche Bobois in crossing the Andes on a hang-glider and was extremely pleased with the garment's weatherproofness. In addition to this practical consideration, he was pondering what arguments he could use to persuade his girlfriend to have an abortion. Marta was inside collecting the result of her pregnancy test and he was a hundred per cent certain that it would be positive, given the intimate link that his life had established with Murphy's law in recent months.

So Giovanni Pagani's brain was harbouring two very different thoughts. They were as tight a squeeze as two sumo wrestlers in a telephone box, yet a third thought managed to find some room.

That guy who had dismounted from a battered old Boxer looked as if he had just escaped from a lunatic asylum, been thrown bodily onto a rubbish collection lorry and finally, for good measure, beaten up by a gang of hooligans.

Giovanni saw him untie a large wall clock from the luggage rack, but then he noticed that Marta, looking radiantly happy, was coming out of the hospital waving a sheet of paper, and as quickly as it had been born the thought vanished, swept away by that of being a father.

In the entrance hall of the Sacred Heart hospital a group of elderly patients were sitting on shabby, savannah-coloured armchairs. Some wearing dressing-gowns, others pyjamas, they were basking like green lizards in the last warm rays of the sun which filtered through the large window that overlooked the car park. They were all saying how strange it was that a night like that should be followed by a sunny day, and that the weather seemed to have gone completely haywire lately.

Sixty-four-year-old Michele Cavoli, who was in hospital for cirrhosis of the liver, maintained that it was all the fault of those Arab bastards, who were putting a lot of chemical poisons into the atmosphere to kill us. If he had been the president of the United States he wouldn't have hesitated five seconds. A couple of nice big atomic bombs on the Middle East to wipe them off the map. He was about to add a historical footnote to the effect that if they hadn't dropped those two bombs on the bloody Japs . . . But he stopped to observe that there was another bastard who deserved to die, squashed underfoot like a cockroach: Franco Basaglia. That fool, with his bill to close the mental hospitals, had ruined Italy, releasing a host of psychopathic maniacs onto the streets and into the public hospitals. That guy over there, for example, the one with the wall clock under his arm, why the hell wasn't he locked away in a nice padded cell? He kept staring at the chandelier like an imbecile and gesticulating as if there was someone hanging down from it. Who the hell was he talking to, the Eternal Father?

Michele Cavoli had hit the nail on the head.

Quattro Formaggi, standing in the middle of the hall with his big nose pointing up in the air, was asking God what he should do, but God wasn't answering him any more.

You're angry. I've done something wrong . . . But what? What have I done wrong?

He didn't understand. Cristiano had told him that Rino had been at home when he'd had the stroke. How was that possible? He had seen him die in the wood with his own eyes.

He was so bewildered . . . If he hadn't had the skull ring in his stomach he would have started thinking it had all been a dream again.

God had helped him and led him by the hand during the storm, he had put Ramona in front of him, he had struck Rino down, he had revealed the purpose of the girl's death to him and then, suddenly, for no reason, he had abandoned him.

He had nobody left now but Rino. He was the only person he could talk to.

He looked around. The entrance hall was full of people. Nobody was taking any notice of him. He had dressed up specially. He was wearing the blue suit Danilo had given him because it had been too small for him. A brown tie. And under his arm he held the barometer clock shaped like a violin that he had found a few months before in a rubbish bin.

The gift for Rino.

The problem was that he hated that place. He had spent three months in there after he had nearly killed himself by touching the high-tension cables with his fishing rod. Three months which he remembered as a black hole, lit up here and there by the odd unpleasant memory. A black hole from which he had emerged full of tics and with a head that no longer worked as it had done before.

He approached the stairway that led to the upper floors. Just next to it was a dark wooden door, which stood ajar. A sliver of golden light came out. Above the door was a blue sign on which was written in golden letters: CHAPEL.

Quattro Formaggi looked around and entered.

It was a long, narrow room. At the other end, right in the centre, was a statue of the Madonna illuminated by a small spotlight and surrounded by copper goblets containing flowers. There were a couple of empty benches. Two loudspeakers emitted, in soft tones, a Gregorian chant.

Quattro Formaggi fell on his knees and began to pray.

203

Beppe Trecca was lying on the lounger where Rino Zena had spent the greater part of his last few evenings. A pair of suede Geoxes lay on the floor.

He was rubbing his chilly feet. He had turned on the electric fire, and the room, fortunately, was beginning to warm up. The dying sun on the horizon was firing its last rays through the shutters, glinting on an empty beer bottle.

Beppe was staring at the television without looking at it. He felt tired and was beginning to feel hungry. The last food to enter his stomach had been the chicken with bamboo shoots that he had eaten in the camper. He could have devoured one of Sahid's kebabs.

How he loved that exotic sandwich! With the spicy sauce, the yoghurt, the tomatoes and that soft bread. In the fridge there was nothing but a jar of pickles and some parmesan rind. In the larder a handful of rice and a couple of stock cubes.

What if I drove over to Sahid's?

How long would it take him? Half an hour at most.

Cristiano was so tired he wouldn't wake up till the next day. Beppe had gone upstairs to check and had found him fast asleep, wrapped up in a double layer of blankets, just like a kebab . . . It was the first time he had been upstairs. He had seen Rino's room. A revolting pigsty with a swastika hanging on the wall. The toilet filthy, with the door broken in. Cristiano's room. An empty cube, without a radiator and full of big cardboard boxes.

The boy couldn't go on living in that squalor. A new home must be found for him as soon as possible. Trecca would find a normal family that could foster him till he was eighteen.

And yet . . . And yet he wasn't so sure that that was the right thing to do. Those two lived for each other, and something told him that if he separated them he would only make things worse. The sorrow would kill them or turn them into two ferocious monsters.

The social worker's empty stomach brought him back to more concrete problems. He realised that the Arab's van was near Ida's house, and therefore off limits.

How about cooking myself some rice?

He could always boil the rice and dissolve the stock cube over it with the cooking water.

He stretched, looking around, and asked himself the same question he asked every time he went to see the Zena family.

How could those two live in a place like that? With no washing machine? No iron? Without even a semblance of order?

He too had been born into a humble home. His father had been a ticket-collector on the regional trains and his mother a housewife. They too had found it hard to make ends meet, but his parents were tidy, responsible people. When you entered the flat you always had to take off your shoes, have a wash and put on your pyjamas and slippers. The dirty clothes were put in a cupboard and everyone, including his father, wore pyjamas at home. He had fond memories of the family suppers. They would sit at the table in their nightclothes, their skin softened by the boiling hot shower.

That's a civilised way of living.

The Zena home, with a bit of imagination and a few pieces of IKEA furniture, could be improved enormously. A lick of paint on the walls and a good clean, and everything would be different.

Since he was going to be spending a week there he could start cleaning it up himself.

If poor old Rino dies I could adopt Cristiano and live here, thought Beppe Trecca, jumping up from the lounger with sudden enthusiasm.

His mind conjured up the image of him with Cristiano, Ida and her children in the house, now completely renovated. All of them in pyjamas. And then the hikes in the mountains with rucksacks. And him and Ida in the tent making love . . .

"*Oh my God, Beppe . . . I'm going to come.*"

He felt a blade slicing through his guts. That dream would never come true. He would never be able to kiss that woman again. He would never be able to give her pleasure.

He collapsed on the sofa disconsolately and started groaning as if they were giving him a proctoscopy.

You must hold firm. If you can't, go away.

Yes, perhaps that was the only way to start living again. To go away. For good. He could return to Ariccia and try to get back into university.

His attention was caught by the images of the regional news.

Against a wall there was a car crushed like a beer can.

'Danilo Aprea must have lost control of his car, which ran into the wall of a building in Via Enrico Fermi. When the rescue services arrived there was nothing they could do. Aprea was . . . '

The social worker gaped.

Rino's friend. Cristiano, in the hospital, had said he would go and stay with him.

So that's why he couldn't get hold of him.

What the hell was going on? In the same night your father goes into a coma and his best friend, the only person who could help you, has a horrific accident and is killed? Why was fate hitting this poor kid so hard? What had he done wrong?

How on earth am I going to tell him?

His mobile phone, which was lying on the floor, gave two beeps and lit up and Beppe Trecca's heart skipped two beats in response.

Another text message.

It was the third since that morning.

Stop it. Stop doing it, please.

He felt stifled. He loosened the knot of his tie with his cold-numbed fingers, and then, on an impulse, picked up the little handset and squeezed it tightly. The bluish light of the display gleamed between his fingers like a radioactive element.

He had to restrain himself from smashing it against a wall. With his eyes closed he breathed in. He opened them again.

MULTIMEDIA MESSAGE
DO YOU WISH TO RECEIVE IT?

Despite instinct, reason and logic, despite his stomach, his throat, the blood that was pulsing in his veins, the hair that was standing up on his head, his trembling hands and even his sagging knees, despite the fact that everything was telling him no, no, and again no, the social worker saw his thumb, anarchic and self-destructive, press the green key.

Slowly an image began to form on the mobile's little screen and Beppe Trecca's soul started burning like newspaper.

Ida was smiling at him a little sulkily, like a little girl whose sweets had been taken away.

Underneath were the words:

Darling, will you call me? ☹

204

'You're praying for a loved one, aren't you?'

Quattro Formaggi, on his knees, turned towards the voice behind him.

He saw a dark form hidden by the gloom of the chapel.

The figure took a step forward.

It was a little man. He must have been about a metre and a half high. A big dwarf. With a round head set between two sloping shoulders. Blue eyes that gleamed like two little lights. Fair hair combed across a balding head. Ears small and crumpled. He wore a grey flannel suit. His trousers, which were too short for him, were held up by a leather belt with a heavy silver buckle. A lozenge-patterned shirt covered, like an air balloon, his distended stomach. He had a black leather briefcase under one arm.

'Are you praying for someone who is suffering?'

He had a quiet voice and a guttural R. But no particular accent.

The little man knelt down beside him. Quattro Formaggi could smell his scent. It was like that soap they used in the public toilets, which gave him a headache.

'May I join you in prayer?'

He nodded, continuing to stare at the weeping statue of the

Madonna. He was about to get up and leave, but the man grabbed hold of his wrist and, looking him in the eye, said: 'You do know, don't you, that our Lord carries off the best people to take them to His home? And that His will is to us, poor sinners, as obscure as the darkest of winter nights?'

Quattro Formaggi knelt there, open-mouthed. The little man's blue eyes bored into him like gimlets.

What if this man had been sent by God? What if he was the messenger who would tell him everything and clear up the muddle in his head?

'You do know that, don't you?'

'Yes, I do,' Quattro Formaggi found himself answering. His voice trembled and the world around him seemed to go blurred and then come back into focus, as if someone was playing with the lens of a camera. The pain in his shoulder grew more acute, and at the same time the sounds from the entrance hall seemed to stop. Now the loudspeakers were emitting piano music played with the lightest of touches.

'It is faith that sustains us and helps us to bear the pain.'

The little man was looking at him with a wise and kindly expression, and Quattro Formaggi couldn't help smiling.

'But sometimes faith alone is not enough. Something more is needed. Something that can put us in contact with God. On speaking terms. As we might be with a friend. May I ask what your name is?'

Quattro Formaggi realised that his throat was dry. He swallowed. 'My name is . . . Corrado Rumitz . . . ' He summoned up his courage. 'Though everyone calls me Quattro Formaggi. I'm tired of that name.'

'Quattro Formaggi,' said the other, gravely.

It was the first time in his life that someone hadn't laughed when he'd told them his nickname.

'Well, I'm very pleased to meet you, Corrado. My name's Riccardo, but I too have a nickname. Ricky.'

Ricky's eyes seemed to grow so big that they filled his whole face.

'May we exchange a sign of peace?'

'A sign of peace?'

The little man hugged him tightly and remained in that position or a long time, squeezing his bruised ribs. Quattro Formaggi forced himself not to scream with pain.

When he released him, Ricky seemed moved. 'Thank you. Sometimes the mere embrace of a stranger is enough to make us feel that God loves us. Sometimes faith is not enough for us to enter the graces of the Lord. Often it takes something more. Often we need . . . ' He looked at his hand, inspired. 'We need an aerial to communicate with the Almighty. I'll show you something.' Ricky picked up his briefcase from the floor and with his short, stumpy fingers opened it quickly. 'You're lucky to have met me today. My instinct, or perhaps the will of God himself, always leads me to people who are in need of help.' The tone of his voice had dropped even lower, if that was possible, and now it was difficult to understand what he was saying.

He took out a little case covered with blue velvet and opened it in front of Quattro Formaggi. Inside, cushioned on white satin, was a small, rusty crucifix attached to a thin golden chain. 'Corrado, you know about Lourdes, don't you?'

Quattro Formaggi knew that once a month a big silver coach left from Piazza Bologna for Lourdes and many people went there, especially the elderly, and the trip cost two hundred euros and took eighteen hours, there and back. When you got there they took you to buy frying pans and porcelain, then you prayed in a cave and there was holy water which could miraculously cure you if you bathed in it. He had thought of going there, for his tics. 'Yes,' he replied, nervously scratching his beard. His right leg, in the meantime, had begun to twitch of its own accord.

'Haven't you ever been there?' The little man's blue eyes stared at him with such intensity that Quattro Formaggi, in alarm, started screwing up his lips. He couldn't speak, he felt as if a thin black tentacle was winding itself round his neck.

He shook his head.

'But you do know about the miraculous water of the Madonna of Lourdes . . . ?'

He nodded.

'And you know that that water has cured cripples, paralytics and people in all conditions, patients considered to be terminally ill by conventional medicine?' Ricky's voice slid down into his ears like warm oil. 'Do you see this crucifix? To look at it, you wouldn't think it was worth a cent. All rusty. Ugly. There are hundreds of crucifixe in any jeweller's shop that are worth a hundred times more. Made of platinum, with diamonds or other precious stones. But not one of them, I tell you not one of them, is like this one. This one is special.' He took it between his thumb and forefinger and picked it up as delicately as if it was a splinter of wood from Noah's ark. 'I don't suppose you know that the cloistered nuns of the convent of the Madonna of Lourdes have a secret pool of miraculous water . . . '

Why did he keep asking him if he knew this or that? He didn't know anything.

'No,' replied Quattro Formaggi.

Ricky smiled, displaying a row of teeth that were too white and regular to be natural. 'Of course you don't; nobody does. Except the people who really count, as always. For thousands of years popes with tumours, dying kings and sick politicians have bathed in that pool brimming with miraculous water. A few years ago the Prime Minister was seriously ill. Cancer was devouring him, just as a serpent eats an egg. Do you know how a serpent eats an egg? Like this . . . ' He opened his mouth wide, with his eyes narrowed to two black slits, and swallowed an invisible egg.

Quattro Formaggi tightened his throat. He would have liked to say that he didn't give a damn about the sacred pool. That all he needed to know was where Ramona's corpse had got to. But he didn't have the courage, and besides, his lips, his teeth and his tongue had gone numb, like that time when he'd had a rotten molar extracted.

'Anyway, the Prime Minister was taken to the secret pool and swam in it. For a mere ten minutes. No more. A couple of lengths, in freestyle. And the cancer vanished. Dissolved. The doctors couldn't believe it. And now he's fine.' The little dwarf dangled the crucifix in front of him like a hypnotist. 'Now look at it! You won't believe what I'm going to tell you, but it's as true as the fact that we're here at this moment. Do you know how long it lay in that pool? For ten years. I'm not joking. Ten long years. While the world was changing – wars were breaking out, the Twin Towers were falling, Italy was being invaded by illegal immigrants – this crucifix lay immersed in the miraculous water.' He sounded as if he was doing a commercial for a pure malt Scotch whisky. 'It was a nun . . . Sister Maria. She hid it in one of the pool's skimmers and then secretly gave it to me. Do you see it? That's why it's so dull and tarnished. I tell no lies.

Now just think how potent the healing effect of this object must be. From the pool it went straight into this box. Nobody has ever hung it round their neck. And do you know why? So that it wouldn't lose its potency. This crucifix can't be recharged like a mobile phone. Once it comes into contact with the sufferer's skin it begins to emanate its . . . ' For the first time Ricky couldn't find the words. But he immediately recovered: ' . . . healingness . . . Ability to heal, I mean. But the important thing is never to take it off. Never to exchange it with anyone. And not to talk about it.' He stared at Quattro Formaggi and then fired a question at him: 'Why are you here? For your own sake, Corrado? Or for someone else's?'

Quattro Formaggi, who had slowly sunk down onto a bench, bowed his head and said: 'No, not for my sake. Rino's in a coma.' He had to break off to clear his throat and then he went on: 'I need to speak to him. I need to know . . . '

'He's in a coma.' Ricky stroked his cheeks pensively. 'Well, with this crucifix he might even wake up in one day. He might easily. Do you know what it means to have such an immense amount of divine energy discharged into you? He might even get straight out of bed, pick up his things and go home, as right as rain.'

'Really?'

'I can't guarantee it. It might take a bit longer. But it's worth trying. This is a wonderful opportunity for you – don't let it slip. There's just one problem . . . '

'What's that?'

'You have to make a offering.'

'What kind of offering?'

'Some money for the Sisters of Lourdes. It's . . . '

'How much?' Quattro Formaggi interrupted him.

'How much have you got?'

'I don't know . . . ' He put his hand in the back pocket of his trousers and took out his wallet, which was full to bursting with all kinds of paper except money. He rummaged through it and eventually extracted one twenty-euro and one five-euro note.

'Is that all you've got?' Ricky's voice couldn't conceal all his disappointment.

'Yes. I'm sorry. Wait a minute, though. Perhaps . . . ' Quattro Formaggi took out of his wallet an envelope, folded in half. The money from the last job he'd done with Rino and Danilo. Four hundred euros. He hadn't even touched it . . . 'I've got this. Take it.' He held out the banknotes, and the little man, with a deadpan expression, snatched them as quick as a ferret and handed him the velvet case.

'Remember, in contact with the skin. And don't talk about it to anyone. Otherwise, bang goes the miracle.'

A second later Quattro Formaggi was alone again.

205

I can't call you or see you again.
Forgive me.

So Beppe Trecca, in tears, had written on his mobile phone.

Now he only had to press the key and Ida would get over it. She would think he was a coward.

"*Beppe, do you really want me?*"

"*Yes, I really do.*"

"*Even with the children?*"

"*Yes, of course.*"

"*Then let's go through with it. Let's talk to Mario and tell him everything.*"

"*All right. I'll speak to him.*"

He would far rather be thought a chicken-shit than a bastard who disappeared without a word.

But he couldn't do it. He would be breaking the agreement.

Perhaps he ought to speak to someone who was expert in pledges and vows to the Lord. Someone who had taken a vow like him. *Father Marcello.*

He must make confession and tell him everything. Though he doubted if the priest would give him the answer he wanted.

He threw his head back on the sofa, gulping down air with every sob. He stared through his tears at his mobile. And then, in agonies of colitis, he deleted the message.

206

Quattro Formaggi opened the blue box, but didn't touch the crucifix.

The messenger had said it would lose its power if he did.

He must put it on Rino, so he would come out of his coma and tell him where Ramona was hidden.

But Rino was very angry. He had gone berserk when he had seen the corpse.

He almost beat me to death.

What if Rino reported him to the police?

The most dangerous people are always your friends. People you trust.

At one time Quattro Formaggi had worked for a while in a fish shop. He gutted the fish and made home deliveries. Every day polystyrene boxes full of large clams were unloaded. The clams were still alive; you only had to drop them in the tank, and ten minutes later they would put out a long white tube through which they would suck in water and oxygen. But the lightest touch on the shell with the point of a knife was enough to make them snap shut and stay closed for at least an hour. But then, when they reopened, if you touched them again they would only stay closed for half an hour. And if you kept on prodding them like this they would eventually get used to it and stop closing altogether.

At that point they were done for. You stuck the point of the knife inside the shell and the stupid little buggers snapped shut with the whole blade inside. Then you twisted the blade, the shell broke and a brown cloud of flesh and excrement gushed out into the water.

What use is a shell if you can be trained not to use it?

It's better not to have one – to be naked – if all it does is help the knife to kill you. Rino was like that knife blade. Quattro Formaggi had got used to him, and that made him a serious threat.

And Cristiano was just like his father – he was hiding the truth from him to thwart him.

Those two are playing me for a sucker.

Rino will open his eyes, pull the needle out of his arm, point at me and start shouting: "It was him, he killed the girl! Put him in prison!"

He would do it. He knew him well. He would never understand that he had killed her because . . .

He saw the white hand and the thin fingers wrapped round his marble-hard penis.

An icy shiver sank its claws into the back of his head. He closed his eyes and felt as if he was falling from a skyscraper.

He found himself on the floor, lying among the hassocks, breathing hard and clutching the crucifix.

He unbuttoned his shirt and put the chain round his neck. The pendant fell among the dark hairs on his chest. He could feel the beneficent power of the crucifix spreading like a warm current through his aching body, into his cracked ribs, into the wound, the torn and bruised flesh.

He brushed the crucifix with his fingertips and felt as if he was touching Ramona's smooth skin. And he saw little Baby Jesus hidden inside the woman's wet body.

"God's will is as obscure to us poor sinners as the darkest of winter nights. We need an aerial to communicate with the Almighty," Ricky had told him.

Now he had the aerial to communicate with.

He got to his feet and limped out of the chapel.

He knew what he had to do. He had to kill Rino.

If Rino woke up he would accuse him.

It was Rino who was opposing the will of God.

God had nearly killed him, and he would finish him off.

In fact he and God were one and the same thing.

He crossed the entrance hall, panting, with his violin-shaped clock under his arm, and pushed his way into the lift, which was full of doctors and visitors.

Quattro Formaggi got out on the second floor.

He remembered that this was where the most seriously ill patients were. He himself had been kept there after the accident with the fishing rod, before being moved to the floor above.

Trying not to attract attention, he went by the maternity ward. The big window with the newborn babies in their cots. A glass door. A long corridor and rows of closed doors. He reached the intensive care department. On the door there was a notice which detailed the visiting hours.

It was out of hours.

He tried turning the handle. The door opened. Scratching his cheek, he peered into the corridor.

The lighting in this department was softer, and the ceiling lower. There was a row of orange plastic chairs along one wall. Through the window he could see a violet strip which divided the dark sky from the plain.

While he waited for a nurse to arrive he thumped his left thigh.

The place seemed deserted.

He plucked up courage and entered. He shut the door behind him as quietly as possible and set off, hardly daring to breathe. To his right there was a big dark room. At the far end of it a sepulchral light shone down on a bed where a man lay quite still.

There were winking lights all around, and a greenish monitor. He walked towards the bed with bated breath.

Rino was lying there with his eyes closed. He seemed to be asleep.

Quattro Formaggi stared at him, twisting his neck. Finally he grabbed hold of his wrist and pulled him, as you might a child that doesn't want to get up. 'Rino . . . ' He knelt down beside the bed and, still holding him by the wrist, whispered in his ear: 'It's me. Quattro Formaggi. I mean . . . It's Corrado. Corrado Rumitz. That's my name.' He started stroking his cheek. 'Rino, will you tell me where Ramona is, please? It's important. I have to do something with her. Something very important. Will you tell me, please? I need the body. If you tell me, God will help you. Do you know why you're in a coma? It was God. He punished you for what you did to me. I'm not angry with you, though. I've forgiven you. You hurt me, but it doesn't matter . . . I'm easy-going. Now, please, will you tell me where Ramona is? You'd better tell me.' He looked at him for a moment, sniffing and scratching his cheek, then snorted impatiently: 'I understand, I'm not stupid . . . You don't want to tell me. Never mind. I've brought you a present.' He showed him the clock and then lifted it up, ready to bring it down on his head. 'It's all yours . . . '

'What are you doing here?'

Quattro Formaggi jumped in the air like a champagne cork. He lowered the clock and spun round.

There was someone standing in the doorway, hidden in the shadows. 'This is not visiting hours. How did you get in?'

The man, tall and thin, in a white coat, came closer.

He didn't see me. He didn't see me. It was dark.

His heart pounded in his chest. 'The door was open . . . '

'Didn't you see the notice with the visiting hours?'

'No. I found the door open and I thought . . . '

'I'm sorry, but you'll have to leave. Come back tomorrow.'

'I came to see my friend. I'll go now, don't worry.'

The doctor came even closer. He was balding, and his head was small. He looked like a vulture. Or rather, a newly hatched pigeon.

'What were you doing with that clock?'

'Me? Nothing. I was . . . '

Answer him. Go on . . .

' . . . looking for somewhere to hang it. Cristiano told me Rino was in a coma and I thought I'd bring him his clock. It might help him to wake up. Mightn't it?'

The doctor glanced at the monitor and adjusted the wheel of a machine. 'I don't think so. All your friend needs is rest.'

'All right. Thank you, doctor. Thank you.' Quattro Formaggi held out his hand, but the doctor ignored it and accompanied him to the door.

'This is an intensive care unit. So it is absolutely imperative to observe the visiting hours.'

'I'm sorry . . . '

The doctor closed the door in his face.

Tuesday

207

At four o'clock precisely the alarm clock started ringing.

Cristiano Zena silenced it with a slap. He had slept a long, dreamless sleep without interruption. He hadn't even got up for a pee. His bladder was bursting. But he felt better.

He turned on the torch and stretched.

Outside, the sky was black and dotted with stars.

Cristiano had a pee, washed his face with cold water and put on some warm clothes. He went down the stairs, trying not to make any noise. It was warmer on the ground floor.

Beppe Trecca was sleeping on the sofa, with his face against the back. He was curled up in a blanket that was too short for him and one of his legs was sticking out.

Cristiano tiptoed into the kitchen, closed the door quietly, took out a packet of rusks and ate them, one by one, in silence. Then he drank two glasses of water to wash them down.

Now that he had slept and eaten, he was ready.

From now on every move he made would have to be weighed up at least three times in advance.

On the kitchen table there was a packet of Dianas belonging to Rino.

Let's have a nice cigarette.

His father always said that when he was about to start a job.

Cristiano wondered whether now that Rino was in a coma he still felt the need to smoke. Maybe when he woke up he wouldn't have the habit any more.

He picked up the box of matches and took one out. He held it against the brown strip.

Right, if it lights first go, everything will go smoothly.

He struck the match and it lingered for a second, as if unsure

whether to light, but then, as if by magic, a little blue flame rose up.
Everything will go smoothly . . .

He lit the cigarette and took two long drags, but his head started spinning.

He extinguished it immediately under the tap.

'I'm ready', he whispered.

208

While Cristiano was smoking his cigarette, Quattro Formaggi, in his underpants and dressing gown, was staring at the TV and drinking Fanta from a family-sized bottle.

There was a cook with a moustache who was preparing some speck and couscous roulades and saying that they made tasty and original little bites for a picnic in the country. Then there was a commercial break, after which the etiquette expert, a short man with dyed hair, began to explain how cutlery should be arranged on the table and how one should kiss a lady's hand.

Quattro Formaggi pressed PLAY on the videorecorder with his foot and Ramona appeared, in handcuffs, in the sheriff's office.

'So what do I have to do to avoid going to jail?'

Henry, a muscular black police officer, twirled his truncheon in his hands and eyed Ramona. 'You have to pay bail. And a high one too. And I don't think you have any money.'

Ramona pushed out her big breasts and said in a knowing tone: 'No, I don't. But there's another way. An easier one.'

Henry released her from the handcuffs. 'Well, the only thing for it is to find the little blonde's corpse as soon as possible. You've got to find her and put her in the crib.'

'Okay, boss. I'll go out and find her.'

Quattro Formaggi took another sip of Fanta and, with glazed eyes, murmured: 'Good man, Henry.' He turned towards the kitchen. There was a strange buzzing noise. Maybe it was the fridge. But it might be the gigantic wasp that had got trapped. A wasp with a two-metre wingspan and a sting as long as your arm.

The insect must have stung him on the chest while he was asleep, because he could feel his guts rotting, and his skin felt as if there were a million white-hot needles sticking into it. And his headache never let up. A fire rose up through his neck and boiled his brain. When he touched his temples he could feel his forehead, his eyebrow arches and his eyes tingling.

The crucifix wasn't working.

He had never taken it off, just as Ricky had told him, but the pain, instead of decreasing, was growing.

God is angry with me. I've lost Ramona. I don't deserve anything. That's the truth.

209

It was cold, but the heavy jacket, flannel shirt and fleece cardigan covered Cristiano well. The ice-cold air went down his throat, which was still irritated by the cigarette, as he rolled up the door of the garage. He turned on the long neon lights, which crackled, shedding a yellowish glow over the large basement room. By the workbench he found a pair of orange plastic gloves, the kind people use for washing the dishes. He put them on.

He went over to the van, took the keys out of his trouser pocket and opened the back doors, hoping that, for some obscure reason, Fabiana's body would not be there any more.

He switched on the torch and shone it inside.

The corpse was there. Dumped to one side. Like a pile of old clothes.

Like a dead thing.

Inside the van there was a faint but sickly odour.

After twenty-four hours a corpse already begins to smell.

One of the few certainties Cristiano Zena had was that, if he did things properly, he would dispose of that body in such a way that nobody would be able to trace it to his father.

This certainty was based on the fact that he had watched all three seasons of *CSI*.

CSI is an American TV series in which a team of highly intelligent forensic scientists studies and examines corpses with technological instruments, while brilliant detectives elicit information even from the smallest and apparently most insignificant clues.

E.g.: they find a shoe. They analyse the sole. There's some dog shit on it. By a study of the DNA they establish the breed. Dalmatian. Where do dalmatians go to crap? They send troops of officers out into all the public parks to study the concentrations of dalmatians and eventually pinpoint with mathematical precision the place where the murderer lives. That kind of thing.

Often Cristiano, in his previous existence, had found himself reflecting, as he watched the television news, on the errors committed by Italian murderers. They always made a complete hash of things, leaving lots of clues, and inevitably got caught.

He would make a better job of it. For everything to work he would have to imagine that that corpse was just like a supermarket chicken when you take it out of its wrapper.

Right, here goes.

He took hold of its feet and pulled it to the edge of the van. He managed to slide it into the wheelbarrow without too much difficulty. He closed the doors.

The cleaning of the van could wait till later.

He pushed the wheelbarrow into the garage, and pulled down the shutter.

He had worked the plan out carefully. He had to remove all clues from the body, then wrap it up and throw it in the river.

He took a transparent plastic dust sheet off the piano, then cleared the ping-pong table of all the cardboard boxes, engine parts and tyres and spread the plastic sheet over it. He found a paint-splashed board which had been dumped in the corner among some iron pipes, and laid it obliquely against the table. He put Fabiana's corpse onto the board, levered it up to the level of the table and rolled it off. Then he laid it out in the middle, as on a dissecting table in a morgue.

Fabiana seemed heavier than when he had put her in the van the night before.

Throughout the operation he had avoided looking at the head, but now he couldn't avoid it. That mask smeared with congealed blood and framed with a mass of curly blonde hair had been the face of the prettiest girl in the school, the one all the boys lusted after.

Why did he kill her?

He couldn't stop thinking about it. He tried desperately to find an answer, but it was baffling. How could he have smashed in the head of such a beautiful girl? And what had Fabiana done to deserve being killed?

His father . . .

Stop it.

. . . kneeling over Fabiana's body as it lay there in the rain . . .

Stop it!

. . . lifted up the stone . . .

STOP THINKING!!!

. . . and brought it down.

Cristiano breathed in and once again smelled the sickly odour of carrion, which entered his mouth and nose and went down his throat like a mephitic gas. His stomach and the rest of his body started shaking convulsively and he had to take three steps backwards to stop himself throwing up the rusks he had just eaten.

He picked up an Esselunga plastic bag and put it over her head in an attempt to conquer his revulsion.

When he felt that the nausea had passed he looked again at the girl's body lying with its legs and arms outspread in the middle of the green table. With the plastic bag over the head it was better.

He observed her. The skin was yellowish. The violet veins, where nothing now flowed, had come to the surface, like the myriad offshoots of a flash of lightning. The clothes caked with grime and blood. The fly of the jeans open. The jacket open. The cardigan and T-shirt torn, as if a wolf had tried to tear her apart. The areola of a nipple emerged from the white lace bra. A few blondish hairs stuck out from the panties.

A thousand times he had imagined seeing her naked, but never like this.

He would have to clean her nails.

That's where they always catch you out. That's where they find a wisp of wool, a piece of the murderer's skin, and all it takes is a DNA test and you're fucked. And then he would have to . . .

'We've found traces of seminal fluid inside the vagina. We've got him.' That's what they always said in the TV films.

So?

So he would have to pull down her knickers. And wash her. Inside and outside.

No, not that.

He would never be able to do it. It was too much. Besides, the trousers were open, but the knickers were pulled up.

He didn't screw her.

No, *he didn't screw her. My father would never do a thing like that to a fourteen-year-old girl.*

He picked up the hosepipe.

But why did he kill her?

And the detergent to wash the grease off his hands.

Because Rino Zena is a homicidal maniac.

Then he ought to go to the police.

"My father has murdered Fabiana Ponticelli. She's in our garage."

No. There must be another explanation. Of course there must. When his father came out of his coma he would tell him and then he would understand everything.

His father was a lout and a drunkard, but not a murderer.

But the other night he hurt that blonde who came into my bedroom. That was just a kick up the backside, though. That's different. My father's a good man.

He examined the girl's right hand, frowning. There was something strange, that didn't seem right, but he couldn't think what. He looked at her left hand. He compared them.

The ring was missing. The skull ring.

Fabiana always had it on her finger.

Where is it?

210

Beppe Trecca woke up with a start, turned over and almost fell off the sofa. For a few moments he couldn't make out where he was. He looked around in bewilderment.

The old television, still on. A folding chair.

This was Cristiano Zena's house.

He sat up and yawned, scratching his head. His back ached and he was itching all over.

Are there fleas here?

Anything was possible in this pigsty. Even crabs and headlice.

He must go and have a pee and drink some water. It seemed as if he had half a kilo of salt in his mouth. The effect of that rice with vegetable stock.

He looked at his Swatch.

Four forty-five.

He stood up, continuing to yawn. He massaged the base of his spine, where he had a cracked vertebra.

He couldn't spend another night on that sofa. The doctor had told him to sleep without a pillow on an orthopaedic mattress, preferably a latex one.

It was that imbecile Father Italo's fault that he was in such a bad way. Three years before, in a village in Burkina Faso, Father Italo, a Dominican missionary from Caianello, had hit him with a shovel and broken his third lumbar vertebra.

Beppe Trecca had been there with a group of volunteers, digging wells for the international project 'A Smile for Africa'. Under a sun that roasted your neurons, among skeletal cows, he was working because he thought it was a worthy cause and because he was going out with Donatella Grasso, one of the group leaders.

It was exhausting work and Beppe, for some unknown reason, had been demoted from a supervising role to one of manual labour.

On the day of the accident, plagued by flies, he had spent the whole morning unloading concrete bricks, under the tyrannical eye of Father Italo. At last lunchtime had come. He had gulped down a thick soup which contained pieces of meat that looked like wood shavings. Afterwards, to get rid of the taste of garlic, he had decided to suck a refreshing mint.

He had searched for the packet in his trouser pocket and found that there was a hole in it and that the mints had fallen down into the seat of his trousers. He had rested one hand on the cement mixer and started waggling his leg to make them fall out onto the ground.

A blood-curdling yell had broken the silence of the savannah. Beppe had barely had time to turn his head and see Father Italo leap forward and whack him in the kidneys with a shovel.

The social worker had gone down like a ninepin while the Dominican yelled: 'Turn off the electricity! He's been electrocuted! He's been electrocuted! Turn it off!'

The excruciating pain and the surprise had prevented Beppe from saying anything. He had tried to get up but the priest, like a man possessed, had with the help of three blacks thrown him down again and grabbed his face and opened his mouth. 'The tongue! The tongue! He'll bite his tongue. Hold it still, for pity's sake!'

Two days later, groggy with painkillers, the social worker had been put on a plane and repatriated with a cracked vertebra and a dislocated jaw.

Holding one hand against his side Beppe went for a pee. He thought he heard noises coming from below. He pricked up his ears, but heard only the trickle of the urine into the water.

He slouched back to the sofa and collapsed on it, yawning: 'What a hard life!'

211

The night, at the end of the plain, was beginning to show the first signs of preparing to leave. A band of fog as thick as cotton wool lay among the rows of poplars that followed the course of the river. The dark tops of the trees emerged from it like the topsails of ghost ships.

Cristiano Zena was panting as he pushed the wheelbarrow carrying the corpse of Fabiana Ponticelli along a track that ran across fields dotted with puddles.

He was steering from memory, since he couldn't switch on the torch.

He had lost a lot of time in the garage and it would soon be light and there was a good chance of meeting someone.

Farmers. Labourers heading for the gravel pits who passed this way to save time. Boys on motorbikes.

You would have to be a complete idiot not to understand that here was a human body under that blanket.

So . . .

So nothing. If I get caught it'll because destiny wants me to be. I'll say I did it. And when papa wakes up he'll realise how much I love him.

His arms were beginning to tremble and the river was still a kilometre away. His T-shirt, under the armpits and on the back, was completely soaked with sweat.

He had been down this track a thousand times. When he had decided to build a raft out of empty jerrycans so that he could go rafting, or when he went fishing with Quattro Formaggi, or when he simply had nothing to do.

Who could ever have imagined that he would come along it pushing Fabiana Ponticelli's corpse?

If only Quattro Formaggi were there with him. Maybe he knew if his father and Fabiana had had a secret affair. Or he could have asked Danilo. But he had disappeared. Cristiano had called him a hundred times. His mobile was always switched off. And there was no reply at home either.

He thought about his phone conversation with Quattro Formaggi. He hadn't seemed particularly surprised to hear that Rino was in a coma.

But you know what he's like, he said to himself, wiping his arm across his forehead, which was beaded with sweat.

He couldn't wait to see him and give him a hug.

He was almost there. The noise of the water even drowned the roar of the lorries which raced along the highway.

He took off his jacket, tied it round his waist and started pushing again. The path, as it neared the river, had gradually turned into a swamp and the small wheel of the wheelbarrow slithered and sank in the mud. Two heavy clods of earth had formed under the soles of his trainers. In front of him, a few dozen metres away, lay a marsh, lit up by the glow from the power station. The trees stood out like pylons in the middle of a sea.

Cristiano couldn't remember the waters of the Forgese ever rising this far.

212

Quattro Formaggi was still sitting on the chair. He was shivering, and the pain from his shoulder spread down through his chest in incandescent waves.

He was holding the crucifix in one hand.

For a moment he had managed to doze off, but a horrific nightmare had wrapped itself round him like an evil-smelling blanket and fortunately he had woken up.

The television, which was going full blast, echoed in his skull, but he didn't want to turn it down. He far preferred the screeching voices of the television to those inside his head.

Besides, if he closed his eyes he saw Ramona naked, lying among the mountains and the shepherds and soldiers, who were walking over her body with the sheep. He desired her with such intensity that he would have cut off his hand to have her.

Then there was that terrible nightmare that he'd had.

He was covered with slimy fur and was one of a pack of dark creatures running along a dark burrow. Beasts with sharp teeth and red eyes and long hairless tails, pushing and squeaking and biting each other in their eagerness to be the first to the end of the tunnel.

Then they all plunged into a carcase covered with blind larvae and millipedes and cockroaches and leeches so fat they were nearly bursting. They began devouring the rotten flesh and the insects. And he ate too, but without ever sating his hunger.

"The dogs of the Apocalypse neither eat nor allow others to eat," Sister Evelina used to say in the orphanage.

But all at once a cold light dazzled him, and in the centre of the ray of light the wraith-like figure of a woman said to him: 'You are the Carrion Man.'

'Who? Me?'

'Yes, you!' and she pointed to him, while all the other creatures fled in terror. 'You are the Carrion Man.'

And then he had woken up.

He suddenly kicked out at the television, which fell off the table but went on shrieking.

Why on earth had Ramona chosen to go through the woods?

She made a mistake. I warned her. It's not my fault she went through the woods.

If she had taken the bypass nothing would have happened and he would be all right and Rino wouldn't be in a coma. And everything would have been as it was before.

'. . . was before,' the Carrion Man murmured and then started thumping himself on the leg.

213

The water had got too deep. Cristiano Zena had abandoned the wheelbarrow, and as he dragged the corpse towards the river dawn had broken over the plain.

He hadn't met anyone. He had been lucky – because of the floods no one had come that way.

Beppe must be awake by this time and would certainly be looking for him.

In front of him a long, rusty barbed-wire fence emerged from the water. Two big black crows were perched on it. Beyond, the pebbly shore was completely submerged by the flood. Cristiano put one foot on the rusty wire, which disappeared into the water, and pushed the body wrapped in cellophane over the barrier.

The river came up to his knees and the current was beginning to pull.

At first he had thought of tying some rocks to the body and sinking it in the river, but now he had decided that it was better to let the current carry it away.

By the time they found it, it would be a long way away and no one would be able to connect it with them. If he was lucky it would reach the sea, and there the fish would finish the job.

He looked for the last time at Fabiana wrapped in the transparent plastic.

He sighed. He didn't even feel sorry for her. He felt tired, drained, reduced to a beast. And alone.

Like a murderer.

He thought wistfully of the days when he used to go down to the river to play.

He closed his eyes.

He released the body as he had so often done with branches, imagining that they were ships and galleons.

When he opened them again the corpse was a little island in the distance.

214

The three hundred and twenty-three metre long Sarca Bridge, designed by the distinguished architect Hiro Itoya and opened a few months previously to the accompaniment of hot-air balloons, brass bands and fireworks, had also felt the fury of the storm.

The south bank hadn't withstood the flood, and the highway, for hundreds of metres, had been invaded by the Forgese's muddy waters.

Teams of workmen had at once set about repairing the embankment, while pumps sucked up the water and spewed it back into the river, which seemed to be boiling as if a flame were burning below.

The traffic, pouring in from all the roads of the plain, had slowed down till it got stuck in a motionless, honking mass.

Now, less than thirty-six hours after the storm, one lane had been reopened and the column, made up of HGVs travelling to or from the frontier and cars full of commuters, was moving fitfully forward, controlled by temporary lights and police.

Right in the middle of the bridge, in a Mercedes S-Class as black as the wings of a condor, sat Mr and Mrs Baldi.

Rita Baldi, thirty-one years old, was a pale, thin little woman, dressed in a pair of jeans and a short T-shirt which left exposed her navel and a strip of seven-month pregnant stomach. At that moment she was painting her fingernails with varnish and now and then glancing up unseeingly at the sombre sky.

The bad weather had returned.

Vincenzo Baldi, thirty-five years old, looked like a cross between

Brad Pitt and the brown long-eared bat which lives on the island of Giglio. His unkempt beard merged with a pair of dark glasses. He was smoking a cigarette and blowing the clouds of nicotine out through a gap above the window.

They had been sitting in the queue for nearly two hours.

In front of them was a German HGV which was transporting organic compost (cow shit) to somewhere or other. The phosphorescent bottle of air freshener attached to the air vent was doing its best, but the smell of excrement filled the car.

They would never make it to the appointment with the engineer Bartolini now.

Bartolini had found what he claimed was a definitive solution to the problem of the damp which afflicted their little house like a mysterious curse. The moisture was rising up through the walls, which were becoming covered with multicoloured moulds. The plaster was cracking and crumbling away. The furniture was warping and the clothes in the drawers were rotting. The solution, according to Bartolini, was to cut horizontally through all the outer walls of the house and to insert an impermeable sheathing patented in Scandinavia, so as to block the fatal rising of the damp.

That queue had raised the tension in the car. And since they had got into the vehicle the two hadn't exchanged a single word.

As a matter of fact they hadn't had a dialogue of more than a few words for a week (they had quarrelled, though neither of them could now remember exactly what about), so Rita was amazed when Vincenzo said: 'I've bought a new car.'

It took her a moment to recover from her surprise and another moment to wet her lips and reply: 'What? I don't understand.' Though she understood perfectly well.

He cleared his throat and repeated: 'I've bought a new car.'

Her nail brush hung suspended in the air: 'What car?'

'Another S-Class. But the next model up from this one. Petrol again. A few more horsepower. A few more accessories.'

Rita Baldi breathed in.

Her childhood friend Arianna Ronchi, who had become a member of parliament, said that, thanks to that profession, she had learned that before replying impulsively and regretting it later you should always touch an object and let out your anger, as if you were discharging the electricity from a live battery. But it was in Rita Baldi's nature to reply instinctively, the same nature that induces a porcupine to raise its quills even on the approach of a predator. So she couldn't restrain herself: 'Why didn't you tell me?'

'Tell you what?'

It is a painful experience shared by many people that, once the conjugal knot has been tied, the man/woman whom you thought to be a brilliant, intuitive creature turns out to be a complete dickhead.

At that point what do you do?

In thirty-six per cent of cases, according to a recent survey, you call your lawyer and ask for a separation. Rita Baldi was one of the other sixty-four per cent. She had resigned herself to the situation, but her husband's idiocy never ceased to amaze her.

'That you wanted to change the car! When did you get this one? Not even six months ago! Why didn't you tell me?'

'Why do I have to tell you everything?'

What drove her wild with rage and gave her an irresistible desire to pick up things and smash them was that Vincenzo always answered a question with another question.

Rita took a deep breath and in an apparently placid voice tried again: 'All right. I'll explain to you why. In the first place . . . ' Another deep breath. 'Because you've just bought a BMW motorbike. Then you bought a Danish refrigerator for . . . ' she didn't want to but couldn't stop herself, ' . . . your crappy wines. Then you bought that thing . . . What's it called? The tractor for cutting the grass. Then . . . '

He interrupted her. 'Well? What's the problem? Who pays for them?'

'Not you. Seeing that we have to pay instalments until 2070. Your son will still be paying them and probably his son will too . . . ' She was too furious to be able to express this microeconomic concept. 'Tell me something. Isn't this car all right? What's wrong with it? Is it crap? Well, if it's crap . . . ' She kicked out with the stiletto heel of her Prada shoe at the air-conditioning control unit. And then at the display of the satnav.

Vincenzo Baldi's left arm moved with the deadly speed of a

scorpion's tail and she was pinned to the back of her seat by a hand gripping her carotid artery. Only then did her husband turn his head and smile. His sunglasses concealed two furrows burning with hatred. 'You do that again and I'll kill you! I swear I'll kill you.'

And she, at this point, like a kid, a fawn or something of the kind, started thrashing about, screaming, wriggling and muttering: 'Oh that's great! That's really great! Go on and kill me, then! Kill me! Kill me and your son, you pathetic . . . ' and she was about to insult him when her survival instinct advised her to stop.

He withdrew his hand and she, gasping for breath, twisted away, picked up her handbag and got out of the car.

Vincenzo Baldi lowered the window: 'Come back here. Where are you going?'

Another question.

Rita didn't reply. She threaded her way through the queuing cars, stepped over a barrier of traffic cones and, holding onto the guardrail, looked down from the bridge.

She knew she wouldn't jump off. Though imagining that she would made her feel much better.

Little one, if I jumped off I'd save you from a shit of a father . . . But don't worry, I'll leave him sooner or later, she said to the son she carried in her womb.

She closed her eyes and opened them again. A pleasant smell of water and mud rose up from the river, which seemed to be exploding between its concrete banks.

Her gaze fell on the remains of some trees which had got caught against the pier that supported the bridge. The branches were covered, like a tramp's Christmas tree, with coloured plastic bags. Nearby two ducks were resting. A male with a shiny green head and a female in her light-brown livery. That couple of fowls certainly got on well. They lay there serenely, one beside the other, cleaning their wings on a big plastic parcel . . .

'What's that?' she said out loud.

Rita Baldi squinted and put up her hand to screen her eyes from the glare.

She couldn't make it out. It looked like . . .

She reached into her handbag for a pair of thin Dolce&Gabbana glasses and put them on.

With an instinctive gesture she touched the place where her baby was growing, and then started screaming.

215

The Carrion Man was rotting.

In his whole life he had never felt so bad. Not even after he'd had the electric shock. On that occasion he had felt fire shoot through him, then darkness.

Now it was different. Now he was slowly rotting.

He was lying on the bed and kept rubbing his stomach, which was as hard and taut as a drum.

He could feel them. The fly larvae moved, they fed on his flesh and corroded his guts. The pain began from there and spread through his whole body, right out into his hair and toenails.

Maybe I should go to hospital.

But they would ask him a lot of questions. They would ask him how he had got into that state and then they would make him stay.

He knew what people were like. People wanted to know. People asked questions.

They would put him next to Rino. And Rino would open his eyes, he would sit up, pointing his finger, and shout: 'It was him! It was him! He killed the girl.'

And you'll go to prison, where at night they take you and . . .

At the thought of going to prison a blade of searing pain cut through his shoulder and released a thousand sparks up through his neck and into his head. He felt the pain spurt out from his tainted flesh, penetrate the sweat-soaked mattress, seep down through the legs of the bed, spread over the floor and down through the walls, through the bricks, into the foundations, along the pipes, into the dark earth and from there into the roots of the trees, which dried up and shed their leaves and withered in silence.

The Carrion Man placed on his stomach the crucifix given to him by Ricky, the messenger of God, and it seemed to bring a little relief.

He got up, shuffled into the bathroom and looked in the mirror.

The skull of death showed through the skin of his face. He raised the hood of his bathrobe and his bony face disappeared, swallowed up by shadows. Only his glistening, bloodshot eyes and yellowish teeth stood out, as if hanging in the void.

That was the face of death. And when it came out of his corpse it would smile as he was doing at that moment.

When he was small he'd had meningitis and his temperature had risen above forty.

'It was a miracle you didn't die. You must thank the Lord,' the nuns said to him.

The fever had been so strong they had immersed him in the fountain opposite the orphanage. He remembered there being eels in the basin and the water boiling and the eels being cooked and turning white.

But perhaps it never happened.

He remembered the aspirin that dissolved. That had happened.

He saw it in front of him. An enormous white disc which undulated in the glass and broke down into bubbles, spray and froth.

He wanted the aspirin that dissolved. He would give everything he owned to feel its salty taste on his dry tongue.

He went into the kitchen. On the dresser was a jamjar full of cents and half-euros. He had enough money to buy some aspirin.

The problem was going outside. The mere thought of meeting people made him feel as if he was drowning, as if he was being seized by a thousand hands and dragged down to the bottom of the ocean.

(If you don't take an aspirin you'll die.)

At first he didn't recognise the voice. Then he smiled.

Cristiano.

It was Cristiano's voice.

How long was it since he had last thought of him? How could he have forgotten him? He was his best friend, his only true friend.

A pang, sharper than the pain he felt in his body, gripped his heart and something hard and pointed pierced his throat.

It had only taken one night and everything had changed.

(What have you done?)

(How could you?)

It wasn't me. It was God. I didn't want to do it, truly I didn't

I swear to you, I didn't want to. It was God who made me do those things. It's nothing to do with me.

'Everything has changed,' he said, and he felt his eyes brim with tears.

He thought of his strolls round the shopping mall with Cristiano, their walks by the riverside, the evenings they spent eating pizza and watching TV with Rino and Danilo.

None of that would happen any more.

He was no longer Quattro Formaggi. He was the Carrion Man now.

He put on – yelping with pain as he did so – some trousers, a high-collared cardigan, his cape and scarf, and stuck a pompom hat on his head.

(You must go straight to the chemist's, buy the aspirin and come home as quickly as possible. If you do that you won't come to any harm.)

He took a handful of coins from the jamjar, crossed himself, walked towards the entrance and opened the door of hell.

216

'Why all the traffic? I don't understand,' grumbled Beppe Trecca at the wheel of his Puma. Cristiano, with his hoodie pulled down over his forehead and his arms crossed, barely heard the social worker.

Drowsily he gazed out of the window at the factory buildings, the sales outlets and the long fences on each side of the road.

They would move five metres, then stop. It was torture. They were on the highway and in half an hour they had only moved about half a kilometre.

Trecca thumped the steering wheel irritably. 'Something must have happened. An accident. It's not normal, this traffic.'

Cristiano observed him out of the corner of his eye. He had never seen him so agitated.

He closed his eyelids and rested his head against the window.

Why hasn't he sent me to the judge yet?

He felt too tired to answer his own question. He wished he could sleep for another twelve hours. And he couldn't face the thought of going back to his father and seeing him on that bed.

The idea that the sun rose and set, that people sat in traffic jams, that they could drop an atomic bomb, that Christ could come back down to Earth, and that the male nurses could take the piss out of his father, laugh at him, while he lay there stretched out like a puppet, made him feel sick, and so angry that his hands were beginning to tingle.

If I catch anyone making fun of him I'll kill them, I swear to God I will.

"Learn to sleep lightly, Cristiano. It's when you're asleep that the buggers will get you!" his father had said the night he had sent him to kill Castardin's dog. It seemed as if a century had passed.

No, he couldn't face going to see him.

He wanted to go back home and look for the ring, that fucking skull ring. After abandoning the corpse in the river Cristiano had returned home and while Trecca slept he had searched for it.

He had turned the garage upside down, and he had looked carefully in the van when he had cleaned it up.

It wasn't there.

He had searched in the jacket and trousers that his father had been wearing.

It wasn't there either.

It had to be still in the woods!

His father's fingerprints on that ring were the only evidence that could link him with Fabiana's death.

'Do you think I ought to turn off down Via Borromeo? I wonder if . . . ' Trecca asked him.

Cristiano pretended to be asleep. Being in the traffic jam meant not being in the hospital.

"Trecca's here. Quick, get out the Monopoly."

The image of him and his father hurriedly setting out the little houses and the money on the board while Trecca parked his car appeared on the screen of his eyelids, and a faint smile curled his lips.

One thing Cristiano just couldn't understand was why this guy was busting his arse for him.

If the roles were reversed I wouldn't lift a finger.

Trecca had gone to pick him up at the hospital, taken him home, done his back in sleeping on the sofa and now he was taking him to see his father again.

"Nobody does anything for anybody. Look behind people's actions, Cristiano." That was what Rino had taught him.

And yet he had a hunch Beppe Trecca wouldn't be getting any overtime pay at the end of the month for looking after him.

Maybe he just likes me.

Anyway, in a few days, if his father didn't wake up, the judge would bung him into a home or foster him out to some shithead.

He must find Danilo as soon as possible. He could adopt him, at least until papa came out of the coma.

If I can find him, that is.

And if they didn't let him stay with Danilo, he would run away.

217

Beppe Trecca was dying for a coffee.

'Why all the traffic? I don't understand,' he said, without expecting any reply from Cristiano.

About a kilometre down the road there was a bar, but with this tailback . . . He couldn't even imagine how long it would take.

The social worker thumped the steering wheel irritably. 'Something must have happened. An accident. It's not normal, this traffic.'

As well as a coffee, he could do with a good massage. The springs of that battered old sofa had given him a terrible backache.

What a hellish night he'd had. Too cold, much too cold. And on top of that the roar of the trucks on the highway. When you closed your eyes you felt as if you were lying on the hard shoulder of a motorway.

He peeked at Cristiano out of the corner of his eye.

He had hidden himself in his hoodie and seemed to be asleep.

Now would be the perfect time to tell him everything.

"Listen, Cristiano, I've got to tell you something. Danilo's been

358

killed in a car accident." No, on second thoughts maybe I'll tell him later.

Later that day he would also have to call the juvenile judge. Maybe he could persuade him to wait a bit longer. A few days.

Long enough for Ida to forget him.

But how long would it take *him* to forget *her*?

He had only spent one day without seeing her or speaking to her, but it seemed like a year. Previously they had met all the time. Once a week they would go shopping at the Quattro Camini. And Ida would stop him buying deep-frozen junk food. Then he would take her to pick up the children from the swimming pool. And if they happened not to meet for a couple of days they would speak on the phone. She was his best friend.

My life partner.

He kept thinking obsessively of the two of them in the camper making love. Of the pleasant smell of her skin. Of her hair, so smooth to the touch. Of feeling her tremble in his arms. It had been the most beautiful thing in his life. And for the first time he had behaved like a man. He had taken their lives in hand and had been ready to face up to his responsibilities.

Suddenly he had understood what it meant to live.

But now, in the desperate state in which he found himself, he would erase that night and go back to the days when they had been just friends. The days when he used to lie to himself.

He looked around.

To the right was Truffarelli's, a big sanitaryware outlet.

He had gone there with her to choose the majolica for the toilet in the house in the mountains that Mario had bought.

Everything on that cursed plain reminded him of her.

I can't stand any more!

He must leave. For some faraway place. For Burkina Faso, to dig artesian wells. It was the only thing for it. Once he had found Cristiano a home he would resign from his job and just go.

218

It had been easy to get as far as the chemist's.

No one had given him so much as a passing glance. Or if they had, the Carrion Man hadn't noticed, because he had kept his eyes on the ground.

The old chemist's shop, Molinari's, with its flashing red cross and its window display with the torso of a brown man covered in bandages and advertisements for skin-toning creams, was there, on the other side of the road.

Now all he had to do was go in, ask for the aspirin, pay and make his escape.

The Carrion Man scratched his cheek, screwed up his lips and thumped himself several times on the thigh.

He couldn't make up his mind whether to go in or not. The chemist was mad, completely out of his mind. He had got the idea, from God knows where, that the Carrion Man was a keen Juventus fan.

The Carrion Man hated madmen, strange people, anyone abnormal. And he loathed football.

He seldom went to the chemist's, but whenever he did that guy, a skinny man with a receding hairline and a goatee beard, would start talking to him about players he had never heard of and the league tables, and once he had invited him to go to Turin to watch a Champions League match.

'Go on, why don't you join us? We're a great bunch of lads. We always have a great time. We're going by coach.'

The Carrion Man had a problem: if anyone said something about him that wasn't true, he couldn't put them right. He was too shy.

Once he had agreed to do a yoga course just because a guy who worked with him in the construction firm had told him he was sure he would like it.

And so it was that he had found himself on a coach crammed with Juventus supporters bound for the stadium. When they had got off the coach, the Carrion Man had pretended to go to the toilet and had hidden behind a police van and only re-emerged after the match to get back on the coach.

What if he now went into the chemist's shop and the guy forced him to go to a football match again?

The Carrion Man sat down on a bench, uncertain what to do. He needed that aspirin.

He could always go to the chemist's at the station. It was a long way and he would have to go by scooter, but that would be better than facing the maniac.

He was about to return home when two women came out of the Boutique della Carne butcher's shop, on the other side of the road, and stopped outside the chemist's.

They looked sixtyish. One was tall and spindly, like a praying mantis, and the other was small and green, like a goblin. The goblin had a quadruped in tow which looked like a Tasmanian devil.

The Carrion Man saw them debating animatedly outside the chemist's shop window. If they would only go in, the chemist would be too busy to talk to him.

Finally the praying mantis pushed the glass door and the two disappeared into the shop.

The Carrion Man got up and limped in after them. He hid behind a rotating display of foot-care products.

Serving at the counter, besides the madman, was an elderly lady in a white coat, who read the prescriptions and stamped them, extremely hard. She was the one he would have to ask for the aspirin.

Standing in the queue, besides the two women, were an old man in a cloth cap and a boy.

The Carrion Man, clutching his coins in his fist, rehearsed his first speech under his breath: 'Hallo. Good morning. Could I have some of that aspirin that dissolves in water, please? Thank you. How much is it?'

Meanwhile the two women, less than half a metre away, were talking conspiratorially in low voices.

'Anyway, he called me five minutes ago . . . ' said the goblin, and showed her friend her mobile phone as if to prove that she wasn't making it all up.

The tall, balding woman knitted her brow. 'But I don't understand. Where is your husband now?'

'On the bridge! He's been there for two hours. The traffic is completely stuck.'

'And what did he tell you, exactly?'

'Matilde, why do I have to repeat things to you a hundred times? Are you taking that medicine for your head that the doctor prescribed for you?'

'Yes I am,' snapped the lanky one impatiently. 'Now will you tell me what he told you? Did he really say there was a corpse under the bridge?'

'Exactly. That's what he said. Listen, Matilde dear, why don't you do something useful? Why don't you call a taxi and go and see for yourself? That way you'll understand everything.'

'Oh really, it's impossible to have a conversation with you!' the mantis intended to retort, but all she managed to say was 'Oh rea . . . ' because a man in a cape who was holding on to the rotating display of Dr Scholl products trod on her big toe and she screamed, partly in fright and partly in pain. On the floor, the man in the cape tried to get back to his feet but like a moose on a carpet of marbles he only managed to slip and slither on the corn plasters and the mint-scented porous insoles, and when he finally managed to get up, limping, sobbing, braying like a mule in a slaughterhouse, he hurled himself at the glass doors of the chemist's and disappeared.

219

'Excuse me, do you know what's happened?' Beppe was asking a lorry driver who had got out of a long, yellow-and-black HGV and was smoking a cigarette.

The man puffed out a mouthful of smoke and said in a bored voice, as if this had happened to him a million times before: 'Apparently they've found a dead body in the river.'

Cristiano, who was still trying to have a doze, winced as if he had been punched in the stomach. He felt a shiver grip the back of his head, his armpits freeze and his cheeks catch fire.

He closed and re-opened his eyes. He opened his mouth. He tried to listen to what Beppe and the trucker were saying, but a buzzing in his ears prevented him from hearing.

He only managed to catch one sentence from the lorry driver: 'In these cases they block everything till the magistrate arrives.'

So they had found Fabiana's body.

Straight away.

He had expected it to be carried down to the sea and be eaten up by the fish, but instead, after less than four hours, it had been found only a stone's throw away from his house.

He tried to swallow, but couldn't. He felt sick. He got out of the car, put his hands on the warm bonnet and let his head hang down.

(Did you really think the body would disappear, by magic?)

I should have buried her.

(Did you really think God or your fairy godmother would help you because you were trying to save your father?)

I should have buried her in concrete.

(From the moment you entered that wood and decided to . . .)

I should have dissolved her in acid. I should have burned her.

(You became an . . .)

He knew the word.

ACCOMPLICE.

I should have cut her up in a thousand pieces and fed her to the pigs, the dogs.

(You're guiltier than him.)

'Cristiano?' Beppe Trecca was calling to him.

(You're worse than him.)

'Cristiano?'

(And now they'll get you. They'll catch you in no time. You're finished.)

'Cristiano, will you answer me? What's the matter?'

He raised his upper lip and growled: 'What the fuck do you want, eh?' He clenched his fists, suddenly feeling an uncontrollable urge to pound that bastard's face to a ball of mincemeat.

The social worker shrank back in alarm. 'Nothing. You're as white as a sheet. Is something wrong? Do you feel ill?'

A gurgle came up from the depths of his throat and then, spluttering, he managed to say: 'Why don't you get off my fucking back What the fuck does it matter to you how I feel? Who the fuck ar you, anyway? What the fuck do you want from me?' As he said all this he noticed that they had been surrounded by a cluster of curious drivers, who had got out of the queuing cars in the belief that they were watching the classic scene of a father quarrelling with his teenage son. Who knows, maybe they were hoping they would start hitting each other, that there would be fireworks.

How he wished he had a nice heavy crowbar so he could smash all their stupid heads in. At least he would have had the satisfaction of carrying out a massacre before spending the rest of his life in jail.

And I killed all these people. I did it with my own hands. So when you come out of your coma – if you ever do come out of it, you bastard – we can see who killed more people, you stupid son of a bitch.

Trecca moved towards him. 'Cristiano! Listen . . . !'

But Cristiano Zena wasn't listening. He was looking up at the sky, at those brown clouds so low he could have touched them with his fingertips, those clouds that would soon pour even more water on this shitty world, and he felt himself levitating, as if aliens had suddenly sucked him up into space. He swayed dizzily, raised his arms towards the clouds, threw his head back and imagined he was puking out everything he had inside him, all that blackness he had inside him, that black anger, that fear, that feeling of not being worth a shit, of being the most pathetic little jerk on the planet, the loneliest and most desperate creature in the world. Out. Yes, out. He must spew out of his mouth all the thoughts, all the anxieties, everything. And turn into a black dog. A black, brainless dog, which ran, stretching out its legs, curving its body, straightening its tail. It barely touched the ground and it spread out, as perfect as an angel.

'An angel . . .' he muttered. He looked with a strange smile at Beppe, the lorry driver in the leather waistcoat, at the car drivers who seemed like mannequins and behind them, beyond the highway, at a green strip of waste land which separated two ploughed fields and across which he could run for ever till he came to where he would be free. Free.

He looked again at Trecca, then sprinted towards the fields and with an incredible leap hurdled the guardrail and for an endless moment felt as if he was flying.

220

The rain poured down on the umbrellas of hundreds of curious bystanders looking down from the bridge and the embankments, it poured down on the silvery spotlights that shed beams of aseptic light on the black waves of the river and on the cellophane that hid the corpse, it poured down on the raincoats of the traffic police, it poured down on a big makeshift tent that had been erected on the very spot where Rita Baldi had first seen the corpse, it poured down on the police cars and the fire engines, it poured down on the four-by-fours of the divers and on the minibuses of the local television stations and on the yellow cape of the Carrion Man.

He was there, squeezed in among the crowd, looking down from the bridge.

Fifty metres below, a red rubber dinghy was fighting the rapids and eddies, trying to reach the body wrapped in plastic.

The Carrion Man's gaze shifted from the black river to the embankments crammed with umbrellas, from there slid over the highway completely covered with stationary cars and over the soaked policemen, rose up into the sky where a helicopter was whirring and finally came to rest on his own trembling hands.

The hands that had produced all this . . .

When an ant finds the corpse of a mouse it doesn't keep the discovery to itself. The first thing it does is to run like mad to the anthill and tell everyone: "Hurry! Hurry! You'll never guess what I've found!"

Half an hour later the carcase is completely covered with ants.

It's exactly the same with human beings.

If he hadn't killed the girl, all those people would now be in their homes. Not standing there shivering in the rain to see what he had done.

It had been him who had created that ten-kilometre queue of cars, too. He'd had those spotlights put there. He had made those carabinieri come. And he would make people sit down at a table to write about him.

And the incredible thing was that nobody could imagine that the man God had ordered to do it was there in their midst.

You see that guy over there? That poor cripple you all think is a pathetic little pillock? Ladies and gentlemen, it was him. He was the one to whom God entrusted the mission.

And they all start clapping and cheering.

"Bravo! Bravo! You lucky man!"

This situation was very agreeable. Very agreeable indeed.

The Carrion Man remembered that once Duccio Pinelli, a welder who had worked in their team at Euroedil, had described to him and Rino how at the age of eighteen, after a booze-up at the pub, he had run over a cyclist on the Bogognano road. Ambulances and police cars had come to the scene of the accident, and the road, just as it was at that moment, had been closed for ages and there had been a tailback ten kilometres long.

'That was the most important thing I've done in my whole life,' he had explained. 'Do you know how many people there are in a ten-kilometre queue of cars? Thousands. Do you realise how many thousands of people wasted four hours of their lives because of me? They missed appointments, arrived late at work, and God knows what incredible opportunities they missed. I changed their destinies. Starting with those of the cyclist and his family. No, *important* isn't the right word. *Important* sounds like something positive. There's another word, a better one, which I can't think of. It's on the tip of my tongue . . . '

'Significant?' Rino had suggested, in a drunken stupor.

'That's the word! Significant! In the rest of my life I must have changed the destinies of two, maybe three people at most. But on the day of the accident I changed the destinies of thousands of people.' He had sat there in silence for a long time, his eyes staring into nothingness. Then suddenly he had added: 'Maybe for the better in some cases, who knows. Perhaps because of those four hours' delay two people had the chance to meet, get to know each other and fall in love.' Then he had stretched his arms and concluded: 'Yes, that was the most significant moment of my life.'

And now the Carrion Man, too, had done something significant. Something a thousand times more significant than what Duccio Pinelli had done.

This would make the front pages, perhaps even the TV news.

221

Cristiano Zena was sitting on the carcase of a burnt-out Fiat 127 and watching as hundreds of seagulls, their wings outspread, wheeled in the rain over a crater piled high with rubbish.

Thousands of tons of smoking refuse, on which crows and gulls feasted and mechanical diggers and trucks climbed.

He had found it in front of him. Quite suddenly.

After jumping down from the highway, he had run as fast as he could across the fields, he had skirted warehouses, followed fences and been barked at by dogs on chains, then all at once he had looked up at the sky and seen gulls circling like vultures that have spotted a dead animal. He had gone on, with his hand pressed against his side and his head drooping, across the weed-strewn, stony ground, and that circular crater almost a kilometre wide had appeared in front of him.

This is where all the shit ends up.

He lit the last cigarette in the packet he had been carrying in his pocket for the past week and took a long drag on it, without feeling any pleasure.

He turned. Through the car's glassless windows he saw that nothing remained of the sun but a violet halo.

The police will have started searching for the murderer by now.

At the thought of hundreds of people all trying to understand who could have killed Fabiana he felt as if he was suffocating.

In fact he had been feeling like this ever since his father's phone call had woken him up in the middle of the night. He couldn't breathe deeply, and even if he opened his chest and breathed in hard, he never completely filled his lungs with air.

Suddenly he remembered the piranha he had seen in the pet shop in the mall.

It was a handsome creature with a red belly. The size of a large sea bream. Three or four hundred grams.

Cristiano didn't like piranhas at all. They sat there motionless in the middle of the fishtank and did nothing. No fish was more boring.

And this one looked really stupid, with that expressionless face, those crooked teeth jutting out of its mouth and those eyes as black as liquorice allsorts. They had put him in a tank that was too small for him, in the company of a large turtle, one of those green ones with orange patches on their cheeks. The ones people keep in bowls with little plastic palm trees till they get fed up with them and flush them down the loo.

Well, turtles are creatures it's better not to mess with. They're tough animals. Cold-blooded. They never die. Tropical beasts, used to living in warm water, but they're perfectly happy in cold water too, where they grow as big as frying pans. And in the natural world there are few animals more voracious and aggressive than turtles. They're worse than crocodiles, which may be voracious, but at least when they're full they flop down on the bank, where even if you kick them they don't take a blind bit of notice of you. But turtles are always hungry.

Anyway, the piranha and the turtle were in this little fishtank in the pet shop in the mall. The turtle flapped those little flippers of his as if he didn't even know how to swim and stretched out his neck and TAC, took a bite with that pointed beak of his out of the piranha's fins. He had already eaten half of its tail and its lateral fins were reduced to two stumps.

Cristiano, seeing what that monster was doing, had run to the owner of the shop to tell her. But she had stared at him with about as much interest as she showed in the tubs of goldfish food.

Cristiano had gone back to the fishtank and the turtle had continued to butcher the piranha, which had accepted the torture with a patience and resignation that made your guts churn in your belly.

But at one point the turtle, after attacking the fin, had turned its attentions to the gill cover. One bite. Then another. And finally it had sunk its teeth into the gill itself, which was swollen with blood. The tank had filled with a red cloud, which had faded to pale pink in the water. And that blood had come into contact with the piranha's nose. Its eye had come to life like a computer screen that has been on standby and the fish had started to quiver, to get excited, just like a shark would do at the blood of its prey: but this wasn't the blood of its prey, it was its own blood, and suddenly the piranha had shot into action, unsheathing a row of sharp teeth, and had ripped the turtle's throat open as easily as you can ladder a stocking.

Cristiano had succeeded, with the help of a net (he wouldn't have put his hands in there for anything in the world), in getting the reptile out of the tank before the piranha could kill it, and had thrown it into another one full of little neon tetras. The turtle, half dead, had swooped on the little fish and was swallowing them whole, but those that were still alive re-emerged through the gash in his throat.

Well, Cristiano Zena, at that moment, felt just like the piranha in the mall, under attack from all sides. And when he finally scented the smell of blood, his own blood, he would spring into action and kill someone.

He threw the cigarette stub on the ground and mashed it to pulp with his sole.

What if somebody saw me?

Suddenly he wasn't quite so sure that no one had seen him when he had thrown the corpse in the river. All it needed was one fisherman, or anyone at all, even at a distance of hundreds of metres, and he was finished.

Cristiano wiped his hand over his forehead. He was sweating and felt sick.

They'll find me. They're bound to find me.

Hold on a minute!

Hold on one goddam minute! You didn't kill her! What are you thinking of? You didn't kill her! It wasn't you! You didn't do anything. You only did what any son would have done.

'Any son would have done what I did,' murmured Cristiano, with his hand over his mouth. 'They'll understand.'

Like hell they will . . . I'll go to jail for the rest of my life.

'Why oh why . . . ? Shit!' He jumped to his feet, and just as he was aiming a kick at the dented door of the 127 his mobile started ringing. He took it out of his pocket, hoping it was Danilo. But it was Trecca . . .

He let it ring and after a dozen rings it fell silent and then he called Danilo again. His mobile, as usual, was switched off. He tried his landline.

It was free. It rang and rang, and nobody answered.

He was about to hang up when a woman's voice suddenly said: 'Yes, hallo?'

'Hallo . . . ' replied Cristiano in amazement.

'Who is it?'

'It's Cristiano . . . '

A moment's pause, then: 'Rino's son?'

Cristiano recognised the voice. It was Teresa, Danilo's wife. 'Yes . . . Can I speak to Danilo?'

There was a brief silence, then in a lifeless tone Teresa said: 'You haven't heard?'

'No. What?'

'Danilo . . . Danilo's gone.'

'What do you mean, gone? Gone where?'

'He had a terrible car accident. He went off the road and crashed into a wall and . . . '

No, it couldn't be true . . . 'He's dead? I don't understand, is he dead?'

'Yes. He's dead. I'm sorry . . . '

'But why is he dead?'

'Apparently he was drunk. He lost control of the car . . . ' Teresa's voice seemed to be coming out of a hole.

Cristiano took the mobile away from his ear and let his arm slide down. He switched it off, staring at the gulls in the sky, the rubbish, the columns of black smoke.

Danilo was dead.

Like Cristiano's heart.

Which felt nothing any more. Absolutely nothing.

He didn't give a damn if Danilo, his adoptive uncle, that fat lump Danilo, had crashed into a wall and been killed.

The only thing that came to his mind was that now he was really in the shit.

I've got to run away. I've got to find Quattro Formaggi and we've got to run away.

But first I must explain to Papa.

222

On the river, a few kilometres away from the rubbish dump, the carabinieri's rubber dinghy had succeeded in approaching the corpse.

The crowd had suddenly fallen silent, and the only sounds were the rustle of the rain on the umbrellas, the buzz of the incandescent spotlights which sent up spirals of steam, and the rush of the river.

A diver in wetsuit, lifejacket and harness jumped off the dinghy. For a moment an eddy seemed to suck him under, but then he was thrown up again and managed to get the current to carry him to the tree on which the corpse was caught. He put his arms round the bundle and was laboriously hauled back onto the dinghy.

From the embankments, and from up on the bridge, there came a burst of applause which was lost in the roar of the river.

The Carrion Man, peering over the parapet, was scratching his neck so hard that it bled.

Ramona.

Who had done it? Who had wrapped her in that plastic sheet and thrown her in the river?

It can't have been God. He doesn't get his hands dirty.

God always gets others to do things. He gives the orders and someone else has the job of carrying them out.

Why didn't you tell me to do it? I would have understood. I would have sacrificed my plan to finish the crib. I've done everything for you.

He looked around. There were hundreds of drenched people. Among them, perhaps, was the person who had thrown the body in the river.

Who are you? Where are you? I want to talk to you. Perhaps you can help me understand.

He took his head in his hands and pressed his temples.

Too many thoughts were going through his mind. Too many voices were talking to him together and muddling him. Though he sensed that soon these thoughts that were infecting his brain would stop and there would finally be silence.

His mobile, in his pocket, started ringing. He took it out. 'Hallo?'

'Hallo, Quattro Formaggi?'

Don't call me that! It's not my name, can't you all get it into your heads? 'Who's that?'

'It's me, Cristiano. Listen to me. It's important. Where are you?'

'Nowhere special.'

'Can we meet at the hospital? I need to talk to you.'

'When?'

'Right away. I've had an idea. Come quick.'

The Carrion Man heard the sound of a siren behind him. He turned and saw a police car advancing slowly through the crowd. Through the rain-streaked rear window he saw a man.

It's him. He's the one who threw the body in the river.

He swayed, his legs were giving way, he clutched hold of the railing.

'Quattro Formaggi, are you there?'

'Sorry.' He switched off his mobile. He began to follow the police car, to stagger among the people, to struggle forward, panting, in that mayhem, frantically elbowing his way through, almost fainting with the pain in his side and shoulder. Everything had dissolved into a darkness crowded with monsters who grew angry, who insulted him, who noticed him, who recorded his face in their memories, but it didn't matter; he had to follow that man.

At last the car stopped and the siren fell silent.

The Carrion Man wanted to get closer, but a cordon of policemen prevented him from doing so.

A woman holding an umbrella and a torch opened the door of the police car. The man got out, covering his head with a newspaper. The two disappeared down an iron stairway that led to the river bank.

The Carrion Man pushed through the crowd and leaned over to watch them.

He saw them go down a long iron stairway and reach the bank, where Ramona had been brought. He saw the man crouch down beside the corpse and then put his hands over his face.

It's her father . . .

He opened his mouth and for a moment a ray of light lit up his heart. He was breathless, overwhelmed by the grief of that man whose daughter he had killed.

What have I done?

But it only lasted for a moment. The darkness enveloped his heart again and he realised that he would never finish the crib. Now they would put Ramona in a coffin and cover her with earth.

Everything that he had done had been in vain. Nobody understood that she had died for something great, something more important. *Because God commands it.*

The people were beginning to return to their cars. The show was over.

There was a child in a blue raincoat with a helmet of black hair who was holding her mother's hand and kept sniffing, with tears in her eyes. The Carrion Man stopped, looked at her and felt like crying too. He raised his hand and, sobbing, waved to her. At first the child covered her face, awed by the figure of that thin man crying under a yellow hood. But then she waved back.

They smiled at each other.

Could it have been Rino who threw Ramona into the river? A flash of lightning lit up the dusk of the Carrion Man's mind.

What if Rino, in the woods, hadn't died as he had seemed to do? If he had only been pretending?

223

Beppe Trecca, sitting in his Puma, was still stuck in the traffic. If until half an hour earlier the queue had been moving at walking pace, now it had come to a complete stop. He could see the turning a hundred metres ahead, like a mirage.

He snapped his mobile shut, irritably.

The little hooligan didn't answer.

He had really gone too far this time. What kind of behaviour was this? He tried to help him and the boy just dashed off like a madman. What if something happened to him?

Who'll get it in the neck? Yours truly!

When he found him he would give him a piece of his mind.

He must have gone to see his father. Where else could he go? But supposing I don't find him in the hospital? What if the little fool has run away?

He felt as if a boa constrictor was crushing him. He loosened the knot of his tie, unbuttoned his shirt collar and started to hyperventilate, trying to dispel his anxiety.

I've even run out of Xanax.

It was impossible to breathe in that damned car. He opened the window, but that didn't help. It was that endless queue that made him feel so bad. He was boiling.

He steered the Puma into the emergency lane, switched on the hazard lights, took his folding umbrella from the back seat and got out.

It's only a panic attack. Once you've felt a few drops of rain on your face you'll feel better.

He leaned with one hand on the bonnet, as if he was exhausted after a long marathon, and looked around. The leaden sky. The honking cars. The never-ending rain.

What am I doing? Why am I still here?

I must go to Burkina Faso.

Cristiano had better go to a home. He had done what he could for him. But now, enough was enough.

And after all . . . I'm a free man.

He didn't depend on anyone. And no one depended on him. He could choose to do what he liked with his life. It had been his decision to remain single, free to travel, to explore new worlds, new civilisations.

So why the hell did I get myself stuck in this lousy wasteland? Helping people who don't want to be helped. If anyone needs help, it's me. No one asks how this poor bugger is feeling! Not even my cousin, not so much as a phone call . . .

He glanced at the motionless queue. A dozen metres away was a people carrier. At the wheel a friar. In the back he could just make out two big St Bernards, who had misted up the windows with their breath.

Beppe gazed at the friar in astonishment.

I've got to talk to him. Right away.

He went over to the car and knocked on the window. The man started in surprise.

'I'm sorry, I'm sorry. I didn't mean to alarm you.'

The window rolled down.

The friar had a thin face and straight white hair. An olive complexion. A pair of narrow glasses were perched on his long nose. 'Do you need help?'

'Yes.'

'Problems with your car?' The huge beasts' muzzles pushed forward to see who this person was and started dribbling happily over the driver's seat.

'Isolde! Tristan! Down!' shouted the friar and then turned back to Trecca. 'They've been shut up in here for hours . . . '

'Can I get in? I want to confess . . . '

The friar frowned. 'I'm sorry, I don't understand.'

'I want you to hear my confession.'

'Here? Now?'

'Yes, now. I beg of you . . . ' implored the social worker. And without waiting for an answer, he jumped into the Espace.

224

The milky glow from the streetlamps bathed the wide stairway of the Sacred Heart hospital. The Carrion Man parked his scooter. His wrapped-round scarf and his hat left only his eyes exposed. All hunched up and limping, he entered the half-deserted entrance hall of the hospital. He saw Cristiano standing in front of the lift.

He went over to him. 'Here I am.'

At first the boy seemed not to recognise him. But then he grabbed him by the arm: 'What on earth's happened to you?'

The Carrion Man was about to tell him the fatuous lie he had prepared (*"I fell off my scooter"*) when he had a sudden brainwave.

He lowered his gaze. 'They beat me up.'

Cristiano stepped backwards and clenched his fists as if he was in a boxing ring. 'Who was it?'

'Some boys on motorbikes blocked my path and then started kicking and punching me.'

'When did this happen?'

'On Sunday evening. I was on my way to Danilo's . . . '

'Who was it?' An expression of hatred distorted Cristiano's features. 'Tell me the truth. Was it Tekken?'

He's fallen for it.

At this point the Carrion Man, like a consummate actor, nodded. 'Why didn't you phone me?'

'I don't know . . . When they went away I picked up my scooter and went home. And then I couldn't get out of bed.'

'Why didn't you tell me when we talked on the phone?'

Quattro Formaggi shrugged.

'You should have told me, Quattro. Tekken beat you up because you're my friend. He's got it in for me so he picked on you. That bastard's going to pay for this. I swear to God he is.' Cristiano looked at the cheek covered with a big, purple bruise: 'Have you seen a doctor?'

The Carrion Man tried to play it down. 'It's nothing . . . I'm fine.'

Cristiano touched his forehead. 'You're boiling. You must have a temperature. You can't even stand up straight . . . There's an accident and emergency ward here . . . '

'No! I said no. They'd lock me up somewhere. They're just dying to . . . '

Cristiano breathed in through his nose. 'You're right, Quattro Formaggi. They want to put me in a home, too. Listen, I've had an idea. A great one . . . '

The Carrion Man wasn't listening. He had turned white and was grinding his teeth as if he wanted to crush them, and puffing his cheeks in and out. It was the third time Cristiano had called him Quattro Formaggi and it wouldn't do. Nobody must ever call him that again.

He restrained himself from grabbing him and hurling him against a glass door in the foyer, shouting: 'Nobody! Nobody must call me that. Do you understand? Nobody!'

Instead he gave himself a couple of slaps on the forehead and with an anguished sigh managed to mutter: 'You mustn't call me that.'

'Eh?' Cristiano had been talking and hadn't heard. 'What did you say?'

'You mustn't call me that any more.'

Cristiano raised an eyebrow. 'How do you mean? Call you what?'

The Carrion Man thumped himself twice on the leg and lowered his eyes, like a child who has done something naughty. 'What you called me just now. You mustn't call me that any more.'

'You mean you don't want me to call you Quattro Formaggi any more?'

'Yes. I don't like it. Please don't do it again.'

225

"So you're Quattro Formaggi."

Cristiano Zena seemed to hear Tekken and the others as they kicked him.

"What a nice tasty little pizza."

That was why he didn't want to be called that any more.

Tekken, you bastard, I'll get you for this.

He moved closer to Quattro Formaggi and hugged him tightly, feeling, under his cape, that he had been reduced to a trembling skeleton. And that he smelled.

He had spent all those days on his own. Suffering like a dog. Without eating. And with no one to help him.

He imagined him lying on the bed in that dump where he lived. Cristiano's throat tightened as if he had swallowed a sea urchin.

In a broken voice he said: 'I promise. I'll never call you that again. Don't worry.'

And he heard him murmur: 'I'm the Carrion Man.'

Cristiano stepped back and looked into his eyes. 'What?'

'The Carrion Man. From today that's my new name.'

It's finally happened. He's flipped.

Rino was in a coma. Danilo was dead. And Quattro Formaggi had gone completely round the bend.

Perhaps the beating they had given him had tipped him over the edge.

'Listen to me . . . ' Cristiano strove to speak clearly and slowly. 'Listen to me carefully. The two of us have got to go away from here. If we don't run away there'll be trouble. I know there will.'

'But where can we go?'

Cristiano put his arms round Quattro Formaggi again so that he could speak in his ear. In the bar behind the glass partition a group of doctors seated at a table were laughing with the barman, who was putting a coin on his elbow and then catching it as it fell.

'To Milan. We'll go to Milan. Listen. I've heard that a lot of people live underground in Milan. People who don't want to live with the people on the surface. There's a king and a kind of army that lives in the tunnels of the metro and decides whether you can enter. I think they put you through some tests. But you and I can pass them. Then we'll find ourselves a secret hole where we can set up home. You know, a place with a hidden entrance that only you and I know about. And we'll put beds in it and a kitchen area. And at night we'll go out and while everyone sleeps we'll find everything we need. What do you say? Do you like my idea? It's good, isn't it?'

Cristiano closed his eyes, certain that Quattro Formaggi would never go with him. He would never leave the village and his flat.

But he heard him murmur: 'All right. Let's go.'

226

The Carrion Man was crying, with his arms round Cristiano.

At last someone had told him what to do. Cristiano, his friend, was there with him, and would never leave him . . .

Yes, they must go to Milan and live underground. And never come back. And forget everything. Ramona. The rain. The woods.

The horror of what he had done made him giddy and he felt as if the ground was crumbling under his feet. He clung to Cristiano. He wiped away his tears and mumbled: 'What about Rino? What shall we do with Rino? Shall we leave him here?'

'Let's go and see him.' Cristiano held out his hand. 'Come on, 'll help you.'

The Carrion Man grasped it.

227

' . . . But in your opinion, father, if I sent her a text message would I be breaking my vow? I wouldn't actually be seeing her . . . '

Beppe Trecca and the friar were parked in the layby, while alongside them the queue of traffic had finally started to flow. The rain drummed on the bodywork of the people carrier.

He had told him everything. The night. Ida. Mario. The accident. The African. The vow. The miracle. It had been a liberation.

The friar had listened to him in silence.

He spread his arms. 'My son, what can I say . . . A vow is a solemn commitment that is made before God. Breaking it is a very serious matter.' He looked him straight in the eye. 'Very serious. Everything else must take second place, whatever the cost . . . '

Trecca, dismayed, pushed back a St Bernard which had mistaken him for a lollipop. 'Not even a text message, then?'

The friar shook his head. 'God has illuminated you. He has given you the chance not to take the wrong road. You would have wrecked a family and hurt your friend. The Lord has put you back on track. You have been very fortunate. Every time you feel the temptation to break your vow you must pray, and you will find the strength to resist.'

The social worker puffed out his cheeks. 'I have. I have prayed. But I can't help myself. She's part of me. The only possible life I see is by her side.'

The friar grabbed hold of his wrist and squeezed it tightly. 'Now stop it, young man! Listen to me. You have been chosen by the Eternal Father. Your prayer has been answered. You have been the witness of something immense. Do you think God performs miracles every day? Forget that woman. Now you have a mission. To tell your story to others as you have just told it to me.' And then, in the grip of a sudden excitement, he began shaking his arm. 'Now you're coming with me.'

Beppe shrank back, wide-eyed, and asked: 'Where to, father?'

'To Switzerland. To Saint-Oyen, and the Hospice on the Great S Bernard Pass. I must introduce you to my superiors. Do you realise how useful your story could be to the young? In this society tha has lost its faith you are like a beacon that shines in the darkness. That is the purpose of miracles – to restore hope.'

Trecca freed himself from his grip. 'An excellent idea. Just let me go and lock my car. I'll be right back.'

228

Cristiano Zena and the Carrion Man knelt down beside Rino's bed. The rain beat against the thermal window panes without making a sound. Now and then a nurse came in and flitted across the room in the half-light like a ghost.

Rino, lying in the same position in which Cristiano had left him, seemed to have got a little colour back in his face, and the two purple bruises around his eyes were turning scarlet.

Quattro Formaggi (Cristiano couldn't think of him by that other stupid name) was holding Rino's hand. 'Do you think he can hear us?'

Cristiano shrugged: 'I don't think so . . . I don't know . . . No . . . ' He must tell Quattro Formaggi about the woods. About Rino and Fabiana. He was the only person he could tell, the only one who would understand. He summoned up his courage. 'Listen . . . There's something I've got to tell you . . . ' But he stopped. Quattro Formaggi was staring at Rino intensely, as if communicating with him, then, without turning, he said: 'Your father's wonderful.'

'Why?'

Quattro Formaggi screwed up his lips. 'Because he saved me.'

'When?'

He started scratching his cheek. 'He always has. Even the very first time we met in the children's home. They'd put me in a barrel and were rolling me along. And he came along and saved me. He didn't even know me.'

Cristiano in fact knew very little about the years of the children's home, when those two had first met. Rino had told him that in those days Quattro Formaggi hadn't had his tics and his lame leg, he had just been a little odd.

'He helped me later, too, when I was electrocuted down by the river . . . When I came out of hospital I walked on crutches. And he used to drive me around. One day he took me to a bit of waste land, where the Opel accessories outlet now is, and he took away my crutches and said that if I wanted to get home I would have to walk there without any crutches. And that if I couldn't do that I would have to crawl on my hands and knees, that he was fed up with helping me, that I could walk perfectly well and that the problems were only in my rotten head.'

'And then?'

'Then he got in his car and drove off and left me there.'

'And what happened?'

'I lay there in the middle of the field for a long time. Some high tension wires passed over my head, very high up, and I could hear the sound of the electricity flowing fast. And those cables, when you looked at them from the ground, one beside the other, were like the strings of a guitar. Luckily I had a couple of Kinder Buenos with me. I ate them. Then, while I was there, on the ground, I saw a black figure, with a hunched back, standing among the ears of wheat. It was a monster. It stood quite still and looked at me. It wore a kind of long black suit and its face was like that of a rook. With a black beak, and wings here,' he pointed to his shoulders. 'It didn't do anything to me. But it looked at me with those evil little eyes. And it had arms with very long sleeves that reached down to the ground. Then it came closer and there were the ends of crutches sticking out of its sleeves, with those plastic tips that stop you slipping.' He paused for breath. 'It was death.'

Cristiano had kept silent throughout his tale, but couldn't help asking: 'Was it papa playing a trick on you?'

'No. It was death. It was waiting for me to die. But I closed my eyes and then when I opened them again it wasn't there any more. So I got to my feet and started walking. I said to my legs: "Walk! Walk!" and they walked. And there in front of me was your father smoking a cigarette on the bonnet of the Renault 5. And I turned round and death wasn't there any more.'

'It was you who drove it away when you started walking.'

'No. It was your father. It was your father who drove it away.'

Cristiano grasped the hands of Rino and Quattro Formaggi, put his face against the sheet and started sobbing.

229

The Carrion Man stroked the head of the sobbing Cristiano and stared in terror at a dark corner of the room.

He hadn't told the whole story. But he couldn't. Death was there with them. He could see him. He was in the room. He was lurking in the corner, to the right. Behind the trolleys with the monitors on them. It looked like a shadow, but it was him. He was identical – he had the same form as death in the field, the same beak, the same wings on his shoulders, the same long arms ending in aluminium crutches.

The Carrion Man was terrified. All the saliva had gone from his mouth.

I know, you've come for Rino. You've come to take him.

230

'Can you believe that? Saint-Oyen, the Hospice, the St Bernards!' Beppe Trecca was driving along and talking out loud. 'The guy thought I was going to go with him to Switzerland, into the mountains, to make a complete arsehole of myself talking about Ida and the camper. Do me a favour!'

He had got into his car, shot past the friar, who was letting his dogs out for a pee, and disappeared into the distance.

For safety's sake he checked in the mirror to see if the guy was following him. There was nobody in sight.

The friar had been very clear, though: the vow could not be broken. It was a very serious matter. He had looked at him with an unequivocal expression, the same expression the Lord would wear when Beppe found himself knocking at the gates of heaven. So no contact with Ida, no text messages, no multimedia messages, no letters or anything of that kind.

The truth was that nobody could help him. This problem was his alone. And he was going to have to solve it with his conscience as a man and as a believer.

And there was only one way of solving it. To go away.

He would take Cristiano next day to the judge and then, after packing his bags, go back to Ariccia and from there fly to Africa.

He stopped in front of the hospital just as Cristiano and Quattro Formaggi were coming out.

He's going to hear me this time.

He honked his horn.

And he cursed himself. He had forgotten there were sick people in there.

Cristiano came over. His eyes were red.

He must have been crying.

The desire to bawl him out had passed.

He opened the door and let him in.

Wednesday

231

Cristiano Zena was woken up at six o'clock in the morning by the door of his father's bedroom softly banging, at regular intervals.

He's back.

Papa's come home.

It wasn't possible. He knew that even if his father woke up he wouldn't be able to move from his bed. And yet he got up, hoping, as a man falling from a skyscraper hopes he won't die, that it was him.

Rino's room was empty.

The door was banging because the bathroom window was open and there was a draught. He closed it. He went back into his bedroom, drank some water, sat down at his table and wrote.

Hi papa,

If you're reading this letter I'm glad it means you've woken up. I'm not here, I've gone to Milan. I ran away because they wanted to put me in a home. They found a way of separating us. You always said they were looking for an excuse and they found one. Come and join me in Milan. I live in the tunnels of the metro with 4 Formaggi.

4 Formaggi is very ill and I think he's not right in the head either. He's scared they'll put him in a loony bin.

Danilo's dead. He was killed in a road accident.

Don't be angry if you don't find me here, I'm fine. Join me in Milan. Or we can meet anywhere you like.

About that other thing – don't worry I've sorted it out but don't talk to anyone it's important they don't suspect anything.

I haven't abandoned you. I'm only waiting for you.
I love you.
Cri

He re-read it and thought it was crap. It was a load of rubbish, he wanted to say millions of things but at that moment he couldn't think of them. Anyway, that letter might be used by the police as evidence and might help the social services find him.

He got to his feet and threw it in the toilet, then started packing.

He would find another way of letting his father know that he and Quattro Formaggi were in Milan.

232

While Cristiano was packing, the Carrion Man was in his own flat, slumped in front of the television.

The fever was devouring him. He was immersed in a shroud of sweat, he felt as if he was boiling. Five minutes earlier his teeth had been chattering with cold.

His mouth was dry and his tongue was covered with cuts and ulcers.

I must call Cristiano and tell him I can't go to Milan today. If we could put it off till tomorrow . . .

'I can't call him! He'd come here . . . He'd discover the crib,' he sighed.

During the night he had been delirious. He had watched the sheets and the walls of the room become covered with daisies. Huge iron daisies. He had started picking them, but they were too heavy to hold in your hand.

He would have liked to switch off the television, which was driving him crazy. But to do that he would have had to get up.

'The latest in a never-ending stream of ground-breaking products from the Garnier laboratories – the new Fructis hair cream, which, when used in conjunction with the shampoo and balsam, help to protect and reinforce the scalp,' someone was yelling from inside the television.

The Carrion Man touched his hair. It hurt and pulsed as if it was made of electric wire.

Then he started spreading that invisible cream on his head, slowly. He felt relief, it was helping a lot and it would soon silence the voices that roared in his head.

233

Cristiano Zena had filled his rucksack with a few clothes, a jar of pickles, the torch so that they could see in the tunnels, and all the medicines he had found, to give to Quattro Formaggi.

He had a problem. Money. He had twenty-five euros in all, which he had saved up to buy, at some far-off time in the future, a PlayStation. That wouldn't get him to Milan. He had searched everywhere among his father's things, in all his pockets and drawers, and had come up with another three euros.

Twenty-eight euros.

And Quattro Formaggi certainly wouldn't have a cent.

Where could he get more?

Beppe Trecca.

He went slowly down the stairs, trying to make as little noise as possible.

The social worker was stretched out fast asleep on the sofa with the television on in front of him. A blonde was explaining how to make a lampshade out of nothing but shoelaces and buttons.

Then the adverts began.

Beppe had hung his trousers and shirt on the back of a chair. And on the floor, by the sofa, he had put his mobile, his car keys and his wallet.

Holding his breath, Cristiano bent down and picked it up.

He was about to open it when the theme tune of the TV news struck up, followed by a summary.

'The funeral of the young girl Fabiana Ponticelli, who was found yesterday in the waters of the Forgese, will take place today in the church of Varrano. The magistrate authorised her burial after examining the results of the autopsy which was carried out that same evening by Dr Viotti . . . '

The image of Fabiana filled the whole screen.

Cristiano, with the wallet in his hand, froze.

It was a rather old photograph, she still had short hair and was laughing.

'What are you doing?'

Cristiano jumped, and almost threw the wallet up in the air in fright.

Trecca was looking at him and yawning. 'What are you doing with my wallet?'

He was speechless, trying to think of an excuse. He mumbled: 'Oh, I just wanted to see if you had any money. I wanted to go and get something for breakfast . . . I was going to pay you back later. Don't worry.' And he laid the wallet on the chair.

Trecca looked at him dubiously for a moment. Then he seemed to believe him. He stretched and started watching the television. 'So she was the reason we got stuck in that traffic jam. Poor girl.'

Meanwhile the report on Fabiana had begun. It showed the parents being pursued by journalists. Then the investigating magistrate, a middle-aged woman in a trouser suit, who said that a painstaking search for the murderers had already begun and that no line of enquiry had been ruled out. Then they went on to discuss the funeral that had been arranged for that morning. The service would be held by Cardinal Bonanni in the presence of the civil authorities.

Cristiano held on to the back of the sofa to steady himself. He felt faint. It was as if he was being sucked down to the bottom of a well of icy water, while his muscles and tendons went limp.

Beppe took his shirt off the chair and put it on. 'She was at your school. Did you know her?'

Cristiano made a superhuman effort to come back up to the surface and reply. 'Yes . . . ' He wanted to add that he hadn't known her very well. But he didn't have the strength.

'Isn't it incredible? They raped her and then killed her by smashing her head in. What kind of man could do a thing like that? To a fourteen-year-old girl!'

Cristiano felt that he ought to reply, but couldn't think of anything to say.

I'm going to throw up.

'Anyway, the murderer hasn't got a chance. They'll catch him in no time.'

'Oh . . . really?' Cristiano found himself saying.

Beppe stood up, still looking at the screen. 'When you kill someone, they get you. Sooner or later they get you. You can be sure of that. It only takes one little detail, even the most trivial, and you're fucked. Only a complete idiot or a madman would think you can commit murder and get away with it. The only possibility of committing the perfect murder is if no one gives a damn about finding the culprit. It wasn't an illegal immigrant who got killed here. It was a fourteen-year-old girl, brutally raped and murdered. Everyone wants to find the murderer. The family, the police, who don't want to be made to look stupid, the public, who don't want a monster roaming the streets killing their children, supporters of the death penalty, people who are curious to see the monster's face, the television companies and the journalists who make a living out of this stuff. Take it from me, they'll catch this guy in a week at the outside. Without a shadow of doubt. It would take a miracle to save him. If I was the murderer I'd give myself up. Or rather, I'd blow my brains out.'

He put on his trousers.

'We'll have to go to the funeral. The whole school's going. You must go too. Then we've got an appointment with the judge. To discuss what's the best thing to do. Okay?'

'Okay.' And for the rest of his life Cristiano Zena continued to ask himself how he had found, that morning, the strength to resist and not to blurt out the whole truth.

234

The Carrion Man saw Ramona smiling at him inside the television. She had made it onto the TV news.

Thanks to me.

He smiled and stretched out his arm, trying to stroke her.

He closed his eyes, and when he opened them again he couldn't understand how much time had passed nor whether he had actually been asleep.

Through the door that led into the sitting room he could see the eastern edge of the crib, which reached almost as far as the front door. That was the most desolate area. Sparse vegetation. Sand dunes. It was the land of the robots, the spaceships, the UFOs and the prehistoric monsters. A dangerous, contaminated zone, where the shepherds didn't venture and even the soldiers dared not go.

The Carrion Man raised his head and looked across to the other side of the scene. He remembered where he had found each figurine, each animal, each little car. For example that black robot there, with the red eyes and pincers instead of hands, had come from a fountain in the little public gardens the year before. A mother had given it to her son. The child had torn open the package, grinding his teeth as if it contained an enemy that he wanted to kill. He had taken out the robot, switched on its eyes, made its legs move and then, already bored, thrown it into the fountain with the goldfish.

The woman had crouched down by her little boy and said to him: 'Antonio, why did you throw it into the water? That's naughty. Mama paid a lot of money for it. You should respect things you're given as presents.' They had left it there, and the Carrion Man had retrieved it and placed it in the future zone.

He wished he could return to those days.

Before any of this had happened.

235

Cristiano Zena was standing in the middle of the sitting room. Trecca was waiting for him outside.

Perhaps he would never see this house again. He looked at the lounger where Rino always lay. He sat down on it.

He had always loathed this unfinished house beside the highway, but the idea of leaving it made him feel desperately sad. He had been born here. He looked around for something, a keepsake to take with him, but nothing seemed suitable.

'Cristiano! Come on. We're late.' Trecca's voice outside.

'Just a minute, I'm coming!'

Then Cristiano saw, dumped in a corner, the threadbare blanket that his father liked to sleep under. He picked it up, sniffed it and put it in his rucksack. Then he went out, slamming the door behind him.

Outside, the sun had only just risen from the horizon, but it was already obvious that a warm, cloudless day was in prospect. The air was transparent and a light wind blew among the foliage of the trees.

'What have you got in that rucksack?' Beppe Trecca asked Cristiano, putting the key into the Puma.

'Clothes.'

'Clothes?'

'Yes, some of my father's clothes for Quattro Formaggi. When we get to Varrano I'll take them to him, then I'll join you in church.'

They got into the car.

The social worker started up the engine and fastened his safety belt. 'I don't think that's a good idea. We'll go to the funeral first. They've set aside an area of the church for the students. They're expecting you. Then we must go and see the magistrate and we can take him the clothes after that.'

Cristiano gave a forced laugh. 'Me? Who's expecting me?'

'Your teachers, your schoolmates . . . '

The car turned onto the highway.

Cristiano put his feet up on the dashboard. 'What are you talking about? They don't give a shit about me.'

'You're wrong. I've talked to your Italian teacher and told her what happened to your father. She's very sad and she hopes you'll soon be back at school.'

Cristiano shook his head, smiling. 'The bitch . . . Aren't people just incredible!'

'What do you mean?'

Cristiano opened the window and then closed it again. 'Oh, never mind . . . What's the point? You don't understand these things . . .' But then he went on: 'What did she say exactly? Tell me, come on.'

'That she was very sorry and that she hoped you would soon be back at school.'

'That's rich, when she's always telling me the best thing I can do is to leave school as soon as possible! Why does she want me to go back, then? I don't understand. And do you know what she said about my father, in front of the whole class? Shall I tell you? She said he's a good-for-nothing. Who the fuck is she to say my father's a good-for-nothing? Does she know him? Are they friends? I don't think so. She's a good-for-nothing herself. The bitch. How much effort do you think it takes to say on the phone: "I'm terribly sorry, I hope he'll soon be back at school?" None at all. Zero. Zilch. The effort of moving your lips. I can just imagine how sorry she is that my father's in a coma . . . I bet she's crying her eyes out all day long. That cow's just hoping he'll die. But she's going to be disappointed, because my father's going to wake up . . . ! I don't want to go to this bloody funeral.'

The social worker flicked the indicator and stopped in an emergency layby, then he looked at Cristiano for a long while before speaking. 'Look, I don't understand this. Fabiana was a friend of yours.'

'In the first place, who told you Fabiana Ponticelli was a friend of mine? I hardly knew her. Friendship is something else. In the second place, the only people at that funeral will be the ones who go there to be seen, so that everyone will see how good they are. Pretending to cry. It's all phoney. Nobody gives a shit about Fabiana Ponticelli. Don't you realise that?'

'Listen, if your father dies will you be sorry?'

'What kind of a question is that? Of course I will.'

'And will Quattro Formaggi be sorry?'

'Of course he will.'

'And if Danilo was alive, wouldn't he be sorry?'

'Of course he would.'

'What about me? Wouldn't I be sorry?'

Cristiano would have liked to say no, but he didn't have the heart. 'Yes . . . I think you would.'

'And won't Fabiana's parents be sorry that their daughter has been beaten up, raped and murdered? Don't you think they'll be sorry?'

'Yes.'

'And her little brother, her relatives, her friends, and anyone who has a heart, won't they be upset that an innocent little girl whose only mistake was to be late going home was killed like an animal in a slaughterhouse?'

Cristiano said nothing.

'You've got your father vegetating in a hospital bed. Your friend Danilo is dead because he got drunk and crashed into a wall. You should be able to understand what it means to suffer and to be compassionate. Do you know what compassion is? To hear you talk I wouldn't have thought so. You hate everybody. You're so full of anger you're bursting. Cristiano, have you got a heart at all?'

'No. I've lost it . . . ' was all he could say.

236

The voices of the television kept pounding away at the Carrion Man's feverish brain. An incomprehensible mixture of music, news bulletins, recipes, commercials. But in the middle of this jumble of sounds one sentence succeeded in carving itself out some space and becoming intelligible. 'Now we are going to discuss the terrible murder in the San Rocco woods with Professor Gianni Calcaterra, the distinguished criminologist and presenter of the show *Crime and Punishment*.'

The Carrion Man slowly turned his head towards the television, like a laboratory monkey on opium. He screwed up his eyes and made a great effort to concentrate.

The screen showed two men sitting on white armchairs. One of them, a skinny man, he knew: he was the guy who appeared on Channel One every morning. The other was a fat man with a goatee beard and long white hair who looked a bit like Danilo. He wore a grey pinstriped suit and had an unlit pipe in his mouth.

'Well, Professor Calcaterra, what impression have you formed of the murderer or murderers of poor Fabiana? By the way, in your opinion, to judge from the first reconstructions, was the murder committed by one person or by more than one?'

The professor looked thoroughly pissed off, as though he had been dragged onto the show by force. 'I'd like to make it clear that given the small amount of evidence in my possession what I say has no scientific value, but is a mere conjecture made in order to help the public understand.'

'Absolutely. We'd like to stress that what the professor says has no scientific value.'

Professor Calcaterra grasped his pipe by the bowl and made a disgusted face, as if he'd just eaten a still-warm turd. 'The first thing to say is that rape is always the result of a man's problematic relationship with his own sexuality.'

The Carrion Man was convinced by now that this guy was Danilo pretending to be Professor Calcaterra. If it wasn't him it must be a close relative.

'Rape arises from a feeling of impotence and inadequacy with respect to the world in general and the female universe in particular. It is likely, in the case of Fabiana Ponticelli, that the rapist killed the girl because he failed to get satisfaction during the rape . . . '

Calcaterra was interrupted by the presenter: 'What you say is really very, very interesting, professor, and certainly adds new perspectives to the understanding of this terrible murder which has shocked the whole of Italy. It's a pity that we don't have much time for talking about it. One last question, professor. Do you have any new information on the case?'

'The search for the murderers of Fabiana Ponticelli is already well advanced and the investigating magistrates and the police, though they are not prepared to say so officially, seem moderately optimistic about the possibility of finding the culprits in a very short time. Somebody knows and will talk.'

Darkness fell on the Carrion Man and a new, immense terror, such as he had never known until that moment, took possession of him. His brain was emptied of all thought and even the voices suddenly stopped.

He sat slumped in the armchair, panting and staring at the ceiling.

Slowly there emerged from the darkness a thought, a name.

Rino.

Rino Zena.

He was the only person who could incriminate him. He was the somebody who knew and who would talk. He saw Rino's arm rising up and pointing at him.

But he must be dead by now. The Carrion Man had seen death hovering near him.

But supposing death had come there for somebody else? A lot of people die every day in a hospital.

He stood up and, swaying on his feet, picked up off the bedside table the pistol he had taken from Rino in the wood and gripped it tightly.

This time they wouldn't stop him.

237

They left the Puma in the car park of the sports club.

'What are all these doing here?' asked Cristiano, pointing to a row of coaches.

Beppe put on some hideous bug-eye sunglasses. 'Schools. People who've come for the funeral.'

Cristiano thought that either Fabiana Ponticelli had known half the nation or some people were going to the funeral without having known her.

The streets of the centre were closed and guarded by the police and nobody could enter without special authorisation.

'The mass is in the church of San Biagio,' said Beppe.

Trecca was watching him like a hawk.

Like you do with a dog the first time you let it off the lead.

He must have guessed something.

There were a lot of people walking in silence towards the church in Piazza Bologna. Along the way Cristiano noticed that all the shops were closed and had black bows tied to their lowered shutters.

He had never seen so many people, not even the previous summer when that TV satire show had come to the village with the life-sized puppet and the dancing girls, but when he reached the piazza he was amazed.

It was an immense human carpet, broken only by the roofs of the minibuses of the TV stations with their satellite dishes, the statue of the marble horse and the lamp posts with clusters of loudspeakers clinging to them. Other people looked out from the windows of the modern blocks that encircled the piazza. Hastily prepared white banners linked the balconies. They said: FABIANA YOU WILL BE FOREVER IN OUR HEARTS. FABIANA TEACH US TO BE BETTER. FABIANA NOW YOU LIVE IN A BETTER PLACE.

'Give me your hand, or we might lose each other in this crowd.' Trecca held out his hand and Cristiano was forced to take it.

They went round the edge of the piazza and finally reached the church. A modern building made of grey concrete, with a pointed roof covered with long strips of tarnished copper. In the centre of the façade was a huge stained-glass window depicting a scrawny Christ. The steps, too, were crammed with people pushing to get in.

'Let's go away. They won't let us in,' said Cristiano, trying to break free of the other's grasp.

'Wait . . . You're a schoolmate of hers.' Trecca spoke to the officials on the door and they let them through. They crossed the right nave, threading their way through the crowd. There was a strong smell of incense, flowers and sweat.

Cristiano found himself face to face with Castardin, the owner of the furniture factory, whose dog he had killed.

Castardin looked him up and down for a moment. 'Wait a minute. You're Rino Zena's son, aren't you?'

Cristiano was about to deny it, but Trecca was beside him.

He nodded.

'I heard about your father. I'm very sorry. How is he?'

'Okay. Thank you.'

The social worker intervened. 'He's still in a coma. But the doctors are optimistic.'

Castardin was shouting as if he was in a seaside discotheque at Riccione. 'Good. Good. Well, when he wakes up give him my best wishes, will you? As soon as he comes out of his coma tell him old Castardin sends him his very best wishes.' He patted him on the back of the head.

Cristiano imagined his father waking up and being told that Castardin sent him his very best wishes. He'd go straight back into a coma and never come out of it again.

A few metres further on was Mariangela Santarelli, the hairdresser, who had gone out with his father when Cristiano was small. She was wearing a veil and a miniskirt. And Max Marchetta, the owner of Euroedil. He was dressed up as if he was going to his own wedding, and was talking into his mobile. Old Marchetta was there, too, on a wheelchair pushed by a Filipino.

They reached the area where his schoolmates were sitting. As soon as they saw him they started whispering, nudging each other and pointing at him.

Cristiano had to restrain himself from turning round and fleeing.

The Italian mistress pushed her way through the crowd, came up and hugged him and whispered in his ear: 'I heard about your father. I'm so sorry.'

The very same words Castardin used.

238

The Carrion Man entered the hospital.

His heart seemed to be trying to escape from his chest. And he was dying for a pee. He held one hand pressed against his stomach, with the fingers touching the steel of the pistol concealed in his underpants.

At last he had managed to get there. He didn't know how he had done it. He had even started the scooter at the first attempt.

The village seemed to have gone mad. All the shutters of the shops were down. All the roads closed to traffic. The car parks full of coaches. The streets packed with people walking towards the centre.

He wanted to ask them where they were all going and what on earth was happening, but didn't have the courage. There were guards and traffic police everywhere.

Maybe there was a Laura Pausini concert or a political rally.

He would have liked to rush upstairs to Rino, but before he did anything else he needed to pee. His bladder was bursting.

He entered the toilet next to the bar. At that moment, thank God, there was no one around. The Carrion Man hurried over to the urinal and let it out, throwing his head back and closing his eyes.

He had to rest one hand against the wall to stop himself collapsing on the floor with the pain. It was like pissing out fire mingled with fragments of glass.

When he opened his eyes he saw that the white ceramic walls of the urinal were splashed with red and that his pecker was dripping urine and blood. The acidic reek of ammonia blended with the metallic tang of blood.

'Oh, shit!' he muttered in despair.

At that moment the spring-operated door of the toilet opened and closed with a creak.

The Carrion Man moved closer to the wall and stared at the hole into which the red piss was falling.

He heard behind him a sound of heels clicking on the floor tiles. Then out of the corner of his eye he saw a figure take up a position three urinals down from his.

'Ahhh! They say it's bad for you to hold it in. Especially after a certain age,' said the man, and at the same time there was a trickling noise.

The Carrion Man turned.

It was Ricky. The angel sent from God.

He was wearing the same grey flannel suit and the same checked shirt. The same blond comb-over which looked as if it had just been licked by a cow. The same everything.

'Ricky . . . ' he blurted out involuntarily.

The little man turned, looked at him and raised his eyebrows. 'Who are you, my friend?'

'It's me. Don't you recognise me?'

'I'm sorry?'

'You must do. You gave me this.' The Carrion Man pulled out from under his cardigan the crucifix he wore on his chest.

Ricky seemed unsure whether to say he knew him or to deny everything and run for it. 'Yes. Of course . . . Now I remember. How are you?'

The Carrion Man sniffed. 'I'm dying . . . '

Ricky zipped up his fly. 'So the crucifix was for you?' He went to wash his hands. 'You should have told me . . . I would have given you something else. Why didn't you tell me?'

The Carrion Man shrugged and admitted: 'I don't know. I know I'm dying and that God has abandoned me.'

Ricky took two steps backwards, drying his hands with a paper towel: 'Have you prayed to the Lord?'

'God doesn't talk to me any more. He's chosen someone else. What have I done wrong?' The Carrion Man limped over to the little fellow and grabbed him by the arm.

Ricky stiffened. 'I don't know. But you must keep praying. With more conviction.'

'But is it up to *me* to kill Rino? Or has God already done it?' He started stamping his foot on the floor as if trying to squash an invisible cockroach.

Ricky broke away from his grasp as if he'd been touched by a leper. 'Look, I'm sorry but I really must go. Good luck.'

The Carrion Man saw him disappear through the door and then screwed up his lips into a grimace of terror, dropped to his knees, hugged himself, bent forward and started crying and moaning: 'Tell me what I have to do. Please . . . Tell me. And I'll do it.'

239

Beppe Trecca was leaning against a column in the side nave with his arms crossed.

He had left Cristiano with his schoolmates and could now see his blond head of hair, prominent among the others.

He looked like an alien, there in their midst. He had completely ignored them.

He's got character, that kid. And he's tough.

He would recover, of that Beppe was certain. He had never complained, he had never seen him shed a tear. That was the way to face difficulties.

Beppe himself, however, felt tired and weak.

He was longing to go home, to take a shower, shave and write his resignation letter. The next day he would close his bank account, gather together the few things he possessed and drive down to Ariccia.

He took off his sunglasses, cleaned them and put them back on again. He screwed up his eyes and saw Ida sitting in the pews of the central nave. Next to her, Mario and the children.

He should have started, choked or hidden away, but instead he stood there, spellbound, gazing at her. During the past few days he had imagined this moment a thousand times and he had never thought he would react like this. He felt peaceful, calm, because he only had to look at her for all his anxieties and fears to dissolve like tempera in water. He knew he was seeing her for the last time, and wanted to fill his memory with her so that he could hold her there for ever.

She wore a black trouser suit and a grey cardigan. Her hair gathered back behind her head. Her neck long and slender. She looked stunning. She was brushing a lock of hair off her forehead with her hand.

What in the name of heaven made me make that vow?

Who said the African was dead, anyway? He was on the ground, but maybe he had only fainted. He hadn't even felt his heart. What a fool he was! It had been his own guilty conscience that had decided for him. In his panic he had written him off. But there had been no doctor there to verify his death.

He was in perfect health. I even bought those socks off him.

Besides, miracles don't exist. They're just an illusion designed to spread the faith. The Lord isn't a merchant you can barter promises with in exchange for favours.

How could I been so stupid as to think you could just say a prayer and God would revive the dead? If that was true nobody would ever die!

There hadn't been any miracle. And if there hadn't been any miracle there wasn't any vow. If he was wrong and had to pay for being happy, he would pay.

I'm in love with Ida Lo Vino and I don't want to lose her for anything in the world.

He felt a sensation of warmth spreading through his body, and his limbs relaxed. It was like being born again. Someone had removed from his chest those thousand kilos that had been crushing the breath out of him.

He filled his lungs, breathed out again and ran his fingers through his hair. He smoothed down his jacket and straightened the knot of his tie.

He strode decisively through the crowd and entered the pew where Ida was sitting.

He smelled the sweet scent of her perfume. He squeezed her arm. 'Ida?'

She turned and saw him. Astonished, she breathed: 'Beppe? Where have you been?'

'I've been closing my account with God,' he said. Then he motioned to her to wait and turned to Mario Lo Vino, who was looking at him and smiling: 'After the service I must talk to you.' He sat down and took hold of Ida's hand.

240

Cristiano had had to embrace all his schoolmates. Some had kissed him. Even that pathetic little pillock Colizzi, the swot, who had always hated him. The only one who had completely ignored him was Esmeralda Guerra, Fabiana's friend.

At first he hadn't recognised her, so smartly dressed and with her long black hair gathered into a plait. She had removed her piercing. She seemed taller, and was breathtakingly beautiful. She was holding a sheet of paper which she kept reading. A group of girls sat around her, trying to comfort her.

Cristiano sat down next to Pietrolin, whom he had once beaten up in the mall with a cardboard cut-out of Brad Pitt.

Pietrolin nudged him. 'Esmeralda's going to read a poem she's written for Fabiana. And tomorrow at three thirty she's going to be on *Real Life Stories* on TV.'

On the other side, standing by a confessional, was Tekken with his whole gang – Ducati, Nespola, Memmo and three or four others whose names Cristiano didn't know. He was so covered in plaster he looked like the Michelin Man.

So that whack I gave you was on target. I hurt you. You deserve it. After what you did to Quattro Formaggi . . .

Suddenly a general murmur arose.

Cristiano looked round.

Fabiana's father, mother and little brother had entered. The crowd parted to let them through. The Ponticellis clung tightly together and made their way forward, looking lost. Some people raised their mobile phones to snap them or make videos. In the dim light of the church the screens of the mobiles lit up like funeral candles.

They put them in the front row, next to the mayor, a lot of important people and the policemen in their uniforms. The mother took her son on her lap while the television cameras zoomed in for a close-up.

'After the funeral there's a procession to the cemetery. I don't know if we have to go too.'

Cristiano stared at Pietrolin, not knowing what to say. Since entering the church he had avoided looking towards the altar, but he couldn't restrain himself any longer.

The white coffin lay on a red carpet. Around it, thousands of irises, tulips and marguerites. Dozens of wreaths and little soft toy white rabbits.

A long queue of people went up to lay down more flowers or simply stroke the coffin.

Fabiana is in there and I was the last to touch her.

He relived the moment when, in pushing the corpse wrapped in plastic out into the river, he had brushed the tip of her toe.

241

The Carrion Man opened the door of the intensive care unit.

His heart was pounding hard in his chest, but its rhythm was regular.

There was a bustle of doctors and nurses going in and out of the room where Rino lay.

An alarm bell was ringing.

He drew nearer, biting the palm of his hand.

Around the bed there was a group of doctors who were talking and blocking his view.

Nobody took any notice of him.

He felt emboldened and moved a little closer. Underneath his cardigan he felt the pistol pushing against his sore ribs.

Between the doctors' backs he saw Rino's body under the sheets. The neck, the chin, the cheeks, the eyelids closed . . . The tattooed arm pierced with transparent tubes was rising. With the forefinger pointing at him. The blue eyes staring into his own.

Rino opened his mouth and said: *"It was you!"*

242

Music started playing and the congregation fell silent. Only the crying of a few babies continued.

At the other end of the church, beside the altar, four girls in black skirts and white blouses were playing a very sad tune on their violins. Cristiano had heard it before in a war film.

Esmeralda looked at Miss Carraccio, the maths teacher, who motioned to her to go, and all her classmates stood up in the pews to let her pass, giving her pats of encouragement.

The church was so quiet that the heels of her black shoes echoed in the reinforced concrete arches.

Esmeralda walked gracefully up the three steps, passed the coffin and stood behind the lectern. She put her mouth to the microphone and had to take three breaths before managing to say, in little more than a whisper: 'This is a poem. I wrote it for you, Fabiana.' Her hand brushed her eyes. 'Fabiana, with your smile. Fabiana, with your great heart. Fabiana who could light up the darkest days . . . Fabiana who made us laugh . . . Now you are . . . ' She bowed her head and began sobbing. She tried to go on. ' . . . now you are . . . now you are . . . ' but she couldn't. She murmured between her sobs: 'We'll miss you, sweetheart.' Then she left the lectern and hurried back to her seat, covering her face.

Alessio Ponticelli looked at his wife and squeezed her hand tightly. He took a deep breath and went to the microphone.

Cristiano had seen him sometimes outside the school. He was a handsome, athletic man, always suntanned. But now he looked ill, as if all the strength had been sucked out of him. He was pale, unkempt, and his eyes were tearful and feverish. He took a folded piece of paper out of his jacket, opened it, looked at it, then put it back in his pocket and started speaking quietly. 'I had written about Fabiana, my daughter, about what a wonderful creature she was, I had written about her dreams . . . but I can't do it, I'm sorry . . . ' He sniffed, dried his eyes and started speaking again, with more vigour. 'They say God can forgive. They say God, in his infinite goodness, created human beings in his image and likeness. But I don't understand: how could he have created the monster that killed my little girl? How could he have stood by and watched all this? A poor little girl being knocked off her scooter, beaten up, raped and then having her head smashed in with a stone? On seeing that, God should have cried out from highest heaven in a voice so loud as to deafen us all, he should have turned day into night, he should have . . . But instead he did nothing. The days pass and nothing happens. The sun rises and sets and a vile murderer skulks among us. And they ask me to speak of forgiveness? How can I forgive him? I haven't got the strength. He's taken away the most beautiful thing I had . . . ' He rested his elbows on the lectern, put his hands over his face and burst into a flood of tears. 'I want to see him dead . . . '

Fabiana's mother got up, went over to her husband, hugged him tightly and led him away.

Behind the altar Cardinal Bonanni, an ancient hunchback, began to read the service in a hoarse voice. 'Give them eternal rest, O Lord, and let perpetual light shine on them.'

The whole congregation rose to their feet and repeated: 'Give them eternal rest, O Lord, and let perpetual light shine on them.'

Cristiano remained seated, crying silently, sobbing so hard he could hardly breathe.

I'm a monster, a monster.

How could he have lugged Fabiana's blood-soaked body about without feeling any pity? How could he have lived through those days without feeling any shame? Without thinking that he had destroyed a family? Where had he found the strength to clean the corpse without any remorse? Why had he been able to do all this?

Because I'm a monster and I don't deserve forgiveness.

243

It was warm in the Carrion Man's living room.

The sun, high in the sky, was shining through the panes of the French windows, and dawn was breaking over the eastern region of the crib.

Through the open window of the bathroom came the twittering of sparrows, the hooting of cars and the blare of the loudspeakers broadcasting the mass that was being held in the church of San Biagio.

The Carrion Man came out of the kitchen holding a chair.

'Out of the depths I call to you, O Lord. Lord, hear my voice; may your ears be attentive to the voice of my prayer,' croaked Cardinal Bonanni through the loudspeakers.

The Carrion Man, taking care not to knock anything over, placed the chair in the middle of the crib. One leg rested on a little lake made out of a blue plastic bowl. One leg on the railway line. One leg in the midst of a pack of polar bears which were tearing a Pokémon to pieces. One leg in the centre of a square lined with tanks and fire engines.

'I hope in the Lord, my soul hopes in his word. My soul longs for the Lord more ardently than watchmen for the morning.'

Then the Carrion Man went back and undressed. He took off his cape. He took off his black-and-white Juventus scarf. He took off his cardigan and vest. He took off his shoes and socks. He took off his trousers. He took the pistol and laid it on the pile of clothes. Lastly he took off his underpants.

'In the name of the Father and of the Son and of the Holy Spirit.'

He spread his arms as if they were the wings of a crippled pigeon, pushed out his swollen belly, cocked his head on one side and looked at his reflection in the French window.

The arms, long and gangly. The right shoulder, purple and swollen. The Adam's apple. The black beard. The small round head. The crucifix among the hairs on the chest. The emaciated torso dappled with bluish bruises. The dark penis perched in front of the balls which dangled like ripe fruit. The right leg, gnarled, withered by the lightning. The scar, as hard as a knot in a tree trunk, running across the calf. The feet with their black nails.

He saw a shadow flit across behind him. He didn't turn around. He knew who it was. He thought he could hear the TOC TOC he made as he walked on his crutches and the rustle of his black cloak brushing across the floor.

'Brothers and sisters, to celebrate this Holy Eucharist for our little sister Fabiana, in the hope that comes to us from the Risen Christ, we humbly confess our sins,' bellowed the priest.

The Carrion Man pulled the plug of the battery charger of his mobile phone out of its socket, strode back, like a colossus, over the deserts, rivers and towns and got up onto the chair. A little black-and-white cow had stuck to the sole of his foot. He removed it and wrapped it in the chain of the crucifix.

'Almighty God, have mercy on us, forgive us our sins and lead us to eternal life.'

The Carrion Man stretched his arms up towards the ceiling. Just above him was the hook for the lampshade and two electric wires which stuck out from the plaster like the forked tongue of a snake.

He passed the wire of the battery charger round the hook several times and then tied it round his neck.

'O God, you are the love that forgives; welcome into your house our little sister Fabiana, who has passed to you from this world; and since she has hoped and believed in you, give her happiness without end. For the sake of our Lord . . . '

How strange. It was as if he was no longer in his body. He was near it. Just to one side. He saw himself, naked, tying the black wire round his neck. He saw his laboured breathing.

Is that me?

(Yes, that's you.)

What on earth had made that naked man get up on a chair and put a noose round his neck?

The Carrion Man knew the answer.

His head.

His small head, covered with hair as black as the feathers of a raven. His crazy head. That head that had ruined his life. There was something inside it that had made him hear too many things, that had made him always feel out of place, different, that had made him do things he couldn't tell anyone about because nobody would have understood them, that had terrified, exhilarated, blinded him, that had made him hide away in a rubbish-filled hole, as frightened as a mouse, that had made him dream of a crib so big as to cover the earth, to replace mountains, seas and rivers with papier-mâché mountains and tin-foil seas.

Well, he was tired of that head.

'Yes, tired,' said the Carrion Man, and he kicked the chair. He hung there above the shepherds, the little soldiers, the plastic animals and the papier-mâché mountains.

Like God.

Gurgling, he raised his arms a little and spread out his hands.

'The Lord is my shepherd, I shall not want. He makes me to lie down in green pastures, he leads me beside the still waters. He restores my soul, he leads me in the paths of righteousness for his name's sake.'

Now that he wasn't breathing any more, now that his desperate lungs were screaming 'air, air!', now that his brain was exploding, now that his legs were thrashing about as on the day they had been shot through with the current, suddenly he understood.

He understood what had been missing from the crib.

It wasn't Ramona.

It was so simple.

Me.

It was me.

Quattro Formaggi smiled. A dazzling flash. Once. Twice. Three times.

Then came the liberating darkness.

244

'Come, saints of God, come angels of the Lord. Welcome her soul and present it to the throne of the Highest. May Christ, who has called you, welcome you, and may the angels lead you with Abraham to heaven. Welcome her soul and present it to the throne of the Highest. Give her eternal rest, o Lord, and may perpetual light shine on her. Welcome her soul and present it to the throne of the Highest.'

Cristiano was still sitting among his schoolmates but his mind was far away, in another church. It was empty. He was standing in front of the lectern beside his father's coffin. Quattro Formaggi and Danilo were sitting in the front row.

My father was a bad man. He raped and killed an innocent girl. He deserves to go to hell. So do I for helping him. I don't know why I helped him. I swear I don't know. My father was a drunkard, a ruffian, a good-for-nothing. He was always hitting people. My father taught me to use a pistol, my father helped me to beat up a guy when I had slashed the saddle of his motorbike. My father has always stood by me since the day I was born. My mother ran away and he brought me up. My father took me fishing. My father was a Nazi but he was good. He believed in God and he never used blasphemous words. He loved me and he loved Quattro Formaggi and Danilo. My father knew what was right and what was wrong.

My father didn't kill Fabiana.

I know he didn't.

The wire of the battery charger snapped. Quattro Formaggi fell down among the shepherds, the Lego houses, the little ducks and the Barbapapas.

Rino Zena, lying in bed, moved his hand.

A voice said: 'Can you hear me? If you can hear me, give me a sign. Any sign at all.'

Rino smiled.

Cristiano Zena opened his eyes.

Everyone stood and clapped as the coffin came by.

He jumped to his feet and shouted: 'It wasn't my father!'

But nobody heard.